tempting
little
thief

USA Today and *Wall Street Journal* bestselling author Meagan Brandy writes New Adult romance novels with a twist. She is a candy-crazed, jukebox junkie who tends to speak in lyrics. Born and raised in California, she is a married mother of three crazy boys who keep her bouncing from one sports field to another, depending on the season, and she wouldn't have it any other way. Starbucks is her best friend and words are her sanity.

tempting little thief

MEAGAN BRANDY

ORION

This edition first published in Great Britain in 2023 by Orion Fiction,
an imprint of The Orion Publishing Group Ltd.,
Carmelite House, 50 Victoria Embankment
London EC4Y 0DZ

An Hachette UK Company

A CIP catalogue record for this book
is available from the British Library.

ISBN (Paperback) 978 1 3987 1953 8
ISBN (eBook) 978 1 3987 1954 5

The Orion Publishing Group Ltd
Carmelite House
50 Victoria Embankment
London, EC4Y 0DZ

Typeset by Born Group
Printed and bound in Great Britain by Clays Ltd, Elcograf S.p.A.

www.orionbooks.co.uk

Prologue
Four Years Ago

The deepest, darkest shade of red runs in a steady stream, filling in the cracks of the concrete, not stopping when it meets the burned grass, but soaking into the roots and panning out like a flame with no fire.

So why the fuck is there a man in yellow trench pants standing ten feet from me, eyes wide and hands raised in the air? His mouth is moving, but if he's speaking, I don't hear shit.

No, that's not right.

I hear something deep in the back of my mind.

Screams.

Cries of pain.

Cries for help.

Cries for mercy.

My vision blurs, and it's as if time rewinds, my fucked-up head forcing me to relive what led me right here, right now . . .

"Please, no. Please, don't. I'll be good. I'll be quiet."

"You're worthless."

Smack.

"Useless."

Smack.

"Trash."

Crash.

More cries.

The scream that tears from me is damn near unrecognizable as I wrench my hands free of the zip ties, a few layers of skin

1

tearing as I do. The electrical cable he used to tie me to this chair holds strong around my middle, but the brutal sounds coming from downstairs tell me there's no time to find something to cut the thickly covered copper digging into my ribs, so I lurch awkwardly to my feet and spin so my front is facing the bed.

Pulling in as much air as the position allows, I run backward with all the speed I can manage, slamming the cheap wood into the wall. A guttural shout rips from my throat as my shoulder crunches against the wall, but I do it again.

"Fuck," I hiss. "Come on, come on, come on . . ."

Wood splinters pierce my bare back, digging into the fresh welts there and tearing open half-healed ones. I do it again. And again, my back teeth at risk of cracking from clenching them so hard.

I gasp, my entire body shaking with rage, as the screams from the first floor grow even louder.

Warm liquid trickles down the entire right side of my body now, and my chest heaves, but I don't stop. I draw on as much adrenaline as I can, and with one last crash, the back bars of the chair split, snapping from the base and left arm enough for me to wiggle my body and crawl out of the restraints.

"You want to cry?!" he screams. "I'll shut you up!"

"No!" she weeps.

My heart pounds wildly as I run toward the voices, the cuts on the bottom of my feet tearing open more and more with every step, but I don't care. I can hardly feel the pain anymore.

I can hardly feel anything. A new, darker form of rage bleeds into my bones, numbing me from the inside out.

"Get back here, you little bitch!" he demands, the front door slamming against the hinge.

"Fuck!" I hurry down the stairs.

She ran outside.

We never run outside when he's like this—or after—but then again, it's never lasted this long before.

My stomach leaps into my throat as the living room comes into view.

2

The broken glass littering the floor mocks me, the bloodstains on the shitty shag carpet a constant reminder, as if I fucking need one, of what he's capable of doing to her, to me.

My mother hugs the now broken frame of the door, cowering against it, and the moment she hears me coming, she attempts to keep me from stepping through, but I shove her away, breaking free when her hand darts out, attempting to latch on to my wrist.

Horror slams into me, and I jerk to a stop on the porch.

My sister's face is even more swollen now, blood seeping from the side of her head where he pistol-whipped her before tying me up, the bullet meant for her still buried in my flesh. She struggles to keep her eyes open, her body growing limp at our father's side as he drags her back toward the house by the hair.

I have to get to her.

I have to free her.

I will save her.

He spots me and comes to a halt, eyes flicking over my shoulder.

And then my mother's body is crashing into me from behind, knocking me unsteady. She's hysterical, afraid for the man she loves more than her children and stumbles. With a slight nudge of my elbow, she tumbles into the dirt, scrambling back and hiding behind a flowerpot when my father pulls the trigger of the gun gripped in his left hand. The harsh "pap" rattles in the trees, the bullet burying itself into the dirt near his feet.

"Son, stop this right now! You're bleeding everywhere! Get back inside before someone sees!" she cries, begging, yet again, for us, the victims, to "be good" and take the fucking whipping we "deserve."

Of course I'm fucking bleeding. I came home to chaos, saw a gun pointed at my sister's head, and with the look of acceptance in her eyes, I jumped in front of her just before he pulled the trigger.

Where I fucked up was turning to see if my sister was okay and trying to check the wound on the side of her head from his beating. He capitalized on my rookie mistake, tackling me from behind when I wasn't looking.

I won't be so foolish now.

But my mother is as dumb as she is pathetic. My dad just shot that same gun in the front fucking yard, where my sister is bleeding and trembling in his hold, her body practically fucking hanging at his feet as if she's a peasant and he's a king.

There's no more "hiding in the house."

No more "swallowing our screams."

No more "covering the bruises under our clothes."

This right here . . . this is it.

This is the day we dreaded but waited for.

The moment we feared but wished for.

This is the end. His . . . or ours.

The fist in my sister's hair tightens, and I bite the inside of my cheek, trying to think of a way to turn this around. To take her place.

She thrashes in his hold, crying, begging, but he keeps dragging her forward toward me.

I step out, curving a bit so I'm no longer in the path of the door but off to its right, my feet now nearly in the center of the yard.

My mom begs me to go inside as she does exactly that, waving all of us in with urgency, but I don't even look at her. I keep my eyes on the bloodshot ones staring right at me.

"You think you're tough, kid?" *He waves the gun at his side.* "Get in the goddamn house. Now."

"Let her go."

You'd think snakes grew from my ears the way the man's eyes bulged at my defiance, shock rooting him in his place.

"Don't!" *my sister pleads, her strangled words stealing her last ounce of energy.* "Just stop. It's o-okay."

She trembles, fear of what he'll do to me racking through her body, just like it is mine for what he might do to her.

I reposition myself, making sure I'm parallel with the front windows rather than leaving my back exposed to my mom and any stupid idea she might come up with to help her husband. I stop moving once the edge of the neighbor's bushes cut along the backs of my legs, both my parents now in my line of sight.

Like I knew he would, my dad follows my movement, shifting his feet sideways to face me once again.

4

He's antsy, head whipping around as sirens sound somewhere in the distance, and his nostrils flare, knowing we can't stand out here much longer. In his mind, he's thinking if he gets us back inside, he can at least try and hide us, manufacture an excuse of some sort—like when I had a "bike accident" that broke bones when, really, he'd shoved me out the upstairs window, sending me sailing into the bed of his El Camino in the driveway because he thought I'd been outside with the fresh black eye he served me the day before. I wasn't outside, but my sister was, and I knew one of us would face his wrath for it, so I made sure it was me.

His hold must loosen because, in the next second, my sister's piercing scream fills the air, and she tears herself from his brutal grip, ripping the hair straight from her scalp as she crawls to me.

I dart forward, grabbing her torso with my arms as gently as I can, and yank her back to me. She goes limp the second she's in my arms, eyes flickering as she mumbles incoherently.

We tumble to the ground, and my dad screeches into the air, charging at us.

My eyes widen when he raises the gun, pointing it at my sister, and then something cold presses into my palm.

I look down in what feels like slow motion but must be no more than a fraction of a second, frowning at the matte-black pistol, my eyes briefly flicking to the split knuckles of the hand passing it to me through the bush.

Hayze Garrett, my one and only friend, because I don't have to hide from him. He lives in hell too.

A branch snaps, and I face forward, lift my left arm, and grin.

Dad's eyes shoot wide, and a cold, dead laugh leaves me. I pull the trigger at the same moment he does.

My body jerks and his gives up on him.

He crashes to the ground with a loud crack that sends a satisfying shiver down my spine.

My pulse pounds heavily in my ears, my mother's cries loud and bellowing, my sister's whimpers of pain deafening and then . . . nothing.

5

I don't feel the bullet he sent through my shoulder earlier or the gashes his belt left in my back afterward. I don't feel the sting of the foxtails embedded in dead grass from the cuts he drew across the bottoms of my feet with his hunting knife to "keep me in the chair," he had said. I don't feel worry or anxiety or dread.

I don't feel helpless or stuck.

I don't feel shit.

I walk over to my father's lifeless body and stare down at the pathetic excuse for a human, the complete waste of flesh and blood.

I blink, my vision clearing, coming back to the present.

My eyes are still on the ground, tracing the path of red backward, from the grass to the cracks to the cement slab . . . up to his ear and temple, to the dead center of his beaded brows, where the blood gushes from.

A perfect fucking shot.

My head cocks to the side as I stare into crystal-colored eyes, the same ones I see in the mirror every morning.

The man the movies say you should trust and love most in the world.

The man who showed us you can trust *no man*. Or woman, for that matter.

My father.

The abusive drunk.

The dead drunk.

A slow smirk spreads along my lips.

Muffled shouts fight their way into my consciousness, and slowly, the echoes in my ears calm, the real-time noises hitting me all at once.

Sirens, shouts, demands.

"You've been shot . . ."

My shot was better.

"Son, it's over . . ."

I'm no one's son anymore.

"Put the gun down . . ."

I will when I'm ready.

"We're here to help . . ."

No one ever helped us.

I point the gun at my dear old dad's cold, dead heart and pull the fucking trigger.

After that, everything goes black.

By the time my mind decides to tap back into reality, I realize I'm sitting on shiny leather seats in a fancy town car, not cuffed in the back of a dirty cop car or belted to a bed in an ambulance on my way to a mental institution. My body feels like it was hit by a truck, and then I remember it wasn't a truck.

It was a custom, *stolen,* steel-bodied Glock shot by my dad. My *dead* dad.

My sister!

My hand shoots for the door handle, and I hiss as pain explodes across every inch of my flesh. Before I can move another muscle, the door flies open, and a man slips inside. He's a big fucker, built like a linebacker, and dressed like I interrupted his fucking wedding or something. He's wearing a suit. An actual *suit* suit with a tie, shiny shoes, and a watch I'd swipe right off his wrist without him realizing if my limbs weren't so fucking heavy.

"Who the fuck are you and where's my sister?" I growl, searching for a weapon in case I somehow landed myself in the presence of another twisted fuck.

"She'll be okay." He speaks calmly like he didn't just climb in the back seat with a murderer. "The doctor is with her now, waiting to see if she will need surgery or not."

"I want to see her."

"I'm afraid you can't. Not yet." The man studies me. He can't be much older than my dad, maybe early forties. "Not until you make a decision."

I don't know what the fuck he's talking about, so I cut the bullshit out and wait, and he doesn't hold out long.

"There's a place for someone like you not far from here. They find kids in your position and offer them an out."

My position. Right. Like there's just a gang of people out there, looking around for beat-on punks who get pushed to the edge and kill so they don't fall over it.

Or maybe killing *is* falling?

"Oh yeah?" I cock my head, ignoring the sharp sting it causes. "Sounds like some shit slick bastards tell young broken girls seconds before they stick a needle in their arm and drop them into rotation at some run-down hourly motel." Panic roars in my chest at the thought. "Where is my sister?"

He watches me a minute, then says, "She's safe. In the hospital, getting the care she needs, but the longer this takes, the less chance I have at keeping social services away."

My brows dip in the center, and the man dips his chin.

Yeah, fucker, you got my attention.

He sits back, screaming money and power as he adjusts the slight crookedness of the sleeves of his suit jacket. I've never even tried on a suit, let alone worn one.

He speaks again. "You have five minutes to decide if you want to step from inside this car and let the badges outside of it take you downtown, where some random person on a set salary will decide if you're a murderer or not—that ends with you behind bars or tossed in foster care—or you can sit back in that seat, and I'll take you somewhere new, and all this goes away."

My eyes narrow. "Where? How?"

"You'll see if you agree, but coming with me means you have a job, a bed, and food in a place free of heavy-handed adults."

Yeah, okay.

When neither of us says a word for several seconds, I lick my lips. "How do I know you're not playin' me?" He's definitely playin' me.

"You don't."

"Who are you?"

"Someone you might never see again, no matter what you choose. Three minutes."

I glare at the guy, trying to make sense of his words, but how the fuck can I? I killed my dad, then shot him in the heart for the fuck of it, in front of who knows how many people, and for some fucked-up reason, I'm not in a jail cell, but in the back of a fucking fancy car with champagne flutes and LED lights on the floorboard.

I've never even seen a ride like this in my entire life, let alone sat in the back of one.

This is a trip. Wild as fuck. Some real-life, otherworld-type shit.

A thousand questions are going through my mind, but right now, I only need the answer to two.

One. "It keeps me out of jail?"

"It does."

Two. "My sister stays out of whatever this is?"

"She does." He nods, looking to his watch then back to me. "So, what do you say, kid?"

"Don't call me kid."

His lips twitch and he cocks his head like a prick. "What should I call you then?"

I think about that a minute, then fall back against the seat, letting go of part of the name I was given and claiming a new one. "Name's Bishop. Bass Bishop."

He nods.

I nod.

And then we're on our fucking way.

Chapter 1

Bass

This motherfucker . . .

Sighing, I crouch down, my knees bent and pointing toward the dude's head. "If I knew you were a bleeder, I'd have stolen a car to deal with you." My words are wasted on him. He can't hear me, not with his ears ringing the way they should be—a pencil to the eardrum will do that to you.

Eavesdropping on conversations not meant for you will do that to you.

A deep groan pushes past the fuckup's lips as he rolls onto his back, eyelids twitching before opening and landing on me.

My smirk is slow, and I cock my head to the side. "You conscious or still stuck in the in-between?"

His eyes close again, and my boy Hayze chuckles from behind me.

"He ain't conscious . . ." he trails off, his voice coming back quieter. "And we ain't alone."

Wiping the blood from my knuckles along the edge of my shirt, I glance over my shoulder to find a sleek and sinful wet fucking dream.

Curves any man would die for—kill for even—and a guaranteed wicked ride.

It's an Aston Martin, shining a custom candy-blue paint job, with a mean-ass black grill, and it only gets sexier. The doors lift straight up in the air.

You'd expect a ritzy fucker to climb out of it: the tailormade type. A stiff prick who flicks his eyes our way in disgust or disregard, but expectations are for fools, a fact that's proven a single second later.

The first thing to come into view is a sharp spike in the form of a heel, nearly equal in size to the switchblade in my pocket, the black strap at the back of it latched tightly around a creamy, arched ankle. A pleated skirt is next. Hitting just above the knee, I follow it upward to where it stops at the fullest point of sharply narrowed hips, a tight white long-sleeve top disappearing beneath it. Large golden cuffs cover the girl's wrists, and the small rings along her fingers gleam in the sun as she reaches up. She pushes a few strands of long, thick blonde hair back, saving them from being caught in the hot-ass pink of her lips, when a gust of wind meets her skin as if she summoned that shit herself, like some kind of fuckin' wind deity.

"God*damn*." Hayze groans.

Yup.

A goddess in the flesh, and no doubt, the girl knows it.

Her steps are slow and effortless, the kind stemming from years of practiced perfection.

She looks every bit the prep school princess, but it's the shade her mouth is painted and the way her tongue slides across that pouty top lip that gives her away.

She's no princess. She's a piranha.

Slick, predatory . . . prone to bite.

Not the petty high school type.

As she heads toward the small building, behind and a little to my right, her eyes float our way, but only her eyes, narrowing on the bulky bastard on the ground at my feet. She can't possibly spot more than an arm and the string of duct tape hanging from it, maybe a hint of his hair, but no more than that.

I shift, slowly pushing to my full height, and her attention snaps my way, holding as I turn to face her fully, ready to move in if needed. This is when we'd normally witness the freezing of the muscles, the widening of the eyes, and the quick flicker of panic that sends someone scurrying away from the big bad wolves.

If her bravado snaps and she bolts, I'm only six steps away. I'll chase her, back her up in the corner where Hayze will be waiting, but that doesn't happen.

It's like I said, this girl . . . she's not what first glances will tell you, so it's not so unexpected when she tsks her tongue instead, her hand running over her long hair as if to make sure it's still perfectly in place. "Boys and their toys."

And she teases. Interesting . . .

"This one malfunctioned."

Her lips twitch, and she hums, keeping toward the small brick building to my right. I watch until she disappears inside it and then turn to Hayze.

"Grab some pain pills and stuff 'em down his throat before you roll him down the hill. He'll wake up enough to run once the ache's hidden a bit."

Hayze says nothing but rushes for the trunk.

Bending again, I empty the guy's pockets, coming up with a wallet, cell, and a busted lighter. Hayze is back right as I'm climbing to my feet.

In tune as fuck with my thoughts, like always, he passes me my phone and I move toward the gas pumps, coming up behind the chick's two-hundred-thousand-dollar beauty for a quick shot of the plate, just in case shit goes south and she's not as immune to blood and bondage as she appears.

The second I toss the items into the trash can wedged between the window-cleaning station and the pump, the door to the convenience store is pushed open, and out she walks, silver-lensed shades now pulled down over her eyes.

She doesn't falter at the sight of me standing two feet from her ride, just keeps on coming, a deep-red straw buried between her lips.

A perfectly arched brow lifts behind the large frames as she places herself an arm's length from me, pressing a button on the keys in her hand. The butterfly door lifts, and she holds her right arm out, dropping her slushy into the trash. The blue liquid splashes up the barrel, but neither of us bothers to look to see if it marked us or not.

"Done already, huh?"

"I only wanted a taste," she quips, tossing her tiny purse on the seat.

One backward step at a time, she changes her mind about sliding into her car, not bothering to close the doors, even though her bag is now sitting right inside, begging to be stolen.

I follow her, my movements slower, eyes locked on her long, toned legs as she crosses the right in front of the left, then spins, her skirt swirling around her thighs, hand coming up to hover over the hood of my car. Starting at the passenger side, her steps follow its contour, palm tracing the body without so much as letting a finger meet the frame.

"Yours?" she wonders as she rounds the vehicle, stepping out wide to avoid the stained proof of the asshole who ate gravel near the front right tire. She leans a bit closer, her eyes trailing over the hood before snapping to mine. An expectant blonde brow hikes up, the girl not used to being made to wait.

"Mine," I confirm, keeping my face blank, but this chick saw a body on the ground before she walked into the store and didn't so much as blink. Now, she skipped over a puddle of blood as if it was nothing but water and is pretending to admire the long, rusty-red hood of my ride . . . right where the VIN number used to be before I took a razor to that bitch. "It's a—"

"A Cutlass, 1972," she interrupts, bending at the knees, and my eyes dart to the curve of her ass so close to showing itself in that skirt. "And with the original grill."

She glances over her shoulder, and I move my eyes to hers.

Hers narrow slightly, but it's a play. Fake as fake can be.

This one knew exactly where my attention would be, just like I knew it was exactly where she wanted it.

She rises to her feet, completely ignoring Hayze's presence when he makes his way back up the hillside. He slows, eyes darting my way in search of a signal—should he bag and gag her or let this play out. Arms loose at my side, I skate my fingertips over my jeans, silently letting him know without a word or glance that all's good.

13

Blondie moves forward, hands folded behind her back like the perfect fucking prep she is, pausing when she's about to pass me. Her left breast presses into the sleeve of my jacket, and her hand lifts, pushing her glasses up onto her head, and as it lowers, the points of her white-tipped fingernails graze along the edge of the zipper.

Mossy-green eyes lock on mine, and she blinks, nice and slow. "Your car has potential. Hate to see it wasted."

"What can I say." My gaze falls to her body, but I bring it right back with a quick flick. "I like a rough ride."

This girl, there's nothing rough about her. She's all satin and silk, with smooth skin and sleek curves.

She doesn't blanch or react in any way, but slow and fuckin' steady, those lips of hers curve to one side. "What you mean to say is you can't afford to fix her up." She cocks her head, speaking with mocking innocence. "Shame."

Yep. Piranha.

I'd let her teeth sink into me, and then I'd bite her spoiled ass back. Literally. And harder.

She steps in closer, waiting for a reaction from me she won't get, but it doesn't take her long to realize as much, and her lips part with a wider smile, her tongue peeking between perfectly pearly *expensive* whites.

And then, on her way past, she shoulder-checks me.

I don't watch her go because I know she expects me to.

Less than a minute later, she peels out, leaving us in a cloud of burned rubber.

I do spin around then, and Hayze comes to stand beside me, our eyes following the taillights down the dark, supposed-to-be deserted road.

A quick, surprised chuckle escapes him, and he shakes his head. "She thinks she's slick, don't she?"

I pull in a deep breath.

She sure as fuck does.

14

Rocklin

The double doors are pulled open the second my heels hit the final step. The second I'm through and closed inside the entryway, the outside light is cut off. Only once the sensors register the entrance has been sealed do the automatic doors five feet ahead disappear into the wall.

As I step into the Distinction room, the room where several sets of eyes you can't see, see *you* and decide which door ahead is to be opened for you, I'm instantly sealed inside what I like to call our lovely little lockbox. Of course, as quickly as the one at my back clicks closed, my team grants my entrance.

The moment my heels click against the white-and-gold marble flooring, Damiano slips from the security room, falling in line beside me. He's as silent as his steps, and my gaze slides his way, the two of us continuing down the hall, passing and ignoring each set of black double doors along the way. We pause in front of the Greyson suite, the largest one in the place, built and designed specifically for me and my girls, Bronx and Delta. It's located at the end of the hall, where the space splits into a *T*, the crossing point of the *hundred-yard catwalk*, as Delta calls it.

It's also the grandest of entrances, the archway carved and crafted from pure white, rose, and standard-colored gold. The three-dimensional serpents weave along thorny vines, their mouths open wide, fangs sinking into broadly bloomed roses, each a soft, delicate shade of pink akin to a ballet slipper. Dead in the center of the flowers, where the pit should be, a diamond sits instead. Rather than leaves framing the stems, they're woven with the illusion of lace, lace that falls into harsh points at the ends and plays like stony icicles protecting the archway. Weapons in disguise, *just in case*.

It's a tether of slyness, Every aspect a representation that only me and the girls can piece together. As was intended.

The door clicks as I step before it and Damiano stands silently at my side, his jaw flexing when I continue past him without a word. I know he'll follow before I hear him lock us inside together.

I go straight for the bar in the far-left corner, tossing my bag on top of it before moving to the large window to its right. The Enterprise is buzzing tonight, a full house expected. Half are people from our world—some eager for the show, some waiting for the business conversations that will follow it. The other half of tonight's guest list consists of those we don't want here but to whom we are forced to extend invites to "keep the peace." They show up from sheer intrigue, shocked they were "lucky enough" to snag tickets to such a "prestigious" event. *Gag me*.

The cocktail area in the gardens below is lively, men and women twice my age drinking the night away as they wait for my girl Delta DeLeon to take her throne—the white leather and suede bench seat of a custom Steinway & Sons piano.

"Is Delta not here yet?" Damiano asks.

"I was told she and the boys arrived a half hour ago but would be . . . *releasing some tension* in the DeLeon suite."

"Good." His shadow grows closer, falling over me from behind, and his palms lift, closing over my forearms. "Everything all right?"

"Why wouldn't it be?"

I spin to face him, only then realizing he's changed from his scholar's uniform, now draped in the finest of black suits, the cuff links at his wrists rivaling the cost of a so-called Ivy League tuition, his golden, secret Greyson Society pin shining proudly along the left trim of his jacket. His blond hair shines under the light of the chandelier and, as always, is swept back from his face in a modern pompadour, making his brown eyes, the same color of watered-down espresso, stand out.

Damiano, or Dom as we tend to call him, is attractive. Abnormally so. He's the kind of man you'd picture when making a list of all the predictably preferred physical attributes: tall, taut, and tempting, with broad shoulders and a square jaw.

There's an allure he possesses, an invisible pull between him and those around him, painting him in the prettiest of lights. People look at Dom and see poise and influence. It's a strong ambience, a coveted one with a potential price tag for desired use in our world, and as we've found, time and time again, a useful one.

He's also oddly . . . basic, as pretty boys with power will be.

Does the vote of an overassertive cougar need to be swayed? Send in the picturesque Prince Charming with an air of arrogance to capture her attention.

How about sending a warning to a man who thinks he's bigger and badder than he's earned the right to claim, who has a pretty princess of a daughter? Send the ideal suitor in to dirty her up and spit her out.

Damiano scans my face, breaking through my thoughts when he speaks. "Your day was tough."

He's right. It was, but his attempt at a therapy session is unnecessary, and the argument with my father he walked in on this morning is not something I want to discuss with him. He knows this.

I tip my head. "Use your big-boy voice, Dom. What is it you would like to say?"

His glare is small, but he nods. "You had an unexpected delay this evening. Your father expected you here at six thirty and started asking at exactly six thirty-one. I've spent the last hour trying and failing to distract him. I can't cover for you if you don't tell me when I need to and where you are."

"In the event I need you to cover for me, you'll be the first to know, and as for where I was, that's what these are for." I flick the golden cuff latched along his wrist beneath his suit jacket.

"We agreed, no unnecessary tracking."

"Exactly. If you had cause for concern, you would have checked. You know me. I needed a minute."

His eyes soften and I hate it, so when he says my name, I cut him off.

"Let my father know I'll be down shortly." I'll smile and say all the right things and pretend he's not making a mistake bound to bite him in the ass, but when it does, I'll happily say I told you so.

I don't tell Dom this, though.

Damiano doesn't respond, but after a moment's pause, he reaches up, his thumb gliding across my cheekbone. He's always been good about doing what I've asked and never pushes too hard.

He knows better than that.

It's no secret he wants me to accept his offer for more, and while I know he cares about me as a person, I also know it's nothing more than a power play.

I know because we spoke of it in direct terms. I'm aware of what he wants, and he's aware of what I do not.

He wants a wife at the tender age of twenty-two, and I want to make my father proud, to claim what's mine as the strongest Revenaw heir, the head seat my father holds within the Greyson Union, an alliance between four families created to keep us on top, without the whispers of a man in my ear. Dom says he wouldn't dare, and I know he's telling the truth.

But today's truth often becomes tomorrow's lie, almost always by accident.

I couldn't fault him for his failure to keep his word, and I'd hate for him to have to die because of it.

Lie rhymes with die for a reason, or so my father swears.

Why Dom's in such a rush, I don't know. We're still stuck on the education train required of us, even though our IQs might surpass every professor on the payroll at Greyson Elite Academy. We both have a place in this world when all is said and done, but no one knows what that place is.

It has to be earned, as anything worth having always does.

Damiano dips his head, softly pressing his lips to the corner of my mouth, and then he's out the door seconds after he releases me.

I trail him to the door, slapping my palm onto the large square on the left side of the wall, not bothering to watch as the steel pins jut out from both sides, piecing together and locking everyone else on the other side—not even my girls could get in now, without me allowing it.

Flicking my eyes to the crown molding above, I return to the bar in the left corner, pursing my lips at the topped-off decanter full of Louis Remy Martin.

Only in my world is it normal for a suite designed for and dedicated to three eighteen-year-old girls to be stocked with liquor worthy of a king.

Or queens, in our case.

Of the criminal underground world, that is.

I pour less than a shot into the short crystal glass and draw it to my lips for a slow sip of the oaky butterscotch flavor. Blindly unclasping and easing the zipper down along my left hip, the heavy-pleated uniform piece falls to the floor.

Resting my elbows on the bar top, I drop my head back, close my eyes, and revel in the moment alone as I release the long, slow sigh I've been holding for what seems like days. In reality, it's only been hours since my father broke the foolish news to me, and it's twisting me up inside in an irritating mix of anger and anticipation.

But seriously, what the fuck is he thinking?

"I'm no expert, but I'm damn sure that's how them heels are meant to be worn." The deep, gravelly words come from somewhere behind me, slicing through my thoughts, and it takes true effort not to jump.

With steady, overly practiced grace, I point my attention over my shoulder to the far-right front corner of the room, where a black velvet armchair sits, the particular nook dark for a reason.

The golden edging along the crease of the wall offers the smallest reflection off the chandeliers, creating the slightest silhouette but nothing more.

No man I know, or woman for that matter, would dare slip inside this suite without permission.

Silence falls, and the dead man leans forward in the chair, the light catching on something shiny along the left side of his face.

Gleaming back at me is a silver loop, curved perfectly around a full, crimson, crookedly hooked bottom lip.

My shock gets the best of me, my eyes widening the slightest as recognition dawns, and he doesn't miss it.

A dark chuckle whispers into the air, the sound deep and rumbly like distant thunder, and then his gaze is flicking over my body. His teeth come out, toying with the piercing before his stare lifts, locking onto mine.

"We meet again, Rich Girl." He cocks his head, an unrelenting, triumphant smirk spreading. "You gonna offer me a drink or what?"

What.

The.

Fuck.

Chapter 2
Rocklin

The urge to pass off this Don Juan wannabe to literally anyone else is high, but the sharp spark of intrigue, or the sheer lack of self-preservation on his part, is somehow greater.

He couldn't possibly have tailed me from the gas station. He was nowhere near his broken-down car and I was pushing a hundred within seconds of pulling from the parking lot, so how he's here right now, I don't know, but I will find out.

I push off the bar, readying to step behind it, but Tall, Daring, and Dreadfully Dressed seems to be against such a move.

In a few long strides, he's a sway away from me, and this time, it's he who tsks his tongue.

My left brow pops up. "Do you or do you not want a drink?"

"I want your hands where I can see them more."

Smart, considering I was going for the weapon strapped to the underside of the shelf behind me.

Lifting my palms into the air, I wiggle my fingers and he creeps closer. "But I'm just a good girl who does what she's told. What threat could I be to a big bad boy like you?" I push my lips into a fake pout.

"Uh-huh." He keeps coming until he's but a foot away, his arms stretching out, hands gripping the edge of the marble at my back. This close, I'm forced to drink him in, from his dark hair to his *dark* demeanor.

His hair is as black as obsidian, shiny like glass, and a moppy mess on top, though smooth and short on the sides. He

21

wears it slightly slicked, but a few pieces have fallen forward, hanging just long enough to create a shadow over his right eye, drawing attention to the slim white scar over his left. His brows are thick, lashes long and sweeping, and his eyes a startling shade of celestine stone.

The invader stares for several silent moments, his eyes nearly too bright to stare into, but it has nothing to do with his mood.

He's bored at best.

"You know why I'm here?" he asks.

"To perve in a corner while an unsuspecting female undresses?"

"Right. That part." His gaze lowers, and it doesn't stop a small frown building along his forehead. "What kind of schoolgirl wears lace and them clip things under her uniform?"

"Clip things?" I deadpan. "Seriously? Have you never bought a girl lingerie?"

Attention still on my body, he says, "Do I look like someone who needs lingerie?"

"Aw." I pretend to pout and his eyes snap up to my lips. "Of course someone like you would assume risqué negligee had a single thing to do with what *you* need. What a selfish lover you must be."

His jaw flexes, and I refuse to react when he jerks even closer, my body now pinned between his and the heavy furniture behind me. For being as trim as he appears, the muscles pressed against me inadvertently reveal there's much more to be seen.

I could easily escape his adorable attempt at an intimidation trap, but he doesn't know that, and I kind of want to see how far he'll push.

Why?

No idea. Maybe because no one ever pushes.

No one ever does a damn thing without asking for permission, but this guy?

I wonder if he's ever asked for anything in his life. He strikes me as the impulsive type, so really he's not the only fool in this scenario because if he's as slick as whatever trick he used to get in here, he could ram a knife into my lung

22

right here, right now. No one would know some emo, grunge, rapper-looking boy toy ended me until they came asking why I never made it down for Delta's performance.

What I *should* do is beat him to the punch, knee him in the nuts, grip the decanter to my right and smash his pretty, scarred face in.

Yet, something keeps me from moving an inch, even when he does.

Hands still flat on the bar top, he slides them farther back, his chest now firm against my own, but I merely lift my chin in challenge.

A hint of amusement flickers in his gaze, sparking something within me. Something reckless and bound to backfire.

"Does the princess wanna find out how *selfish* I can be?" he offers, but his tone is falsely flippant.

Someone's confident, but somehow, it's not in the usual way. I get the feeling if I laughed at him or went with the obvious attempt to tear him down, like pointing out the well-worn shoes on his feet or the faded, threadbare jeans stretched over his thighs, he'd go full-on Eminem in *8 Mile* on me, lay all his shit out and let you judge, because *fuck you*.

Or that's what I imagine he would say.

It's in the steady way he stares and the playful yet purposeful manner he moves.

It's the fact that he's here right now at all, while half the state's biggest crime families pretend to enjoy each other's company on the other side of this wall.

"In your dreams."

His tongue comes out, flicking along his lip ring, and like a lightning bolt in a stormy night sky, my attention strikes down.

The tall, tattooed tyrant leans toward me, and I narrow in on the gleaming silver loop on the tip of his pink tongue as it teases the spot demanding my notice.

His feet shuffle in, bringing us nose to nose, and my lips flatten as his jeans meet my bare skin, the heat of his breath rolling over my jaw and neck when he dips the slightest bit.

"Them legs, those heels . . . I don't know, Rich Girl, there's a good chance you might be *exactly* what I see when I close my eyes tonight."

"Careful." I yank my head to the side when the presence of his mouth is felt closer to my cheek . . . and the tingling sensation it creates travels farther south without permission. "We don't take kindly to those who touch what doesn't belong to them."

"Would you look at that. Guess we've got something in common, after all," he whispers. "See, I'm always careful. Why do you think I'm here?"

His body retreats in an instant, and I snap to attention, mouth parted in a brief moment of surprise as I realize his play but clamping into a flat line as he takes a few backward steps.

Once again, his lazy, *brazen* gaze licks across my skin, his teeth sinking into his swollen, recently split bottom lip. "Such a shame," he murmurs to himself.

And then he turns to leave, lifting his hand to press on the sensor lock beside the door.

I could almost laugh. Truly.

Did he think it would be so easy?

He must assume he's clever.

He's not . . .

Bass

My palm comes down on the large, lit-up square, and the high-tech fuckery of a lock shifts . . . right as I'm kicked in the ass—a weak-ass kick.

Whipping around, I frown when Little Miss Priss isn't standing behind me but now sitting on top of the bar, one long, naked leg crossed over the other, coin rolling a miniature dagger over the knuckles of her left hand, without so much as looking at it.

She cocks her head, lengthy, silky blonde hair spilling over her shoulder and teasing the edges of her bare thighs. My hand slaps out once more, and the door behind me relocks.

She curls her fingers over the edge of the bar, her brows bouncing once.

Keeping a careful eye on her, I shift, quickly glancing at my back pocket. A small silver blade sticks straight through the worn denim. I yank it free and toss it to the side before pulling my phone out of said pocket, the phone she fucking swiped from me with her little kitty cat game of brushing her body against mine at the gas station. The back is pierced, the techy bullshit on the inside staring back at me.

Sure the fuck enough. When I flip it over, the screen's black.

Great. Now I have to figure out who to jack for a new phone and blackmail some asshole into jailbreaking it before they use the damn FindMe app.

My eyes snap up to the blonde brat who keeps creating more work for me—as if I don't have a full enough plate as it is. I lower my arm to my side, my phone dangling loosely from my fingertips. I tap it against my thigh. "Lucky shot."

25

She smirks, glancing away, and in a blink, the knife in her left hand is tossed to the right, my phone flying from my grasp as both the knife and it clank to the floor.

I glare and she smiles brightly, like a fucking straight-up beauty queen. Bet she could snap her fingers at almost anyone, and on their knees they'd go.

Pretty little Piranha.

"If you wanted me to stay, sharpshooter, you could have just asked."

"I'm not well versed in asking," she fires back.

Glancing around the room, from the marble floors to the vaulted ceilings, weird-ass designs curved and carved along it, leading to giant pillars in each corner. Everything is shiny and crisp fucking clean. Expensive and unnecessary, like the three chandeliers, the dozen or more bundles of white and pink roses randomly scattered around the space, and the crystal containers holding them. They're useless. Wasteful.

I give a half shake of my head. "Nah, I bet the fuck not."

"You couldn't meet the minimum," she quips.

My gaze sharpens.

Interesting choice of words.

"You don't know me, girl. Don't play like you do."

"We do have a single table that's a short five *K*, but it's a one-hand walk. Win and walk or win and play again." She rolls along, believing she's speaking a language I don't know or can't follow.

It's like I said, the girl knows nothing about me.

"Let me guess." I cock a brow. "Game two is a ten *K* hand?"

Her eyes narrow slightly before she has a chance to stop them.

Not as clueless as you thought, huh, Rich Girl?

She covers her suspicion with a prissy press of her lips, smashed tight and puckered as if she tastes something sour. "Get them where you want them, right?"

We study each other for a long, silent minute.

"Why take my phone?"

26

Picking up her abandoned drink, she brings it to her lips for a slow sip. "You know why."

"Why do you care if I had your plate number?"

"Why would I tell you the answer to that when I did what was needed to make sure you didn't?" She uncrosses and recrosses her legs in the opposite direction, flashing the small triangle cloth hiding her pussy for a split second, and leans forward.

When I say nothing, she adds, "Only someone with something to hide would go through the trouble to *attempt* to retrieve what was stolen."

"And that right there's it, ain't it?" She took my phone because I *took* her plate number, but what's someone like her know about hiding or getting dirt beneath her fake fingernails? If I allowed the first glance to dictate the answer, it'd say not a damn thing.

She hums, her lips twitching, though her stare homes in. "What's your name?"

"It doesn't matter."

"It does if you want it on your headstone."

"I'd rather burn than be buried."

"Would you look at that." She grins, using my words against me as she picks up a third dagger she had tucked beneath her ass. Blindly pressing the sharp tip into her middle finger, she twirls it with her other hand. "Yet another thing we have in common."

Ever so slowly, her gaze pulls from mine and begins traveling across my face. She pauses on the scar near my left eye and then moves to my lips, swollen and straining against the lip ring—the one shot the fucker I left bleeding got on me tonight when he threw his head back in a last-ditch effort to get free.

Such a bitch move. He knew he had a debt to pay. He should have taken his punishment like a man. *Listen to words not meant for you, lose your ability to do so.* It's fair.

He's lucky I left him with one intact eardrum.

Honestly, he's lucky I left him with his life, but my bosses aren't exactly keen on unnecessary bloodshed.

Doubt this girl realizes it, but she's now drawing with the tip of the blade she holds, re-creating the smooth lines of the tattoos crawling up my neck from under my T-shirt, where her forest eyes are now glued. The blood spilled from tonight's cleanup job has dried, the large stain turning the thin cotton crisp against my skin, but I didn't exactly have time for a fuckin' wardrobe change in my rush to get my shit back from the little thief in front of me.

I don't have much, so no one gets to take what's mine. It might be broken now, but that's all right. So long as she has no use for it, I don't care. It's mine, and what's mine no one else is allowed to touch.

"If you walk out now, I might not send security to hinder your escape," she says, tipping her head as if to try and spot where the chain hanging at my left side leads.

"They couldn't stop me from gettin' in. What makes you think they could stop me from gettin' out?"

Green eyes meet mine. "How *did* you get in?"

My smirk is slow, and she glares.

"I will find out." She quickly adds, "Security might be a little lax tonight for the event, but all I have to do is pull up the surveillance videos."

I don't know what event she's talking about or why any kind of security would ease up instead of double down for an open event, but I don't say that.

I nod, taking slow strides toward her, and curiosity flicks across her face.

"Maybe, but then them *men* you got running around looking like a gang of Ask Jeeves would ask questions and *I'm* bettin' you don't wanna shed no light for them." I'm right in front of her now.

Her chin lifts defiantly, the slenderness of her throat causing my fingers to twitch. "You don't know me, fuckboy."

"Nah." I look from her long legs to the lacy cuffs circling her thick, toned thighs and the small clasps latched to the tips, connecting the thin material to her G-string. "But you're

28

quick to call me as you see me . . . and now I'm feelin' some type of way."

Interest sparks within her, the slight shift of her legs, that internal need for friction between them giving her away as she speaks. "And what, dare I ask, is it you're feeling?"

"The need to live up to it." My eyes slice to hers, just in time to witness yet another accidental reaction.

But for real, how shocked can she be?

Where I come from, a five-star meal is as rare as the car she was cruisin' in tonight. When you find it in front of you, you sure as fuck don't pass it off to the next asshole when you *know* it's within reach. Even she should recognize this much.

"You're insane." She shakes her head.

"Yeah." I nod mine, reaching forward to flatten my palms on either side of her as I creep in closer. "Are you?"

Slowly, her frown deepens, and she straightens up, her chest pressing into mine. I allow her to force me back a bit, but she says nothing, so I push a little more.

"Got to say," I keep on. "My radar for crazy is blaring, Barbie girl, and it's pointing back at you."

She hops down with a loud clink, her heels bringing her eye level with me. "I don't even know you."

"It's not like you'll see me again after tonight, so what's it matter?"

"You speak as if you'll make it out of here alive."

"Tell you what." I let my arms fall to my sides. "I make it out tonight. I'll consider coming back."

A rich, throaty chuckle works its way up her throat. "And why would I want that?"

"I don't know . . ." Gripping the folds of my leather jacket, I peel it off one sleeve at a time, tossing it to the side. My shirt's next and her attention instantly snaps from the ink on my forearms to the ink on my chest. Reaching out, I skate my knuckles along her bicep, covered in her long-sleeve white top. Still, she shivers. "Why would you?"

29

Her gaze pops up to mine, and I can see her wheels turning, a voice at the forefront of her mind telling her to back away. To end this. To do what she knows she should, be the good girl she spoke of but isn't. She knows she should send me out the door, yet she hesitates . . . but only for a quick fucking second before those green eyes sharpen with resolution.

And then she's on me, leaping with zero effort, those long legs locking along my belt at my back. She hauls herself forward, arching her back so her chest is resting just above my pecs, her lips begging to be bitten. She rolls her hips slightly and my chest rumbles in approval.

As if she's been waiting for the opportunity, her tongue comes out, flicking across my lip ring and my mouth opens instantly, but she's quick, denying my bite and causing my teeth to snap together on a harsh clink.

"In case you missed it," she shares, her voice thicker than before as reckless need swells within her. "I pressed the silent alarm."

I glare, and she smirks, saying, "You've got five minutes."

Bumping her ass with my knee, I toss her up a few more inches, catching her with a tight grip on the underside of her thighs. "I only need three."

"That's pathetic."

"Nah." I whip us around, going toward the chaise in front of the window. I lower to my knees, perching her ass on the edge of the fancy material I couldn't name if I tried. "That's skill. Now shut that pretty mouth unless you want me to fill it and put those heels on my shoulders."

She sucks in a sharp breath, her eyes darkening with desire, but her glare deepens as she tries to rein herself in, to stay in control. "Bossy much?"

"You have no idea."

Air whooshes past her lips when I unclip the shit along her thighs, the rough pads of my fingertips enticing her silky skin from nothing but the contact. I'd bet she's used to smooth, unworked hands touching her. Hands that are used to lotion and don't touch more than pens and paper. The green kind.

30

Unhappy with my pace, she tears her shirt over her head, revealing a bra the same shade as her sunbathed skin. "And in four minutes and fifteen seconds, no one else will either."

A gruff laugh leaves me, and I unbuckle my belt, freeing myself from my jeans. Her chin begins to dip, but my right hand flies up, catching it between my fingers before she can peek.

"You don't get to look."

Her brow quirks. "Afraid I'll judge?"

Yanking her ass to the edge, I dig a condom from my wallet, stuff it back in my pocket, and tear the package open with my teeth. "More like beg to taste." I keep her chin in my grasp as I roll it on and then jerk forward, pressing the tip of my dick to the triangle of her panties. "But there's no time for that."

A scoffed laugh escapes her, but then I press harder, and she hisses.

She feels it, the cool, smooth circles stretching against the rubber trapping them in. Her eyes widen, the muscles of her jaw fighting to be freed from my hold, but like I said, I have no intention of giving her a glimpse.

Maybe if she was a good girl and hadn't hit the alarm, I would.

If she were a good girl, we wouldn't be where we are . . .

She can drive herself mad, wondering what it was she felt sliding along her insides later.

Reaching between us, I pull the thin cloth aside. She cheats, swiftly swiping her thumb down, the tip brushing along my swollen head before I can fully buck my hips away, but she doesn't cop a single feel of the jewelry there, and I know that's what she was hoping for.

Her shoes slide slightly down my shoulder blades until the pointed spikes dig into the space just below my collarbone. She'll leave a mark for sure, and something tells me that's her intention.

I ease into her a few inches and her back bows, her golden hair spilling over her shoulders. I push the rest of the way in, following with slow, solid thrusts, and she pushes, her ass smashing against my dangling belt to match my pace. She's battling for dominance she won't gain, but I won't tell her that and ruin the fun.

Leaning forward, I put pressure on her legs. "Come on now, little thief." I skate my fingers along her outer thighs. "You can go wider for me."

Instantly, her legs fall wide open, her hips lifting, willing me deeper while keeping her heels pressed into my skin. I groan, my fingertips stretching along her waist and down to dig into her ass. I swear I'm in her fucking stomach now, a barrier reached, and I prod against it, over and over. She's full to the max, stretched so good around me, and when I adjust my hips the slightest bit, tipping them a little to the left, her back flies off the furniture.

"There it is," I groan, keeping my position, my dick rubbing along her walls, working her G-spot and this girl, she starts fucking dancing.

Straight up dancing, eyes closed, hips spinning in a circle, ass lifting off the seat and coming down just as fast, rolling in a crazy eight-like pattern. She doesn't lose her pace, doesn't stop pressing against me. She keeps moving, taking my cock like a champ as she chases her orgasm. And good for fucking her. She should since she hasn't a clue if I'll give it to her.

I will. But what she doesn't know is it won't be until the *very* last second when she starts to wonder if her earlier guess about selfishness is true. It ain't.

There's no fun to be had if the female isn't in it. I never would have touched her if I didn't sense how much she wanted me to. What's the point of fucking someone who's only out to make you feel good when you can do that shit on your own without the risks?

Real pleasure comes into play when you show your partner how well you can.

When she's gasping and panting and begging. When she's hooked.

My blood boils in pure approval at the thought of hooking a woman the likes of her.

32

What a sight we must be right now, a ritzy, pretty thing laid out, a dirtbag with dried blood and grease slicked on his hands standing over her, railing her perfectly pink pussy while she tangos on my rock-hard cock.

Fuck, I want to talk to her. Tell her how good she feels. How tight this pussy is, how her arousal is coating me, allowing me in even deeper. I want to tell her my dick loves the feel of her and that, for the first time in a long fucking time, I want to stay buried where I am, grind my piercings at every angle in her heat and watch her fucking thrash beneath me, pleading for more.

Then I want to ease her to her knees and watch her clean the crossing barbells with the tip of her rosy tongue in slow, delirious licks. After that, I'd drop beside her and take her tongue with my own, tasting us both before starting back at step one.

But I don't say any of that, and I'm betting she doesn't lick like a sweet little thing.

Nah, this one'll bite like a tiger. Draw blood and say it's your fault.

Maybe even punish you for it.

My kind of woman . . . yet the exact opposite, somehow.

Gripping her heels, I lower them to my sides so I can move in closer. My hand trails up her stomach as I press at the hard point between her ribs, skating beyond her breasts until my long fingers reach the magnet calling to them. My tongue glides along my lower lip as I curl my fingers around her throat, testing the shape against my palm.

What do you know, a perfect fucking fit.

Rich Girl gasps, her mouth hanging open, body lifting off the cushion as if I conjured her to me with my mind.

Long, silky hair meets my slick, sweaty skin, and I drop my eyes to where my dick slides in and out of her, faster and faster, and still she dances. Girl's got serious control of her rhythm, moving her body just the way she likes it. Again, good for fuckin' her.

Damn good for me, too.

"If you're going to grab me . . ." Her delicate fingers curve around my own, eyes two shades darker than before, like moss under the midnight light. "*Grab me.* I know you want to."

"I want to see the indents of my rings marked on your skin."

"Tease."

"Mm." Pulling my lip ring between my teeth, my hand closes tighter around her throat, and her mouth parts, curling up into a honied smile a moment later. Her palms flatten at her sides, eyes closing as if she's getting a fucking massage, not a solid pounding of her pussy.

I like it, like how she's not embarrassed about what she likes. She's flying high, and I put her there.

I rise to my feet then, leaning over her while keeping her half suspended in the air, and give my hips a better angle to finish this. "Legs up, knees against my sides, nice and fucking high," I growl, my eyes shut as I sink farther into her. "Pussy's good, gorgeous." The words had to be said. "Wet and tight."

"And stubborn."

I chuckle at her unexpected, slightly pouty tone, dropping my head so I can taste the peaked, peachy nipple in need of some attention. I press the cool metal of my lip piercing against the taut skin and she clenches around me.

"As it should be," I murmur against her. Grazing her with my teeth, I lick along her breast, past my hold at her neck, and close my mouth over her upper throat, just below her jawline. "Your cum should be earned, no?"

"Men should be capable of earning, *no*?" she mocks.

I dip my hips then, pressing to the left a bit, and she moans, loud and heady.

I do it again, and her arms give out, her elbows falling to the cushion on a gasp.

I do it a third time, but when I'm all the way in, I grind against her, flexing my cock to deepen the pleasure the magic cross piercing provides while applying pressure to her clit with my body. Time's running out, so I move back to her G-spot, hit against it with deep, repetitive nudges, not pulling out by even an inch but shoving all the way forward with each minimal retreat.

She grows impossibly tighter, suffocating my cock, and my thighs begin to burn, the muscles there tightening, heat swirling in my core.

Fuck yes, it's been a minute since my *cum was earned.*

She shatters, and she ain't quiet about it.

The girl has no shame, and as my eyes fixate on her flawless face, a dangerous desire simmers beneath my skin, sending my pulse hammering against my temples, my neck, my fucking fingertips as the devil on my shoulder whispers, *"mine"* his lie hot and heedless.

But I can't look away. My gaze is glued to hers as pleasure ripples through me, but I hold off, gritting my teeth as I grind into her. I try to wait for her walls to release their death grip on me, to loosen, but she begins to spasm all over again.

I pull my hips back, groaning as my hands replace her pussy on my cock. She whimpers from the loss, and a rough chuckle escapes me as a growl rattles her throat. Eyes on her dripping center, I tear the condom from my skin, my dick swelling angrily once freed. I yank once, twice, and cum spills, hot and thick, trickling down over her clit, warming the sensitive nub and making her entire body twitch.

I want to stay and watch, to rub my head over it, then trail it down her slit and push back inside for that after-sex finale, dragging every last bit of tension from our bodies.

Allow her to come again.

But I don't.

On my feet, I tuck myself back into my jeans, buckling the belt as I lean forward, yanking the tie off the thick, gold-and-white curtains guarding the window.

One of her eyelids pops open, then the other, slowly. The signs of a well-fucked woman.

"Satisfied?"

She smiles coyly, shrugging as she stretches her torso. "I will be once you get caught, and I can torture you for answers."

"What kind of torture you got in mind?"

She wants to smile wider but fights it.

"Question." She pauses for a breath, hers still labored. "Why hunt if not for the kill?"

She doesn't have to say it. I know she's talking about the dumb fucker we rolled over the hill.

A pretty little privileged girl who pulled up to find a man leaning over an unconscious one should have run off screaming at such a sight, yet here we are.

"Sometimes the tricks are understood better when coming from the clown."

"But a clown wears many faces, so who's to say this one won't hide in the shadows?"

"He can hide all he wants; I'll hear him coming. He, on the other hand, won't be hearing shit."

Small creases form along her forehead, smoothing out as she puts it together. "His eardrums."

I don't confirm or deny, and because my subconscious is on to something, I press my knee into the spot beside her satiated body, grasping her chin to hold her gaze to mine.

"Keep the blond James Bond out of your bed."

Surprise flickers through her. At my words or just remembering I was in here when he was, I don't know. Don't care.

She lifts a single brow. "How would you know if I did?"

Trailing my knuckles along the swell of her breast, I bring my eyes back to hers. "Fuck around and find out."

An unexpected scoff bubbles out of her, and I run my tongue along my bottom lip.

Her thighs clench, and I groan, then bend forward and tie the sash from the curtains over her eyes.

I'm down to twenty seconds, if that, but I take two to press my body into her naked one and bring my mouth to her ear.

"Thanks for the ride, Rich Girl."

And then I'm gone.

Chapter 3
Rocklin

"Ms. Milano, I *completely* agree. I'll speak to the student's adviser, and we'll come up with a proper punishment," I say into the air, my phone on speaker.

Bronx, the oldest by six months and the chameleon of our girl gang of three, rolls her eyes, sticks her tongue in her cheek and pumps her hand in front of her mouth. Always with the dirty mind, our sassy little Scorpio.

I clear my throat to hide a laugh and toss my lipstick at her, which she blocks with a pillow before falling over on the sofa in full-on dramatics as if this conversation is boring her to death.

"I know you will, Ms. Revenaw. We can always count on you girls to help guide the others into notable achievements," our sweet, yet incredibly underqualified dean—reason number one why our families were so keen on hiring the woman in the first place—sings our praises.

"Of course. We'll make sure she's given exactly what she needs, so when the next exam approaches, she will be prepared." I push on my eyebrow to perfect the arch, shifting in the mirror to make sure my uniform is pressed properly. "Cheating is most *definitely* unacceptable."

My eyes lift, finding Delta's porcelain face in the mirror as she slips behind me, whispering in my ear, "Unless you're the headliner in the nation's most prestigious prep school musical ensemble or the world's youngest Olympic diving champion or the next Pablo Picasso. Then it's entirely acceptable, yes, Coco Rocco?"

"Don't forget the tallest!" Bronx whispers.

I flip Delta off at the use of the rhyming nickname, and an airy laugh leaves her.

She and I were born two weeks apart, but it might as well have been two decades.

Delta is all regal and renaissance. She breathes grace and poise, whereas Bronx and I have to remember ours the older we get. Being the sole grandchild of a notable senator will do that, even if her mother is all the things she aspires *not* to become. Like a conniving, title-and-trust-fund-chasing bitch, for example. Delta is the very opposite.

She's coy, and while cunning is called for in our lives, Delta has a moral compass. Most of the time anyway.

"Thank you so much, dear. We'll see you soon."

"Bye, Ms. Milano." I smile as I speak, my tongue falling out the second I end the call and my bedroom door opening at the exact same time.

My spine goes rigid, eyes narrowing as my heart rate spikes, but then Saylor, the "lady's maid" of the north wing, my wing, steps in, a stack of towels piled high in her hands.

She jerks to a stop, her light eyes widening as they meet mine. "I'm so sorry. I thought you had left already, or I never would have—"

"Saylor, it's fine." My shoulders ease. "I didn't expect you is all, and why are you carrying all that? I told you, you don't—"

"Please." She yanks them back when I approach, so I pause. "Let me do as I'm assigned. It makes everything easier."

The way she says "easier" and the quick break in eye contact doesn't go unnoticed, but I simply nod, and then what she said hits me. "Why exactly did you think I was gone?"

Her features contort—no one likes being a rat. "Jasper called about twenty minutes ago, saying I could start my tasks early if I wanted. He thought you left with Mr. Donato and his wards."

Bronx rises, dark, thick curls bouncing around her slender face. "Of course he did." She looks to me. "I wonder where he got that idea?"

Jasper is the house manager here, the one who divvies out the tasks and is in charge of making sure life at Greyson Manor flows as smoothly as the silk curtains draped along each and every window. Unlike the coarse embroidered draperies in the Greyson suite at The Enterprise, something I didn't discover until it was lowered over my eyes. Even the sash was roughly textured, the golden threading scratchy to the touch, almost as coarse as the fingers that tied it in place . . .

Memories of last night flash before me, still fresh in my mind, as I run the tips of my nails over my lips.

Fingers of a felon, if I had my guess. I bet he comes from chaos. The depiction of death represented in bold ink along his skin is hint enough if the healing of busted knuckles and the small nicks and scars along his skin didn't make it obvious all on their own.

Yeah, I bet his world is as dark as his ink-black hair.

Could it be as fucked as mine?

He *did* have his man roll the bloody and beaten one down a hill, so . . . maybe?

I didn't spot any family crests on his skin, and his rings were inconsequential, random shapes of personal expression he likely picked up—or stole—here and there. His car, while the VIN was scratched and the license plate removed, was nothing special and held no markings. He didn't utter a key name or code word to reveal who he was or that he was aware of exactly who *I* was.

We are at The Enterprise, the "event venue"—or so the description reads when you look it up online—we established a few years ago as a power move. A new venue allowed us to play the game, offering suites and a sense of superiority to the families of the surrounding areas, who believe they are just that. Important, superior, worth more than they actually are. Like the mayor of the bordering town and the governor, the widowed philanthropist, and the district attorney, one for his wife and one for his mistress—those last few come in handy more often than my father would like.

The point is, it's not just the Greysons and those attached to us who are in attendance this weekend. The suites are open to our strategically chosen "equals," as well as those we allow to acquire tickets to the concert. That's a lot of possible entry points.

It's not like the nameless intruder worked his way into Greyson Manor, knowing exactly who he'd find inside. Father hasn't mentioned a breach, and Bronx isn't fixated on her computer screen, typing away at hyperspeed.

If he was spotted or captured, I would know it, but he wasn't.

So, if he *is* a gangster, he's an insignificant one.

"Damiano needs to rein in his wards." Delta pulls me from my thoughts when she speaks of the bothersome brothers, the newest pains in the ass, to join us here in the manor. "They did this to Sasha last week," she mentions the dedicated maid of her wing. "The poor girl and what she walked in on." Delta's skin pinkens at her own memory.

"What *did* she walk in on?" I tease, knowing the possibilities are endless with her and her two boyfriends. They'd do absolutely anything she asked, and they'd do it well.

Delta only smiles as she grabs her purse off the vanity and heads for the door. "The point is, those Greco boys are causing trouble, just as we were warned they would. They've become a handful."

"Couple handfuls, if I had to guess." Bronx smirks as she slips into her blazer, refusing to button the front until she absolutely has to. She waggles her brows when she meets my eyes. "Tell me they don't scream Big Dick Energy?"

"No. They scream gonorrhea."

Bronx laughs loudly as Saylor's cheeks turn as red as her sparkly shoes and she quickly disappears into my closet.

"I'll have Dom talk to them." I frown, irritated by the entire situation, and head down the stairs. "In the meantime, we'll beat them at their own game. Serve them a little trouble right back." I might have been warned to keep my distance, but I was also instructed to be sure they never forget their place.

As if we would allow anyone to.

"Ooh, yes." Bronx's hips sway a little more. "Now I almost hope Dom doesn't do as he's told for once, but this is you we're talking about. Everyone is so quick to submit."

Not everyone, my mind whispers, flashing back to a silver loop wrapped around a faultlessly full lip before my eyes.

Frowning, I force a smile as the girls share a laugh as we continue to the main floor.

The Greyson Manor truly is a thing of beauty.

The centuries-old castle of sorts sits on a one-hundred-acre estate, a seventeen-foot iron gate wrapping around its entirety—the first level of defense against outsiders.

Rumor has it the original deed included another thirty-five acres, that land extending beyond our back gardens, and currently covered in rows of giant trees, hiding the abandoned mansion at its front, but greed is said to be the reason proof cannot be found.

The manor itself is made up of four wings: north, south, east, and west, one dedicated to each of us girls and those we wish to move into them, with the others' approval, of course.

The single and sole entry leading to each wing meets in the same place, off the sides of the sixty-foot entryway. Only the first dozen stairs are visible from the foyer, keeping what lies beyond a mystery to those uninvited to ascend. Each wing's stairway curves and curls in the same way, so the final step of all four meet against the same marble flooring at the same distance, representing equal ground.

The west and south wings land on the left side of the room, the east and north on the right.

If I look to my right, I find the giant oak doors trimmed in gold leading to the outside, and if I look to my left, the far wall parallel to the front door and beneath the overhanging balcony of the lounge is another set of doors, these ones larger, thicker. Bulletproof. *Sound*proof.

It's the chancellor's chambers.

As a cardinal girl of Greyson, the four points of the compass that make us go round, we are chancellors ourselves, which is our world's way of saying our words outweigh all . . . with a little bit of coercion from our families, of course. But to be head chancellor is the highest point of power. The empress of all.

Or emperor, as it stands. Calvin Greyson—a.k.a. Calvin Moore—is a good chancellor, but he's not meant for the seat he occupies. He represents the Greyson name as a whole to the outside council, unrelated to our core four families.

Calvin's job is to work with those that are sort of like us but not a threat to our operations on the outside of our districts to keep us under the radar, so we can function within our own laws and way of life, cities hidden within cities, so to speak. He doesn't deal in the things we do. His hands stay pristine, as intended.

He was raised, hell, he was *born*, to represent our generation and the one to follow. In a few years' time, he'll start making political moves, slowly sliding into office, and eventually, when the time comes for Delta's grandfather to step away from the Senate, our people will do all that's necessary to place Calvin in his position.

As my father says, we have to have an ear within the government at all times. How else would corrupt organizations get away with all the shit they did if they didn't have someone of "legitimate" power in their back pockets?

Head chancellor of the Greysons, which includes both the manor and the academy, was intended to be a solitary position, but when our Helena, our last chancellor and Damiano's great-aunt, was found dead in her bathtub four years ago, Calvin was asked to step up, and so he did.

He was a decision of circumstance. We know this. *He* knows this, and we respect him all the same. He's harsh, brutal when the situation calls for it but fair and honest. Basically, if you fuck up, you earn the outcome, and so on.

The moment Bronx lowers her left heel to the shiny floor with a soft clink, the man himself steps out.

Calvin's eyes lift to ours, a single brow rising. "All hail from the north. That can't be good," he teases.

"I would take the trip *south* if you allowed me the pleasure, Mr. Greyson." Bronx not so subtly purrs.

Calvin's jaw clenches, but he says nothing, simply nods his chin in farewell and saunters off, the tension of his faintly impressive muscles visible through his tailored suit.

He doesn't make it out of earshot before laughter flows from us, and we step through the front doors, already being held open, our car waiting right at the edge of the steps.

Sai, the man who drives us as a trio and my own personal guardian every other second of my life, is there, ready and waiting.

He winks as I approach, the slight wrinkles at the edge deepening with the action as he crosses his right hand over his left, thrusting his chin high, proud to show off the markings of his neck—the double-walled *G*, identical to the ring on his right hand, he's put on display, burned and branded into his skin, a representation of the oath he took to protect and serve at all costs. To always put me and my safety above all others at all times, including at the risk of his own life.

It sounds a little over the top but in my world? It's necessary, and the fact that Sai chose to dedicate his life to protecting mine means more than I can express.

Delta is the last to slide in. "You should have asked Calvin to travel south, doubling the chances of him taking one of the two offers—your wing or your hoo-ha."

Bronx sighs dramatically, playfully fanning herself. "Or I could just spread my legs *very unladylike* the next time I'm called into his office and asked to sit in the chair across from him."

"Why does it sound like you need to add 'again' to the end of that sentence?" I flick my eyes her way over my compact mirror, triple-checking I didn't get lipstick on my teeth.

"One chip at a time, Rocco. You know the game best. Dom took a chisel to your ice years ago and only just broke through."

"Which is awfully sad when you think about it." Delta joins in on Bronx's fun. "It's not like he requires a Magnum-sized hole."

"Poor Damiano and his six-inch grower not shower," Bronx adds with a faux pout.

I roll my eyes but chuckle along with them.

They're only teasing. All three of us have seen Damiano naked, be it out at the Greyson lake house, when we'd go late-night skinny dipping or, on occasion, his suitless laps in the pool on the grounds. Or simply when he decides to strip down to his birthday suit on fun, drunken nights of partying.

He's far from girthy challenged, and he *has* worn me down over the last few months. If 'wore me down' refers to the fact that his argument of being a capable, wanting young man as I am a capable, needy young woman, and the idea that we could benefit sexually from one another has finally begun to make a lick of sense.

Sai loops our car around the long driveway, through the first set of iron gates, blocking us off from the rest of the estate, and starts down the long road that sometimes feels never ending.

Most of my life is spent within these walls and when I'm not here, I'm shadowed everywhere I go.

Sai may come off as the perfect, silent chauffeur, and he is as far as everyone else is concerned. He pretends he doesn't hear whatever is said and that he doesn't see whatever is to be seen, when really, he sees everything, hears everything, *knows* every-freaking-thing. He has this sixth sense when it comes to me.

Ten years as my guardian will do that.

When I was a little girl, he was my dad's shadow, the man with the muscle when my dad wasn't in the mood to use his own, and then just before my mother died, he became mine.

He's taller than tall and built like a bull, with wide shoulders and arms that threaten to shred the seams of his suit jacket. His nose is a bit crooked and he has small scars littering his features, but not in a way that makes him appear rugged. His hair is as dark as his eyes, but over the last few years, hints of gray have popped up in the hairline near his temples. Him and my dad both.

44

When they stand beside each other, they look every bit as menacing as they did ten years ago. Age has only made them stronger, as it tends to do when everyone is trying to be the next you.

I know why my dad put his oldest and his most trusted friend with me.

There is no doubt in my mind, or anyone who knows the man behind the mask, that if anyone ever dared come after me, he'd go full-blown John Creasy on their ass.

The car continues at a steady pace, rolling through the parallel rows of palm trees, the peak lights that normally illuminate their height no longer glowing under the morning sun. As the last set disappears behind us, the road widens and curves, taking us around the dormitory and out the second gate that blocks it off from the academy building.

The only way for students, all of whom are required to live on campus, to get to the school and outside the estate grounds is through the bottom floor of the boarding house. It narrows into a single tunnel, leading straight into the Power Play Hall of Greyson Elite. People often ask why the school isn't protected within the grounds of the Greyson property, as if the third and final iron fence locking us in isn't protection enough, not to mention the guards all around, but if they gave it even half the thought they should, they would find the answer quite simple.

Greyson Elite is a prestigious private school for young scholars: the geniuses of our world and the rare few lucky enough to be invited. We're a nationally accredited academy, though we don't publicize such a rudimentary term.

If a concerning complaint or perilous predicament were to be whispered into the county sheriff's ear or reach the district attorney's office before we had a chance to sweep our own halls, we couldn't exactly keep them off "academy" grounds when investigating. Pay the right people to make things disappear, yes. Keep them off the grounds, no.

But preventing them from sniffing around the problems in our own personal place of residence? Easy as the SATs.

It's rare for an issue to slip under the radar, but it has happened in the past, and we're not naive enough to assume it couldn't happen to us.

It all comes down to one idea: Greyson Elite is no joke.

It's competitive and cutthroat. We've allowed enough rumors to roam, strategic ones, of course, alluding to what our personal interests are in the students of this place, so everyone is constantly slicing the ankles of the person in front of them in hopes for their time to shine. We encourage it. People either graduate and move on, get stepped on, or are *hired* on if they show promise or possess a specific skill our founders, a.k.a. our fathers, are after—reason number one most are presented with an invitation into the school to begin with, to help build our teams.

Tech whiz? Check.

Ties to prominent families overseas? Check.

Can hang five minutes sparring with Bronx or Damiano? Check *and* a golden star.

If you're connected to our world in any way with a kid in their last year of high school, you're waiting next to your mailbox on May 1 with bated breath, the official invite day.

There is no waiting list for those who decline, which is a rarity in itself.

You're in, or you're not, and once you are, you better be ready to work.

There are dozens of positions to fill and new ones to be created when promise shows itself.

That's the beauty of the Greyson Empire. We aren't stuck in a time loop where our elders know best and we don't fix what isn't broken. Buildings crash and crumble with no sign of a crack.

Tsunamis arise and destroy with little, if any, warning.

Here, we don't hold on to what was but look toward what can and will be.

If you're worthy, the possibilities are endless.

If there's no place for you, you can create one.

It can be that simple . . . or it can be the hardest thing you'll ever do.

No one can ever say Greyson Elite Academy is easy, and that's exactly the way we want it. It's as I said . . . only the supreme is selected, and only the strongest survive.

Heiress or not, no one can claim my girls and I haven't earned our birthright.

And no one will know about the secret society we've created within the Greyson world unless we decide we want them to.

"Game faces, bitches." Bronx straightens her shoulders, preparing to be seen once the door is pulled open, and the two of us follow suit. "It's time to play plastic."

She is first from the door, and I follow.

As per usual, at the top of the steps, leaning against the wall closest to the entrance, stands Delta's boyfriends, Alto and Ander. Beside them, Damiano is propped with one foot against the wall, and his arms crossed over his chest with his wards at his side, the slightly psychotic, potentially problematic Greco brothers. The five of them stand back, watching as we step out, patiently waiting to fall in line behind us. They're careful not to make eye contact with me but smile slyly at my flirty friend.

Delta is the last to get to her feet, and then Sai closes the door, folding his hands loosely in front of him and giving a curt nod to the boys. And then he waits, as he always does. I'm not exactly sure how long he stays at the edge of the curb, but he's always there when I look back.

Together, we girls hit the brick steps, our strides the same width, paces mirrored, and pastel pleaded uniforms pressed to perfection.

We're the picture of poise: calm and collected, intriguing and intuitive.

Outright unattainable yet utterly approachable.

A brilliant example for all to aspire to.

Just before we pass the threshold into the exquisite, Roman-inspired building with its high arches and hand-carved woodwork, we pause beside the gold-infused beams, a dozen more stretching along the walls ahead. I meet my girls' eyes, and a flicker of humor grins back from each. With hidden smirks and stimulated minds, we glide into the school, prepared to assume our roles for the day, secretly desperate to *own* the night.

And we will.

We always do.

Chapter 4
Bass

The heavy beating in the background has my body jolting upright, palms slick with sweat as I clench the bat in my hand, ready to swing at a moment's notice, but then the pounding sounds again and I recognize it for what it is, heavy knuckles coming down on the cheap wooden door.

"Up, Bishop. Now." Keffer's voice comes through right as the room shifts into focus, and I spot the morning light streaming past the cracks of the broken blinds.

My shoulders ease and I pop my neck, tossing the wooden weapon—the only fucking "weapon" I'm allowed to keep in this house—on the bed.

"Yeah," I call back, running my hands down my face.

I've lived in this group home for almost four years now. Came here after I put a bullet in my old man . . . two seconds before he pulled a trigger himself, the barrel of his gun pointed at my baby sister.

She's all right.

He's dead.

Too kind of an ending for a heavy-handed motherfucker like him, if you ask me. I'd have liked to drag it out a bit, maybe tie him up, put him through half the shit he put us through, but that would have given my mom time to try and save him, and turning a gun on her wasn't necessary . . . at least not in front of my sister. That, and a bullet, is too merciful anyway.

She didn't deserve the air she was left to breathe. She was everything a mother shouldn't be, a real piece of shit who loved her husband more than her kids, went along with all he did because he was more important. He never hit her, and she never did raise her own hand to us . . . just helped him ice his own after he would. She is a weak, worthless woman who will get what's coming to her, wherever the fuck she is.

My sister Brielle and I, we're nothing like them.

Nah, that's a lie.

My dad was an angry piece of shit, and so am I, but it ain't the same. I get pissed, annoyed, vindictive when I feel the need, and yeah, I'm pretty fucking violent, but when you grow up in shit you can't control, controlling the shit you willingly put yourself into is a whole lot different.

I made a deal when I moved to this group home, and that deal meant the scrappy motherfucker inside me gets to come out to play when the situation calls for it. Lucky me, it just so happens the situation always seems to call for it.

Rich pricks mixing with poor punks will do that.

Thankfully, what I said about my sister is true. She might share our blood, but she's different. Better. Brielle is gentle, kind, and quiet. She's thoughtful and selfless, and I miss the hell out of her, but after the life we were born into, the last thing I wanted was her living in a group home full of teenage girls angry at the world, so when I was offered a job in exchange for a room in this twisted town, I countered the offer, asking Brielle be shielded from any more bullshit.

How she isn't as jaded or as screwed up as the girls in the home across the yard from this one, I don't know, but she ain't, and I'll die trying to keep it that way.

She's staying with our aunt a state over, still has a couple years of school left, which should be enough time for me to set us up someplace new. Somewhere that will be ours, where the only rules I'll have to follow are the ones I set for myself.

I don't hate it here. The house might be old and worn down, full of teenage punks with more problems than sense, but the hot water works, and the food's free. Money ain't much, but at least they pay me, and the job feels like shit I was born and bred for. But the biggest fuckin' bonus? I'm here because I choose to be, not 'cause some jackass judge, who knows nothing about the streets or the kids who come from it, says I have to be.

I aged out a while ago, but this place ain't like most, and I'm here until I'm ready to leave.

Or until I fuck up.

Only, I won't fuck up.

But I *will* level up.

I don't want to be the poor punk. The hands' man. The go-to guy.

I want to be *the* guy.

My mind itches for more. I just have to figure out where to find it.

"Bishop, let's go!" Keefer's voice slices through my thoughts.

I quickly tug on a pair of faded jeans and a T-shirt, then snag my jacket off the bed, making it as quick as possible—something we're all required to do. I don't have the same rules as everyone here, but I do the basic shit so no one bitches and causes unnecessary problems.

Slipping out of the room, I close the door behind me, meeting Keefer in the kitchen.

He's a big dude, tall as me, but with muscles that bulge like a beast. The man's shoulders are so wide he has to turn his body to fit through the doorframe. His physique is probably part of the reason he's "caretaker" of this house—it takes a monster of a man to keep all these punks in line. He can rein in a gang of teenage assholes with ease, most times with just a look, depending on the situation.

Keefer leans against the counter, coffee cup in hand, watching a kid named Wyatt finish up his chores. Wyatt nods my way as he walks out, and once he's gone, I pull open the fridge, pushing aside the piles of vegetables to find the energy drink I buried.

Fucking thing's gone.

Sighing, I stand, flipping off Keefer when he laughs.

"Take it your skipping classes again this mornin'?" he asks.

"I'll be there." Late, but I'll be there.

He nods. "Warehouse again tonight?"

Filling a cup of water, I look at him.

Am I going? Yes. I go every night we open the place, but I have other shit to do today before I head over to run the fights I'm paid to handle, but none of that has anything to do with Keefer. He might be in charge in this house, but when it comes to the jobs of this town, he's told only what he needs to know, and that ain't much. We all have our roles, and until you're the one assigning what those are, you fill yours, or you're gone.

But I didn't earn myself the spot of the man in charge of the ring by simply doing as I'm fucking told. I do shit my way, always, and no one says a word because what's asked of me gets done. If, at the end of the day, no rock's left unturned, no hint that can't be hunted, then no one gives a fuck how it happens, and all's good. And me?

I'm damn fucking good.

I know it.

They know it.

And later tonight, the fucker who thought he was slick from last week's fights will know it too.

I'll show him why you don't fuck the hand that holds the honey, one broken bone at a time.

Rocklin

It's never fun breaking a girl's spirit.

Well . . . that's a lie. Depending on the situation, it can be entertaining as hell, but fun or not, it's a necessary evil.

Ms. Milano caught a second-year attempting to cheat, and Greysons do not cheat. They're the best of the best because they work for it. She didn't, so her privileges at The Enterprise are no more.

"Back to being as equal as any other student she goes," Delta singsongs, waving as she heads out the door, her class on the other side of the building this morning.

"So much for a Wednesday girl." Bronx drops onto the mini sofa, slipping a sucker between her lips. "And speaking of downgrades. I need a date for the fundraiser next month."

"What happened to going with Victor, the *dirty politician with a dirtier mouth*?" I tease.

"You know that one Cardi-B song? The hook, the lean . . ." She smiles. "Turned out he had neither."

Laughter bursts from me, and she winks, then pops up and heads out, closing the door behind her.

I move across the room, toying with my necklace as I stare out the large window that makes up the entirety of the back wall of the room.

This building sits on a large platform of sorts, bringing us two stories off ground level, and the school itself is three, this room located on the highest one. The view, while not extraordinary, is far from pedestrian.

In the distance, large city buildings block the sun from destroying the gardens, both built and managed by the prospects here to learn about giving back to the earth—basically young men and women looking to add some check marks to their portfolios, so when they seek investors or run for political positions in the future, they find it easier to swing the farmers and hardworking citizens their way. Or their families use farmlands as a cover business, so no one comes asking where their wealth comes from, which means they better know the difference between a hoe and a ho.

Separating us from the city is a small river. The only way in or out of our zone, once you wind back down the hillsides, is a single bascule bridge—talk about the perfect location.

Behind me, the door to the room opens and closes, but I don't bother looking, the soft cedar scent of his cologne giving him away with a single inhale.

Damiano's palms close around my shoulders, and he glides them down my blazer, giving me a light squeeze. "Everything will work out, Rocklin."

"I'm not concerned. There are plenty more students in this school to pick from." None of which we're interested in that we're not already testing, but I don't need to tell him this. He already knows.

"I'm not talking about the girl and her ranking." He steps closer. "I'm talking about what your father told you yesterday, but you knew that already. I tried to talk to you about it before, but you cut me out."

He's right, I did, but if he's brave enough to ask, he needs to be required to actually do so.

"Don't cut me out. You're stressed." His voice ends in a low whisper, and from behind, he brings my knuckles to his warm, soft lips. "I can help with that." His free hand slides around my body, pulling me further into him.

This is typical Damiano behavior, dying to be the white knight and waiting for the moment I need one, a moment I hope never comes.

The girls know about his offer of marriage, just as they know it's not going to happen, and of course, it's not due to my late mother's one marital condition that her children would never be the victims of an arranged marriage—I guess her death overrode that little clause.

It's because I'm not interested in becoming my sister and the disaster she's become. Plus, my father would never allow the union, and it has nothing to do with the relentless efforts of my father's business associate's heir, Oliver Henshaw, shooting his shot with me every chance he gets.

Damiano is the son of a henchman who succumbed to greed and trusted the wrong man with his treachery. His mother was a random beauty paid to provide his heir and never heard from again after his birth.

I'm the daughter of the most notorious kingpin my world has ever known, the man all men must come to if looking to cross from the eastern to the western borders. My mother was the sole heir of the largest real estate enterprise in the nation, giving my father the furthest reach a man in his position has ever had.

His family is falling.

Mine is nearly limitless.

My father isn't an ignorant man. He knows Damiano is a fantastic asset, the kind you want on your side, and he does admire his dedication, but as of right now, it stops there.

As for me as a person and not as a Greyson or the daughter of Rayo Revenaw, Dom is only relevant when he and I wish to capitalize on matters of a *personal* nature.

It works for us. It's easier, safer. He doesn't have to worry if a woman will claim foul play in search of a quick payout, and I don't have to worry about a gun being pressed to my neck when expecting lips instead—that was one of those lessons you need only learn once.

Dark hair and crystal eyes flash in my mind, and I frown.

Or maybe I didn't learn a damn thing . . .

The best part of it all, outside of not being potentially murdered or kidnapped as a bone for barter, is Dom still does as he pleases, with whomever he pleases, *whenever* he pleases, which I more than appreciate. The last thing I need is him coming after me to the point of obsession, and exclusivity always leads to something to that effect. I've led enough welcome wagons for girls dumped here for this very reason to know firsthand.

Fucking rich boys, I swear.

Damiano Donato, while a lover of all things love and the truest romantic I've ever seen, wants me outside of the bedroom for one reason, and that is what a position at my side offers him. But it's as my father says, *money does not give you power and love destroys everything*.

Damiano would fall in love with me if I allowed him to, and that love would get him killed.

Just as it did my mother . . .

"You didn't have to put yourself at risk by relieving Sai last night and taking off in your favorite car."

Irritation prickles along my skin. I don't like to be psycho-analyzed, but I am stressed. Tense. So I stand silent in his arms a moment but say in the next, "I'm giving morning announcements in five minutes."

"You're right." He releases me as he steps away, and it's only when he adds, "Not nearly enough time anyway, is it?" that I realize my irritation isn't only coming from this conversation and the fact that he dared to have it, but also in the direction I took it.

Dom's words should be enticing, the statement sensual, alluding to naughty things, but it doesn't quite ring right when you happen to know that while, yes, he's known to last the night . . . he took my five-minute warning as his hint to exit, when he could have read it as a challenge.

I only need three, the raspy roughness of my intruder replays in my mind.

What a smooth bastard he was.

With one last kiss to my knuckles, Dom makes his way to the door.

"Before I go." He pauses. "Sergio mentioned a security alert came through."

I don't allow my frown to slip into place, my focus remaining out the window while my lungs expand.

Did he get caught after all?

"Oh?"

Damiano doesn't respond right away. "There was a ping of your Aston Martin this morning. Someone ran the plate number, but the system was unable to pick up from where . . ."

He doesn't ask why someone would feel a need to run the plate in the first place like he wants to, hoping I'll offer the answer on my own.

I spin to face him, meeting his gaze with a fixed one of my own. "Thanks for the heads-up."

When I say nothing else, he takes the hint, leaving me alone once more.

I walk around the desk, lower into the seat, and pull the microphone over, placing it directly before me.

So Tall and Tattooed dug a little deeper. The Aston was stored the minute I stepped out of it, which means he memorized my plate number in the six seconds he saw it, but not only that. Our security couldn't figure out where the search came from?

Interesting.

Well, interestingly irritating.

As I watch the clock tick toward game time, my phone screen lights up with a silently delivered text, and I glare at it a long moment before clicking on the unknown sender's message.

Unknown: Shame, Rich Girl. Thought we were on the same page.

My lips press into a small smile, and I lean back in the chair.

Me: Should I know who this is and to what it is you're referring?

Unknown: Cute. In a bratty, not at all attractive type of way. You know who this is, and you know what I mean. James Bond. His lips. Your skin.

I fly to my feet, spinning and flicking my gaze along every inch of space beyond the glass window. No sign of a black, moppy mess in sight. He can't possibly be on the grounds. Eyes flick from my screen to the glass and back.

Me: Careful. Stray dogs get put to sleep.

My warning falls on deaf ears, or maybe dumb ones, as he responds in kind.

Unknown: Listen. Bad pussies don't.

The innuendo couldn't be clearer. If I were less trained in the art of composure, my jaw might have fallen open, and a laugh might have followed.

He's ridiculous.

Clueless.

He's also quite bold and, yes, clearly lacks any sense of self-preservation, but bold nonetheless. So he thinks he's capable of wearing me out, of "putting me to sleep," does he?

Me: I create rules. What gave you the impression I would follow any?

I wait for that instant response, for his quick wit and ready remark.

It never comes, and irritation turns in my stomach at an irrational, not to mention uncharacteristic move such as that one.

The clock ticks its final second, and I quickly reclaim my place behind the desk, but my mind is reeling, my fingers twitching with the need to tap the trigger of cool steel.

So, Dom knows I was somewhere I shouldn't have been.

Tall and tattooed knows who I am and where to find me.

My dad knows I don't agree with his decision.

And *I know* those are all facts, meaning there is nothing I can do about all the above.

What utter bullshit is that?

Boiling with irritation, I flip on the gem-covered switch in front of me.

"Good morning, Greyson, Rocklin Revenaw here . . ."

My smile is wide, my voice welcoming.

Not a care in the fucking world.

58

Chapter 5
Rocklin

Swiping her rich-red lipstick across her full lips, Bronx winks at herself in her compact mirror, tossing it in her clutch the same moment Sai lets off the brake, the car rolling forward for our turn to exit.

Delta and I lean back into the seat as Sai's shadow passes the window, and seconds later, he's tugging the door open, and one long leg at a time, she climbs out. Once he closes us inside, the blackout windows providing no insight to those around us that two girls still sit inside, we shift in our seats to watch.

Spine straight, shoulders stretched and squared with perfect form, Bronx floats her way toward the door. The dress of choice tonight is the exact shade of her lips, an enticing contrast against the smoky softness of her golden skin. Her curls are tight and pulled back in a sleek, low band, leaving her collarbone and neck completely exposed, ebony ringlets teasing the nape of her neck.

Delta and I chuckle when not one but both men positioned at the bottom steps—security disguised as the welcoming committee—lift their hands, dying for a chance to test the smoothness of her skin against theirs.

Our girl is happy to oblige, of course, making direct eye contact with both and lifting her arms slightly so their fingers brush and guide along her forearms, purring her thanks and even managing a hint of a blush along her high cheekbones.

With the grace of an angel, she climbs the steps outside of the Cia Bella Century Hall, where the next set of men is ushered forward. They tip their heads as if to bow, sweeping their hands out as the doors are pulled open for her.

It's not until she disappears inside that Sai rolls forward, looping us around the back. We're at a complete stop for no more than five seconds, just long enough for him to place a hat on his head, glasses on his face, and a ring on his left hand. Slowly, we ease back into the line of arriving cars as if we hadn't yet driven through.

"Two at the edge of the carpet, two at the top, and now *four* at the door." Delta smooths two fingers down from her perfect middle part, making sure every piece of hair is slick straight against her scalp, her bun so tight, the almond arch of her eyes seems even more defined than normal.

I eye the men, but as the two newcomers settle into position, the other two disappear to the left. "They're rotating."

"That could be a problem."

I nod but straighten as someone comes forward, opening the door when Sai doesn't step out. "Ready?"

"Starved."

My smirk slips free. Of course she is. She's been locked away in the music room for a few weeks now, perfecting her fall performance for the Greyson Gala, the largest and most prestigious event of the year set to take place in six weeks' time.

Unlike Bronx, Delta and I keep our heads pointed straight, our chins high, *too* high. So high, the doormen sour, their gazes not once seeking or lingering on the two spoiled socialites, especially not when not only our attitude is the polar opposite of our south-wing siren tonight but our clothing of choice as well.

Delta wears a tailored tan dress, the hem modest at the knee and sharp across the shoulder, little to no skin beyond her arms and calves showing, with flat white pumps. Mine is as equally dull, a classic ivory with half-cuff sleeves and a slight slit down the back seam, offering no more than an inch above the bend of my knee. My shoes are identical in color and two inches shorter than my staple.

We're basic and boring and utterly forgettable.

"I'm going to burn this shade of lipstick when we get home." My lips hardly part as I speak, but Delta's answering hum tells me she hears and the slight brush of her fingertips along the hips of her dress says she plans to do the same with her wardrobe.

As we step into the foyer, Delta settles her gaze on a group of men conversing around a tall cocktail table and pivots with grace in their direction. They look like your standard fundraiser attendees—dime-a-dozen suits, lack of excitement, and wrists wrapped in flashy watches. Basically, someone told them they had to be here, and while they like to pretend they're men of many decisions, they're not. Someone said show up, so here they are, being seen and making small talk no one gives a shit about as they wait for the moment to make their donation and be on their way.

I recognize some attendees from past events. A bigwig banker and the lawyer who made this small town's latest indiscretion disappear, to name a few, but we didn't hop on a helicopter for an hour's trip several towns over to be spotted by people who may or may not know who we are.

So I curve away from the familiar faces, leisurely weaving my way through the room, accepting a flute of champagne from a stone-faced brunette, her bow tie sharp and high at her collar. She continues past me, skating along the edge of each cluster of patrons.

Bringing the glass to my mouth, I tip it the slightest bit, pressing my lips along the rim as I shift a bit, giving myself a full-access view of the space.

The Cia Bella is a pretty place, the art all replicas rather than originals, the frames painted with gold rather than made of it, but the design is quite nice, even if the architect did essentially rip off one Charles Lameire with the dome-like design, sharp tunnel-like sides framed by paneled windows that sweep above as well.

Musee d'Orsay, anyone?

Out of the corner of my eye, I find Bronx where intended, three men towering over my friend's five-four frame, her heels sleek but decisively on the shorter side tonight.

Be the picture of desire, utterly unmissable in a space full of powerful men, but to get the attention of the one you want, pretend you're not the baddest bitch in the room when, little does he know, you are more than he could handle on his best day. Smile shy, gasp when he accidentally grazes your skin, and fake a flush when his eyes tell you he's envisioning you bent over his bed.

Sadly, it really is so simple, and my nympho friend is a master of the craft—something the women positioned beside the hedgehogs, dying for five minutes alone with B, hate. Especially since she spent the last two days memorizing every detail and running numbers related to their corporation. She's full of stats and ideas and fake-ass fascination for their mildly performing, highly unstimulating pharmaceutical corporations—it always pays to have a photographic memory.

She's dazzling them with digits and details, making them wish the women on their arms stayed home tonight. As predicted, the women don't want to stand beside a woman more brilliant than them, so when the brunette server passes by the very next moment, without pausing beside them, they follow her toward the open bar.

Delta's eyes breeze past mine at that moment, and then she weaves right as I move left. At the last second, she turns, smiling at a random person as she shuffles forward, her elbow nudging Bronx in the back.

B falls into the tall, blond man in front of her with a gasp, and his eager palms clasp her forearms in an instant, steadying her against her chest.

Her chin dips, eyes flicking up to his, and I almost let a laugh slip as I use the slim space now present between the other men, who instantly shuffled back at the sound of B's gasp.

My chest brushes one, and I smile at him. "Excuse me."

I ease through the small space, tucking my champagne flute closer to my chest.

The man smiles, opening his mouth to speak, but I curve behind him, and he doesn't care enough to spin away from Bronx completely.

"Think they've already placed bets on who she leaves with tonight?" Delta whispers when she falls in line beside me in the hall.

Tucking the man's wallet into the sleeve of my dress, I smirk. "Blondie most definitely believes it's him."

Pulling two giant diamond bands from the edge of her bra, Delta passes one to me with a raised brow. "If he keeps looking at her like he is, he might be."

The both of us laugh under our breath, slip the rings on our ring fingers, and curve into the lounge.

Cedar and ambrosia swirl in my senses, the first indication we've found what we're looking for, exactly where we knew we'd find it. Cigar after cigar sends steady streams of smoke into the air, eye after eye falling to our left hands as we pass through the *men's only* section of the place, quickly dismissing our presence with a single glance, just in case we "belong" to a man at their table, let alone one they're attempting to get to open their wallets after tonight's networking is complete.

Delta winks and I shift slightly, walking backward as I speak to her, my arms bent at my sides as I extend my hands outward. "It was quite entertaining. I—" My arm bumps into a hard body, the liquid in my glass sloshing over the rim, and I jolt, my free hand coming up to my mouth as I spin.

"My apologies," I rush out, glancing around for a waitress.

Shiny brown hair is at my side in a moment. "Here we are." She offers the man a dry cloth, passing one to me as well.

"Sir." I shake my head. "I'm so sorry. Please, allow me to have it cleaned?"

The man, also known as Jacobi Randolph, owner and CEO of Randolph Investments, dabs at his jacket before simply tossing the towel and peeling it from his body. "Now that won't be necessary, mis . . ." His eyes roam over my body as he hangs his jacket over the nearest chair.

Pretending to tuck a loose strand of hair back . . . with the ring-adorned hand, I smile. "Mrs. Brown, sir."

His smirk slips oh so quickly, replaced by poorly concealed annoyance. "It's all right, Mrs. Brown. I'll survive." He nods toward someone over my shoulder, and a moment later, an elderly man steps up beside me with a warm smile.

"Sorry, miss, but this is the *men's only* lounge. If you exit through the side doors there, you'll find a connecting hall that will lead back to the main floor."

"Oh! How silly of us. We didn't realize."

"Have a nice night, ladies." Randolph 'excuses' us, arm swinging out as if to point us toward the hall leading back into the main area before turning back to his friends.

Delta and I play good girls and head where we were instructed, but we don't slip into the connecting hall. We continue straight out to the patio, where Sai already awaits, car door open for us to slip right inside.

I toss the man's watch into the open safe on the floorboard and kick it closed.

"Well, that was so easy, it was almost boring." Delta reaches for the actual champagne in the fresh pile of ice, bringing the bottle to her lips before passing it to me.

"Yeah, and apparently"—I make a show out of looking around to the empty seat on the left, where Bronx should have already been firmly planted—"so is our friend."

Our eyes meet once more and we both begin laughing.

The glass blocking us from Sai's view rolls down, and he grins over his shoulder. "Where to, your Greysons?"

"Back to the airstrip, Sai, and then The Enterprise."

Time for the real fun to begin.

Bass

Twisting my torso, I slip through the cut wire fence, Hayze on my heels. I roll right while he cuts left, looking for leeches trying to hide out between the stacks of crates framing the gate and following the length of the abandoned lot around until we meet again, making sure we're all clear. No homeless hanging around or overeager partiers looking to secure a spot before we allow it.

I yank on the chains of the old warehouse door, making sure no one's decided to be real fucking stupid and pick the lock. The last thing we need is this place collapsing on some punks who think they don't have to follow the rules when no one's looking.

Hayze sends the text, letting people know bets are open, and within ten minutes, body after body is slipping through the fence, ready for a show and some Friday night fun. If watching poor assholes punch each other to the point of split flesh for a small stack of cash counts as fun. And if it doesn't, most of us out here turning a ten into a quick twenty, that's enough incentive to slide this way. Not much feels better than taking cash from spoiled rich kids, and these fools love to throw bills around. It leads to a lot of dick-measuring when you mix the rich and the poor, but that's why I'm here. To keep all these assholes in line, to remind them the second they crawl through that gate, who they are on the other side of it, means jack shit.

This is a dark spot on the edge of town with no electricity, a makeshift fighting ring in the dirt, and wooden flats stacked all around, the only seating option.

Bring drama here, bleed here. Run, we chase you. Disappear, we find you.

Sing? Well . . . better say your goodbyes before it's too late. Rats die. It's as simple as that.

Three hours later and the place is louder and fuller, the air pungent with the scent of weed and tobacco. The dirt is stained red, pockets have been pinched or plugged, and the patrons are good and buzzed.

Holding the joint between my fingers, I pull in a long drag, letting it roll out over my lip and inhaling through my nose. My phone beeps in my free hand and I glance at the screen.

Hayze: your ten. Green jacket.

My eyes flick up, skating past Hayze, who is positioned on the opposite side of the yard but directly across from where I'm sitting. I don't look in the direction he gave. Don't need to.

If trust exists in this cesspool, Hayze holds most of mine in his greasy hands. He doesn't live at the group home with me but stays in a tent behind his sister's trailer on the south side. He's two years older than me, got his GED in juvenile hall, found me again the minute he got out, and hasn't left since. He's my friend before he's anything else, but he doesn't work for anyone like I do. I prefer it that way. It will make it easier for when my time comes to leave this place, to find something better out there and to bring my sister home. He's coming with me.

Right now, to keep the peace with my bosses, I don't tell Hayze what he doesn't need to know, and he understands it. I know the drill of bringing someone else into my jobs—I give him a cut of my money and if he fucks up, I pay the price. I wouldn't risk my spot or my sister's safety by bringing some fool I wouldn't bleed for into the mix.

He was my neighbor before I came here, heard and saw more than I'd like, but it goes both ways. I wasn't always from a group home, and he wasn't always squatting in the back of a trap house. His situation is worse, which is why I leave him my car most of the time.

It's an old beater that breaks down every couple weeks, but it's a fucking car with a back seat that can serve as a bed when needed. More than he would ever ask for or expect, and that's why I do it. That, and there's no telling when he'll need a quick escape or when I might have to call on one for my damn self.

He's got no one but me, and I don't take that loyalty for granted.

Like I said, when I leave, he's coming with me.

It takes longer than I would have liked, but we're finally rolling into the fourth and final fight. The hype guy in the center of the makeshift ring with a megaphone lets everyone know betting is open, then moves right along to shouting and clowning on our back-to-back contenders.

Greg Moyer, a nineteen-year-old asshole with a snow problem that's led to some shitty decisions on his part, got his ass beat last week and came back again, but anything for a bag of blow, yeah?

Fucking weasel.

I take names and money, and it only takes a few minutes for the line before me to dwindle. Sensing eyes on me, mine cut to the dark-haired dude who hit me up after the last fights. Sure enough, he's looking this way, but after our eyes meet, he slowly looks away, stuffing his hands in his jacket to hide the jewelry he doesn't want jacked as he talks to the guy he came with, the same one as last time. The interaction is no more than a quick glance and I'm facing forward again.

"Bishop, I got ten on Moyer." One of the regulars comes up, a sophomore from the group home who has seen shit that would make ex-cons cry.

"Boy, where'd you get twenty from?" I lift a brow, taking the bill he won't be doubling like he hopes, and give him back his change. At least he won't be ass broke again after he loses.

His smirk is as crooked as his teeth are. "Popped some chick's tire at the grocery store, waited for her to come out and offered to change it for her for a fee."

Chuckling, I shake my head, keeping the frown from my face when the dude in the green jacket shoulder-checks him out of his way.

The guy grins, pulling out a wad of bills. "Three-fifty on Thomas."

Pulling smoke into my lungs, I blow it out into the guy's face, mentally logging the name he gives.

Matt Jones.

Yeah, fucking right.

He might as well have said Joe Blow. He picked the whitest, most basic fucking name his little mind could conjure. Dumbass.

Still, I take his cash, sealing his fate and dismissing him with a flick of my eyes over his shoulder.

A few more shuffle my way, then the dark-haired guy is in front of me. He holds out two bills between his fingers. I stare at him a long second then jump off the crate. Everyone who tried to line up behind him scatters, knowing the drill. Bets are closed when my feet hit the ground, but I snatch the money from his fingers as I shoulder past him.

I go to stand at the edge of the ring, and Hayze slides up directly across from me on the opposite side.

Just like the dark-haired dude, I forgot his fuckin' name, said he would, "Matt Jones" doubled his bet from last week.

Hayze wiggles his fingers at his sides, eager to close them around something, and my own adrenaline beats against my chest, but I keep it locked down.

No movement. No emotion. No tells.

The crowd goes crazy as the two come to blows, rocking and bobbing and landing hit after hit. Blood spills from Thomas's mouth, and Moyer has a gash over his eye, but seconds before the first round can end, the fight does. Thomas catches Moyer with a clean fade to the jaw, and the guy goes down instantly.

Now we know for sure.

Some cheer; others complain, and my eyes lift to Hayze.

I bend, sliding under the rope and coming up next to Thomas.

I clap his shoulder, pay him off, and send the smiling man into the gang of girls waiting on him.

And then I turn to Moyer.

He chuckles, shrugging his shoulders as he tries to catch his breath. "Fuck, maybe you were right, Bishop. I should have waited another week to recover from last week's pounding."

I nod, glancing at the crowd, noting the whistleblower is nowhere in sight, and with moves too fast to be anticipated, I grip his head, slamming it down into my knee, kicking behind his a second later. His body jolts backward, and he drops flat on his back, his head bouncing against the ground with a hard thump, his bottom teeth now sticking through his lower lip. His eyes roll back as consciousness slips away and everyone around falls silent.

I whip around, locking my eyes on Green Jacket Guy, and his widen. I know what comes next. Everyone paying attention does.

Green Jacket tries to make a fucking run for it. He spins . . . right into Hayze, his throat wrapped up in Hayze's eager hand.

Hayze stares up at him, his eyes dead and cold as he shifts, so the dude is facing me again, now forced to watch.

I bend down, take my knife from my pocket, and cut the protective tape from Moyer's hands. I look up at Jennings, another guy who works out here, and lift my chin.

He dumps a bucket of water over Moyer's head, and the fucker gasps himself awake.

It takes him a moment to remember where he's at, and panic flickers across his face.

He knows he threw this fight like he threw last week's, just like I know the guy in the green jacket pulled up in a black ride . . . Greg Moyer in his front fucking seat.

His eyes go wide, and then he screams, jerking in my hold as I snap his pinkie backward until his knuckle is flat against the back of his hand. And then I do the same thing to the middle finger and, lastly, his thumb. He doesn't fight, doesn't ask what I'm doing or why.

He just jerks and shakes and cries like a bitch, accepting his punishment, knowing it could be far worse . . . that it will be if he fights me.

I don't tell anyone why I did it and I don't stick around to see what Hayze will do to Green Jacket, but I know it will be worse than what I gave to Moyer.

Serves the fucker right.

A snake can't slither into a wolf's den and make it out in one piece. We will sniff it out, and then we'll take you out. Forgiveness doesn't exist here—reason number one my mother is nowhere to be fucking found; she ran right out of town with no word of where she went.

Bet she just fucking loves that, never having to look the son she fed to the devil over and over and over again in the eyes.

Wherever she is, she's probably rebuilt a new life by now. Working at some fast-food joint and going home to a shitty but clean apartment without a care in the fucking world. No hungover husband to nurse, no kids to keep her awake with their cries for help that won't come.

I will find you, Mother Dearest.

I roll my shoulders, blocking that shit out. Tonight ain't about the past. My energy is boiling beneath my skin, begging for the release it didn't get. I almost wish Moyer would have fought back, but a bitch is a bitch, so I knew he wouldn't. My work for the night might be finished, but I haven't yet.

So I nod my goodbye to my boys and slip out the hole in the gate. I pull my headphones on, slide my hands in my jacket pockets, and off I fucking go.

Might have to steal me a ride, but that's all right.

I'll pick a decent-looking car with a pile of shit under the hood, and if the night goes well, I might even torch it after and let the owner get a nice little insurance check as a thank-you.

Yeah, that's what I'll do.

Ready or not, Rich Girl, here I come . . .

Chapter 6
Rocklin

Sai bypasses the first-level parking garage, now completely empty, and as we near the outer edge, rolling over the track grips, the back wall slides left, and we enter the underground lot.

Standing just outside the double door is a fresh wave of shiny brown hair . . . and a perfectly placed bow tie.

As Delta and I step out, the girl stands taller, stretching both her arms out in front of her, a black suit jacket hanging from her fingertips.

"And the glass?"

"Mixed in with the dozens of others, likely already being polished and restocked." Valley, one of our Greyson Society hopefuls, stands tall but chews her lip anxiously, her shoulders relaxing when I give a slow nod.

Delta sighs like a proud mother and folds the coat over her arm right as her men, Ander and Alto, appear. Delta and her boys head inside, and I follow on her tail, but just before I enter, I pause, turning back to our newest recruit.

"Back left pocket."

Her brows furrow and I lift one of mine.

She jerks, catching on, and hastily reaches into her back pocket, her eyes widening when she pulls out the glittered key card, her personal ticket to The Devine lounge here at The Enterprise. She looks from it to me, a smile taking over her features.

"You earned it. Keep doing so."

She understands what everyone afforded the opportunity to join us does—there is no cementing of status for prospects. We give when earned, we take when taken advantage of. What kind of power would our coveted coed crew hold if we didn't?

Valley nods, and I push the door open, waving a hand to allow her to step in before me.

She squeals, stomping her feet a little, and I can't help the low laugh that escapes, but before she passes me, she pauses. "I don't want to walk in front of you."

My lips curve the slightest bit, and I link my arm with hers, leading us into the building side by side.

Valley's eyes widen, her lips parting and hiking up high. "This is . . . wow."

"It's only the back." Bronx appears on our left, her curled hair now a tattered mess at her back. She winks, snagging Valley's wrist. Who the hell knows how she arrived as quickly as we did. "Come on, girl. Let's get you out of that penguin suit and into something silky. The Greyson changing room is orgasmic."

Valley follows after her, eager to slip into something more her flavor, and I grin, heading toward our private quarters to do the same.

"Meet us in The Devine lounge in thirty!" Bronx shouts, the two disappearing around the corner.

The Devine lounge is the golden ticket. It's much like the Greyson suite, only less than as far as regalness goes, and open to *all* Greysons, hopefuls we're testing and those who've earned the golden pin alike. It's something for them to look forward to, to work toward, because, yes, sometimes the only things that matter to spoiled rich kids are shiny things and private parties their peers aren't privy to or allowed to attend.

To attend Greyson Academy is to *join* the elite, but to be a true Greyson is to *be* elite.

My lips curve and I feel lighter on my feet, a familiar zing tickling along my spine. It's always a good night when one of our girls takes a step forward, and a scheme is put in motion with ease.

72

Ready to get into something far more formidable, I follow the long hallway around, coming up to the edge of the private entry, but before I reach the double doors of the Greyson suite, the second one to the right captures my attention. The light along the frame is glowing a soft blue, an indicator to all who come across there is someone inside.

There are only two people who can enter that room, outside of myself, of course, and they both share the name curved along the center of the door. *My* last name.

It's my family's personal suite, and it's occupied.

My father is away on business, so there is only *one* person it could be, and she's got a lot of fucking nerve.

Heat explodes behind my rib cage, and I storm forward, my hand flying out to slap over the scanner, but just before it can flatten onto the small lit security square, fingers wrap around my wrist. I see the shadow coming, though, and spin in time to slip beneath their extended arm, swiftly winding behind their back, my hands positioned so my lower left palm is pressed at the tip of their chin, my right against the back of their head.

My eyes narrow on the blond hair before me. "I could have snapped your neck."

"Better than you storming in there and snapping hers."

"Is it, though?" I press firmer, and his hands lift into the air in front of him. "If I remember right, we both agreed I should have done *exactly* that three months and seven days ago."

"Nice to know you're no longer obsessing over that day, and in case it needs to be said, you know you can't kill your sister. That was a conversation to make you feel better."

Shoving Dom away, I whip around, moving quickly to the main Greyson door, and of course, Dom follows. His arms wrap around me from behind just as the doors open for us.

Clenching my teeth together, I allow him to walk me inside, his hold tightening once we're out of the hall. The back entrance to the suite faces nothing but a narrow hallway, allowing for an extra hint of anonymity, *just in case.*

73

Dom's left hand slides lower until it's clasped over my hip, his right coming up to glide down my arm. "Don't be upset with me."

"Don't get in my way."

"Not my intention." His lips press into my hair, the warmth of his breath against my skin causing the anger boiling in me to slide farther south. Damiano senses it, and the hand on my hip squeezes.

"Your prospect did good. Calvin said she didn't make eye contact with a soul all night," he murmurs.

"She didn't," I confirm, the level of eye candy slipping to the forefront of my mind. I tip my head slightly, meeting his brown eyes. "Hell of an attendee list, by the way."

"The Sandsburn row team was passing through on their way to a conference. They were happy to have a night out."

"Well *done*, Mr. Donato. They were a perfect test of temptation for the girl."

At my compliment, Damiano stands taller, his tongue slipping free to wet the natural swell of his lips. He dips closer and I keep my gaze on his. He smiles as his mouth comes down on the corner of mine, applying the smallest bit of pressure, testing to see what I might do.

"Can I help you out of this dress?" he whispers, and when I don't pull back, he shifts slightly so he's more at my side. His fingers span out, lowering from the curve of my hip to the curve of my ass, and then continue lower until the hem is in his grasp. He lifts it slowly, eyes growing darker before me.

He leans in again, and then his body stills, his hand going up to press on his earpiece.

"On my way." He steps back, dropping a quick peck to my cheek. "They need me in the control room."

I nod, facing forward as I remove the horrendous pearls from my ears.

"Hey, Dom?" I call out, knowing he's yet to cross the threshold into the hall. "Let Valley come to you."

Glancing over my shoulder, I meet his stare as I take off the other earring. I don't have to say what I mean. He knows.

The man has a knack for *welcoming* the girls once they enter, but there's something about Valley. I don't want her mind to swim into still water if she's not the one who jumps in first.

Damiano can't help them swim, he knows this, and while most of our girls who fall into him are aware, every so often, there's one whose common sense gets lost in translation. I don't want to risk her being one. Again, unless she puts herself there.

A small smirk forms on his lips, and he gives a curt nod, disappearing out the door.

With a sigh, I contemplate my next move. To change and go to my girls for a guaranteed good night, or slip back into the hall with a fresh set of daggers, ready to dip them into the girl in the room two doors down from this one?

I close my eyes when Dom's footsteps come right back as if he knew I might sway on my decision to play nice the moment he left. "You've convinced me to control myself tonight, Dom." Lie. "Go."

His hand comes around me, pressing firmly against my neck, and my head falls back against his shoulder, his warm breath at my ear once more. "That's all that was, huh?"

The thick, throaty question tickles along my skin, and a low, derisive laugh pushes past my lips. My eyes flick open, narrowing on the ceiling. "You have got to be kidding me."

"Maybe I got you wrong, Rich Girl." Tattooed knuckles come into view, but I don't so much as breathe when they come around, locking along my jaw. He tips my head to the side, and our eyes clash.

Mine flare, the sight far more intoxicating than I remember.

Glacier-blue eyes impale me, long, thick, *black* lashes framing them. He cocks his head, his blink a low, lazy one. "You the white knight needin' type?"

"I can swing my own sword with ease."

His head bobs the slightest bit, as if he figured as much, as if he knows I'm not some docile duchess who needs direction but can think for and handle myself without question. I can, but who the hell is he to assume he knows more about me than the sound of my moans?

Lifting my shoulder in an idle shrug, I continue, "But there's something about a man willing to put his *sword* to use when I'm in need of a distraction."

I watch his face, waiting for a reaction, but he gives none. Not even a slight tic of the jaw.

Why I expected it, I'll never know.

Annoyed with myself, I jerk my head from his grip, focusing forward, but he isn't deterred. He simply presses closer.

Leaning in, he nips at my jaw from his position behind me, following it down to the curve of my neck, playing the strings he somehow knows are my favorite. His teeth graze gently, and then he sucks the skin there, his tongue slick, warm. *Rough.*

Heat explodes in my core, spreading by the second.

His finger presses firmly into my waist, and he murmurs, "Bad day?"

His heated breath wafting over the wet kiss he left behind has my body betraying my calm bravado, and I quake in his arms.

"Nothing a steaming bath won't fix."

He hums against me, and my ass presses into him without permission. The groan the move earns draws goose bumps to the surface of my skin. "Who is he to you?"

I almost laugh at his ping-ponging thoughts, but his mere presence is distracting.

"He's mine."

The vibration from his low rumble along my back has my muscles coiling, and then I'm shuffled forward toward the dark corner of the room, the corner he shadowed himself in the day he found me here.

His head lifts, mouth aligned with my ear. "Careful choice of words."

"Was it, though?" Damiano *is* mine.

He's my housemate back at Greyson Manor. My peer. My occasional lover.

My open-ended offer of more.

So yes, Dom is mine in various ways . . . minus the one he's referring to.

He presses me flat against the wall, the buckle of his belt digging into the swell of my ass.

My lips part and I don't have to look to know his tongue flicks along his own.

"*Rocklin Revenaw*," he purrs my name for the first time, and it sounds naughty leaving his lips. Like a dirty secret he'll keep for himself.

He continues, his fingers finding the skin of my thighs, "Five-eleven, earthy-green eyes, and a natural blonde. Nineteen, third-year and adviser at Greyson Elite Academy, a school for young scholars. A stepping-stone to greatness, offering an education more coveted than any Ivy League in the nation."

"Memorized the brochure?" My words come out breathy.

A pleased grin meets the skin of my neck and I let my head fall back, wanting *more*, but he's in no hurry, slowly tapping his fingers on the inside of my leg in a rolling-like motion, pinkie to pointer, and again, each time the point of contact a little higher than the last.

"I did. Among other things." His hands continue upward, taking this wretched dress with them as they glide up and up until his thumbs tangle with the turquoise string of my underwear. "Can he call you his?"

I say nothing, and his movements halt.

Suddenly, and I do mean *sudden,* no part of him is touching me. His hands fly from me so fast I nearly lose balance, and in absolutely no hurry, I face him in all his degenerate glory.

Same black jacket.

Same white T-shirt.

Same electric pull pulsing through my every vein, summoning me closer.

"So fuckin' tempting." His heated gaze has zeroed in on the space between my thighs. "But what belongs to someone else ain't somethin' I'm into." Lower lip sucked between his teeth, piercing and all, he shuffles backward toward the door. "Damn shame, though, Rich Girl."

His tongue comes out, gliding over the ridiculously shiny hoop. Counterfeit silver, I'm sure, but that doesn't lessen the sudden urge I have to taste it.

But he's . . . leaving . . . because he thinks I'm Dom's girl? *Is he serious?*

"An honorable intruder. Never knew such a thing existed." I try to keep the frustration laced with sass from my tone, but I'm not as successful as I would like.

Not that it matters, as he ignores me completely and just keeps *walking*.

He's almost to the door now and my pulse jumps with each shuffle of his feet, but why do I care? He's no one. He doesn't belong.

I don't even know his fucking name!

Apparently, my conscious doesn't give a shit, as my leg begins to bounce, and I drop my head back, eyes rolling to the ceiling, the decision already made.

"Oh, for fuck's sake." I tear myself from the wall, headed right for him.

Gripping him by the tattered leather jacket, I slap my hand over the square on the wall, and the doors begin to close, but I don't wait for the hard click.

I yank him forward, smashing my lips to his.

He doesn't move.

Doesn't touch or kiss back.

He holds still, eyes steady on me. Waiting.

No, not waiting. Wordlessly *demanding*, and I have no idea why it kicks my desire into the greediest of need.

I give him what he wants in anticipation of the reward that will follow, sucking the breath from my lungs. "No," I breathe. "I am not *his*."

My stranger needs no other words. I'm in his hands, ass to the wall in seconds.

He squeezes, tugs, and presses, growling against my lips as he tears his away, but only so he can whip my dress over my head. His mouth comes back, licking. Sucking. Biting.

He moves lower, his fingers curled over the edge of my bra, pulling it down, so his heated tongue can toy with the pebbled peaks there.

My eyes close, my head falling back on the soundproof wood behind me.

His hand slips between my thighs, seeking out the proof of my arousal, but he doesn't give his approval. He growls. "This for me or him?"

An incredulous laugh escapes, rolling into a moan when he edges his finger into my underwear. "You're ridiculous."

"And you're soaked, *throbbing*. Needing to come." He presses inside me, and my walls clench around him, desperate to hold him there. "Wet for me or him?"

"He hardly touched me."

"Pathetic if he has to touch you at all to make you drip." A second finger presses inside me, and I arch into him. "But he did touch you, and that's against the rules, ma."

My eyes begin to roll but clamp shut when he follows his words with a nip to my collarbone, swiftly bringing his lips to mine. He claims my mouth as he works his fingers in and out in slow, determined motions, his thumb bent, playing at my clit like the strings of a harp, each stroke purposeful, leading into the next.

"We've been over this."

"We have." His words are a deep rasp along my shoulder, and then my bra is gone, one leg lifted and locked along his back.

His hand slips from me, looping around from behind instead and diving back into my slick heat. "This pussy's good, Rich Girl. Let me have it."

I'm panting now. My hand shoots up over my head, latching on to the light fixture attached there, and I grind against him. "If you think I'm about to stop you, you're highly mistaken."

His chuckle is low, dark. "Nah, you're not gettin' it. Let me have it. Let me . . ." His buckle unclips, and then the head of his cock is at my entrance. "Call it mine a minute."

I tense, shoving his chest slightly, so I can see him better, but he's focused on where our bodies are bare and touching.

He's insane, likely—*highly* likely—in the literal sense.

But he has me in his hold, so I must be too . . .

He's slow to bring his eyes to mine, and when he does, sheer determination shines back.

He presses inside, filling me as he waits, head cocking to one side.

Stretched like this, with his glass-like gaze on me, I can't think, so I don't. I roll my hips instead, and already, with the little bit of foreplay, my orgasm is crowning.

He pulls out a few inches, rocking into me with deep, rhythmic strokes, palming my ass and rolling me into him as he slides inside, guiding my hips back with each glide out.

He feels it, I'm there.

"So soon, Rich Girl?" he teases, sucking on my bottom lip.

His tone is almost playful, charming, if a guy like him is capable of such a thing. It's a dangerous, adorable sound.

A whimper leaves me, beads of sweat building along the base of my neck, and I reach out, clenching onto him.

My insides spasm, and I moan, ready for release, but that moan morphs into a gasp when he tears out of me. My eyes snap open, and I blink into focus, swiftly narrowing in on his form.

His already *retreating* form.

I didn't see him press the button to open the door, but it's open, he's smirking, and then . . .

He's gone.

A sharp breath hisses from my lips, my body falling against the wall with a soft thud.

"Are you fucking kidding me?!"

I don't mean to shout, but there it is.

I think I hear him chuckle, and then I'm *positive* I do because it grows an alto deeper when the chair I kick over in the next second topples with a harsh thump.

Annoyed and flustered beyond reason, I press my fingertips into the corners of my eyes and catch my breath.

It takes a moment, but I get myself together, and then a low laugh slips past my lips as I bend, reaching beneath the small table to my left. When I stand, it's with a small, simple, single-fold wallet in my hand, black leather, of course, that I slipped from his pocket and nudged from view.

Slapping it in my palm, I smirk and look inside.

My lips quickly turn down when each card slot is as empty as the next, with nothing but a small sliver of white where the bills should be. Taking it out, I let the wallet fall to the floor and unfold the piece of paper—the bottom corner of a menu.

I read over the single line written in sharp, dark, quite flawless cursive, my teeth sinking into my lower lip.

Call me Bastian, little thief.

A low laugh leaves me, and I drop into the armchair with a sigh, staring at his name a little longer than I'll admit.

"Well played, Bastian."

Well played.

Chapter 7
Bass

The metal fence presses at my back as I cut a quick glance at the curb. No Hayze, so I don't bail on the new group home girl yet.

She's trying to get back on the cards at the warehouse, in need of a quick buck for reasons that are none of my business, as all the girls at the home are, but she's been the first one of them to step in that dirt ring and whoop ass like she's bored, the shit comes so easy to her. It makes for good business for me, but my boss has taken an interest in the scrappy, sassy chick with two chips on her shoulders, and he wants her ass far away from there. And me.

I laugh on the inside at that.

"What'd they say?" She blows her black hair from her face, glaring at me, trying to hear from the horse's mouth why I won't let her back in the ring and knowing damn well the order came from the top.

I don't entertain her shit, and she doesn't expect me to. She comes from where I come from, not literally, but punk kids from the gutter are born understanding what these privileged pricks have to be taught.

"Come on now." I bend my knee, pressing the bottom of my foot against the fence as I slide my eyes her way. "You know how this shit works."

She nods, frowning forward. "No singers."

"No fucking singers, Rae."

The girl snags my cigarette from my hand and takes a drag, dropping her head back.

I frown her way as she blows the smoke into the air, watching it until it disappears.

She looks up. "Guess there's no chance you'll add me on then, huh?"

My phone beeps in my palm, and when I look toward the road this time, Hayze is pulling up at the edge of the school parking lot. I take my shit back, and with one final drag, I stomp it beneath my foot, pushing off the fence. "See you around, Carver."

I don't look back, and I'm out, sliding into the passenger seat a minute later.

"You know you could hit that, right? If you really wanted." Hayze whips us around, heading toward the edge of the city.

He might be right.

Rae should be my type from *A* to fucking *Z*. She understands the world I come from, not as an eye on the outside, but from deep within. She's tough as shit, jaded and pissed at the world, a self-sabotaging asshole with something to prove.

Too much like me.

"Rae's good people. I'd have her back if she needed me to, but that's where that dies."

"Ain't she fucking your boss anyway?"

"Probably." I look in the rearview mirror, ensuring no one's tailing us. "Turn right."

He does, cutting me a quick glance. "So that girl's too hard, but did my boy discover he likes something a little . . . softer?"

"And blonder."

Hayze howls with laughter and my lips curve up on one side.

"Aye, eat that shit up, my boy. Rich girls love to play in the dark . . . until they realize we never step out of it." He grins, turning the music up high.

He's not lying. There's a lot of money around here, and with that comes spoiled socialites who want a night with a guy they couldn't—and wouldn't—stand in the light with.

But Hayze said "something softer," and when it comes to my new favorite blonde, I'm not convinced he's right.

There's something hidden behind this prep-school princess's green eyes, a sharpness built like armor but worn like silk. A sly sort of sadist enveloped in a pretty fucking package that's yet to be unwrapped. It taunts me, making my teeth ache with the need to tear into it. To shed the smiling shadows in her gaze, one sharp bite at a time until I peel her back enough, the real her shines through.

Spoiled socialites don't have that, and they sure as fuck aren't surrounded by armed guards. My smirk deepens at the thought.

Straight-up TAC team fuckers were all around that building and I still got to her, left her pissed and pantin' the last time, and I enjoyed every fucking second.

The girl's used to getting what she wants when she wants it, so I had to show her who the boss would be, and it ain't her. Her frustrated little growl replays in my head, and a low chuckle leaves me.

Pulling out my phone, I shoot her a quick message.

Me: What'd you use?

Not long after I press send, her text comes through.

Rich Girl: Am I supposed to detect a hint of intellect behind such a question?

Damn, she even texts like a ritzy bitch.

Me: When you thought of me these last three nights. You use a vibrator or your pretty little fingers?

A grin curves my mouth, and I don't have to wait more than a few seconds for a response.

Rich Girl: Bastian, if you would please . . .

Rich Girl: Fuck.

Rich Girl: OFF.

My tongue slips over my lip, spinning the silver ring there.

A frown pulls at my brows, and I shove my phone into my jacket pocket.

I shouldn't have told her my real name. I *never* use my real name. Just Bass. Sometimes Bishop.

Never *Bastian*.

Maybe that's why I gave her that name, so she couldn't find me, couldn't search for my secrets. When I moved to this town, I was told my file was erased, that what I did disappeared the same way I did, but I don't know if that means completely. I used to trip, waiting for the day someone came banging down the doors with shiny silver bracelets, asking for me, be it the cops or even the dude who dropped me here. After a year or so, I stopped waiting and said fuck it. If they come, they come and they never did.

Took a while to prove myself and start getting paid, but the minute I did, I started saving. After a good six months, I bit the bullet and bought one of those hundred-dollar prepaid credit cards from the grocery store. I found a website that helps you find people, and after the ninety-nine-dollar fee, plus five more months of waiting, they found jack shit on my mom.

I've dug a little deeper since then, and still, four years and not a fucking blip on the map. So now, I'm wondering if money *can* move mountains, and there really is zero record of me to be found, the way there's nothing that helps me find her.

For all I know, Rich Girl doesn't give a damn who the criminal she let fuck her is, but I was inside that big ass, highly guarded building. Twice. That's sure to make the wheels spin, ain't it? Have her wondering who I am and where I came from?

I'm no one, and I came from shit, but would she let me play with her body if she knew I stood over my dad's dead one with a smile?

I bet the fuck not.

Then again, she's not what she seems, so maybe she would. Maybe . . . she'd stand beside me, her lips curled just the same.

A low laugh leaves me, and I shake my head.

Yeah, fucking right.

Hayze rolls to a stop behind the drugstore, and together, we climb out.

I push all thoughts to the back of my mind and allow it to go numb.

I've got a list of shit to do this fine Monday morning, and a long-legged, smart-mouthed blonde ain't on it.

Rocklin

"Should I ask Saylor to deliver a fresh cappuccino and a warmed blanket to your room, Miss Revenew?" Jasper asks as I stand from the breakfast nook on the back patio.

"What makes you think I plan to go straight up to my room, lock myself inside, and sit on my balcony?"

Jasper fights a smile, scooting in the chair I slipped from. "The same way I know you will take a book with you, one that will not be recreational reading, and you will not move until the clock strikes eight a.m.

"I won't?" I playfully wonder.

"You will not."

Folding my arms in front of me, I allow my lips to curve up as I tip my head. "What do you suppose I'll warm my soul with this gorgeous Saturday morning?"

He passes me my phone before standing tall and clasping his hands behind his back. "Some light reading, of course. Perhaps *Investment Management and Fiduciary Service*?"

"Am I that predictable?"

"Focused. Not predictable."

A low laugh leaves me. "Well, good guess, but this morning I'll be diving into the life of one extremely spoiled royal."

"Ah yes, academy invitations go out in a few short months. Get to know them better than they know themselves."

"Exactly."

His lips arch in response, and he gives a small bow as we part ways.

I head toward my wing with a smile.

When I was first dropped onto the grounds of the Greyson

Estate, I thought the place was too big, the rooms and other girls too far, but a separate wing per Greyson was the only solution its curator could come up with to represent equal command, something about offering the Greysons of that time the illusion of control—create a cardinal system, a compass rose, and give them each their own mini kingdom, as a mansion as exquisite as ours can feel, and allow them to rule over it, offering the room in their sections to whomever they like and keeping out those they don't.

I say they're lucky that didn't backfire on their asses tenfold.

Only a man would assume creating distance between those who are supposed to work as a team was a good idea, that their private quarters would cut out the jealousy or need for one to rank higher than the other. It didn't and all those before us proved that.

It wasn't until Delta, Bronx, and I slipped into our roles that it changed.

We're the first generation of all female successors set to reign, meaning none of us has brothers who will ease into our family's positions within the Greyson Union.

There are no heirs, only heiresses.

We *are* the future.

While my father is the most powerful, and his name alone is enough to make a man piss where he stands, to identify as a Greyson is to let others know to wrong one is to wrong all. So if someone wants to take an arrow to my heart, it won't only be the Revenaws who tear theirs from their chest, but my girls' families as well. It's a safeguard, so to speak. An unshakable alliance every small fish in the criminal world is aware of.

If Delta, Bronx, and I weren't as tight as our corsets on gala nights, we would be the generation to explode the foundation the ideal sits on.

There isn't a record in the books one of us didn't break or create during our first two years here at Greyson Elite Academy.

They don't call us prodigies for nothing, but when no one is around to hear it, some do call us weak. The overly ambitious assholes, looking to take our families' places, believe the influence our last names hold will die with the men in charge today if left to our order.

They're wrong.

My sister might have failed to fill the role my father granted her with her latest bullshit, not that that was a huge shock considering, but I won't.

When my family needs a leader to hold the Revenaw name high, I'll step up with pride . . . and a semi loaded down with ammunition of all kinds. Especially those of the secret kind. Thankfully, the girls and I keep none from one another—reason number one why living here in the manor with them works as well as it does.

"A Greyson princess not dressed and pressed before daylight. I didn't know such a thing was allowed. Guess a lot can change in three months' time."

Ice, hard and heavy, fills my veins, stiffening my spine and pricking against my skin like a thousand tiny needles, the largest and sharpest stabbing straight into my back.

Speak of the devil and she shall appear . . .

My brain sends a sensation to my body, triggering it to shake, but I'm a fucking genius and that pathetic reflex is stopped before it starts.

She will never be given the satisfaction of catching me off guard. Not after what she did and sure as hell not after what she's trying to do now.

Slowly and with the grace of a fucking Greyson, I turn, resisting the urge to clench my jaw at the mirrored image before me. I should tear her tongue out for mocking me, even if she did deliver her words in a teasing, unmistakably uneasy tone.

Mine, of course, is as flat as her chest. "How would you? Only Greysons know what Greysons are and are not allowed to do." Nothing has changed. There isn't and never has been such a rule about pajamas or how we dress in our own home on our own time. I could walk around the place buck naked if

I wanted and no one would bat a lash. The staff would greet me just the same, pretending it was completely normal.

My sister has the audacity to appear regretful, her eyes lowering with her chin, though it has nothing to do with what she said.

She's always been the submissive type.

Weakness, that's what submission is.

Giving in is giving up and giving up is not allowed, not for Greysons and surely not for the daughters of Rayo Revenaw.

We have to be strong. Dominant. *Supreme*.

My sister missed the memo.

My gaze flicks over her head as the culprit who snuck her in with his entrance stalks around the corner.

Instinctively, my posture straightens.

Shoulders wide and level, chin high and solid, eyes sharp and mouth carefully curved. *Never let them see your worries, daughter*. It didn't take long for that message to sink in.

Another lesson my sister couldn't seem to learn.

"This is what I like to see." He slides up, his mere presence alone intimidating, his expression soft yet deceiving. "Both my girls in one place, as it should be."

"And how about the circumstance?" I smile. Big and fake. "Is it ideal as well, or are you still pretending she didn't—"

"Not the time." My father's voice is lethally calm, though his eyes flash their warning.

"I look forward to the invite on my calendar."

I've never been great with warnings.

Rayo Revenaw stares, giving nothing away, but I know my father well, so he doesn't have to.

He wants me to stay quiet. To accept his decision. To offer my sister the protection the manor provides. That we can provide. He wants me to simply say "yes."

Abso-fucking-lutely *not*.

He may control many things. His influence may reign over me in most ways, maybe all ways, even if I like to pretend differently, and at the end of the day, if he wants something to happen, chances are it will.

In this instance, though, to make such a command would piss off *a lot* of people, and in our world, the enemies you make along the way do not talk shit behind your back.

They take a knife to it.

To force my hand would be like taking the Bandoni and DeLeon names and spitting on them. Bronx's dad and Delta's grandfather would be knocking down the doors at Revenaw Towers by nightfall. Of course, my girls and I are tight, so I could very easily say yes, and fill them in later. They wouldn't fight me as I wouldn't fight them, but we don't make decisions without each other unless we must.

This is not one of those situations.

My sister won't die before dinner.

I mean, it's not likely, anyway . . .

No, Father will just have to do what he hates.

He'll have to wait.

I smile sweetly, and he knows he'll be walking out of here today with my sister in tow.

His chest rises with a full inhale, and while he speaks to my sister, his eyes stay on me. "Boston, wait in the common room."

"But—" she dares to argue.

Both our heads snap her way, and she smacks her mouth shut, shooting me a sharp look before waltzing away, nose in the air like rotten royalty. She hates to be dismissed, even if her attitude is nothing more than hurt she's trying and failing to hide. Why she would expect anything less, I don't know. She did this, not me.

Once she's gone, my father begins.

"I heard you lost a girl this week."

"Did you hear we added one as well?"

"You should add more males," he dismisses my comment. "More strength."

I don't respond, simply giving him a single curt nod.

Sure, Dad, I'll get right on that, as it's just so easy to trust males who already think they're special simply because they were born with some prestigious pedigree.

He holds my gaze a long moment and then clears his lungs, his features and shoulders softening. "Darling, it's not safe for your sister to be in our home."

"That's her problem. She needs to be held accountable."

"It will be her head or her hand. That is the kind of accountability we're talking about."

My heart beats a little harder, but I don't show it. "She knows this. She *knew* this, and still, she chose to come home. She's playing you, Dad, looking for an out she can't find. She expects to be saved by someone when she was taught to save herself."

"She's fragile."

"She's a disgrace," I fire back, the words stinging more than I want them to. "To our family name and to the union."

The union was created to tie power families together, to close the gaps and make us stronger so we're less susceptible to treachery. A *cross-one, cross-all* situation because each of our families has seen and experienced how fleeting trust can be.

Boston's little half-cocked plan, the one she apparently couldn't even go along with when she's the one who came up with it in the first place? It's the complete fucking opposite.

My father's eyes narrow with disappointment, but as quickly as the expression settles, it's gone, and a smile spreads across his lips. He climbs the last few steps I refuse to come down and wraps his arms around me.

I lean into his chest, my eyes closing a moment.

We used to be a normal family.

Well, as normal as life can be when your dad became who he is by unaliving people for a living before switching things up.

Now he pays people to do it for him.

"That, daughter," he whispers into my hair. "Is why you are the prize of this family. I know I can count on you to do what you must, no matter what that calls for. The strides you'll make will set this world ablaze."

My brows pull into a slight frown, but I erase it as he releases me, looking up at him.

I fight the urge to sigh and instead ask the important question. "Have they come looking for her yet?"

"Not yet. From what I've gathered, he's not yet aware she's gone. If there was a plan being made, I would know," he says, beyond sure. Then again, he probably is.

He has men everywhere, even where people think he can't reach.

"It's been nine days since she came back." It makes no sense. "How can he *not* know?"

"Ask her."

I glare, and he raises a brow.

Say you're right and not overconfident, I want to begin with, but instead go with, "How long do you think you can keep this quiet? How long until they come for her?"

"A few weeks, maybe less, maybe longer. I'm told he's away on business."

I eye him. The sharp, ever-present glare isn't as deep as it should be, considering.

"How are you so calm about this? This is a big deal, Dad. This is Caesar and Brutus big."

"It's not a betrayal, it's simply . . . a shifting point in a larger picture. One that isn't yet clear to all the players on the board. In time, it will be."

My head tugs back, shocked by his lack of, well, murderous rage, even if his daughter is the one at fault.

"Rocklin." My dad merely tips his head. "You'll do as you must, no matter what?"

There's that line again. Conform, conform, conform.

My jaw clenches, but I give him what he wants yet again—obedience and a curt nod of agreement, to which he nods back.

Ever the dutiful daughter, I wait until he's turned his back to me to turn mine on him and head up the stairs, but not before he calls over his shoulder, "Sai has taken a leave, but he'll be back sometime tomorrow. No joyriding in his absence, Rocklin. We wouldn't want someone to mistake you for your sister."

My spine stiffens, and I nod without looking back, taking careful steps as I climb the staircase to my suite.

My sister creates a disaster of epic proportions and gets a free pass.

I drive the countryside and get fucking *grounded* like a pedestrian?

And what's this with Sai?

He and I have an agreement. He doesn't go running to my dad about things so long as I don't give him a reason, forcing his hand, and an hour with a sports car isn't one. He knew about my little need for an escape as it's a repetitive one. He even has the GPS locked in on his phone and probably stares at the little blip on his screen the entire time I'm gone until I return to where I'm supposed to be.

So what the hell is this about?

In all the years Sai's been my guard, never *once* has he "taken leave." Sure, there are certain hours of the day, some days, depending on what's going on and where I am, that allow him to, at the very least, sit in peace. So does he accept his allotted time for himself? Duh.

What he does not do is *take a fucking leave*. He's never even been late, let alone "called in!"

So where is he and how did my dad find out?

Did he punish Sai?

Threaten him?

Does my sister have something to do with this?

Probably, not that my dad would tell me if I asked. I'm next in line as head of the Revenaw name and he still has me on that "need to know" level because "the less I know, the safer I am."

Grinding my jaw, I throw my door open and stomp inside.

My father says I'm the perfect daughter, that I'll "change our world" and "lead us into a new era," whatever the fuck that means.

He pushes me but pacifies my sister.

My girls don't know this, but I'm "not allowed" to rank below them. When I was forced to walk away from swimming, he was angry, as we all were, but his anger went beyond the situation. He suggested we find a "nonviolent" way to make Delta stop playing piano and to get Bronx to retire her paint brushes, so we girls would remain "equal."

I guess my Olympic gold medal, literally topping me out in the sport, my perfect GPA, and my role as captain on both the fencing and the skeet shooting team doesn't mean much to the man who has the Mafia in his back pocket. Without him, they would have a quarter of what they do.

He's indispensable and he wants that for me, but it's never enough, not for the man who took over the northern district organizations as a whole at the young age of twenty-one. Took down his competitors before he turned twenty-two, and after that, men twice his age traveled from across the nation to kneel at his feet. Literally, I've seen the photos.

Ignorant people believe I have it easy, but they couldn't be more wrong, and now, as if I don't have enough on my plate, my sister's problem has become mine, but that's how it goes, right? The strongest cleans up the weakest's mess.

Not sure how exactly her royal fuckup can be "cleaned," but I'm sure Rayo Revenaw has a plan.

A plan he won't include me in.

He can't risk her being seen at our childhood home in the city, and he can't stay home to make sure she's not, even if he does have a dozen guards on-site at all times. It's bullshit to put those of us at the manor in this situation, but I can't say I don't understand his reasoning.

Still . . .

Fuck her, fuck him, and fuck this.

Chapter 8
Rocklin

When a hunter explains such a sport to her class, she will say something along the lines of "you have to block everything else out" or "a clear mind is key." She wouldn't be wrong. That is the easiest way . . . and *that* is precisely why we teach things differently at Greyson Elite Academy.

We focus the chaos in our minds on our problem, envisioning the prime frustrations long before the target is released. We teach them to let the noise take over, to drown in it to the point of desperation, where the only way to find the air they need to survive is to take out the person threatening it.

Mine takes the shape of the person I see in the mirror every morning, her blonde hair a single shade darker than mine.

I mount my shotgun, drawing the stock close to my cheek and blow out a long breath.

"Pull."

The first target is released. My weight is focused on my front foot, my eyes tracking the target, the muzzle of the gun following. I gently squeeze the trigger so as not to disrupt my shot, and the clay pigeon shatters in the air, as does the second and each one after that.

My body shakes with anger and I lower the gun to my side, staring up at the final smoke spot in the sky.

"Perfect, as always," is spoken from about ten feet behind me.

My lips press into a tight line and I blow out a harsh breath, annoyed even more than before. "You really shouldn't approach me when I have a gun in my hands. I might pull the trigger by accident."

"And allow a single mistake on your perfect record? Not like-likely," she stutters over the word when I whip around to face her, small creases forming along her temples.

"Watch yourself, *sister*, and get the hell out of here before I humiliate you more than you're humiliating our family."

I shoulder past her, handing the gun off to Dante, the roundsman who handles the skeet-shooting training zone both behind the manor and on the academy grounds.

"What do you care about family?!" she shouts in anxious urgency. "I'm the one who—"

I spin, step into her, and have her by the throat, shoving her into a pillar before the next word can leave her mouth. My nails dig into her trachea, pinching and drawing small beads of blood to the surface.

Alarm widens her eyes, but she doesn't even attempt to get free. She's not as physically weak as she is mentally, but she *is* weaker than me, and we both know it.

Everyone knows it.

I don't feel bigger or better because of it.

I just am.

I tighten my hold, shoving her back, even though she's already pressed as far against the statue-wielding beam as she can be. "You're the one who cheated on her entrance exams because you couldn't be bothered to study, and you weren't intelligent enough not to. The one who allowed a boy to videotape her in bed because he said he wanted to take a piece of you with him overseas, forcing Dad to take a *piece* of him as retribution. The one who was so desperate to be number one in our father's eyes that you arranged an unsolicited union between you and the son of our father's greatest fucking enemy. The one who realized her mistake *after* signing a contract that promises you as his wife. And you're the one who ran away from said man, knowing full well he owns you now. Literally. He fucking bought you, Boston!"

Tears cloud her eyes, and my throat burns in response. I hate this. Hate how I feel like I hate her.

I release her, my gaze following as she dramatically drops to the ground, coughing uncontrollably and rubbing along her reddened skin, her tears threatening to leak now. "Don't cry. You did this to yourself."

She nods, looking everywhere but at me. "We can't all be emotional zombies, Coco."

"Good thing one of us can, or we'd both be blinded by Balenciaga, wouldn't we?"

We stare at one other for a moment, and I note the fairness of her skin is even fairer, her cheeks even thinner. She's doing it again, making food the enemy. Waging war on her body to combat her brain.

"I told Dad to send you back, but he's afraid if he does, they'll return you to our doorstep . . . in a casket with his name on it. What you two don't seem to understand is your running already warrants one. They'll have Dad's head for this if it gets out. They won't allow their family to be humiliated." I swallow the bile threatening to rise as the truth burns across my tongue like acid when I add, "Any more than I will."

Relief washes over her in an instant, and she reaches for me but quickly catches herself, her hand falling to her side. "Really?" she whispers. "I can come back to the manor?"

"I have to get the girls' approval and sit down with Calvin to talk about how the students could be affected if this goes bad faster than Dad seems to expect." Her gaze flicks away, guilt settling along her shoulders as she draws them back. "We might even run this by Damiano, too, as it affects him. He approved admission to your fiancé's little sister. Did you know this?"

Her eyes widen. "Is she already here?"

"She's finishing her semester in Paris. She'll be here next term."

Boston nods, looking away.

My attention falls to her arms, both frail looking, her body as willowy as ever—the perfect ballerina. If a ballerina is a malnourished, oversensitive bitch.

She's not actually a bitch. Well, not any more than we all can be when pushed, but she pulled some bitch shit, so it's fitting. Honestly, she's the kind one of the two of us. The understanding and caring one. All of which makes her weaker in the ways the heir to Rayo Revenaw cannot be.

"You've been gone three months. Have you been training?"

A haunted look falls over her. "No."

"Dancing?"

She looks away.

That's a no.

My eyes narrow, and I bite into my cheek, telling myself to walk the fuck away and fast.

To avoid anything unnecessary, like grabbing on to her wrist and tugging her to me for a hug I shouldn't want to give her. Like telling her I missed her and I'm glad she's back because I'm not.

I would be if things were different, but they aren't, so here we are.

She's too unpredictable and runs on a whim when we've been taught to do the opposite.

I spin on my heels and head back down the stone path. "Go and stay gone unless you're called back. Meet me in the throwing room of the manor at two tomorrow afternoon."

She says nothing and I head straight for the lower-level pool.

The second my feet hit the inside of the glass elevator doors, I start stripping. Tearing my fingerless gloves from my hands, I toss them aside, yanking the earplugs from my ears and letting them fall where they may.

My beret is next and then the white vest and boots. I'm unzipping my body suit as the doors ding open, the scent of specialized chlorine thick in the dewy air. My throat thickens instantly, but I swallow beyond it and push forward.

I clap my hands and the long glass windows disappear into the rocks, and a swoosh of fresh air seeps into the space, filling my lungs.

I climb the steps, up and up, my feet freezing at the second platform, glaring up at the third level.

Fuck it.

Up I go until I'm fifty feet high.

My chest tightens in warning, but I push forward.

I step up to the edge, spin, and curve my torso backward, dropping so fast toward the water the air whistles past my ears. It's only seconds, less than really, but my mind doesn't compute the limited time, my lungs opening up, and for just a moment, *everything* disappears. There's no noise. No worries. No betrayal.

No plans or schemes or enemies. No work to be done, good or bad.

There's just me in the air, hurdling toward the water at rapid speed.

My body is slightly arched, arms locked straight, my left palm positioned over my right, palm facing the water, ready to create a break in the surface to allow my body to pass through without a splash.

A perfect ripple.

My body shoots back for the surface, but after a quick breath, I drop my head back, floating a moment, and then curl into a ball, sinking myself.

I think of nothing as I lower toward the pool's bottom, my mind and limbs blissfully numb.

Weightless.

Only once my lungs begin to shrivel, and the pounding in my chest issues its final warning, do I rocket to the surface.

Diving meets no longer fill up my free days. There's no concert tonight that requires Delta's pristine performance. No art exhibit Bronx is required to reveal. No scheme to run or ruin that isn't already in motion.

So once I'm showered and perfectly presentable, the girls, Calvin, and I load up in Cal's car, and his driver takes us to the outskirts of our territory for dinner. Mid-drive, I have the urge to look behind us, even though I know if I do, Sai won't be tailing close behind.

What would he even do on a "leave"?

I bet my father has him doing a job or something, but if that's the case, why him? He's my guardian for a reason, and with the threats we could be facing, it's an odd time for Sai to be away.

Calvin chooses a quiet restaurant without a dress code or need for reservations, so we wait for the far corner booth to become available.

I knew going into this there were no obvious resolutions for my sister's stupidity other than shipping her ass right back and waiting to see what happened next, but I guess I was pathetically optimistic the four of us together could suggest, at the very least, an idea of some sort on what to do.

Sighing, I drop back in my chair. "This is fucking pointless," I complain. "She fucked us. Plain and simple."

Bronx scoffs her agreement while Delta offers a soft smile.

"I think your father is right, Rocklin," Calvin says, glaring at Bronx from across the table.

She dips her finger straight into the fondue kit the waitress dropped off a little over fifteen minutes ago, the group of us two hours into a meeting that has got us nowhere. She sucks it from her skin, seeming completely oblivious we're watching, but Delta and I know better.

She is fully aware.

Calvin drags his attention back to me. "You're going to have to talk to your sister, get the full story straight."

Delta nods her agreement. "There isn't much we can say without it."

Groaning, I press my middle fingers into the corners of my eyes. "I know. We need her side so we can tear it apart and determine if it's utter bullshit or not. Just so you guys know . . . I'm betting on bullshit."

The table laughs lightly, and I let my hands fall, releasing a long, harsh breath as I look around. "And the last item on the menu for tonight?"

Calvin sits back, tossing a few bills on the table as he raises a brow in my direction. "You already know."

He's right. I do, and it might be the most annoying part.

As per usual, my father will be getting exactly what he wanted.

"Then it's settled." I set the cloth napkin down, pushing to my feet. "Boston is officially moving back into Greyson Manor."

Hoo-fucking-ray.

I down what's left of the champagne in my glass and the others rise with me—here's to hoping her *fiancé* doesn't kill her when he figures it out.

Sadly, that would be the easiest ending.

No, that won't work.

Back in the manor, I charge for my wing and then my room.

If my sister's fiancé kills her for her runaway-bride bullshit, then my father will kill his sister. And brother. And mother. Basically, anyone the shark of the south district has ever so much as smiled at, while the man himself is forced to watch—Father is nothing if not thorough.

No one harms his family and lives.

The problem is the Fikile family is as powerful as they are because Enzo Fikile is as ruthless as Rayo Revenaw.

Blood for blood.

Tit for tat.

Wife for life.

Boston fucked them over, and the moment they realize it, they'll fuck us right back. Returning the steep price paid for her won't fix the issue.

In our world, it will only insult Enzo more.

He misses the money as much as my father notices he has it, which he doesn't.

The fee was more of a technicality, a show of good faith that if Enzo were to fall and nothing be left in Boston's name, that stipend would go to her. It's literally wasted money sitting in an account that technically doesn't exist, so Uncle Sam can't come knocking.

The real transaction will be the tying of our names, the contract she signed alongside her wedding license, which is set to be filed soon. A union between two powerful families, merging the northern and southern district crews once and for all—something no one has ever been able to accomplish. Something the eastern and western gangs won't take kindly to when—not if—this goes public.

Something the youngest, *hidden* heir to our cardinal compass, the girl who belongs in the east wing here in Greyson Manor would be forced to do when the time came.

This is why my father wants Boston here, because you can no more storm the grounds of the Greyson Estate than you can the White House.

Greyson Elite is neutral territory and the only of its kind, a boarding school for children of power. We have gangsters' daughters and cartels' sons, future kings and secret princesses, be it the royal or Mafia kind, and the rare few who are hoped to be or heard to be worthy of more than their parents' rank in our world would offer—finding those jaded gems is the job of the chancellor and his most trusted. It's how Kenex and Kylo, the Greco brothers, found their way here, much to my father's dismay. An outside council member had worked with them before, but they needed proper training.

Boston was born into this life and was once worthy of it, though the head position was given to me. Now she's a liability, one I'll have to handle as it's my blood she shares. My family name.

And for the first time in a long time, I don't have the answer to fix the problem. I *always* have an answer, but a deal was made, and she broke it. There is no way around that. You're nothing if not your word where we come from. Forgiveness is not a practiced action in our world. My sister could literally pay with her life.

Damn her!

Frustrated, I step into my closet, kick my heels wherever they may land and tear my dress over my head, dropping it to the floor. My closet is color coordinated, so I move to the black section, slip on a long-sleeve bodysuit, and wiggle into a pair of dark, formfitting slacks that come up to my belly button and choke my ankles.

The mirror glows and I cock my head, looking over my outfit.

Yeah, knee-high boots are a must.

I eye a royal-blue pair, but in the end, I'm in a mood.

"Black it is." I slide them on, zipping them up behind the calves, grab my bag, and head for the stairs.

I pass Saylor and Jasper on my way; Calvin's door is ajar as I step onto the landing, but no one stops me, and I don't look back. I curve through the hall, past the music and dining rooms, and press the code for the garage.

The giant glass doors slide open and the slight chill from the massive underground space smacks me in my face.

When I press the key fob, my baby purrs to life, the rumbling of the engine a strong, settling sound that causes the haywire sensation in my chest to settle slightly.

The door rises for me on my command, and I climb inside, my fingers curling around the steering wheel, following it around until my fists touch.

I close my eyes and slam the gas pedal to the floor before the door has even sealed shut, smashing my foot on the brake just as quickly. Only then do I open my eyes, and a smirk pulls at my lips.

Three inches is all that separates me from the steel doors leading to the underground tunnel. That's closer than last time.

Entering the gate code on the screen we added to the car, it opens.

I'm free, under the summer night's sky, in forty-five seconds flat.

The car wraps around the winding roads effortlessly, floating along the lanes with ease, and I crack the windows, the scent of pine mixed with a smoky floral note filling the air. And something savory. Someone's cooking and it smells delicious, but just as soon as the aroma fills the cab, it's gone, the speed

I'm going carrying me long past it. I keep driving, curving along the coastline you can't see this time of night.

Before I know where I'm going, an hour has passed and I'm slamming on my brakes, staring across the empty lot leading up to a small brick building in the middle of nowhere, my eyes slicing to the curb at the edge of the hillside.

My brows pull together as I put the car in park, but I don't climb out.

I sit back and wonder why the hell I drove here.

That night, when I stumbled upon the half man, half boy in a leather jacket and faded black jeans, was the first time I had ever been here, and I don't even know how I found it then.

Hell, I don't even know how I found it now.

Last time I had to take a few wrong turns on my way back to figure out where I was.

Okay, so maybe Sai *did* tell my dad. Did I venture into a point of pizzo where the man behind the counter pays the Mafia for his protection, meaning there's trouble to be found here?

Is he paying my dad?

The Fikiles?

That's a sobering thought and my hand instinctively dips into the space at the edge of the seat, my fingertips brushing over the small dagger stored there. If I reach beneath the seat, there's a gun and, in the glove box, a knife. Beneath the custom floorboard in back is a shotgun, and in the event silence is necessary . . . a bow and arrow are tucked beside it. All are safeguards Sia and my father demanded when I argued my case for having my own vehicles. If it were up to them, I would be kept locked tightly behind the bulletproof black glass of a town car forever and always, or preferably, in Greyson Manor, unless I absolutely "had" to come out.

I pretended to argue against the stash of weapons, so they would feel they were winning something, but I'm no dunce. I'm the best leverage a man could have over my father: my sister as well, foolish or not.

My father would rage for less, so dare to touch his daughters without our—maybe even without his—permission? That's a surefire ticket six feet under.

Though I doubt I'll have any need for a weapon tonight. These coordinates are no one's territory—I checked the minute I got home that night.

So how is it Bastian was able to . . . address his problem without the local authorities being called? A small business owner with no ties or knowledge of the organized crime families circling this town and the ones connected to it would panic, would he not? Lock his doors, call for help?

So why didn't he?

Does he fear the wannabe bad boy in the rusty old Cutlass?

If so, what's there to fear?

So, he's stealthy and can make his way into places he doesn't belong. All rats do. That's why exterminators exist; ours just happen to have silencers at the end of a six-inch barrel. I bet he couldn't even buy a gun if he wanted. One, they're expensive. Two, he probably has a record, scrappers like him always do.

Then again, he wasn't caught sneaking around The Enterprise, though he could have passed for . . . no. He wouldn't pass for anyone I can think of. Perhaps a distant cousin of the Vails from Saint Charles. Their grandson, who started at Greyson Elite last fall, adds more ink by the month.

Tattoos aren't frowned upon in our world, per se. In fact, many crime families bare their family crests on their body somewhere, the same those of us with guardians do ours, but if you're not a man everyone should know and remember, you're a man who should blend in if needed. The last thing you want is for someone to see you coming, and a body covered in art is sure to turn heads.

Bastian didn't allow me to turn mine when he teased me with the toy along his tip.

On that thought, I recline my seat a few inches and pull out my phone, typing the basics of what I know was there.

Dick piercing.

I hit search, my brows jumping and caving in the next second when the first set of images pop up.

There are a few with bunches of sagging skin stretched between hoop-like rings, two and three in a straight line down the shaft and others with a hook straight through the hole.

"Definitely not . . ."

My lips smash to the side, and I close my eyes, remembering.

The jewelry strained against the rubber jacket he suffocated it in, but it didn't prevent the chill of the metal from shocking my heated center when he teased me with the tip . . .

The tip!

I try again

Dick head piercing.

My phone thinks for a second, and then a new image pops up.

My mouth drops open, and as I read the name of the piercing, I realize I knew what this one was, but damn. "Fucking *ouch*."

It's a Prince Albert, a curved barbell, almost like a hook, right through the piss hole.

Why the hell would anyone do that?

I begin reading the description, all the way down to the benefits, and okay. Now I get it.

I scroll back up to the photo examples, zooming in on the thick, proudly erect head of the dick on the screen.

"Good guess, but wrong."

My phone falls to my chest, dagger between my fingers in a split second, but as my eyes slice to the window, and the familiar shadow looms there, I drop it.

My heart starts pounding, the adrenaline crashes back down and my head falls against the seat.

Jesus, Rocklin, wake the fuck up. You'd be dead already if it were anyone else.

Wait, what?

My muscles lock, the thought ghastly and unwelcome. I don't even know this guy. He's no more than a stranger who pops up when he wants and sends creepy texts, making me think he's watching from god knows where, but he *is* watching. He wouldn't know when Damiano's hands are on me if he wasn't.

What would he do if I let Dom lay me down and climb on top of me?

Would he watch and whisper angry words later?

Burst in and bust the *pretty boy's* lip?

Or would he walk away and never look back?

"What's the frown for, Rich Girl?"

The humor in his tone snaps me from my thoughts, and I glare straight ahead, but I do unlock the doors, pressing the button for the passenger one to open.

He doesn't move for a full fifteen seconds, but then annoyingly slow, he curves around the back, my eyes popping up to the rearview mirror to catch a glimpse before pointing forward once more.

What are you doing, Rocklin?

This is everything your father has warned you about.

Maybe that's exactly why I'm here, for a taste of rebellion. Maybe I'm more like my sister than I care to admit.

Bastian eases into the seat, nothing but the soft swish of his leather jacket heard as he does.

He reaches over and my head snaps his way, hand darting up, nicking the butt of his palm.

He pauses mid-move, raising a brow, and I raise one right back.

"You invited me in here, 'member?" he asks, crystal eyes swimming with mirth.

"I'm still trying to figure out why."

"It's 'cause you want me to clear this up for you."

I frown. "Clear what up?"

His mouth curves now, and I follow the lazy path his eyes make to where he is reaching . . . for the phone in my lap, face up, angry, purple-ish dick lighting up the screen.

Instantly, horrifyingly, my cheeks heat. Legitimate warmth washes over my neck and face and now I kind of want to stab myself.

I'm blushing, like I have a damn thing to be embarrassed about, like the opinion or thought of the biker boy, minus the bike, at my side matters. If it weren't dark out here, I might push him out and take off, but it is, so my humiliation is only my own.

Still, Bastian chuckles as he sits back, a low whistle leaving him.

I flick my eyes his way, watching the fascination on his face as his gaze traces every inch his greedy eyes can reach as he licks the itty-bitty blood drop my dagger left on his palm. He takes in the candy-blue leather, following the stark white stripe across to the large screen in the center, his pupils dilating as the rim rolls around it, the color fading into a new one with each full spin. His lips curve higher and higher with each second, and his eyes flick to mine after he spots the shifter.

"A touchscreen twelve-speed?" he confirms.

I nod, my gaze skimming across his features, the cynical harshness nowhere to be seen.

He sits comfortably beside me as if we're old friends and tonight is like any other Saturday night. As if he doesn't notice the stark difference between the two of us or how batshit crazy it is we're two strangers who "met," and I use that term lightly, under criminal circumstances.

I stole from him.

He broke into my building.

We fucked without exchanging names.

He looks so . . . calm and casual in his own chaotic and careless way. There are wrinkles in his shirt and a streak of something smudged along his cheek, as if he was carrying something greasy and wiped his hands down his face but didn't care to look at his reflection after, too busy going about his day.

His hair is all over the place, no strands brushed any which way but lying in crisscrossed curls where they may. It's as if he runs his hands through it often but switches off which one, maybe even using both sometimes.

Giant headphones hang around his neck, they're brandless and bulky, and there's a wire attached, tucked beneath his shirt, but he doesn't seem to mind it. The cut on his lip is gone, but the swell I assumed it caused is still there, pressing against that same silver ring.

My attention falls to his knuckles. While they haven't healed completely, they did a little and now reveal a permanent dark mark, almost a shadow along each, one too many tears of the skin if I had to guess.

His fingers fold then, fist flexing, stretching the scarred skin taut before opening once more, and my eyes lift to find his frown pointed at his hand.

"Didn't have to use 'em much this week." Slowly, he looks my way.

I don't know why, but I nod.

We stare at each other for several moments, and then he cocks his head.

"What are you doing out here, Rich Girl?"

"I have no idea." The response leaves me instantly, and I realize it's the truth.

I have no idea why I came out here.

I didn't plan it, that's for sure.

Bastian is watching me, something swimming in his light eyes I can't name. What's worse, I don't feel an incessant prickle beneath the ribs, the one that triggers my mind to spin, demanding I dig dagger deep to find out what it is, as it does when I meet the eyes of most.

My life is complicated, one issue after the next, one worry that trickles into ten.

Someone is always trying to earn their way into the Greysons' good graces or befriend the Revenaw heir, or catch the eye of the team captain. If it's not those things, then they're searching for a slipup, waiting in the wings with a secret camera disguised as a new brooch or family crest or something else as equally unoriginal, trying to come up with the smallest scrap of dirt they can call home to Daddy with— everyone wants to know if Rayo Revenaw's prize daughter is all she's said to be.

I've never claimed to be a damn thing, though the expectation has always been there, and the target branded into both mine and my sister's back from simply being born, then I started beating everyone . . . at everything. And so the red ring grew.

Bastian isn't looking at me the way my peers do, though. There's no calculation in his gaze, no triumph. Curiosity, yes. Attraction, duh, but if I told him to get out and go away, he wouldn't try and find a way to stay. He'd laugh and then he'd leave, probably without looking back.

He wouldn't be upset, though, and he'd still text me when he thought to. I shouldn't be so sure of this, but I am.

I have a feeling he's hard to offend. Actually, I'm not sure anything I could think of would offend this guy.

It's . . . interesting. Intriguing?

Everything offends people in my world. Look at them too long, they're insulted. Don't look at them at all, double the insult. There's a fine line to tread when surrounded by formidable people. It's exhausting.

"How did you know I was here?" I break the silence.

He makes himself more comfortable in my passenger seat. "How do you think I knew?"

"The man in the store." Obviously. "He called you."

Bastian nods.

"This is neutral territory," I warn, my voice snappier than intended.

His brows bunch together. "Neutral territory. You're not talkin' off the path, are you?"

Shit. Okay, so he's either a bottom-feeder, low in rank or clueless that an organized crime ring owns this city . . . and everyone within a three-hundred-mile radius.

Pivot.

"How did you find this place?" I ignore his question.

"Heard about it."

"From who?"

"Nobody."

111

My eyes sharpen. "Do you know a lot of nobodies?"

He shrugs unapologetically. "Everyone I know is a nobody, Rich Girl. What's with the twenty questions?" he asks but tells me more without waiting for my answer. "Buddy of mine came across this place after a cabin trip, said it was dark and quiet and hard to find, so I came down and talked to the owner. If I show up, he turns a blind eye, and in exchange—"

"You pay him for his silence."

He scowls slightly. "I power wash his dumpsters twice a month and show up on his restock days. The man's pushing seventy with a bad knee. He can't lift shit over ten pounds and can't stand for more than twenty. I help him out; he helps me out."

That's . . . sweet.

He could simply threaten the guy since he's not under anyone's protection, and it wouldn't be an act against a powerful family to do so, but no. It's an even, fair trade, and the man hasn't been backed into a corner he's not allowed out of without penalty.

It's an odd way to do business, but again, *interesting*.

"Have you ever had barbeque?"

His eyes widen at the random subject change, a low chuckle slipping past his lips. "Yeah, I've had barbeque." He laughs again. "Why, have you . . ." he trails off. "You've never had barbeque."

It's not a question and I'm not sure why I don't want to explain.

Probably because Bastian looks like he could use the iron a solid steak would provide and I'm a different kind of rich. My meals are strategically planned, prepped, and prepared by cultural, notable chefs. Very rarely is a meal repeated unless we specifically ask, and we do. Sometimes.

It's the same at Greyson Elite. Based on your profile, extracurriculars of choice, and yes, even field of study, your meals are managed.

"You don't feed the body, you feed the brain," is our nutritionist's favorite line.

I guess barbeque doesn't fit the bill.

I push my hair over my shoulder and his eyes follow the movement, slowly coming back to mine.

He studies me. "You hungry?"

"No."

He nods, glancing out the window a moment before looking back, a joint suddenly in his fingertips. "Wanna get hungry?"

Do I?

I don't know, but what I do know is I should go home.

If my dad finds out I'm here, he won't call and warn me back to the manor.

He'll show up with two SUVs leading and three tailing, each loaded down with armed guards. He might shoot Bastian for fun, and by fun, I mean most likely. Of course, it won't be a lethal shot, he'd go for the foot or calf.

I think.

Either way, Bastian would leave with a hole in his body and not one he could fill with body jewelry. So, if I'm going to risk getting busted, I might as well get high first, and that's the only reason I open my palm, waiting for him to drop the joint into it.

It's definitely not because I want to stay here a little longer. With him.

Chapter 9

Bass

The sky's dope out here. The smog from the city below is not quite as thick, letting a bit of the stars show themselves, shining false hope over all of us, whisperin' *there's more out there*, and *all you have to do is reach for it*.

I've been reaching, stacking nonexistent rocks, and climbing invisible, never-ending ladders, and I get no closer to a single thing I want.

A better life for my sister.

A clue to where my shitty mother is.

A fucking purpose of my own.

Thing is, I'm a catch-22.

Poor as fuck but rich in brainpower. Careless but cautious. I'm black-hearted, but that bitch still bleeds.

I don't need or want a quiet little life. That shit ain't for me, not after what I've done and what I *enjoy* doing, but I can't figure out a way around my darker needs that leads to what I want most.

My sister happy in a home where she feels safe inside.

Never once has she brought up our mother, and I can't say for certain if she thinks of her at all, but I hope she doesn't since there are no happy memories that would come to her mind.

I, on the other hand, think about her all the time. Every day and every single fucking night.

There will be no sense of prevailing while she's still out there, free and clear. She might not have physically touched us, but she's as much of a monster as our dad was, and I'm

114

frothing with the need for her to understand that now. I'm not a lanky, unhealthy boy afraid to speak up or act out.

I'm the shadow that lurks.

The bigger monster.

The stronger one.

Bigger and stronger or not, I still don't know how to give my sister what she needs that allows me to take what I want from this life, and there lies one of the million fucking problems being born Bastian Bishop buried me in.

Glaring at the flickering lights in the sky, I blow smoke rings into the air, blocking out every speck.

Silence must stretch too long because, in my peripheral, Rocklin turns her head toward me.

It took some convincing to get her out of the car, but for the last fifteen minutes, we've been lying side by side on a blanket on my rusted hood. The joint's gone out twice already, both of us lost in our own thoughts, and neither of us has spoken a single one out loud since we started.

Maybe because we don't know each other or maybe because we don't trust each other.

Probably both reasons.

I'd bet it also has something to do with the fact neither of us knows what the fuck we're doing here.

No matter, she's staring at me now, her lips sealed shut, so I'm thinking she's got something on her mind. Not sure she'd have ended up out here if she didn't.

This—I—am against her better judgment, as I should be, just like she's against mine.

There are a lot of rich folks in the town I live in, and I'll happily take the fuckers' money when they want to play big baller, betting a ridiculous amount on a fight with no clear winner. It's always for show, to get the girl or to piss off some guy or some other dumbass reason. The rich pricks where I'm from go to school and get good grades, but other than that, they spend their time partying and chasing tail.

Basically, they're normal-ass high school and college kids.

115

Rocklin ain't like them, that's easy to see.

"You like your life, Rich Girl?"

When she says nothing, I roll my head against the frame, so I'm facing her as she is me, our backs flat, hands lying on our stomachs, minus the one holding the joint.

She's glaring, searching, so I let her. Ain't nothing for her to find, after all.

She blinks a few times, but that's all I get.

"That a hard question?"

"It's a personal question," she quips.

"Right, and only my dick gets the pleasure of knowing you personally, yeah?"

Her lips purse, eyes narrowing, but then a small laugh leaves her, and she snatches the joint from my fingers, facing the sky once more. "If I were smart, yes, but then again, letting a stranger fuck me wasn't the brightest idea I've ever had. I had myself tested, by the way. Turns out you're clean," she teases.

A smirk pulls at my lips. "Thanks for clearing that up. I was worried there a minute."

She bounces her brows once, waving the dead joint, so I reach over and spark the lighter.

She puffs a few times, her nose scrunching. "This tastes like shit."

"Yeah, 'cause it's been lit five times. Quit bullshittin'."

She tries to hide her smile, taking a few long pulls before handing it back.

A long, loud sigh pushes past her lips, and then she says, "My sister's a cunt."

From the corner of my eye, I glance her way.

So, she has a sister. She's not alone in some fancy house she can't escape. That's good.

"Sucks to be you. My sister's an angel."

Her head snaps my way. "You have a sister?"

"Yup." I frown at the sky.

Why'd I tell her that?

116

I don't talk about my sister. I keep her in my mind but out of my mouth. She's good and the world isn't.

Fuck it, it's not like it matters. This . . . friendly little adventure Rocklin's on will pass when her moment of rebellion does.

Daddy's little princess doesn't play in the dirt for long.

The thought shouldn't taste so sour on my tongue.

Rocklin rolls onto her stomach, her forearms flat on the car, and her hair falls over her shoulder.

I'm tempted to touch it, to run the silky golden strands between my fingers.

"Is that another thing we have in common?" she jokes, and it looks good on her.

No practiced sass or head-held-high bullshit.

Just a stoned girl, looking like the sexiest version of Catwoman I've ever seen in her all-black, skintight getup—the Barbie version, pink lips and all.

I push up, roll myself, and like I thought she might, she rolls with me, once again on her back, in perfect timing for me to throw my leg over her body. I hover a few inches above her.

She stares, lips slightly quirked, waiting to see what I'll do.

My knuckles come up, and I decide to do what I wanted to, pinch a strand of her hair between my fingers, bringing it to my cheek. It's as soft as it looks. Smells like flowers dipped in sugar.

Her chest rises and falls quickly, palms flattening on the blanket. I've got a feeling she wants to reach out, grab me, yank on me, and demand all the things she wants. In her life, I bet she gets exactly what she expects, yet she holds back.

Good girl.

"Another bad day, ma?"

There's a moment's hesitation, but she nods. It's subtle, but it's there.

"Is it the bitchy sister's fault?"

Her eyes narrow, yet still . . . another small nod.

"Want me to kill her?"

Shock flickers across her face, and then she laughs. It's a deep belly laugh, eyes crinkling and all. Her hand comes up and slightly covers her face. When it finally falls back to her side, there's a flip in her features.

They're softer, less cagey. Less . . . suspicious.

I press my knee between hers and those green eyes flick to my lips, so I run my tongue along my bottom one.

"Waiting for me to kiss you?"

At her glare, a chuckle leaves me, and I dip down, running my mouth up the side of her neck, groaning when she stretches it wider for me. I kiss her throat, reveling in the sharp breath she draws through her nostrils.

"Does it make you feel better to know I want to?" My hand glides down her side until I can fold my fingers with hers, and then I lean back, pulling her with me, our shoes meeting the pavement.

A small frown tugs at her brows, but she shakes it off quickly, studying my expression as I pull her hair over one shoulder.

"Time to go, Rich Girl. I got a curfew."

"Oh, please." She rolls her eyes. "As if your parents could make you do a damn thing."

"Good thing ain't got none, then, huh?" A darkness washes over me, but I blink it away.

Rocklin eyes me but doesn't ask, coming to me when I pull her hand.

"No, but for real, I've got shit to handle, so you gotta go, and I don't want you coming out here like you did tonight."

"You don't make the rules."

"I won't always be able to show on a dime." I ignore her. "You're lucky I could this time."

She puts space between us, scowling. "I told you I don't know why I came."

"Oh, I believe that." I erase the distance she created and draw her chin between my fingers. I tilt her how I want her, and she lets me.

"Do what I said, Rich Girl," I whisper, stretching my thumb so the tip of my nail scrapes along her lip, my other fingers

118

meeting the skin of her jaw and neck. I test the skin there, and it's as soft as I remember. Dragging my touch lower, my eyes leave the point of contact, seeking out hers once more. "Go home, but don't worry. Way I see it, you came to me tonight, and I have every intention of rewarding you for it."

"Reward me like I'm a dog?" Her question is bratty, but her tone gives her away.

It's low and raspy and goes straight to my dick.

"Nah." My smirk is slow. "Like a bad *bitch*."

She shakes her head, but a soft chuckle pushes past her lips. She gives me a playful yet challenging glare. "I like shiny things."

"I've got something shiny for you, but not tonight. Soon. Now . . . *go*."

"Yes, daddy," she sasses, taking backward steps, but I dart forward, loop my arm around her waist and yank her to me.

"Careful, ma . . ." I whisper against her lips, "I might like that."

She smiles now, a big, real one, and damn.

I like it.

Like her.

What a fuckin dumbass you are, my man.

"You know I could get out of your hold, right? That if I didn't want you to touch me, I would have already used the dagger in my waistband and stuck you in your eye?"

"You mean this dagger?" I grab the edge of my jacket, pulling it out, so she can see the shiny silver handle sticking higher than the inside pocket.

Her jaw drops and now I'm the one who chuckles.

"You're not the only one with sticky fingers, Little Thief." I swat her ass to get her moving and step away.

Slowly, she turns, not sparing me another glance as she slips inside her fancy ride and pulls away. I stare after her, knowing I should change my number, tell Donny behind the counter not to bother letting me know if she pulls up out here again.

Cut it and cut it quick.

A girl like that will leave you bleeding on the floor.

What I want to know is why she came tonight. What drove her to me? What problems is she running from?

And the most deranged of questions, what can a low-class, poor motherfucker like me do to fix it?

The likely answer?

Not a goddamn thing.

Chapter 10

Rocklin

Bastian is a liar. Sai is acting odd, and my sister is in worse shape than I thought.

Sai has become a constant presence, looming no less than twenty feet away—far enough so I can speak freely but close enough to stop any escape I might try to make, which is exactly how he's acting: as if I might take off at any moment. My dad must have really laid into him.

Boston is weak, and while she's always been on the feeble side mentally, it's never affected her physically. It is now. Her stamina is lower, so she's whining for more breaks between grappling and starting fights to avoid sparring. She falls to her ass after twenty minutes of wrestling in the steam room, and even her concentration is off—her shooting average has split in half. She's sleeping through breakfast and staring into space more than she listens. I've been working with her for five days in a row now and it's not getting any better.

And in those five days, not once has a liquid-eyed bad boy made his existence known.

I've been to The Enterprise twice and nothing. I'm annoyed, which only annoys me more.

What kind of girl twiddles her thumbs, waiting for a single-named stranger to break in and have their way with them, anyway?

The kind who appreciates a good dicking down, apparently.

Pathetic? Maybe.

I must be because I've even considered asking Dom to pop in, figuratively, of course, where I would then wait for him to touch me, all to see if my tattooed shadow shows up, but who's to say he would?

He did say he had 'shit to do' and couldn't simply show up like an employee on call.

It's not like I want to see him, so who fucking cares. I just wanted the reward he promised me.

I scoff, shake off my gloves, and wipe the sweat from my chest with a towel. A promise from some back-alley bad boy? Please.

"Someone's frustrated." Boston smiles. "Something on your mind or maybe . . . someone?"

My eyes slice to my sister, narrowing.

We used to talk boys, but that was before she signed herself over to the worst one she could find.

I give her my back, and she follows me to the gym shower, stripping down beside me and stepping under the spray as I do.

"Come on, Coco. Don't shut me out. I fucked up. I know, but—"

"But nothing, Boston." I quickly scrub my scalp, diving farther beneath the warm spray. "You made a choice that will taint our name. If you weren't Dad's daughter, you'd be dead already."

"Okay, that's dramatic."

"It's the truth."

"Enzo doesn't even know I'm here, so you can stop expecting him to bust through the gates and break your perfect record of control."

I turn my shower off and face her.

"How is that exactly? How does a man who's nearly as powerful as Dad *not know* his *fiancée* ran away?"

She shrugs, turning toward her towel. "Because he doesn't care. It's not like he wanted me. He knew it was a good deal, that's all."

A frown builds along my brow. Is that . . . hurt? Bitterness?

It doesn't matter. Her response doesn't answer the question, so I ask again. "*How* does he not know?"

"Trust me, he doesn't."

"*Boston.*"

"Oh my god, fine! Because he's gone, okay?!" she shouts. "You know how Dad dropped me off for this stupid 'three-month get-to-know-each-other' clause he put into the contract, with a midpoint 'check-in'? Well, shocker, but Enzo Fikile didn't hold up his end."

"What do you mean?"

"Isn't it obvious?" She looks away. "My husband-to-be didn't do what he said he would."

My head tugs back, and I blink. "You were there for three months. Are you telling me you have spent no time with Enzo at all?"

"You can't tell Dad!"

"*Boston!*"

"No, okay!" she shouts back. "Unless you count the three minutes he stood in my doorway the day of the 'check-in.' I was dolled up to the max, full-blown heiress mode, Coco, and he didn't even blink. He looked me in the eye, told me Dad had just arrived, and then he said, and I quote, 'I like it here. It's nice, and Enzo's people treat me well. This is a good choice, Dad. I'm sure.'" Boston frowns at her clothes as she pulls them on. "I didn't realize until he said his own name those were the words he expected me to say to Dad when he asked for my final decision, so I did." Her eyes find mine. "That's the only time I saw Enzo outside of the day I arrived when he showed me to my room, which was on the complete opposite end of the estate than his, by the way." She turns, picks her gym clothes up off the floor and sets them in the hamper for the staff. "He was gone the next morning and hasn't been back since."

Damn. I would go stir-crazy alone all that time, but really, her explanation only makes this worse.

She knows it, adding, "It would have been better if I said he beat me or let his team have their way with me, wouldn't it?" She looks away, chewing on her lip. "God, this turned into a mess. I should have just . . ." She swallows, facing away from me.

I walk up behind her, laying my chin on her shoulder, and she reaches up, her palm flattening on my cheek as she leans her head against mine.

"I'm sorry," she whispers, tears thickening her tone.

"I know."

She hangs her head and we both understand.

She's sorry for what she did, but she's also sorry for lying because she and I both know she *is* lying.

Why and about which part is yet to be seen.

Back in my room, I get ready for class, meeting Bronx and Delta at the car two minutes later than usual.

Sai narrows his eyes. "You're never late."

"And you never take days off." I widen my eyes mockingly. "Guess it's true what the mundane say, 'some things do change.'"

I slide inside and the girls follow, their wide, entertaining eyes flicking from me to where Sai closes the door. I roll up the soundproof window and click the button for the privacy setting. A sheet of darkness slips over the glass and the girls' gazes sharpen.

"What's going on?" Delta asks.

"My sister is up to something and my dad won't talk to me about what he knows. It's been five days. The man knows something." I look to Bronx, who is already waiting expectantly. "Think you can find out where Enzo Fikile is without alerting him someone's looking for him?"

"Finally, you asked." She grins, making some notes on her phone, before looking up again. "I have a lot of ideas for where to start, just waiting to be explored."

I grin at my girl.

"Now that we covered one, how about the other? What's going on with Sai?" Delta wonders.

"I don't know. Ever since his random two-day leave, something has been off."

"Yeah, he never used to linger on campus before," Bronx agrees.

"Right? It's odd. He's following me through the training yard in the evenings now, and he shadowed me into The Enterprise this week like he's refusing to let me out of his sight, but then he'll turn around and disappear randomly and I won't see him for an hour or more."

Wait. What if he knows the grounds were breached by my MIA intruder?

"Coco Rocco?"

"Hmm?" My head pops up, and I lick my lips.

Delt frowns, asking, "It makes the most sense this is about Enzo."

"Maybe, but my dad acted like the threat of Enzo showing up was as worrisome as flies in the summer, guaranteed, but no big deal."

"To be fair, your dad is top notch when it comes to intel, so maybe it isn't?" Bronx suggests, even though I know it bothers her too.

For including us in so little, our fathers sure do expect a lot from us.

What would they do if we just . . . stopped being perfect twenty-four hours a day?

"Boston finally spilled a little," I share, and then repeat what she had to say.

"So Boston doesn't think he knows and your dad's acting like he's unconcerned, but Sai is on one," Bronx lays it all out, trying to make sense, but that's the problem.

It doesn't.

"Let's shelf this for now." I eye the campus outside the window, the boys exactly where expected, up the steps. "Time to shine."

Delta runs her hands down her jacket.

Bronx sighs, buttoning hers.

With practiced smiles and devising minds, we climb out.

The minutes tick by, one class rolls into the next, and with each one, my focus dims further. I couldn't tell you what we went over in my international dynamics class and I have no idea what topic we're tackling in debate next.

Now I'm sitting in my last class before break and all I can think about is the situation with Boston. If Enzo didn't honor the deal of the ass-backward courtship my father demanded, is that not enough to potentially call a foul and cut the contract?

My dad, Boston, and Enzo all signed it. Enzo paid. My sister was 'delivered,' and the wedding is being planned, but it hasn't happened yet. Could his failure to spend any sort of time with her be her ticket out without causing a war?

If that were the case, why would she not want Dad to know this?

Maybe that's the lie she told?

I swallow my sigh, trailing the feather of my pen along my chin, tuning in for the first time since I sat down in advanced investment management.

Professor Fredric asks a question, his gaze falling on me for the answer, even though more than half the class have their hands raised and I do not.

Rocklin Revenaw expected to have every answer to every fucking problem known to man. Gag. Me.

What would they say about me should I give the wrong one?

"Entrepreneurship requires balance. You must account for risk and growth and can't have one without the other. Your investment portfolio should be approached the same way." Textbook response.

The professor praises.

My classmates offer terse smiles.

I want to fucking scream.

I'm sitting in a classroom full of people dying to take my spot while a credible threat looms over my family.

I know how to handle money, massive quantities of it at that. The entire idea behind The Enterprise was mine. Not Bronx or Delta. Not my dad's. *Mine.*

Did they find a way to make it more to help cover the truth? Yes.

But the added zeros of net worth growth and the potential for more . . . stable relationships with other outside organizations became possible because of me.

126

Any man with half a brain and a gun can find himself a million or two if he plays his cards right, but what happens once he does? What's he going to do with all that cash and no paper trail for where it came from? With all those marked bills?

He's going to come to The Enterprise and *play cards*, that's what.

The professor dims the lights and goes into a PowerPoint about the many risks that come along with investments, so I allow my shoulders to slump the slightest bit.

I look at the clock.

Fifteen more minutes.

My phone vibrates on the table, so I flip it over, my pulse jumping slightly when I see the name on the screen.

Bastian: outside.

My brows snap together, and I glance around, catching the eye of my desk partner.

I force a smile and then face forward again.

Outside. As in, outside of Greyson Elite? There is *no way* he got inside the gates. None.

The guards are ex-military and act like they're still at war.

Me: show me.

The three little dots appear at the bottom, and then an image comes through.

My lips quirk instantly.

So my little intruder couldn't get in. He's standing outside his car, parked in front of the emergency walking gate. It's seventeen feet of stone-cold steel, a latch locked in place every two feet. He couldn't open it with a shotgun. But how long has he been there? The guards round the grounds like clockwork; they work like a merry-go-round, every inch touched by sight every nine minutes.

Bastian: come to me, Rich Girl.

My insides do *not* turn to liquid mush.

I look at the clock.

Twelve minutes until class ends. Four minutes until the guards approach him, question him, and unbeknownst to him, scan his body with supersecret software that will then run him through a recognition program, where everything from a second-grade root canal will come up.

Before I know what I'm doing, I'm standing in the middle of class, my bag in hand.

All heads turn to me, eyes narrowing, widening, questioning.

Dom meets my gaze and tenses, preparing to rise, but I shake my head subtly and head for the door.

"Miss Revenaw?" the professor calls.

"Emergency." My single-worded lie is all he gets and then I'm in the hall, rushing down it.

I burst through the garden doors and weave along the path, slowing as I reach the gate.

Bastian leans against his passenger door, one leg crossed over the other, arms folded over his chest. He spots me, cocking his head, and waits until I reach the gate to push off.

He comes to me.

His long, tattooed fingers wrap around the steel bars and he stares at me. "Rich Girl."

"Poor Boy."

His lip quirks and he steps back. "Well, come on, then."

"Where?"

He ignores me, opens the passenger door and moves to his. He doesn't look my way as he climbs inside; he just does it, and then he waits.

My eyes dart around the space on instinct, just in case this is a setup and I've been blind this whole time and he's trying to infiltrate the grounds like some black ops badass shit, but there's no one in sight.

I have two hours of free time that technically won't start for another handful of minutes, but I'm already here.

My phone starts buzzing in my pocket and I know it's Dom, likely the girls too, wondering what happened and ready to help with whatever it is.

I don't dig it from my bag, but I do slide the golden cuff down my wrist and lift it to the scanner. The gate creaks as it opens, and I slip through the gap before it's done, slamming it closed.

I sit on the towel covering the torn leather of the ancient Cutlass and look to Bastian. "So. Where are we going?"

He pushes my hair over my shoulder, ignores me, then off we go.

My eyes are glued to Bastian. Stuck like a fly to honey.

When he said he was outside, I figured he wanted . . . honestly, I have no idea.

All I had time to process was the fact that he was outside of Greyson Elite and he wanted me to come to him, and as slightly troubling as it is, I wanted to. More than that, though, I didn't want the guards to find him.

Maybe somewhere, deep down, I'm afraid he's not a random guy I met in the dark, but I'm a trick he's turning.

Maybe I don't want to know who he really is and where he really comes from.

Maybe . . . I do want to know him better and that's why I couldn't allow our little bubble to be popped by what would follow if he was found lurking outside a school full of influential men's kin.

Either way, no part of me expected to be propped on top of a park picnic table that's been painted one too many times, watching as Bastian glares at a grill.

We haven't said a whole lot outside of our usual banter, but he's been moving nonstop.

There's foil beside me and a small grocery bag he digs into every once in a while. When he lights a wad of napkins on fire, dropping them on top of a pile of half-burned coals, I almost worry he's playing it by ear, but he seems to know what he's doing.

What he's doing . . . is barbequing.

Apparently, he's getting hot doing it because he sets down the switchblade he's using as a utensil and peels off his jacket, tossing it at me.

I catch it at the last second, narrowing my gaze on him, and he cracks a small smile.

"Just making sure you weren't zoning out on me," he says, turning back to the grill.

I fold the weathered leather and set it neatly in my lap. "Oh, I'm zoned in. Wondering how you became so domesticated," I tease.

"Used to have a chore rotation at the group home." Bastian shrugs. "Punks love them some barbeque."

Group home? He doesn't elaborate, so I leave it be.

"I can't believe you're cooking for me right now."

"I'm not." He flashes me a grin over his shoulder, a few dark strands of his hair falling over his forehead with the move, and my god, the heat that spreads through me. "I'm cooking for me, but I'll share." He glares then as if thinking better of it. "Food. I'll share food . . . wait." His features sharpen more, gaze, once again, darting my way. "This kind of food, feel me?"

A laugh bubbles up in me, and I look down, realizing my fingers are running across the cool leather in my lap. My eyes catch on the sewn-in tag at the collar. Written in the same perfect cursive on the note from his wallet. "Bishop."

Our eyes meet, and he frowns, dropping his to the jacket.

He pauses a moment as if working through the slipup and deciding if he's pissed I found it, but then he nods, turning to squirt sauce onto the meat right out of the bottle.

Bastian Bishop.

I look him over.

"*Episcopos.*"

He frowns my way, but only for a moment.

"Your last name," I tell him. "It means overseer." I pause. "What do you do, Bastian Bishop?"

It's such a generic, cliché question. He's around my age, so he should be in school. I skipped my senior year and went straight into the scholar's program, now in year two.

"Oversee."

I roll my eyes, watching as he grabs a strip of foil, drops the meat inside of it, and walks over, nodding his chin for me to move, so I scoot toward the other end.

Bastian places the tinfoil he's using as a serving tray between us, sauce-coated chicken legs on top of it. I've never seen tinfoil at the dinner table, and I've never eaten chicken legs before, but it smells divine. So much so I lean forward for a stronger hint.

"All right, Rich Girl." He holds the end of a drumstick and takes his switchblade, cutting into the meat and then lifting the blade to my lips.

"Forgot to pack the forks, did you?"

"No forks, no plates, and limited napkins." He frowns in warning. "Now, open."

I do as I'm told, and he eases the blade forward.

I snap my teeth closed over it and he tenses, making me laugh on the inside as I lean back, taking the bite with me. I flick my tongue out to touch the tip of the blade for fun and then chew.

My eyes widen, my palm coming up to cover my lips as I finish it.

"That's . . . good."

He nods, grabs a drumstick between his thumb and pointer finger, and bites right into it like a caveman, coming up with sauce along his cheeks.

Chuckling, I lean closer, and he narrows his eyes when I keep on coming. Gazes locked, I lick at the sauce, and before I can pull away, his free hand locks around my neck, and his mouth is on mine.

It's hard and firm and wanting, and I open for him, welcoming the heat of his tongue and shivering as he rolls the silver ring across my lower lip. He pulls it into his mouth, growling as he tears away.

He glares, but it's liquefied and hooded. "Eat."

I look down at the mess between us, and he adjusts to cut me off more, but I nudge his arm away. Looking to where he still holds his piece between his fingers, I settle my gaze on mine.

And then I pick it up.

131

Bass

It's comical. Truly.

Her face scrunches, and she stares at the mess of meat like it's foreign, and she has no idea what to do next. To guide her, as fucking weird as that seems when we're only eating fucking chicken, I bring mine to my lips, taking a more careful bite from the edge and she does the same, her hand coming up to hover beneath her mouth to protect her little schoolgirl uniform, just in case a rogue piece falls with her careful nibble.

Now that I think about it, she's probably never had a chicken leg before.

"Okay, this is so going on the menu." She sets her half-eaten bone down, stares at her fingers a moment, and then licks the tips clean.

"Menu, huh?" I toss my bone in the bag, going for a second one. "Your family own a restaurant or something?"

Her eyes fly up. "What? No. Why?"

"On the menu . . ." I raise a brow.

Her mouth opens, but then she looks down, and I'll be damned. Her cheeks grow a hint darker, like the day I had her on her back beneath me. Well, not that deep of a flush, but a flush nonetheless.

Suddenly her shoulders square and her face goes all plastic on me, the fun, flirty girl going into *dare to judge me* mode. "We have house chefs with a rotating menu."

Okay, definitely never had a chicken leg before.

The only chef who ever made me dinner was Darleen at the local Denny's.

She's waiting for me to judge, flipping her hair and pulling her mirror from her bag to check her reflection.

Still perfect, Rich Girl.

"What's your favorite thing they've made?" I ask.

Her eyes slide my way, searching, but when she decides I don't give a shit she's got it all and I've got nothing, she answers, "I like all food, but sushi is probably my favorite at the moment."

I nod and then shrug. "Never tried it."

Her eyes bug out, but then she gives a sassy smile. "So does that mean next time it's my turn to make you a dragon roll?"

I push the garbage into the bag at my feet and grip her by the hips, lifting and setting her on my lap. She spins, straddling me right here in the middle of the park, and I bring my hands around, making sure her skirt is covering her ass.

"There's gonna be a next time, then?" Using my pinkie, I push her hair from her face, lifting my chin to meet her lips, but I only skim mine along her soft, pillowy ones.

"Depends."

"On?"

"Whether you're a liar or not."

"I'm no liar, Rich Girl."

"Then where is the reward you promised me?"

My mouth curves slowly. "Someone's been waiting."

"Someone's been busy." She looks pointedly at the purple beneath my left eye. "Catfight?"

"Dog fight."

Her lips quirk, but her gaze holds mine. She wants more.

"I run a fighting ring close to where I live. I find fighters, take bets, and solve problems." I point to my eye. "This was a free shot I gave an asshole who thought he was tough."

She nods, wiggling in my lap a bit, so I slide my hands up her thighs, stretching my fingers wide to see how much I can fit in my palms.

"Sounds illegal."

"Only if you get caught."

"Or if someone rats you out."

"Songbirds get their voice boxes ripped out, Rich Girl. I don't play."

Her pupils grow larger and she reaches up, touching my lip ring with her thumb. "My life isn't exactly straight and narrow either," she admits, though it's low and hesitant. Her gaze snaps to mine. "As in not at all. People who . . . *sing* in my world are fed to the sharks."

She stares hard, studying my reaction, and I kinda get the feeling she's trying to figure out if I knew that already.

I get her concerns more than she knows.

"Hard to trust outsiders, ain't it?" I slide my hands along her ass beneath her skirt. More fancy clips and clasps locked tight to another G-string. "Never know who's after you or who's *after* you."

She rubs her lips together. "Are you after me, Bastian Bishop?"

"Way I see it . . ." I lean forward, forcing her to latch on to my neck or fall back onto the concrete below. "I've already got you."

Her attention falls to my lips, and she frowns, whispering, likely to herself more than me, "I think you might."

"I do. You'll see." I focus on the exposed skin on her legs and the pleated uniform lying against it. "There's something about this skirt." I fist it between my fingers. "Kinda like it."

"Of course you do," she mocks. "It's a common fantasy, one I would bet you've never found yourself living in."

"Not exactly the crowd I hang around, so no, I haven't, but . . ." Her ass sits on the roughness of my jeans, the strip of lace on her panties a useless form of protection. "I was *in* you, wasn't I?"

"Doesn't count."

"No?"

"No." Her grip on me tightens as she draws herself closer. "I had already dropped the skirt that night."

Her long, soft fingers toy with the hair on the nape of my neck, and my eyes close as I think back.

"Yeah," I agree. "It was the shoes for me then . . . and the legs, the ass, the hips, but that mouth and the sass that came from it? That pulled the trigger."

She fights a smile. "You sure it wasn't the knife throwing?"

"That too. Maybe even the eyes. I love me some green."

"Don't see much of that, do you?" She pops a brow like a brat.

I nod, owning it. "Your guess is right, Rich Girl. I'm nothing but a poor punk, but this punk made you come."

"I think it was a fluke," she sasses, but her voice is raspy and breathy. "You should prove it wasn't."

"Should I now?" I glide my thumb along her jaw, tipping her head a bit, and she does what I want.

She comes to me.

Her mouth finds mine, lips gliding along like silk against sand, soft against rough, parting, and my tongue breaks through, tangling with hers in long, slow strokes. Getting to know her mouth by feel, since last time was a fucking frenzy. *Literally.*

Her body hums, skin heating to the touch, and when I bite down on her bottom lip, she sighs.

Suddenly, she freezes, her eyes bulging. "What time is it?"

"Almost three last I checked. Why?"

"Oh my god!" She squirms, so I stand, lowering her to her feet, and then she spins, grabs her phone and winces. "Fuck, fuck, shit. We have to go. Now."

Chuckling, I start grabbing my things, and she wraps her fingers around my wrist, my jacket hanging over her arm as she yanks me along. "I'm comin'. Chill. You act like you've never ditched before."

"I haven't." She glares at me from over the hood as I round the car. "Greysons don't ditch," she explains. "We're shiny and perfect. Always. But that's not the problem. You know that shark I mentioned?" She slides into the car, forcing me to follow.

"Uh-huh?" I turn the engine over, meeting her gaze.

135

"I call him Dad, and he has a thing for machine guns."

"I like machine guns."

"He doesn't trust outsiders."

"I don't trust anyone."

"Bastian," she snaps, and her eyes sharpen. She hesitates, but only for a split second, and then says, "He will murder you and no one will ever find out."

My gaze narrows on her, falling to her preppy uniform and then the spot she keeps her weapon.

Fucking knew it.

I pull onto the road and grip her thigh before hitting the gas. "Schoolgirl, my ass."

Chapter 11
Rocklin

Ten missed calls and too many texts to count, I dial back the last one who called. Bronx answers in half a ring.

"Bitch, what the fuck?" Bronx hisses.

I glare at Bastian when he grins. "I'm almost there."

"I know. I have your location, remember?!" she whisper-shouts. "Hurry the fuck up!"

"What's Sai—"

"What's your mammoth of a guard doing? Sweating. Bullets. Threatening to *shoot* lots and lots of fucking bullets. Girl, he's in full-blown panic mode!"

"What did you tell him?"

"You were held up by your professor in your last class."

"And?"

"And then your professor walked by and said, 'Ladies, I missed Miss Revenaw today.'"

Bass laughs and I smack him.

"Okay, I—"

"Hold up," Bronx snaps, and then there's some shuffling. "Was that a chuckle?"

"A male chuckle?" Delta adds.

"A sexy, raspy, deep *male* chuckle?!" Bronx nearly squeals.

"Shut up!"

"Oh, she doesn't like us talking about how hot her little secret sounds—"

"I will hang up right now." She's not wrong, there's unexpected heat in my stomach.

"So, I'll call right back. Who is he? That new hot professor? Did the freaking Henshaw heir finally get his way? Oh, is it the—"

"I'm pulling up," I cut her off, eyes snapping to the steering wheel when Bastian's grip causes it to squeak, his knuckles growing white. "Where's Sai?"

"Throwing open doors near Calder Hall."

"Okay. I'm getting out now."

"Hurry, and bye, Coco Rocco's new dick, hope you like sharing! Don't get attached, or she'll spit you out."

The line clicks.

"Sharing?" Bass glares.

I throw my seat belt off and dash out, but he catches me by the arm, yanking me back.

"*Sharing*?"

Growling, I lean over and smash my mouth to his and squeeze his junk until he growls, pressing it up into my hand. I massage him, sucking his lips until he pants and then I'm gone.

"That's for holding back on my reward!"

"I'm gonna punish you, girl!"

"Can't wait!"

I hear his door open and then he shouts. "I do not share, Rocklin Revenaw!"

I smile brightly, slamming the steel gate and peeking at him through the gaps. "See you later, Bastian Bishop!"

He stares at me over the hood, his teeth sunk deep into his bottom lip, eyes hard and piercing.

I blow him a kiss and then I run. I head down the garden path, straight into the doors of Calder Hall, stopping short as Sai's red face flashes at the opposite end as he, too, reaches the dividing door. His shoulders visibly relax as he spots me through the glass, but his bunch as he flings the thing open, stepping inside.

"Not funny." His voice is stern, but he makes sure to keep it controlled.

I level my breathing, ignoring the cramp-like feeling in my chest. "What?"

138

"Don't. You can be mad, we can have a conversation, but you do not go off without notifying me. Not now." It's a demand from my guard, slash Dad's old bestie, slash second father figure. Still, he pretends to ask, "Okay?"

"Tell me why."

His eyes narrow and he looks around, and when he faces me again, he says one word. Or one name, rather. "Boston."

Awareness prickles and I stare back at him. What he means is *Enzo*.

So there is danger creeping in from somewhere, but if that's the case, what's with his disappearing act?

Understanding this isn't the place to talk about it, I don't push. I'm not even sure which questions I need to ask yet anyway, so I stay silent.

"Can I take you home now?" He frowns, stepping aside with his hand swept out.

I lead us to the car where the others wait. I meet Dom's gaze as I step out of the building, and he nods his chin.

I nod back, glancing from him to Delta's boyfriends, to the Greco brothers, before sliding into the back seat with my girls.

Sai and I will talk, but first . . . time to spill the juice on my "new dick."

Delta tightens her robe, and we drop into the seats on Bronx's balcony, glancing down at the boys wrestling on the platform sixty yards away.

"They're getting better," I note, also watching Kenex and Kylo's match. "Faster."

"Kenex beat Alto in a firing contest this week."

I nod. That's good. Something I'll store for later in case my dad decides to try and get us to kick them out. Again.

"But they did corner Sasha yesterday," Delta shares. "Not sure what they said, but she was as red as a tomato when she walked away, so it was definitely on the naughty side."

"We did say we'd give them a little taste of the trouble

they bring." Bronx pours two glasses of wine, keeping the bottle for herself.

"We did." I grab mine, leaning back once more and kicking my feet up on the stone railing.

"Now." She drinks straight from the bottle. "Details. All of them."

"You're not going to like it," I tell them both.

"Oh, this sounds like it's going to be good!"

"Was it the heir?" She scrunches her face. "I mean . . . he's drop-dead, *do me now and do me good* gorgeous, but imagine all the family dinners you'll have to go to with that mama's boy."

Running my finger over the rim of the glass, I smile down at it. "No, it's not him. And that won't be a problem because *Bastian* has no parents."

"Good. We hate parents."

A laugh leaves me and I take a sip, shrugging lightly. "I don't know. I like my dad."

"You love your dad. You don't like him."

True . . .

"So . . . Bastian, hmm?" Delta smiles. "Is he Italian mob? Greek cartel?" She gasps. "Oh my god, you said parentless, so is he already in his position?!"

"No, nothing like that."

Confusion takes place along both their expressions as they wait for more.

"He's . . ." He's what? How do I explain him?

An "associate," as we call the grunt guys at the very bottom of the food chain, but he's not even on it, let alone at the bottom.

A petty thief, perhaps, but really, I'm the one who stole from him.

An armed robber, but again . . . I was the one with a weapon the night we met. I'm sure he had one, but he didn't show his cards.

He never shows his cards.

He's like a vault, giving nothing away, yet radiating dominance someone like him shouldn't so easily possess.

Or maybe he should. What do I know?

He's just a hot guy with a wicked mouth that knows how to use his dick. An orphan who was taught to barbeque and has a sister somewhere, who apparently has a halo hovering over her head, if his words are true.

He's a guy I hardly know but can't stop thinking about.

I look to my girls, my best friends. "He's an outsider."

"An enemy crew?" Bronx's brows dip in the center.

"Unaffiliated."

"Rocklin . . ." Delta speaks with caution, not wanting to question me but needing to nonetheless. "Are you sure?"

I understand their concern. It's the same shit I worked through myself when I first met him.

Who he is and where he comes from. How he gets in and who sends him.

I've asked myself all the right questions and looked for all the answers, but at the end of the day, I'm trusting my gut.

Bastian Bishop is a nobody, just as he claimed.

No, that's not true.

He's not a nobody.

He's . . . mine.

"You like him," Delta whispers softly.

My head snaps her way. "I hardly know him."

"But you want to know him more," Bronx guesses.

"I *will* know him more."

"Your dad—"

"Won't allow it?" I finish off my glass, snagging the bottle from her hand and pouring more into mine. "Yeah, I know."

"So, okay, he's unaffiliated, but what's he like?"

"He's . . . annoying." My lips quirk. "Bossy."

"So, he's you," Bronx teases, taking another very unladylike chug from the bottle, snagging the second one from where she stuffed it under the table, the cork already out. "Imagine the power struggle."

I frown.

Is there one?

"Come on, give us more," she urges.

"He's sly. Confident."

"Still you."

"He's poor." I look to them. "Wears jeans and old Jordans and I think he's alone, but I'm not sure."

"So the opposite of you . . ." Delta gives a tender smile. "Sounds like Ander when we first found him and look at him now."

"Shacking up with a queen bee and her boo." Bronx wiggles her brows.

The three of us laugh.

"You won't be laughing when I tell you how we met." I pause. "Well, maybe you will laugh about *that* part, but not what followed."

Both girls sit forward, eyes dancing with excitement.

I go into full detail about the gas station and how he broke into The Enterprise, not leaving out a single detail until I get to the sex. I do tell them, but I keep the good parts to myself, much to their dismay. I tell them about the texts and his warning about Dom. How I plan to heed it and keep Dom out of my bed because I'm not done with him yet.

Before he spoke up from that dark corner in the Greyson Suite, my life was starting to feel uniform, frustrating rather than fulfilling. Even with its changing parts, it was all the same: superficial smiles and designer gowns, perfect grades, and weeding out worthy prospects.

I give orders.

Demand excellence.

Always have to shine.

Forever in control.

It's tiring, and sometimes, I just want to . . . let go.

People go out of their way to appease me; they listen and wait for direction. They don't take charge and would never dare tell me what to do.

Bastian does and he expects me to listen, threatens me even, in a way my twisted mind finds entertaining. Adorable even.

"I can't believe he got into The Enterprise without being seen."

"It's kind of badass." This comes from Delta, and it makes us all laugh loud enough to gain the attention of the boys yards away.

Dom pushes to his feet from where he's crouched in full-on training mode, now staring our way.

"Think he could take Dom?" Bronx wonders, cocking her head to the side.

It's no secret Dom's our strongest fighter, everyone knows it, but Bastian doesn't.

I bet he'd see it as a challenge, and my money would be on him.

A wicked idea sparks and I look to my girls. "I have an idea, but we'll need to dig a bit."

Bronx kicks her legs in excitement—she's all about the hunt; she wouldn't be the daughter or Torin "The Tracker" Bandoni if she wasn't. Owning and operating a national transport facility allows for eyes everywhere. She meets him once a month, if not more, and he gives her some crazy kind of code and challenges her to crack it.

It's how they bond, daddy hacker teaching his daughter all he knows.

"I'm sorry I didn't tell you guys about Bastian sooner."

"You wanted something for yourself. We get it. If I told you half the shit I hide," Bronx jokes, but her eyes are gentle.

We love each other and we are happy to be in this together, but there's not a lot in our world that's ours and ours alone. We deserve something for ourselves. At least one thing, right?

I think I want mine to be him.

For now, anyway . . .

"So do I get free rein?" Bronx asks, meaning can she dig as deep as the file goes to find his secrets?

I want to say no, but this isn't about what my gut tells me. This is about us and our future. This is bigger than me. I can recognize that.

So I nod, and it's settled.

"Now, back to this idea of yours . . ." Delta finally finishes her first glass, tipping it forward to ask for another. "What is it?"

143

Bass

My leg bounces, my temples pounding the entire way back to Hayze's crash pad. I snag my headphones from the back seat, hide the key in the broken gas cap and leave, sending him a quick text to let him know the car's back in case he'd rather crash in the back of it. It's colder than normal tonight.

Rocklin's friends probably have fat mansions and vacation homes.

My man is sleeping in a fucking tent behind a crack house.

I'm walking back to one that ain't mine but on loan, so long as I do as I'm fucking told, like the bitch boy I agreed to be when some rich prick in a suit dropped me here.

I'm grateful I'm not behind steel bars, but I'm also done.

For the hundredth time, Rocklin's homegirls' words spark in my brain like an engine misfire, popping and cracking and rustling awake parts of me that have lain dormant.

Professor.

Heir.

What was she about to say next? Fucking King of England or some shit?

I knew she was top notch, the ultimate luxury, but damn. I'm missing something bigger.

And share?

I don't fucking think so.

I warned her from the gate I wouldn't, and she'll learn the hard way if she thinks I was playing. I wasn't, and something tells me she knows it.

Something also tells me she likes it, and if my little rich girl thought she scared me with her machine gun and murder comments, she's mistaken.

I remember how it felt to stare down at my dad's dead body. I liked it, the power the shot fired through my veins, like a fucking blowtorch, heating and numbing me all at once.

I've kept the feeling close in my chest, pulling it to the surface when I need a little reminder of what I'm capable of when the world around me grows bleak. When using my fists on dumb fucks ain't enough and that little needle in my brain starts to prick at me. Demanding more.

Yeah, my shit's been locked up for a long time now, so I'm *dying* to let out some real rage.

Let a motherfucker give me a reason.

Touching her will be a reason.

Taking her will be a death sentence.

Some might call that irrational since I hardly know the girl, but obsession knows no rules and I wouldn't listen anyway.

There's a fire in her eyes that speaks to the devil buried in mine, and he wants to play.

To worship.

To possess.

There wasn't much mentioned about her family when I looked her up, nothing but a squeaky clean, prim and proper social media account—or so it would look to the outside eye, but gray recognizes gray—linked to the school's website. Now I know why.

Her pops isn't just a man with more money and property than the Pope. He's something more.

Some*one* big, and I bet she's his pride and joy, his perfect princess.

My eyes narrow at nothing, my chin lifting into the night. *That's all right*.

Every pretty little princess needs herself a prince.

I'll be her dark, daunting one.

I dare *Daddy* to try and stop me.

My phone rings in my pocket and I fish it out to find Hayze calling.

I hit answer on the FaceTime call, smirking when a waft of smoke is what I see first, his grinning face second.

"Sup, my boy?" He pulls a blunt to his lips again.

"Just letting you know the car's out front."

He nods, but the gleam in his eyes has me stopping.

"What happened?"

"Counted out the cash."

"And?"

"Two hundred in counterfeit bills."

My face falls, anger swimming in my gut as face after face flashes in my mind until I land on one. "What a brave little bitch, rats on one dude to try and cover his own ass," I mutter. "No wonder you're fired up."

"Love making little boys bleed."

I scoff and start walking again. "That sounds fucked up."

"Nah." He grins, dropping back on his sleeping bag. "Fucked up would be cutting off his dick and feeding it to him."

A chuckle leaves me, and I shake my head. "Find him. Call me when you do."

"You got it, boss."

Boss.

I like the sound of that . . .

Chapter 12
Rocklin

There's a soft knock on my door, and then it's opened, and before Saylor can issue a warning with her wide eyes, my dad strides in.

Bronx slams her laptop shut, and Delta throws the pillow in her lap over the papers just as I drop onto my side over the stack.

"Dad. Hi. You didn't tell me you were stopping by."

His eyes narrow, his gaze slicing from one of us to the next, settling on me. "Daughter . . ." He trails off. "What are we up to this evening?"

"Studying."

"Working."

"Planning."

We all answer at the same time, but thankfully, all responses are cohesive enough to be convincing.

"Uh-huh." His lips pinch and he looks to Bronx. "Your father is still joining us for dinner tomorrow, I hope?"

"He is," she confirms.

My dad nods and then it's Delta's turn. "Your grandfather said your mother has finally taken the hint?"

"No contact for a few months now." Delta places a hand over her heart, sighing dramatically. "It's bliss."

My dad's lip twitches. "I know the feeling."

I frown but erase it as his attention returns to me.

"I wanted you girls to see this first." He passes the folded paper from beneath his arm.

Accepting it, I unfold the simple sheet of printer paper, and the girls lean toward me, the three of us reading the print in silence.

Breaking News: Jacobi Randolph arrested after his brand-new, six-million-dollar building burned to the ground just five months after its opening. Randolph allegedly filed a claim with the insurance company early Wednesday morning, but officials have now stepped in. Sources said during a routine search of Randolph's vehicle, the county sheriff seized a suit jacket suspected to be the same one Randolph was photographed wearing the night of the fire and is believed to have traces of kerosene. Now, authorities say they will be looking into the overnight success of Randolph's financial firm as they suspect foul play . . .

I chuckle, shaking my head, not bothering to read over the last few paragraphs of the report.

It's scary how easy running schemes can be sometimes.

Jacobi Randolph didn't do his research. He fled a small city on the East Coast and thought he would come this way, reinvent himself and come up on a couple easy millions.

But again . . . he didn't do his research.

No one steps into Revenaw territory without permission, not when tricks are to be played.

There's an order and a hierarchy that must be followed, and Randolph will be the newest reminder of what happens when you do as you wish. Well, a warning of it anyway. This is what we call a "friendly" reminder.

You don't bring heat to hell. You'll burn before you even reach the gates.

This is my father's territory, and if anyone is going to rob from the rich here, it's him, not some wannabe who figured out how easy it is to swindle men worth millions out of a couple they won't miss.

"This is going to print?" Delta asks, smiling up at my dad.

"Front page tomorrow morning. Be sure to take the girl to celebrate."

I smile down at the fruits of Valley's initiation efforts. "We will. Thank you for letting us know in advance."

"Of course." He nods, his brown eyes sliding to mine. "I hear your sister is all settled in now."

"She is." I fight a smirk. "The studios in the basement suit her well."

His brows snap together, and I fight to keep my muscles from tensing.

Shit, she didn't tell him that little detail. I'm kind of proud of her, but I also want to smack her as now I'm the fool.

His jaw muscles tic and I know what he's thinking, even if his words are carefully chosen in front of the girls. "Are we sure it's safe for her there?" He delivers his question calmly when he really wants to growl, *are we sure the degenerate boys I told you not to bring here won't do something I'll have to kill them for*?

"Damiano's suite is just across from hers. Our weapon supply is in the same area. She's safer there than anywhere in the house," I assure him.

"Couldn't give her her old room back, hmm?"

"I gave it to Saylor."

"Your maid has an apartment suite?"

"She does."

My father nods, holding my stare for several silent seconds, and I know this little random visit he's not entirely unknown for isn't simply about the paper in my hands, so I stare back.

He will speak when he's ready.

I swear his lip twitches when he recognizes the stubborn streak he gave me, but it's gone too fast to say for sure.

"I'm having a drink with Mr. Henshaw and his family tonight. Oliver will be there. Join me?"

I fake a yawn and the creases along his temples deepen. "I'm going to turn in early tonight, actually. Classes were so intense today; I need to go over my reading a few times just to know what was covered."

Bronx laughs but covers it with a cough, facing the window as if it suddenly became interesting.

"Right, well, we wouldn't want you to fall behind, now would we?" He pulls in a deep breath, smoothing his suit jacket down when it's already as smooth as it could possibly be. "*Next time*," he warns, letting me know no invitation will be given.

It will be a demand I must obey without a fight.

I smile, and when he holds his arms out, I climb off the bed, ignoring the crinkle of papers beneath me, and go to him.

He wraps his arm around me, whispering into my ear, "Behave, Rocco. Do not give me reason to believe you're not."

Releasing me, he steps back.

Before he can escape, I have to ask. "Have you heard anything about Enzo?"

My dad's stance widens, and I know before he answers that he will be giving me one single word in response.

"No," he says, and then he walks out the door.

I wait several minutes before poking my head out to make sure it's clear and turn to my girls.

When I spoke to Sai, all he would say is it's his job as my guard to be extra cautious, to consider all possibilities, from all angles, at all times, and make sure if those threats come from unlikely sources, that he's prepared to face what that means—whatever the fuck *that* means. He wouldn't say much and I get it. He has to be careful of what he says, as the wrong choice of words could sound a lot like going against the boss's orders, and that's not allowed.

Dad would have his head, oldest friend, and the man who swore his allegiance to his daughter aside. Defiance is a sure way to the Revenaw cellar, and I'm not sure anyone's ever come out of there in one piece. Literally.

I open my mouth to speak, but Jasper appears before I can, giving a small bow.

"There's a problem in the basement."

"What time is it?" Bronx takes a sip of her cappuccino cocktail, her attempt to drown out the wine and keep her focus.

"Thirty minutes before schedule," Delta answers for her, looking to me.

Eight in the evening.

I shrug a shoulder, picking up the pile of papers that, so far, has led us nowhere, and stuff them beneath the pillows. "We improvise."

Our grins grow in unison, and Jasper's eyes widen the slightest bit.

The three of us climb to our feet, slide into slippers and wind our way toward the lowest level of Greyson Manor, the basement studios. Though basement is a general term and not a very good one to describe the area. It's as exquisite as any other area within the manor, if only a little "less than" the upper floors, in the sense that they don't have the balcony views or staff of their own.

As we reach the end of the stairs, Kylo has Kenex by the throat, his fist coming down on his brother's jaw, but Kenex only grins, his right hook whipping around just as fast, slamming into Kylo's nose.

Blood starts pouring instantly and the brothers take each other down, swinging and wrestling, headbutting and choking one another until both nearly put each other to sleep. Only then do they finally let each other go, flopping onto their backs on the marble floor.

"Well, Coco Rocco, maybe your father was right after all." Delta tips her head. "They're degenerates who cannot be trusted." Her tone fills with amusement with her last words, and she holds her palm out.

I slap it with mine, cocking my head, waiting for them to realize they have an audience.

What Delta said is true. My dad did go out of his way to drill into me why they shouldn't be allowed to move into the manor. Hell, he didn't even want them accepted into the school or on the grounds at all, a firm believer only those of "notable" blood are worthy, and I can't say I completely disagree. It's risky and we only have the word of others to go off, but the hardest part for me is my father is never wrong. His concerns always prove themselves valid. Every single time. There are too many snakes looking to slide into our fold to trust blindly, but at the end of the day, it wasn't solely my decision.

The problem was they were trusted enough by his colleagues to do small-time work, so the others saw no reason not to offer them the same, after some rounds of testing, of course.

To which they passed, so what could I say outside of "they don't belong" and "you can't trust anything an outsider claims," as my father has taught and demonstrated as truth. He was furious and wouldn't set foot in the manor for months, but when it comes to matters of the school and the decisions surrounding it, Greyson Elite Academy is ours to control.

Everything outside of that? Well, it depends on the day.

"You can come out now," Bronx calls.

Delilah, the Grecos' current merry-go-round girl, slips out of Kenex's room, a small hint of guilt in her eyes, but there's a sly smile on her lips as she steps over the duo.

Both boys pant in place, frowning at her back as she comes our way.

"Jasper," I call. "There's a wire transfer pending on Delilah's account."

"I'll send it through, Miss Revenaw." Even he can't keep the hint of amusement from his tone as he bows, excusing himself.

Kylo sits up, tearing his hoodie over his head, wiping the blood from his face and neck with it. "Yo, what the—"

"Fuck's goin' on?" Kenex finishes, his shirt torn down to the waist, nothing but his collar intact.

"What happened, dear Grecos?" Delta cocks her head, Ander coming up at her back in that exact moment, his arms looping around her.

Ander smirks. "Someone walk in on something they shouldn't have?"

"You mean on something that *shouldn't have* happened?!" Kylo hops to his feet, glaring at Delilah—because his brother is faultless, of course. "Today was my day. He had her yesterday."

But his eyes quickly grow sharp, and that self-assuredness that gets them into trouble takes over. He lets his arms fall, his chin lifting as his shoulders seem to widen, and Delilah takes an involuntary step forward.

My arm shoots out, stopping her from advancing, and Kylo's eyes narrow.

This is their favorite part of the game: the let-go.

The dismissal.

When the rule is broken, so is the girl and the rule is *always* broken.

They see to that themselves, always with a new twist, of course.

Not this time.

We may or may not have reiterated to Delilah about this part, but then again . . .

"You knew the terms before you played with these pups." I look to her. "You took my deal, which ends theirs. Your little contract is now void."

Delilah faces the boys again, frowning. "But he's—"

"But he's calling you to him without a single word leaving his lips? I know." I push off the wall, moving toward the duo. "But that's because the Grecos are predators, Delilah. They like to hunt, and once they find the sweet, vanilla girl they are searching for, they turn her inside out. Make you crave things you never even knew existed . . . right before dismissing you. So have some grace and go."

While the girl does hesitate it's only for a moment, and then she's gone.

I turn to the boys, pinning them with a warning glare. "If you want us to allow you to bring your little contract play-things into this space, stop sneaking off at night if you can't show up the next day bright-eyed and ready. Stop messing with Saylor. Stop trying to occupy Jasper so you can do God knows what—you're risking someone slipping where they don't belong by doing this—and *stop* trying to traumatize Sasha. The last thing she needs to see is my girl on all fours between her men. Do it again, and they won't allow you to watch anymore."

Both boys give a curt nod and behind me, I hear Delta and Ander's footsteps carrying them away.

"Go."

My eyes slide toward Bronx, who tugs the younger Greco closer by his torn collar. "Go," she whispers this time. "I'll take care of this."

Nodding, I look to the two, unable to hold in my frown. "Don't forget, B, this is still a punishment."

Bronx's smile is more heard than seen. "Oh, I'm aware."

I don't stick around to see what happens next but head back up to my wing to finish off the so far useless pile of papers waiting for me.

Bronx found very little on my . . . on Bastian.

So little, in fact, all we know for sure is his name is real, his father is dead, and his mother isn't. He said he had no parents, so there could be cause for concern there, but I can name a solid dozen people at Greyson Prep who claim the same, even though their families show up for most of their allotted visits.

Despite the lack of a paper trail on him, though, Bronx figured she would find what she needed from the car, but, of course, the DMV had no record of it. In the end, she was able to track his car via satellite by going back to the time and place we knew he was and seeing where he went from there. She found out where he resides.

He stays in Brayshaw, a place Calvin knows well, located nearly two hours north of here. It's a town our name holds no weight in, but even so, it doesn't rival our own. The family there runs a solo operation of sorts. Basically, they want nothing to do with our world and keep to their own problems.

Which means Bastian Bishop is what he said he was.

A nobody who does morally gray work.

It's both a best- and worst-case scenario.

There is no knife he's waiting to thrust into my back, but also no trust he can be given.

Outsiders are what they are for a reason.

Greed and the need for power are hard enough to handle for the people bred into our world, and it's only that much harder for those who stumble upon it.

And the ones who stumble tend to fall flat . . . right into a pre-dug plot at Greyson Cemetery.

My father would have his head, without a second thought, if Bastian so much as lingered too long.

Curious minds cause conflict, as he would say in justification, just as he loves to remind me, *some paper trails need not be forged, daughter. We're only dishonest when we must be.*

That is his favorite line when I argue my case as to why I should be sitting in classes all day and not privy to his business meetings, being that I'll take his place one day. We could easily forge my transcripts to reflect I completed all that was required, but he won't allow it because "paper trails."

Truthfully, he's not being entirely overcautious. I know there must be tracks inquiring minds can touch, just in case, and every once in a while, someone *does* decide they want to know more about who we are and what we do. Paper trails point them in the direction we want them to go, allowing us to control the narrative.

For instance, if you look at my transcript, it shows an eighteen-year-old Olympic gold medalist. Honor student, doubling her studies in international business and investment management with a perfect record. The average man reading my file would see it for what it is, an academic genius, likely due to being a spoiled rich girl with every resource available at her fingertips, just as they believe Greyson Elite Academy to be some kind of rich kid club.

But if, say, an enemy of my father was to look at this, he'd begin strategizing immediately. Seeking allies in favor of keeping Rayo Revenaw from expanding his reach any further than it already is—which I fully intend to do in time.

So poor Bastian, and his lack of living proof, won't sit well with my father, should he take an interest in him, but I won't give him reason to.

My father knows I'm no angel, even if he and the other elders demand we pretend to be in the presence of most, but he's fully aware of who his daughter is and likely knows some of the things I might be up to. It's his job to keep me in line, focused and headed in the right direction, but he allows a bit of leeway as I never give him reason to worry.

He expects me to be cunning and ruthless when the situation calls for it, as it does when dealing with potential prospects. So long as I continue to do what's expected of me, be pretty and perfect in all areas, and poisonous to the ones that matter most, he pretends to leave me alone, expecting Sai to report if the reality reads otherwise.

Sai *does* report to my dad, but as his lifelong best friend, Sai knows how to work my dad when necessary. He would never directly lie to a pointed question, so he's strategic with the things he shares and always has to give him more than I would want because if he didn't, my father would grow suspicious, Sai would be relieved as my guard, and who the hell knows who would be put in his place.

So, basically, if I want to hold on to my new naughty friend for a while, all I have to do is keep him away from my dad.

It shouldn't be too hard.

Right?

Chapter 13
Rocklin

The prospects are abuzz, the result of Valley's scheme having posted early on the town's social media sites, and the need for a celebration works perfectly in our favor.

The girls want to meet Bastian, as is their right, since he took it upon himself to slip into the space that belongs to them as well. Besides, they're my girls. They should know who to blame if blame needs a name.

Tonight, we're partying in The Devine Lounge.

The space is larger than our Greyson Suite to allow room for all of us. There's shiny shit everywhere and reflective glass makes up ninety percent of the room, representing a strong and solid front—cracks are for the weak, and those who create them are thrown out.

Valley passed her first test, as well as her second, though she doesn't know it yet.

Everyone we've ever allowed within these four walls knows the mark of a Greyson when they hear one, but nobody knows who carries out what task. It's a way to track loyalty outside of the unspoken threat against their families should they dare to breathe a word, of course.

Most are smarter than that, and the rare few who crave approval from their parents, running to them for what they hope will be their first pat on the back of their lifetime, learn the hard way doing so will earn them the opposite.

The parents know the drill and would hit them with a litany of disgrace they'd feel through the phone.

Once accepted, all parents who send their children here are after something. That's literally the point to them living under the same roof and attending the same school as other high-profile attendees. No one leaves here without something. If you aren't brought into the fold of one of our worlds, if not the Greyson Society directly, you still leave with a golden stamp of acceptance. Being invited to Greyson Elite is an honor in itself. Graduating from it is an open invitation to hold your nose as high in the air as you wish.

Not to mention the connections gained along the way, and some come solely for this reason.

Some are *invited* solely for this reason.

You never know when you need a friend somewhere.

Where the fuck is *my* friend?

Glancing at my phone, I pull up the security app, searching every crevice of the Greyson Suite, but he's not in there, waiting like I assumed he would be.

Delta's soft, floral-scented perfume wafts over my shoulder. Her whisper-soft, drunken voice sounds like a true, good girl having her first glass of wine. "Maybe he's waiting in the hall somewhere with another blindfold, anticipating whisking you away?"

"You mean like your boys over there?"

Both of us look up and to the right, where Alto and Ander sit, one on the seat of a white, tufted chair, the other on the arm of it, glasses half-full, gazes locked on their reason for breathing.

Delta sighs, leaning down even more until her forearms are folded over the back of the chaise I'm lounging in. "They do look a little deprived, don't they?"

The grin in her voice has mine stretching, and I drop my head back to meet her gaze.

She winks, pressing a small kiss to my lips, and the laughter that leaves her is silent when two glasses can be heard slamming onto the tabletop, even through the soft music.

"Go away before the Grecos get a show they're supposed to be on a time-out from."

She giggles, then sighs, a big, fat, fake sigh. "Fine. We'll take the DeLeon Suite, just in case lover boy shows."

"He's not showing." Bronx falls next to me, her little sparkly dress riding up her thigh. "Maybe he's not as obsessed with you as you think?" she teases, sipping on some bright drink. She has no flavor of choice.

Bronx loves everything and nothing at the same time. She's picky like that.

Stealing her glass from her fingertips, she pouts as I toss it back, refusing to make a face when fire spreads inside my throat.

I move to the large glass window, smiling as I pass a couple girls dancing and drinking in the center of the room, the large circular couches framing them. With a wide-open floor plan, and tall, bistro-style tables all around, the space allows for privacy without offering too much.

While there is a small open bar in the back corner anyone allowed in this room can use, there are also two members on staff at all times, who are paid well to tend to everyone's needs, even before they're asked. This is why, when I look back, Bronx already has a brand-new glass in her hand. She lifts it as she stands and saunters over to join in on whatever conversation Marcus and Gabriel, two third-years who joined the Greysons a little over a year ago, are having.

As I face the window wall once more, I toy with my necklace, looking out into our pride and joy.

The Game Room is locked and hidden when The Enterprise is open to all, like on music or mela nights. *This* is what brings the big, bad boys to our doorstep.

Everyone thought we were crazy when we proposed the idea, but at the end of the day, I knew the opportunity for control would burn bright in my power-hungry father's eyes, and if Rayo was in, Delta's grandfather and Bronx's father were sure to follow.

In ancient times, the king would gather in the hall and feast with his people, sharing the fruits of their labor, if only to a minimal extent.

Now, the people feed the king.

Or, well, *queens*.

It was our little way of keeping a semblance of control, making sure we, as individuals, were cut into the profit.

"Look at Lena." Damiano joins me in front of the glass, his hands in his pockets as he stares at one of our advanced girls. "She's killing it tonight."

I hum my approval, watching the redhead closely as she deals a fresh hand, her table full of suited men. She's wearing an all-white piece tonight, the cut modest over her chest and not so much as a slit in the side, the lacy hem stopping midthigh. The card tables are custom and glass for a reason, allowing us to see every inch of the people behind them at all times.

Lena's hair is braided in two pigtails, pink ribbons tied at the end, the same color as the fuzzy bracelets around her wrists.

"She went all out virgin-ness tonight, didn't she?"

Dom nods. "And look at her numbers."

Our eyes lift to the screen on the far wall to see tonight's standings.

Lena is leading all twelve girls on the floor in tips by a whopping two hundred K, and she still has twenty minutes left.

"Someone is getting a nice little bump in their account tonight."

"The way these girls like to shop, it's probably already as good as gone."

Damiano laughs, sliding in behind me.

My muscles stiffen as his arms settle around me and he catches it, his doing the same.

"Something wrong?" he asks, a hint of suspicion in his tone.

I sigh, watching as a man pushes a half million in chips to the center of the craps table. "What do you know?"

Slowly, his grip shifts, and he spins me to face him, his eyes locking with mine. "I know someone ran your plate a few weeks back and we couldn't figure out where it came from. I know you know who it was because you didn't so much as bat a lash when, normally, you'd be suiting up for war or sending me

160

out to handle the problem before it became one. I know you went off Greyson grounds without protection the other day."

"I had protection."

"Not the kind of protection your car has inside it and not the kind that comes from letting us watch out for you." He frowns. "I know your sister showing up is a big problem for your family, and we will help any way we are able, but I don't have to tell you this. You already know that."

"Get to the but, Dom."

He licks his lips, glancing around us to make sure no one is tuning in. "I don't want you making a mistake you can't take back and since whatever it is you're doing, or whoever it is you're doing, requires you to be outside of our walls, I can't help but think you know it's wrong."

"Wrong is subjective."

"Wrong is putting yourself at risk for someone who couldn't even pretend to protect you."

"You know nothing about him," I snap before I can stop myself, the need to defend Bastian catching me off guard, but Dom doesn't fret.

"I know I'll be here when he's gone."

The thought tugs at something behind my ribs, and I have to work to hold back the frown threatening to settle along my brows. Damiano's words, spoken strong and undeniably . . . true. The time will come when Bastian must go. It's inevitable.

"Yes." My voice sounds scratchy, even to me. "You will be."

The golden boy before me settles, his hand coming up to cup my cheek as he leans in to whisper in my ear. "Just be careful, gorgeous, and remember, I'm here. Always." His lips press gently to my jaw, and he releases me without another word, joining his friends at the bar.

The soft-blue lights around the tally board in The Game Room blink white, indicating the round is up and it's time to switch dealers. Around the room, the girls who have yet to have a drink—only the sober allowed on game nights—hustle their way through the side door, eager to claim their table of choice.

The betting is halted for two minutes during the shift when the men at the tables order new drinks or spark fresh cigars, some even standing to stretch their legs.

That's when I see him, there at the entrance to the room.

Everything inside me turns to stone as he saunters in like he owns the place but sticks out like a ruby in a bed of diamonds.

The men here wear suits if only to hide the markings of what gangs they're tied to, and they walk in with a sense of ease, almost a pep in their step if men like them are capable of one. Why? Because they know, win or lose, at the end of the night, when the tables are closed, the money they came here to wash will end up right where it's supposed to be.

That's the beauty of this place.

We've erased the threat of a setup or worse.

The hard part is whatever the hell they did before coming here that led them to need to make a visit, and we don't ask where their money comes from; we just accept it and take our cut. Should whoever handles their money once it's squeaky clean ever fuck up and make the government wonder, they have something to fall back on.

Gambling winnings or losses.

It's a win-win, and they send their most trusted into our space, the ones capable of relaxing, who can sit back and enjoy a drink and a pretty face because they know she's not placed there as bait.

Bastian is *not* relaxed or calm or anyone's most trusted.

I'm not so sure I can claim to trust him at all, though I think a really dumb part of me might.

He's the picture of aggression, dark hair seeming somehow darker. Tattoos, somehow fiercer, stand out against his fair skin like the scars of a soldier, and the shadows under his eyes seem to double.

Even though I'm not in the room, I feel the air shift, the little hairs at the nape of my neck standing on end, the sleuths in my soul beckoning me to him one shiver at a time.

How can a man—a boy, as some might call him—with nothing to his name step into a room where the name you claim is your worth and appear the dominant one?

How did he get into the room in the first place?

The answer comes in the form of a silent alarm.

Wide-eyed, I whip my head toward Bronx, cupping the cuff on my wrist as it vibrates against me.

She jumps up, as does Damiano, the only others in this room who were alerted.

She follows my gaze back to the window right as Carson, the man running the room tonight, makes his way to Bastian and a sharp breath slices down my throat.

I prepare to dart, the hem of my dress in my hand, but Damiano catches my wrist with his, his other darting up to his earpiece.

"False alarm." He glares at me, his hand shaking. "I said false alarm," he repeats even more sharply. He's pissed, aware now it's not just a guy from the outside . . . but that the guy has found his way within our inner sanctum.

The bracelet stops vibrating right as Delta, her men right behind her, burst through the door.

Worry creases her brows as she rushes toward us, but then her eyes slowly slide to the one-sided window.

Carson's shoulders ease and he sweeps a hand, giving his okay for Bastian to pass.

"Is that . . ." one says.

"Damn, he's . . ." trails the other.

I can only nod, my gaze tracking his every step as he weaves through a few of the tables, head after head turning his way, sizing him up as he passes.

He steps up to the bar, and a moment later, the bartender hands him something, leaning over a little too far, but he doesn't accept the view down her top she so *sweetly* offers.

No, his eyes snap up, and my lungs jump when they lock onto mine.

My pulse beats harder as I stare into the endless marble pits before me.

"He can't . . . I mean, there's no way he sees you . . . right?" Delta whispers.

"No." It's Dom who answers, his tone strained yet curious. "He can't see her."

Once again, I steal the drink from Bronx's hand, downing it in one go right as another couple boxes on the screen flash white. With Dom's hand off me, I tear my dress over my head, leaving me in the lingerie I didn't intend on showing to all tonight, and rush out the same door the other girls did.

"Rocklin, wait!" Dom shouts, but I'm already gone.

The girls, some prospects, some already donning their golden Greyson pins, part for me without a word, and I mask my expression as I step up to the door, waiting for someone from the security room to buzz me in.

It feels like a century passes before I step inside.

The room is thick with the scent of cigars, and what is supposed to be a safe zone for all reads a little heavier.

Or maybe it's just me who feels the change, the air of power.

The *shift* of authority.

Out of the corner of my eye, I assess the room, and no, it's not only me.

Some are sitting back, flirty smiles gone as they mask their expressions in favor of something more intimidating. These men aren't the bosses.

A boss wouldn't willingly walk into a snake pit without a weapon, but they are important men, higher than soldiers but not quite a second-in-command. Cousins maybe, loyal brothers who follow orders like well-trained pups.

Bastian is different.

He comes from the streets, not a bassinet protected by bullets.

The world is his weapon, and so is everything in it.

I'm less than four feet through the door when Bastian's head snaps over his shoulder as if he senses me coming, and the marbly shade of his gaze changes right before my eyes. Darkening. Pupils *dilating*.

If he looked threatening before, he's downright menacing now. His jaw ticcing as he takes in my outfit . . . or lack thereof.

See, one little blip we choose not to tell our fathers is the friendly little competition we allow our Greysons to have while secretly helping them gain some independence. No one wants their parents privy to everything they choose to buy, and who knows, maybe some plan to run once they find the courage to stand up to the person making their decisions for them.

The girls aren't strippers and they aren't allowed to trade sex for anything they may be offered, so they must keep the goods hidden, but the rest of their skin is free game. The more they make, the more they take home, and the highest of the night gets a bonus. If they make it to the five-hundred-thousand mark, the frosty wall on the left side of the room grows clear, and she gets center stage in the cage.

Some do it for the thrill, something we desperately need after being prim and proper all the time. This allows a safe place to let go without ending up on social media or some TMZ story about "Heiresses Gone Wild."

Others do it looking for a golden ticket, a marriage proposal to a powerful family. Two girls have accepted offers already and we've only been up and running at full steam for eighteen months. If my memory serves me right, both girls were wearing the same shade of red I am those nights.

Judging by the murderous glare in Bastian's eyes, he's not a fan of the corset bodysuit.

Or more, judging by the perilous flame soaring behind the white-hot rage, he doesn't like that others can see it . . .

I wonder what he'd say if he knew I wore it for him?

Smile and shred it to pieces, if I had to guess . . .

Bastian tracks me like a gazelle he's already claimed, his glare slicing to John Grecko, the Greyson who replaced the girl who poured his drink, as John looks at me.

With a flick of my hand, I send him to the other end, stepping in front of Bass, a three-foot-wide bar the only thing keeping him from yanking me against him. I thought it would be a safe distance, but apparently it isn't.

He doesn't hesitate, instantly jerking forward so his torso stretches over the space, his pointer finger hooking into the deep V of my top, ready to haul me across the granite, right to him.

"Don't do it," I warn quickly, plastering on a saucy smile while my eyes beg him to listen. "All hell will break loose."

"I was born in hell. Lived with the devil for fifteen years. I can take it."

A frown builds along my brow, a million questions running through my head, but all I say is, "Let go."

"Don't want to." His voice rumbles, his jaw clenching and then a low growl leaves me. Reluctantly, he releases me, but he doesn't sit back. His eyes bore into me and something that feels a lot like guilt washes through me, though it makes no sense. I have nothing to be guilty about.

Sure, I was trying to draw him out by coming here tonight and partying with the group as a whole—if he knew when Dom was near me, surely he'd show if he knew eight other guys were. By show, I meant snatch me in the hall or wait in the dark corner of the suite.

He's the one who came in here unannounced as if he had any idea what to expect when he arrived. I bet he still doesn't have a clue what he walked in the middle of. Not that it matters.

I don't think he cares.

But the closer I look, the more my concern builds as this man in front of me is showing none . . . nothing.

He's pissed, that's for sure, but other than that, he almost looks like he's enjoying himself, like there's a secret I don't know and he's not going to tell me.

Now I'm the one leaning forward.

"Bastian."

He brings his drink to his lips. "Rich Girl."

"You better be careful. You have no idea who you're dealing with."

I realize as I say it that I'm worried but not for me, for him.

166

I don't want him to get hurt.

What would I do if he was?

Resisting the urge to swallow, I pull in a slow breath.

Something intense flares in his piercing orbs, and I wonder if he knows. If my fear *for him* is written all over me . . . or if he can simply read me better than I'd like. Slowly, his attention falls, gaze scorching across my skin like the threat of a flame too close, and I fight the urge to cover myself. Not from his searing appraisal but from some ridiculous emotion I can't quite name.

It's sour and irritably similar to shame, but that's ridiculous. I have nothing to feel ashamed of and now I'm getting annoyed.

To distract myself, I pour us both a shot from the blue whiskey bottle closest to me. Without looking away from one another, we empty the contents of our glasses.

As he swallows, I'm called to his Adam's apple, stuck staring as it pops slightly beneath the tattoos there, and then his tongue pokes out, demanding I follow its path as it glides along his lower lip, spinning the lip ring as he loves to do.

Maybe he doesn't even notice he does it.

Maybe he does it because he knows I like it . . .

"So." He pauses, the air thickening and not in the good way. "This is why you wear them little clip things. For a bunch of motherfuckers in monkey suits."

"Careful," I edge quietly, eyes flicking over his shoulder a brief moment.

"Oh, I'm sorry," he deadpans, not lowering his tone by a single octave. "Motherfuckers in monkey suits . . . with lots of money, yeah? I get it right that time?"

My pulse jumps and I grip the countertop, hating the anxious tension crawling up my spine.

Bastian sits back, throwing one arm over the chair beside him, and glances behind him when a table close to the door cheers, obviously being dealt a winning hand. When he turns back, he's grinding his jaw. "I don't like it."

"You don't have to," I defend. "You don't—"

"Belong?" His eyes flash. "Yeah, I know."

"That's not what—"

"Don't lie."

God, he's infuriating! I study him for several long moments, unsure of what to say, but then he folds his arms over the granite before him, cocking his head.

"You playin' with me, Rich Girl?" He speaks each word slowly and purposefully. "Cause if you are, it won't end well. I might be broke, but I'm not dumb. I'm a clever piece of shit. It would do you some good to remember that." He drums his fingers against the countertop, eyes following the movement a moment before popping up to mine, this time full of anger I don't quite understand. It's deeper. Darker. *Something's changed. Something's . . . wrong.* "Street smarts beat out nine to one every single time, and by the looks of it, you ain't got no one around who has 'em. You willin' to *bet* against those odds?"

This guy. He has absolutely no sense of self-preservation. None.

A soft vibration sounds and my eyes bulge as he begins shoving his hand in his pocket, mine darting across the table to grip his wrist.

His gaze slices up to mine, pupils doubling in size.

"That is a sure way to get a bullet in your brain," I hiss. "Guaranteed privacy, that is what we offer here. No exceptions. How the hell did you get that past security?" I demand, then think better of it. "Don't say it."

"Who is the Henshaw heir?"

His question catches me so off guard I stiffen. "What?" How does he know about him?

Bronx!

"Is he in here?" he asks. *Demands* really.

The hairs on the back of my neck prickle, tingling for all the wrong reasons. "Do not make a scene," I warn.

His eyes sharpen, and terrifyingly slow, he stands, his grip on me unrelenting. "So he is in here."

"No," I hiss.

He's behind the glass.

He cocks his head a little, studying me, and after several silent seconds, rounds the counter.

I should pull away.

I should issue another warning and make it count, but something deep beneath my bones won't let me. Now I'm playing the part of that gazelle, waiting for the rogue lion with bated breath.

I can accept his touch, his kiss, but I've never allowed anyone in this room close enough to try.

Bastian isn't interested in my permission but is prepared to take what he wants, to *take* from me. The girl everyone gives to.

My stomach erupts with a tingling sensation. I have no business feeling at the thought, yet there it is, growing, spreading through my every vein, and he sees it.

He's in front of me now, and this time, his arm does hook around my body, and in one swift tug, I'm flush against him, the zippers of his leather jacket scraping along my arms.

His knuckles come up, pressing at the underside of my jaw, but then he holds.

Freezes.

He waits.

Gaze bold and sure, he places a bet in his mind, one I hear.

One I am going to win, as stupid as the move may prove to be.

I lift my mouth to his, feathering it across his bottom lip, and the corner of his mouth hitches the slightest bit as he applies pressure, sealing our kiss airtight, but he doesn't take it further.

Doesn't force my lips to part or choke me with his tongue like I expected.

Like I hoped?

Slowly, Bastian pulls back, eyes on mine, satisfaction swimming in his own, but when he blinks, it's gone, nothing but a harsh, wicked glare in its place.

And then they flick over my shoulder, his chin lowering at the same time as he stares into the mirrored glass at my back, the glass the others are standing behind. Watching. Waiting.

Rough, long fingers thread into my hair, tugging harshly but not yanking, just a solid, firm grip that teases and tingles the scalp. Tipping my head, he leans forward, the warmth of his breath fanning along my neck as he moves toward my ear.

He holds there, eyes strong on the mirror, grip tight and possessive, and then he whispers, for only me to hear, "*Behave, Little Thief.*"

He pulls back, his teeth sinking into his lower lip as he tugs mine down with his thumb, eyes narrowing. "Do not test me."

All at once, I'm released. He steps back to adjust his jacket and saunters toward the door, patting Carson on the shoulder on his way as if he owns the fucking place.

Carson laughs at something he says and bows.

Bastian's brows betray him, lifting, but only by a fraction at the show of respect, of superiority, and then he walks out the door.

It's not until I realize the world keeps spinning, as if he were never here, that I snap out of my shock and press the button on the bottom of the bar so someone knows to swap me out.

The second I get to the side door, it opens, and Valley slides in as I move out.

Bronx, Delta, and the rest of our tight-knit group are waiting by the exit and say not a word as we rush into the hall, scurry down it and into the Greyson Suite as I tug my dress back over my head, my skin itching to be covered once more.

I no sooner slap my palm on the side door to lock us inside the private space when Dom starts speaking into his wired microphone.

"What do you mean you don't have eyes on him?" he snaps. "It's been two fucking minutes, max!"

I whip around, dread drawing led to my limbs like a heavy weight.

No.

Did they snag him?

Did someone break contract and call my dad?

Holy shit! Does my dad have him?

Does Sai?

Before I can ask, Damiano looks to Kenex, and I realize then there's one person missing.

But wait.

Two minutes. Eyes on him . . .

I whip around as Damiano charges for the door he's already reopened, and I swiftly tear a dagger from the center of a bundle of pink roses closest to me, throwing it in the same second.

"Fuck!" Damiano jolts, torso twisting as he digs the one-inch blade from his ass. His features harden as he points them my way.

I rush him. "You sent Kylo to follow him without talking to me first?!"

His jaw clenches. "You were kind of busy."

My head rears back and he has the brains to cool his tone.

"It was necessary, Rocklin," he pleads his case. "It's my job to help keep everyone, including you, safe. I only asked Kylo to shadow him and make sure he left the property without issue since we have no idea how he got inside."

Bronx had the feeds tapped in, watching for him so we could intervene if he showed and erase him from the log, but she never saw him coming. I cut a quick glance at her, and when she holds my stare, I know she saw nothing. "Was he not on the footage?"

Dom's nostrils flare. Answer enough. "Nothing."

Interesting . . .

My features pull as I try to process everything all at once. "Kylo? Where is he now?"

"Not answering his call, not wearing his cuff, not on any of the surveillance screens." Dom narrows his eyes. "How does he know about the cuff?"

He didn't. I used it to open the gate, but I didn't think he paid attention, and I sure as hell didn't mention we could track each other with it.

He's a smart criminal.

"Not the time to smirk." This comes from Alto, who half shields Delta with his body.

He gets a pass for his attitude since he belongs to her, and his aggression only stems from his worry.

Looking around the room, I say, "No one is at risk when it comes to him."

"If that's true, Coco Rocco, then where is Kylo?" Delta whispers.

My blood pressure spikes, my head growing nauseous as her words seep in, but before it can take hold, before I go down the rabbit hole of what-ifs that can't be ignored, considering the man we sent to watch him disappeared with him and what that means, the oldest Greco steps forward.

"I know where he is." All eyes snap to Kenex as he hangs his head, dark hair falling into his eyes.

I look to Damiano, he looks to the others, and we settle our glares on the ward. "Take us."

I'm not sure what we're about to find when we get wherever we're about to go, but I hope, for Bastian's sake, this hasn't been some elaborate game he's been playing, that this is all a misunderstanding, though something tells me . . . it isn't.

I'd really hate to have to kill him . . .

Chapter 14
Rocklin

It was not a misunderstanding. Not at all.

Not even a little bit.

In fact, it was a plan, and it had *nothing* to do with me, though I was the decoy.

The mouse caught in the clutches of a six-foot-something tattooed trap.

It seems the wards were doing worse than causing trouble and wreaking havoc at the manor, as they do best. Before we issued our little warning of no more foul play, they had already gone a little farther south to get their kicks, planning to ease up on us here.

They traveled to a little town two hours away, where boys box for a buck, but they made a mistake in the form of a fitted golden cuff. Of course, as Kenex tells it, that was only the first one, and if anyone knows consequences must be dealt, it's us.

This is why we tell him to keep his mouth shut, agreeing to watch this play out, and the only reason why we stay hidden, tucked behind giant crates in a busted-down warehouse or junkyard, or whatever you would call a place that looks like it should be demolished and has dirt as a "floor." Well, that, and it would take all of two seconds for someone to look at us and know we don't belong, but we have an easy enough time getting in, though I'm not convinced they are trying to keep people out.

Sure, no one really parks out front, and there are a couple of guys who look like they sniff their supply more than sell it hovering around, but the cuts in the metal fence and thick cloth tied along the top don't do anything to prevent the unwanted from entering.

"This place is . . . different," Delta whispers, peering around Ander's shoulder to try and catch a glimpse of the crowd, and there is one.

No less than five dozen people mingle around, shouting and laughing, marijuana thick in the air and the scent of stale beer not far from where we stand.

A crate rattles to our left and we look to find Bronx has jumped up to use it as a seat, but Damiano shakes his head, gripping her by the hips to lower her back down. "Don't touch anything, or you'll likely need a tetanus shot."

"Relax, Damiano," she teases. "You need to take your feet off the pearly floors you're used to once in a while."

"This is the last place I would choose to be if I did," he bites back, facing forward and searching the crowd once more.

"Oh, we know, pretty boy." She crosses her arms, ready with another quick remark, but a loud bullhorn has all of us straightening.

We shuffle backward a bit as the crowd moves in, and finally, we can spot what we have been missing.

There's a circle in the center, a few barrels with ropes linked to each one to keep people out, and it clicks.

I run a fighting ring close to where I live. I find fighters, take bets, Bastian's words replay in my head, and I spin around, glaring at Kenex as I curse my father for never being wrong.

"What in the hell did you do?" I seethe.

He huffs, opening his mouth, but then *his* voice fills the air.

"Come out, come out, wherever you are . . ."

My muscles lock and I drop my head back. Of course! *Of course,* he knows we're here. That *I* am here.

I sigh, flicking my gaze to my girls as I spin, but before I can face forward, Damiano is in my way.

His chest bumps mine. "You are the one that insisted we ditch Sai back at the house. You're not walking out in the

174

middle of this crowd. There is no one at the gate. Every person in here could have a weapon!" His expression is tense, angry, but most of all, he's concerned. "This could be a trap."

"It isn't."

His face grows red. "You don't know that. You hardly know *him*."

A sharpness shoots through me, causing my muscles to stiffen along with my jaw. "I know him well enough to know if you don't get out of my face, I'm not the one you will need to worry about."

Damiano's head yanks back as if slapped. "You would sic him on me?"

"Of course not," I snap. "He would come to you on his own and if you believe for a single second he will stop on my command, you're dead wrong. He won't."

Damiano's eyes narrow, searching, *speculating*, but he isn't allowed to do it for long.

"Move," the deep, deadly baritone booms through the speaker, sending a shiver down my spine. "Right the fuck now."

Damiano scoffs, standing taller, and a jarring "pop" sounds a second later—the microphone dropping to the ground.

Quickly, I jerk past Damiano, just in time to witness Bastian hopping over a post with zero effort, chin down, eyes up, and headed this way, but he comes to a halt at the sight of me, and then every other head follows suit.

"Fuck," is cursed from the corner we're in.

"I'm not taking Delta out there," Ander says.

"You don't have to." *He only wants me*.

"Bring the brother with you."

Okay, apparently, he wants Kenex too.

I look back, eyes wide, when I find Kenex grinning from ear to ear.

Bass waits for us to be almost to him before walking back-ward and dipping beneath the rope. We reach its edge a moment later, finally spotting our missing Greyson—also grinning.

Idiots.

"In the ring," Bastian demands.

I swear Kenex almost runs, excitement bright in his eyes, the fool.

I look to the dirt beneath his feet, already stained with streaks of blood someone did a poor job trying to cover with a second layer of dirt.

"I thought Leo and Maddoc were the last fight of the night?" someone shouts out random names, confirming my previous thought.

Blood was already spilled here tonight.

That's why he didn't show sooner. He was working.

"Change of plans." Bastian stares Kenex down, speaking to the crowd. "No hype man. No bets. Just . . . seizing the opportunity." His jaw tics. "Bitch one, in the ring."

Kylo stands, stepping in so he's on one side of Bastian and Kenex is on the other.

He's going to make them fight each other?

Until . . . what, one concedes? Because that won't happen. Damiano has to peel them off each other all the time. Almost every single training session and the brothers *do* train daily, in fact, and that's not counting other areas, just hand-to-hand combat.

We'll have to jump in to stop it, but then what?

All these renegades attack us at once?

Bastian wouldn't allow that . . .

Right?

I look to him, and his eyes find mine in the same second. He stares long and hard, and then it gets worse. Slowly, he begins to peel his jacket from his body, walking toward me.

Without a word or warning, my body obeys the command he didn't have to give, turning, and then my arms are sliding into the thick, heavy sleeves until it's draped over my shoulders. "Do not look away, Little Thief," he whispers.

Facing the ring once more, I watch, transfixed, as Bastian's shirt leaves him next, and holy. Shit.

His art really is everywhere. All over.

His entire left rib cage, designed to look like a reaper tore his skin from his flesh, but instead of reaching his insides, a monster of sorts is released, its talons breaking free.

Bastian breaking free, but from what? or more . . . who?

Suddenly I want to know all his secrets, the deep, dark ones that sting. The ones that leave the circles beneath his eyes. The shadow within them.

Though now is not the time, as he's backed up a few more feet, and both Kylo and Kenex are still in the ring. The crowd gets loud, swarming in, and Bastian's gaze flashes to mine, then over my shoulder for a curt nod.

Suddenly two arms cage me in, gripping the rope steady and keeping those around from touching me.

I get a look at who it is, but the sharp bark in my ear makes me pause. "What'd he say, prep?"

I grit my teeth. "I could smash your windpipe in right now if I wanted to, just so you know."

"So I heard, but I ain't hurting you and as much as you pretend to hate it, me standing here is his way of protecting you, so shut the fuck up, face forward and give him what he wants."

I do as he says, but only because Kenex and Kylo look to each other, both their gazes snapping to me, then back.

A second later, Bastian holds his arms out wide, cocks his head and my eyes bulge, my heartbeat thumping erratically in my chest as reality crashes into me all at once.

"He's not—"

"He is."

"He can't—"

"He can."

"He will—"

"He won't."

I slam my heel into the foot of the asshole caging me in and cutting me off, and he growls into my ear, pressing his body firmer into mine.

177

"Careful, schoolgirl. My boy will be real mad if I have to shut you up with my tongue."

I can't even threaten him back as the mood shifts once more.

The air buzzes, and the Greco brothers smile, tearing the shirts off their backs, bumping knuckles with one another as they too realize what they've been granted.

A free shot.

Bastian wants them to hit him. To *fight* him . . . at the same fucking time.

He told me about the free shots he gives, but if he assumes a Greyson, which I can't say for sure he realizes they are, is remotely equal to the little boys who come out here to play fight club, he is mistaken. Plus, there are two of them.

Yet Kylo's shirt was already half torn before he tore it from his body and there were some fresh scrapes across his arms, as well as a small scrape across his left cheek as if he were knocked down and dragged. There are no marks on Bastian's skin, no fresh ones at least, which makes no sense because Kylo would have fought back.

None of that matters now, though, as the boys raise their fists.

Bass holds his hands behind his back, lifting and tipping his chin the slightest bit, offering his jaw, unaware he's about to have it broken in two.

Kylo and Kenex are second to Damiano in combat, trained by professionals who show no mercy, but on the flip side, Bastian probably doesn't acknowledge such a word. That doesn't mean he's stronger, and if somehow he is, it can't be enough to take on two . . . yet here he is, prepared to do so.

I grip the rope, my chest inflating as the nonexistent bell dings.

The twins rush forward at once, one swinging right as the other spins, leg flying through the air in what is sure to be a bone-cracking kick—attacking from both levels, on opposite sides.

But Bastian must have been a fucking gymnast in his past life as he bends at the knees, dropping him a few inches and

178

simultaneously strengthening his stance as his upper half folds backward, torso stretched and suspended parallel with the ground. Kylo's fist no more than slides off the skin of Bastian's cheek, the momentum with which he dives forcing him to bring his left foot forward for a single step and right into the path of his brother's boot.

Kylo's knee buckles but recovers quickly, spinning back and coming up with a backhanded punch that finds nothing but air.

Bastian dips low, sweeping under his outstretched arm and comes up beside Kenex, his left arm flying around and smashing into his cheekbone, waist twisting in the same move to protect his position as Kylo throws himself at Bastian, going for a takedown.

Bastian sprawls, dropping his legs back until they're completely outstretched behind him, the tips of his toes balanced in the dirt. He presses his chin into Kylo's shoulder blade, forcing him to let go and adjust, using the moment to wrap his arms around Kylo's middle. Bastian swiftly spins, taking his back and folding his left arm beneath Kylo's neck, yanking back before jumping to his feet.

It is all a quick ten-second move, and now Kenex is there, ready to make his.

Bastian squeezes, then tosses the gasping brother to the dirt, leaping over his body in the same second and fists start flying.

The crunch of bone rings over and over, splotches of blood flying as they beat into each other.

One, two, uppercut.

Cheek, chest, chin.

Sweat beads along both boys' brows and Kylo is on his feet again. He comes up from the back of Bastian, and Bastian spots his shadow, swinging once before dipping and spinning to face the other, but Kylo knew he would. He's prepared for it and serves him with a left hook, connecting with Bastian's right eye.

His head whips to the side, left foot shooting back to brace himself, and Kenex kicks at it, dropping him to his knees.

My chest heaves and I push closer, the body behind me following as silent support.

Kenex swings and Bastian's head whips in the opposite direction from the impact, blood rolling in a steady stream from his temple and the corner of his mouth.

Kylo circles for a better vantage point, coming around and gripping Bastian by the neck, his brother taking the position beside him in the same second, and I start to shake.

I jerk, and the body behind me squeezes itself closer, preventing any escape I might try to make.

Am I trying to make one?

To protect, to give my loyalty to the man who broke into my club and stole one of my own?

That's . . . wrong.

Right?

Kylo draws back, prepared to give Bastian all his momentum, and my entire body coils with tension I can't fight, but when I look at Bastian, my eyes narrow as, I swear, his mouth hooks up in one corner.

He's . . . *grinning*.

And then his hands come up, locking onto Kylo's wrist, his legs swinging up as he balances his weight like a fucking boneless acrobat. His legs come up a split second later, wrapping and locking around Kylo's neck, swinging and slamming him to the floor with a booming thud that sends a cloud of dirt into the air. The same moment he's whipping through the air, he swings, the angle of his fist a downward motion, driving right into Kenex's temple.

He's knocked out cold.

Kenex is bent, gripping his side.

And Bastian pushes to his feet, spitting at theirs.

If the crowd was loud before, they're deafening now.

People scream and shout, whistling and screeching sounds you'd never hear in the training studios at Greyson Prep. It's pure drunken debauchery.

Fingers wrap around mine, and a swift inhale zips down into my aching lungs, reminding me to breathe. I look down to the large, inkless hand as it peels mine from the fraying rope. Slowly, the guy flips it over, and I frown at the small drops of blood pooling around the crescent marks, a perfect match to my fingernails.

"You hurt yourself," he whispers in my ear. "He won't like that."

"I didn't know." I also don't know why I answer . . . or why, when he lifts my hand in his, tugging it beyond my line of sight, I allow him to do so.

A warm tongue flicks along my palm and I frown but don't pull away.

If Bastian trusts him, I can too.

Wait.

What?!

I yank away and the male chuckles.

"Your blood tastes the same, but it ain't, is it, blue blood?" he rasps.

"Hayze."

My eyes fly forward, gasping at the sight of Bastian standing tall, not three feet away, staring right at me.

The body behind mine disappears as the crowd does.

His lip is split once more, the small gash at the edge of his eye bleeding less, the blood now gathering near his hairline.

But he stands solid and strong. Unfazed.

Suddenly, Damiano is in the center of the ring, bent and checking Kylo for a pulse.

"He's alive," Bastian tells me.

I nod. I know. I saw Bastian peek at his chest when he pretended to only be spitting at Kylo's feet. Something tells me he wouldn't have cared if it weren't for me.

Not that he cares if they're hurt, but it would probably suck for him to kill someone in my circle, not knowing what such a move would lead to. At the very least, he recognizes this much.

We stare at each other for several long minutes and I'm pretty sure it's my smirk that's set free first, though I try to squash it to the side to hide it.

Bastian chuckles and comes closer, stopping right in front of me, his dark hair stuck to his forehead and hanging over his left eye.

He's slick with sweat, smeared in blood and dirt, yet I still want to reach out to him, to touch him. Trace his tattoos. But now is not the time, as the rest of my crew steps up to join us.

He gives me one more second of himself, then a mask slips over his face, and I know the part we can't avoid comes next.

He stole one of ours and it's time to find out why.

For his sake—or maybe mine—it better be a damn good reason.

Bass

The crowd wasn't expecting a second show.

When I left the building, I knew someone would follow, and I knew, if it was going to be one of them and not some beefy security dude, he'd be quick to volunteer to be the one to tail me out.

He—they—didn't want anyone to find out what they'd done. That was my thought, one that proved right when I got sight of the angry faces that didn't belong on these dark and dirty grounds.

Like my Rich Girl, these *Greysons,* as their little rich kid club like to call themselves, are all big and bad . . . so long as they don't tug their leashes too hard, reason number one why they came my way. I didn't put it together right away, but all it took was five minutes of working through my thoughts to link the bracelets.

Now I'm sitting on a crate staring into the eyes of the pretty motherfucker who knows what my girl feels like on the inside.

Not sure how I feel about it.

"We should speak somewhere more private," blond James Bond suggests, trying to take the lead.

"Ain't no privacy out here, pretty boy." Hayze hops up beside me, tossing me a white shirt he found in the car since I used the one I had on to wipe the blood off me as best I could. "This is as close to alone as you're gon' get."

James Bond narrows his eyes, glancing around the space.

Most people are gone already, the ones who aren't are too drunk or high to pay attention, and they're also clustered in their own little cliques closer to the front.

I brought us all the way to the back, on the edge of the old building my bosses have been talking about fixing up.

"Why don't we let the Grecos tell us how we ended up here?" a dude with freakish white-blond hair pipes in.

"I want to know how this guy got into The Game Room." The one at his side, I'm talking *really close* to his side, disagrees.

"This ain't your spot, homeboys. What you want don't mean shit." Hayze pops a beer, pointing it forward before taking a long drink.

"You should watch how you talk to them," a soft little voice adds, but I don't look.

In my peripheral, the dudes she speaks of shuffle closer, drawing Hayze to his feet.

"Why not, gorgeous?" he goads, taking small steps toward her.

"Watch yourself," one warns.

"Or what?" Hayze fires back.

"Or I'll cut your skin from your—"

"How many times you fuck her?"

The conversation cuts, all eyes flying to me when I speak, but mine haven't left the handsy motherfucker. Not once.

The dark-haired girl's cheeks bubble up with a laugh she tries to hold in, the other princess's jaw hits the dirt, and Rocklin's eyes close for a long second, or at least that's what I got from the corner of my eye, 'cause I'm not about to look away.

He needs to answer.

"How many times?"

He shakes his head, looking off.

I jump down, temples tic, tic, ticcing. "I asked you a question."

"She can answer if she wants to."

"Don't be a little bitch."

The charge in the air zaps stronger, and he darts forward, offended like a weak little prick, more so when I meet his single step with two of my own.

184

Rocklin moves between us, her front to me, and she yanks my head down by the tips of my hair. My eyes don't stray from the pretty fuck behind her, so she shifts some more, blocking him from my view.

I glare.

She glares.

And then I realize with us this close, her chest touching mine, her ass has gotta be touching him.

I whip her around, backing her up until her knees hit the crates.

Her eyes flare, desire brimming, but still, she hisses nice and low, "Not now. Get this done."

My hold on her tightens, jaw clenching. My eyes stay glued on my girl, but I speak to the others. "Which one of you had the bright idea to come here?"

"Both," the brothers answer in unison.

I just discovered the "brothers" part tonight, but it makes sense. They're the same height, same build, dark hair and dark eyes to match, only one's skin is a single shade lighter than the other's.

"How did you find out about this place?"

Don't say my pretty little thing, or I might have to—

"A contract girl."

Rocklin rolls her eyes, and a frown builds over my brow. Reluctantly, I release her, moving to lean on the crate at her side.

I face forward, looking into James Bond's eyes when he glares from her to me before meeting the brother's gaze who's closest to me. "And that is?"

"A chick we vet, hook up with for a while, and then let go of." The one with the knot on the side of his head shrugs. "She ditched us one night, said she was going to an event, so we followed her to make sure she wasn't meeting up with someone else. Led us here."

"Who was she?"

"I'd have to look it up. Been a couple months now," he says.

The other one adds, "Name was white girl basic. Chelsea or Clair or something."

Chelsea, Clair . . .

No . . .

I raise a brow, guessing, "Chloe?"

I feel Rocklin look to me, but I stay focused.

"Yeah. Daughter of some guy our guardian knows. That's how we met her. Went with Sai on some security situation, and he told us to wait outside. Wasn't long before she pulled up in a little red convertible." He smiles and his brother looks to him with a matching one. "Remember that one time—"

"I know who she is," I cut off their bullshit. "Is she the one who told you to ask me if you could fight here?"

Oh, Blond Boy doesn't like the sound of that, he's all beefed up, pulling the dominant card on his little soldiers—facing them head-on, chin lifted.

The one with the broken rib lifts a finger. "That was my idea."

The way the other one snaps his head his way tells me he's covering for his brother. I'd bet he's the oldest.

"Kenex," says Rocklin, and then she points to the other. "Kylo."

Kylo is the one I brought out. The odd fucker grinned at me when I put my blade against his chin and climbed in the car like it was nothing.

"You did all this, showed up in our space, took one of our people, cut into our government-grade security surveillance because he *asked you to fight*?" Blond Asshole clips.

I run through my brain for this punk's name, replaying every word from mine and Rocklin's conversation, if you could call it that, and come up with it.

Damiano.

Dom.

"Tell me something, *Dom*." I cock my head. "Do the people at your little poker tables know they're trading real cash for fake cash?"

His face falls.

Yeah, I saw the swap.

Yeah, I know that's the fucking point.

A secret cardroom would only exist for two possible reasons: a way to flip for big money or a way to hide it.

It's the dark-haired girl who moves first, thrusting her left arm out to knock the air from Kylo's windpipe, the other sending a small knife straight into Kenex's right thigh.

Both groan at the same exact second, and I lift a brow at Rocklin.

Are all these chicks some secret assassins or some shit?

"Idiots!" the brunette seethes, tearing her knife from Kenex's thigh, and pointing it between the two of them. "You took cash from the fucking club and brought it here?!"

Kenex glares. "We were just having some fun, and I told you it was my idea."

"Kenex—" his brother interrupts.

"Shut up," he cuts him off, looking around again. "I don't see the big deal."

"You threw down two bills on a bet. Bills that were fake but grew the pot. The pot had to be paid at the end of the night. You cut into my money."

Money I don't have, but I don't have to add that part. They know.

"Yeah, well, you kicked my ass," he volleys.

"He kicked your brother's ass too." Hayze grins. "Probably gonna kick this fool's ass next if he keeps moving his eyes to Barbie over here."

My gaze slices to Damiano's, his already narrowed in on Hayze.

"If he wants to fight me like a man, that can be arranged." Dom squares his shoulders.

"What a pussy boy's cop-out. Like a man." Hayze scoffs, pulling his leg.

Damiano shakes his head, turning away as if he's below him, dismissing him like the prick he is. He turns to face me. "Two hundred dollars? That's what he owes you, right?"

He pulls his wallet out, flashing the center fold more than necessary like he's trying to blind us with the green it's thick with. He pulls out two bills and holds them out for me to take like I'm a dog and he's offering me a treat, expecting me to jump on it. Maybe even drool a bit.

I move forward slowly, and a shitty look of superiority flashes over his face, making him feel really big right now, but I don't take the money.

I take the whole fucking wallet and heave it somewhere to the left.

Damiano's jaw snaps closed. His face turns red as he steps toward me.

This time, Kylo slips in his way.

A chuckle leaves me as I lick the corner of my mouth where the blood has dried. "Don't insult me, rich boy. It ain't about the money, but you knew that before you opened your wallet." We stare at each other a moment, and he doesn't deny it. "I'll give it to you, though. You trained your pets well. They fought hard, got back up and didn't bitch out. So well, I might take 'em from you, offer 'em something that doesn't come with a collar."

"If you plan on being around Rocklin, as bad of an idea as that is for you, you might want to watch yourself," he warns. "There are no games to be played in our world. What you did here tonight is for children."

"So you think I should cut them at the throat and watch them bleed out?" My blade is in my hand, flipped open in a split second, pressed to the pulse point of Kylo's neck, and at the move, everyone goes on the defense.

Each girl has a knife of sorts in hand, pulling them from who the fuck knows where, and two are in the hands of the manic-looking dude they called Ander, and the white-haired one's hand disappeared beneath his coat jacket. He's packing something better.

Rocklin is braced and ready, facing both our bodies, and Dom has an Ace between his fingers, a literal playing card, the edge razor sharp.

I lift a brow as a challenge and his nostrils flare. "That's what I thought." Slowly, I flick the blade closed, stuffing it back into my pocket. "I'm no fool, as much as you wish I were. I end one of you. I'm ending this." I nod toward Rocklin. "And that ain't in the cards, so why don't you put yours away. Then go away."

We stare off for several minutes, and slowly, everyone eases, silence falling over all of us.

That is until Hayze jumps down with a loud clap.

"So." He smirks, eyes on the angelic-looking girl who seems to already have two men of her own. "Who's down to party?"

Chapter 15
Bass

Surprise, surprise, Damiano was *not* down to keep the night going, pulling the group away for a long, private conversation before realizing he was the odd man out.

The others might not have wanted to party as much as they were curious, but then again, secret underground world aside, they are spoiled-ass rich kids. Partying is what they do best, though I bet it looks a lot different than this—a fully furnished showroom house Hayze broke his way into, swiftly removing the "model home" sign from the window before they caught a glimpse of it.

He took off a few minutes before we did to secure the spot, a place he's been watching for a while. Of course, that was after he went and found Dom's wallet and used the cash that was in it to buy beer and snacks, something I realized when we walked in, and he tossed the now lighter item to the dude.

Without saying a word to avoid the others arguing against it since he wouldn't have listened to them anyway, Hayze called a few people to join us, not more than a handful of girls and a spare dick or two to occupy the others. My boy's got my back like that.

The stiff is sitting in the corner of the couch, talking to the brothers, who are more relaxed now, a cloud of girls around them. They might not be the kind they're used to, but then again, if Kenex and Kylo hooked up with Chloe, maybe they are. She's what I used to look at and call a rich girl, but the label's less fitting now that I know these girls. She seems more normal now, being she's got too much money, but isn't a ninja, billionaire Barbie like these ones.

I walk up to Rocklin, lowering a bottle in front of her from behind, and those big green eyes meet mine over her shoulder.

"You're not above beer from a bottle, are you?"

Her glare is playful as she accepts it, and I watch as she brings it to those glossy lips, my teeth sinking into mine as she does, tasting the blood there.

Glancing up at the girls who hover close by, boldly staring right at me, I wait as they do.

Rocklin stands taller, pointing to the one with shiny, dark curls and a saucy smile. "This is Bronx." She moves to the next. "That's Delta and her men, Ander and Alto."

I nod my chin. "Bass."

Bronx smirks, eyes trailing over me as she cocks her head, tongue trailing along the edges of her teeth, and Rocklin shoves her in the forehead, making her laugh.

Delta smiles slyly as she eyes me. "You know, I want to say I'm surprised by you, but somehow I'm just . . . not." Her giggle is light and airy as she pushes her lips to one side.

I glare, and Ander, the one with a tattoo on his hand, something I didn't expect from these people, grips her chin, lifting her eyes to his as he arches a single brow in question.

"And why is that, baby?" the other one, Alto, says.

She smiles reassuringly, eyes shifting my way, so he tugs her closer, forcing her to look back to him, fully expecting his woman to answer. "Think about it. All the pretty boys begging to be in her bed, yet she gives them not a glance, and then here he is . . ."

"Finish the sentence, beautiful," Ander commands, his voice low but not *that* low.

I meet Bronx's smirk with a raised brow 'cause I'm pretty fucking sure I'm becoming the starting point of this trio's foreplay for the night.

"The opposite of what she knows, but seemingly all the things she craves. Rough, *tough*, and oh so enticing."

Ander's eyes narrow but snap to Hayze when he says, "So is this like an invite-only situation or . . ."

Ander chuckles, but Alto stands tall, frown sharp.

Shaking my head, I dip toward Rocklin's ear. "I'm gonna rinse your boys' blood off me. Do not leave."

I kiss her neck, winking at Delta when she traces the movement, grinning once I've turned, so they can't see, and I hear a soft little smack on my exit.

See, not all rich boys are different from me. Rocklin would have gotten her ass tapped for that too, a little harder, but tapped nonetheless.

I find a towel in the cabinet in the hall and move to the room farthest in the back. I'm not surprised the place has no hot water, but the soap bottles in the shower have actual soap in them, so I can't complain, making quick work of washing off.

I'm out as fast as I'm in, stepping into the room with my jeans hung open as I towel off my hair and step out.

I come to a halt when I find Rocklin stepping inside, closing the door behind her with a soft clink.

She leans her back against it, hands folded behind her, head flat on the cheap wood. "Bass?"

I nod, and she says it again, testing the way it sounds.

Rubbing her lips together, she nips at her lower one. "Does anyone call you Bastian?"

"No."

She breaks eye contact, smiling at the carpet before refocusing on me.

"Tonight didn't go the way I thought it would." She pushes off, trailing her fingers along the dresser as she steps left toward the bed.

I trail around the right. Swiping the towel down my chest, and her eyes follow the contact. "Nah, I bet not."

"You'd win your hand." Her gaze snaps up to mine. "It was dangerous what you did," she says. "Walking in like that."

I nod, curving the bed as she stops at the edge of it. I step up in front of her, pushing her hair over her shoulder. "You gonna get in trouble, Rich Girl?"

Her lips twitch and she reaches up, her touch featherlight against the script above my collarbone. "You're kind of a badass, aren't you?"

"Kind of?" I trace her mouth with the pad of my thumb and she closes her eyes, leaning into my palm. I step closer, my left knee wedging between hers and she rests against it.

"Okay, fine," she rasps. "You're a total badass. A dumb, reckless, unreasonably beautiful badass."

"You want to punish me, ma?" I lean in so we're breathing the same air, the towel falling from my fingertips, so I can drive them into her hair on the opposite side. "'Cause I'll let you if you do, but fair warning . . ." I nip at her lower lip, "I might like it coming from you."

"You would," she nearly whimpers, palms burning across my chest as she explores, floating across scars you can't see but *can* feel. She doesn't so much as pause but continues to the next part of me she's eager to touch. "You might even beg for it."

"I would." I press my nose to hers, my tongue slipping out, needing to taste the seam of her lips again. "But how 'bout you, hmm? My little racketeering, money-laundering, bad bitch."

She opens up, chasing my mouth, but I evade her, dropping my lips onto her neck and sucking hard at the skin beneath her ear.

Her nails dig into my pecs, and I growl against her.

"I owe you a reward, don't I?" My left hand drops to her thigh, inching up and up, until the curve of her bare ass is in my hold. "So tell me, my little kingpin in training, what is it that you want? Tell me, and I'll give it to you."

Rather than speak, Rocklin pulls back a little, eyes on mine as she lifts her hands over her head, and I don't wait, I gather the sparkly red number in my palms and pull it off her.

Her hair falls in long, soft waves, and I want to wrap it around my fist. I want to tug on it until it stings her scalp, but only a little, only enough to make her gasp and wiggle. But I don't because this is her show. She's in charge.

As I wait for her next instruction, though, I'm reminded of what everyone saw tonight when I look down at what's

193

before me—a perfect fucking body wrapped in ribbon and lace.

A corset that pushes her tits up high, begging you to touch and taste and claim.

Making you wish you could do just that, and it only gets worse when you follow the slimming thing down to the clasp of her upper thigh, little red jewels hooking into thigh-high stockings that round her thigh like shorts without a waistband, cheeky chonies, the only thing hiding her pussy from all who wished to see.

Make no mistake, they *all* wished to see. I know this because while she was watching me, I was watching them, and while I was part of their intrigue, she held most of it. The queen fucking bee who shone brighter than any other in that room—a beacon in a room of night-lights.

My eyes flash to hers as I fold my fingers in the strings at her back.

She stares knowingly. "Does it help if I say I wore it for you, that I was waiting for you to come to me tonight?"

"No."

"How about if I said I didn't plan on going in that room until you walked into it?"

My jaw clenches and she reaches into my open jeans, cupping me over my boxers, a small smile curving her lips as she massages me, my length growing more by the second. "I'm here to be rewarded, remember?"

I'm about to tell her I remember well, but this cancels that out. Now she's about to be punished, but something has me pausing, and the reason reveals itself quicker than expected.

Rocklin steps out of her shoes, gently pushing them to the side, purposefully making herself lower than me so she's looked down upon.

Something I would never have expected from my rulemaking queen comes next.

A blush, one born of uncertainty, not embarrassment, and maybe a little shame. Definitely vulnerability. It clicks in an instant.

194

"I see . . ." I lick my lips, eyes eating her up as I take a step back.

The *contessa*, the knife-throwing, money-laundering daughter of a murdering man, isn't craving control.

She has that in spades.

She makes rules, punishes those who break them, and bosses others around all the time. People come to her for answers she's expected to have and they look to her to lead.

Pretty and perfect all the time, that's what she said.

Always poised and in control.

Control she must take.

But not here.

Not now.

Not with me . . .

My cock twitches as she holds my gaze, the crimson of her cheeks spreading lower, all the fuck over.

This girl, she's offering herself up to me on a pretty little platter, knowing mine's nothing but a tarnished sterling silver compared to the gold her wrists are wrapped in.

She wants me to do what I want.

To take what I want.

To take control, lead her where I want her, trusting me to get her there.

She *wants* to be the submissive little lamb and me, the big bad wolf.

I'd go as far as to say she needs it.

I couldn't get any fucking harder, my dick throbbing, aching to be freed.

As if reading my mind, her eyes fall to my waistband. Her attention holds there, thighs clenching when she spots a hint of the tip peeking through the elastic.

I reach up with one hand, gliding my thumb along her bottom lip, the swell thick and full, soft, the perfect contrast to my jagged, broken skin. "Bet these will feel so good wrapped around my dick."

Her lips part as if ready.

"Bet you'd suck me so good." I tip my head, my knuckles brushing down her cheek. "Wouldn't you, gorgeous girl?"

She nods.

"Say it."

"Yes." She shudders. "I would."

"Would what?"

Her gaze slices up to mine. "I would suck you so good, Bastian," she promises. "I would treat you like a king and take you as deep as you'd allow. I wouldn't stop until you were ready to come, and then I'd beg you to let me taste you on my tongue."

Right before my eyes, the forest green of hers grows into the deepest shade of dark hunter green. She loves this shit.

I step out of my jeans, and her attention snaps back to my bulge, stiff and straining. Her chest heaves, her mouth watering, forcing her to swallow.

I fist myself over my boxers and she whimpers at the sight.

At the fucking *sight*, with no part of us touching, my balls appreciate the sound, drawing up tight.

Slowly, I walk backward, and she tracks my every move, toes curling into the carpet to help hold herself still.

"Close your eyes."

She listens.

I push my boxers down, kicking out of them, and lower into the armchair in the corner. I stare at her a moment, at the perfect arch of her ass, toned and bubbled, cheeks hanging from the thin panties I'm taking home with me tonight.

My fingers wrap around my dick and I squeeze, my jaw flexing. I give it a little tug, once, twice, and a long, tight third time, my groan filling the room.

She sucks in a breath, her hands flattening at her sides as she squeezes her eyes to keep from peeking.

"My dick is so hard. It's aching, Rich Girl. Looking at you, knowing what's next." I stroke myself again, my legs falling open wider as I rest my head against the back of the chair. "Fuck," I groan. "There's precum on the tip already."

A tremble works its way through her.

"Do you want to taste it?"

"Yes."

Instant fucking answer.

"Do not open your eyes, but come to me, perfect girl." She moves instantly. "Find me and you can taste me." I keep talking to direct her, and my girl's got perfect, well-trained senses.

Her legs brush mine, and she pauses, burying her hands between her thighs for a split second.

She waits, and I let her, crawling my fingers up her inner thigh but stopping *just* before her pussy.

"You know what to do."

She lowers to her knees, eyes still closed.

I take her hand, threading my fingers through hers and draw them to my lips. I kiss each knuckle, biting on the pinkie and she moans.

"Ready to taste?"

"Yes."

"Go on then."

Her fingers graze my shaft and I jolt, but she quickly wraps them around and a heavy breath rushes from her lungs. She leans forward, and when her tongue pokes out, it's like a heavy weight falls on my chest.

The anticipation fucking heady.

She tastes along the head of my cock in a long, greedy lick, and then she gasps.

I smirk through my moan. "You feel them?"

"Y-yes."

"It's gonna feel so good inside you and it's going in raw this time."

"Yes."

Leaning forward, I take her lips and she moans into my mouth, panting, and my dick swells in her grip. She's so fucking desperate for me.

"Be my bad girl and do what you said you would. Take me deep. Make me come." I nip at her lip. "Do that, and what you earn is yours to do with what you please."

She wastes no time, dipping down, her mouth forming an O, but right when my tip touches her lips, I snap, "Wait."

Her brows crash, but she listens, freezing there.

And then I make her wait some more, pulling at restraint I didn't know I had 'cause all I want is to sink inside her pillowy mouth. I want to shove into her throat and stay there.

But she wants her control stripped, and I want what she wants more, so the agony of making her wait is necessary.

"Such a good little listener," I praise and that frown of hers, built of overwhelming need, doubles, her hand on me shaking. Her control is slipping, but she's a fucking trooper. Her mouth's opened wide, drool slipping and sliding down her chin, but she doesn't move to wipe it away. She shakes as it slides down her skin, wanting me to dirty her up. To use her.

She wants to be my naughty little whore, if just for tonight.

"Slide your tongue in a circle, count quietly in your head."

She does, a little flicker of excitement washing over her with each ball she finds.

I run my hand through her hair. "What did you find, Rich Girl?"

"Four," she cries.

"Four," I confirm, scooting my hips farther down the chair. "You want to see me, Rich Girl? Want to look at what's about to fill your throat? What you already had buried deep inside you?"

"Please," she whispers, and I hiss as her lips brush over my head a bit.

"Open those eyes for me then."

Her lids flick open so fast, she has to blink to focus, gaze pointed right where she wants it.

She stares at my dick in awe, eyes skipping to mine, but only for the briefest of seconds.

The green is almost gone now, nothing but black pools of desire, her pupils blown wide.

Her lips twitch and she looks to me, waiting.

Fuck me, with her on her knees like this, my dick in hand, peeking up from under those black-painted lashes.

My muscles fucking melt, and I reach out, needing to touch her, grazing my thumb along her cheek. "Suck your king, my queen."

The cutest fucking cry escapes her, and then I'm in her mouth, deep into her throat on the first try. She gags around me instantly but doesn't pull back. She hollows out her fucking cheeks and sucks, licks, and moans.

"Fuck," I hiss, my toes folding into the carpet.

She bobs and squeezes, suffocating my cock with her mouth.

She might have been the one looking to be ruled over tonight, but her mouth is owning me right now.

"So fucking good, my queen is," I whisper, and I'm the one rewarded this time.

Like a fucking tornado, her tongue twists around my shaft, dancing in ways that shouldn't be possible with her mouth as full as it is, and it's fucking full.

I nod, drop my head back and peer down my nose at her.

Her speed increases until my muscles are constricting, then slows, sending a shudder through my body, and then she does it again.

My brows dip in the center and she smiles around my dick, taking me deeper, moaning around me as I pulse inside her mouth.

My eyes close and my hips start to pump faster and faster, and she settles, letting me take her how I want her. My long-ass arms come up, gently holding her face as I fuck into her pretty, pouty lips. My dick will be covered in that ruby red when we're done, and we're almost fucking done.

"Fucking velvet tongue . . . mmm. I'm close now. Decide where you want me."

She bobs furiously, getting as many extra strokes as she can, her hands coming up to massage my balls and I jerk in her hold.

"There you go," I groan, jaw clenching, a sharp hiss of air pushing between my clasped teeth. "Make me come, my little thief. Take from me. Make me yours."

She whines around me, feels the pulsing, and then pulls all the way back, her hand wrapping around my dick, and pumps, those eyes locked on mine as she rests the head on her lower lip.

My eyes flash from her eyes to her mouth, flicking between them as white ropes of cum spray into her mouth, growling when she tips her head back and pumps again, forcing more cum to leak further. She purses her lips, pushing it from between them and her eyes close as it runs down her chin and neck. Then she stretches her neck long, and I know what she wants.

Panting and loose-limbed, I reach forward, swiping it along my finger and drawing it to her lips.

She moans, taking both fingers in and sucking them clean before diving down and cleaning the head of my cock, not leaving behind a single smear, swallowing with a satisfied sigh.

Her chest heaves, her tits jutting up, ready to be let loose, to be played with.

Swallowing, I try to catch my breath. "On the bed. Legs open."

She scrambles, climbs and scoots all the way back, where she lays herself flat, hand already clenching at the sheets as she rubs her thighs together, trying to find the friction she needs.

"I said, legs *open*."

They drop wide in the next second, knees to fucking blanket, and the wet spot it reveals has me flying off the chair, swooping my pants off the floor and tossing them to the side, so I can crawl over to her.

Teeth bared, I scrape them along her thighs, kissing my way up her left arm until I'm right above her, hovering over her.

"Does my girl want to be fucked?" I ask, licking her lower lip before sitting up and pinning her down with my hips over hers.

I grip the strings on the front of her damn corset and dig into the pocket of my pants I set beside me, coming up with my switchblade.

Eyes on hers, I flip it open, swinging it in the air and bringing it down to the center of her tits in a single second.

She gasps at the feel of the cold steel against her heated skin, but she doesn't so much as stiffen. In fact, her tongue pokes out, licking along those luscious lips.

Slowly, I drag the blade down, and with each little popping sound the ties make as it cuts through, her breath quickens.

It falls open beside her, her tits bouncing free, and I swoop down, taking one pert pink nipple between my teeth. I tug and she moans, her hand twitching as if wanting to touch me, but she doesn't. She waits for my permission and that makes my dick throb, the hairs on the back of my neck standing.

She doesn't want any part of this halfway. She wants me to own her.

"Touch me," I demand.

Her hands fly up so fast I grin against her skin, moving to the other nipple to tease the same, her soft fingers diving into my hair. The second she comes in contact with the dark strands, she sighs beneath me, and I reward her little tugs by sliding my hips back and grinding once, twice . . .

"You're wet for me." I slide my hands down until I'm slipping beneath her panties. "Soaked these things through."

"Yes," she pants.

I pull back quickly and she nearly pouts.

"Show me," I tell her. "Show me how ready you are for me. Show me what a slut your pussy is for me."

Her nostrils flare and she moans, her hand flying between her legs, desperate for the touch I've yet to give.

I thought she'd swipe her fingers through her folds, but no, she's too good for that.

She does me one better, thrusting two fingers inside herself, her back bowing slightly as she sings into the air. She pumps once, the little cheat, and pulls back, bringing her fingers close for my approval.

I open my mouth and she feeds herself to me, limbs trembling at the sight. I slurp like a nasty motherfucker and then dive down, taking her lips as I push her panties to the side and I don't delay.

Give no warning.

I fill her in one thrust.

We moan together on instinct, and I hold there, buried to the hilt, from base to fucking tip.

"So fucking ready for me, aren't you?" I grind my pelvis against her clit, tugging on her hair enough to sting. "Aren't you?"

"Yes," she wheezes. "God, this is so—"

"Good?"

"Fuck yes." She squeezes me. "It's warm and the stretch . . ."

Her body quakes, dying to move, but I don't give her permission to.

I rock slow, deep, barely pulling out an inch and pushing back in, keeping her full of me. "I want this pussy to choke on me. I want her to spit on me, then I want to drown her."

She nods.

"Grab me." I bury my face in her neck, licking up the column of it. "I want to feel how greedy you are."

She's happy to give me what I want, her hands far from hesitant as she traces every groove of my skin, feeling across my scars and over my tattoos. She squeezes my biceps and grips my neck, testing her strength against it, and I clench the muscles there, pushing against her hold, encouraging her.

She squeezes harder, and when I slap her inner thigh, she lets out a little yelp, flinging her legs up and around. She locks them behind my back, so I tap her ass in thanks, her pussy squeezing in appreciation.

I sit back on my knees, and her long legs keep their hold as I grip her hips and incline them a bit, pushing back in.

"Fuck," she hisses, moaning right after.

"I'm deeper now. You feel it, don't you?"

"I feel all of you." She gasps. "God, you're everywhere. This is . . . I've . . ."

My eyes narrow and then it clicks.

She's never fucked this way before, never given herself over to someone else, at their mercy, and not just that, but never raw. Just me.

Only ever me.

Fuck me, that does something to me and it ain't normal 'cause I knew that, right? Felt it even though she didn't say it. Maybe not the condomless part, but the rest, fuck yeah, I knew.

My ego sails, obsession peaking to an all-time high, skyrocketing. I need to mark her, to claim her so everyone knows whose she is. For now, I settle for my stamp on the body that belongs to me. I smack her ass hard, the slap a sharp echo, and she spasms, coming with no warning, and it's a fucking sight.

Beauty fucking queen.

My fucking queen.

I don't pause or let up, but I do flip her, hauling her up on all fours and bracing myself behind her.

Her knees widen for me, and I slide inside, my hips slapping at her pussy, balls smacking her clit over and over, and then she's trembling once more.

Her muscles give, her left elbow collapsing, so I nudge the right one down too, her cheek now flat on the comforter, ass nice and fucking high.

I bend forward, licking my way up her spine as my hips drive into her. "Look at you, Rich Girl. Bent over like this, offering this ass to me. I should take it now." I press over the tight ring of muscle, and she lets out a long, muffled moan, clenching even more around me. "Yeah, you like the sound of that, don't you?"

She nods, clamping her eyes closed, nails shredding through the comforter.

"I'd be so fucking filthy to you. I will be, maybe soon." I kiss her left shoulder, then her right, and push up again, massaging the sharp red palm print across her ass cheek.

"I should punish you for what you did tonight," I force past clenched teeth, eyes rolling back as my thighs clench in warning, finale number two right fucking there, begging to be let loose into its home. "But this pussy is too good, so tight and warm and mine. I can't, and to know no one's ever had you like this . . . raw, heat to fucking heat . . ."

Not yet, not yet, not yet . . .

I hold off, drawing blood from my cheek. "Imma need you to give me one more." I bend, folding my back over hers, using her shoulder as a pillow as both my hands drive beneath her.

My hips bump furiously, and I pinch her clit, rolling it between my fingers as I tweak her nipples, tugging and pinching in rapid succession.

"I can't, I can't . . ." she whines, body taut.

I bite her shoulder. "You can. You will."

I shove in hard, again and again, and she gasps, shaking.

"Bastian—"

"Give me what I earned," I cut her off.

She breaks, and my cock loves it, letting go as she flutters around it.

Pushing in as far as I can, I jerk, twitching as she falls to her stomach, and I give her my weight. She must not mind it because her hand manages to come up, loosely threading into my hair.

We lie like that, naked and piled together for several minutes before I roll off, lift her and tuck her into me.

Her body is dead weight, limp to my touch and slick with sweat. Her hair is wrecked, makeup smeared and lipstick all the fuck over.

"Why are you smirking like that?" she rasps.

"You're good and fucked, and you look it."

"And you like that."

I climb over her again, lowering my body onto hers. "I fucking *love* that."

Her eyes hold mine and something passes between us, and while neither of us says a word, we lean in, in the same moment, our lips meeting in the middle.

The kiss is slower than any other we've had, almost like we're exploring, memorizing. Searching? For what, I don't know, but I'm thinking we already found it, and you know what they say . . .

Finders keepers.

And losers can get fucked.

Chapter 16
Bass

She sits on the edge of the bed, slipping her spiky heels on, her hair falling forward, hiding her from me.

Not okay with that.

My hand comes up, pushing her long golden locks over her other shoulder, so there isn't a spot on her face I can't see.

Her head turns to peek at me, eyes gliding along my face. "You do that a lot."

"What?"

"Touch my hair." She watches me for a moment, gaze settling along the bruising on my face. "Your eye is turning purple."

"You should see the other guys . . . plural."

Her lips lift with an airy laugh, and she leans back, lying across my lap.

It's such a normal, comfortable move to make that it digs at something inside me. I can't stop staring at her.

"Bastian the badass," she teases. "*My* badass." She glances up, but only for a second before going back to following the path her fingers trace over the tattoo on my side, her thumb gliding over the eye of the monster down to its mouth. "There's a scar here."

"Scars all over if you look close."

"I felt them," she whispers, quietly wondering. "From the devil?"

That's right, I tossed that one out there, didn't I?

Swiping my thumb beneath her eyes to clean off the streaks of black makeup there, I find myself nodding. "My old man. He was a real piece of shit."

Frowning, I bring my gaze to hers. I don't talk about this shit. Not because I have issues or try to bury my past, but because no one wants to hear my shit. Why would they?

It ain't pretty, and most have their own problems to worry about. They don't need mine.

I expect her to look at me with prying eyes, searching for a way to fix the broken boy, but I'm not broken and there is no fixing to be done. I am who I am. Period.

So she shocks me when I get none of that, and the girl smiles up at me instead. "But did he kill people so he could *take over the world*?"

Chuckling, I lift her by her ribs, and she twists, wrapping her legs behind as I lower her into my lap. "Nah . . ." I think better of it, and I can't help the smirk that follows. "Tried to, but nah."

She eyes me, her gaze slicing to the perfect circle, the bullet wound on my shoulder, to the zigzagging slashes beneath the ink on my chest. She touches the tattoos on my neck, the barbed wire made to look like it's cutting deep, tearing at the worthless skin that means nothing. Mine's marked up in the worst way, scarred and mangled from shitty at-home stitch jobs in places. I don't give my marred body a single thought in the day. It means shit to me.

But the ink that covers it? It all means something.

Rocklin's quiet, but creases have formed along her brows, so I draw her gaze to mine with a tip of her chin.

I wait, and it takes her a minute, but then she says, "When you said you had no parents, what did you mean exactly?"

"Ask me the real question."

Her submissiveness was gone the minute we were done playing, so she goes full sass on me now. "Did you lie to me?"

My eyes narrow. "What if I did?"

"I don't like liars."

"You like me." I rub my palms along her thigh. "And you've got no clue if I am one or not."

"Do not fuck with me, Bastian."

"Then tell me what you think you know."

She concedes. "Your father is dead."

"Uh-huh . . ."

"Your mother isn't."

I flip her so fast she yelps, and I've got her hands pinned above her head a second later. She thinks she's fast, slick, and she is.

I'm faster. Better. "You went digging."

"I had to." She lifts her chin defiantly. "You snuck into a place no one has ever snuck into before, and that was before The Game Room. I let it slide, don't ask me why—"

"Because you want me."

"—but I couldn't expect my girls to do the same. We're a unit. Three against the world, that's how it has to be."

"Tell me what you know," I repeat myself.

She clamps her mouth shut, and my palms start to sweat, wondering if, just maybe, she found what I couldn't. If she knows something I don't.

If my little rich girl has the answer I've been looking for, but as I stare into her big green eyes, I realize something.

While the gleam within them is hard, it's not from anger. Or it is, but that little bit of rage isn't for me. At least, not yet.

All she's trying to do is see if she trusts a man she shouldn't, someone she had no intentions of having any faith in, and maybe she shouldn't. Only time will tell if that was a mistake she never meant to make. Regardless, she trusts me. She never would have dropped the veil for me tonight if she didn't. But she did.

She let me in. Showed me who she wants to be when the world's not looking, a secret insight to the socialite no one has ever earned the privilege of seeing.

She gave me something I had no idea I wanted.

Now, she's looking for a little reassurance, wants me to add a bit of fuel to the little flame that's sparked in her belly, the one with my name written in the vapors, damn close to the combustion zone, where I'd brand her from the inside out.

Branding her. Now that's an idea . . .

Moving her legs, I wrap my arms around her once more and fall back, taking her with me.

"You know what happens when you shoot a man in the skull, Rich Girl?" I cock my head. "He dies, yet he's not dead. His body's still alive, heart still pumping, lungs still fighting, holding on to a bit of hope, but the motherfucker's already gone. Nothing but flesh and bone and a slowing heart. And then . . . nothing."

She nods, understanding. "Punishment or mercy?"

"I'd call it mercy. I hate guns. Guns are too kind. Mercy is for the weak."

"You sound like my father."

"Smart man."

"And you killed yours?"

"Smart woman." I hold her gaze, watching for a sign of disapproval or fright.

Instead, her palms flatten on my chest, gliding up and around my neck.

My pulse settles, and I realize that's why she did it. To reassure me. Comfort me.

I just told her I murdered my old man, and instead of running, she wants to wash my worries away.

Will she be my ride or die?

"My mother ain't dead," I tell her what she already knows, adding what she doesn't. "But she is to me and definitely deserves to be. I've been looking for her a while now, but she disappeared the day I did."

She nods. "There is no record of you. How is that not on file?"

"A man in a monkey suit came to me. Dropped me somewhere that offered me a job, and I took it. I'm every bit the poor punk I look. I've got nothing of my own and I live in a group home with half a dozen others like me."

"How old were you?"

"Fifteen." I kiss her left cheek, then the right. "I got into that little club, ma, 'cause my pops beat silence into me, and

208

those beatings taught me how to be invisible. You can't touch what you can't see and you can't find what you can't hear. I was inside before they knew I'd arrived, and the silent alarm that was triggered wasn't them catching on. It was Hayze, and it was on purpose."

"To draw the attention to you."

"That's right."

"The guy we came here with, the one who was behind me at the fight, that was Hayze?"

I nod.

"He licked my blood."

A loud laugh bursts from me, and I drop my head into the crook of her neck before falling to the side of her. "Yeah, he's got a thing for blood."

She glares at me, pushing up on her elbow.

"What?"

"I thought you'd, I don't know, jump up and run out there, choke him out or something."

I grin, tucking her hair behind her ear. "I will if you want me to."

Her eyes only narrow further. "This is shocking. I'm shocked."

I can't help but laugh at how serious she looks.

"Bastian, you're jealousy in human form."

"It ain't jealousy."

"No?"

I shake my head. "It's a matter of what's mine and what's not theirs. No one should touch what's not theirs without permission."

She glares playfully, likely remembering when she said something like that the night she became mine.

"In case you're wondering, Hayze is the only male I won't have eating concrete for touching you. I love that dude."

"So if I wanted him to . . . play with us?" Her eyes spark in mischief, attempting to call my bluff like a good little gambler.

My phone is in my hands in seconds, and not five after that, my boy is opening the bedroom door.

Her head swings toward it, eyes wide when they come back on me.

"Come here, my man."

He steps inside, closes the door behind him, and walks to the edge of the bed. His eyes never leave mine, even though my girl has a lot of leg showing, her panties are at our feet and nipples poking through her thin dress since the corset that acted as a bra is shredded somewhere in here.

I sit up, pull her with me, and set her on my lap. "She wants to know how you taste. Ain't that right, Rich Girl?"

"Yes," she says, no airy, soft rasp in her tone.

My dick twitches against her ass at that.

She's not turned on. Just testing me.

Hayze smirks nice and slow, his attention finally moving to her. He tips his head, trailing a thumb along his chin. "Can I put my tongue in her mouth?"

"If she lets you."

He nods, lowering to his knees and shuffles between mine, hers crossed over my right thigh.

His palms come up, tracing her face without touching it, and he nods.

Licking his lips, he whispers, "Come to daddy, gorgeous."

Rocklin leans forward.

Hayze leans in.

Their lips are a breath away.

I kick him in the chest, taking her around the waist and burying my face in her neck.

They both laugh loudly, and I growl against her skin. "Yeah, fucking right, Rich Girl. Ask me some shit like that again. I dare you."

She flips me, climbing on top, and I let her pin me down, her satisfied smirk spinning something low in my gut. "So jealous." She beams.

"So mine."

She freezes, but only for a second, before lowering, holding her hair to one side, so she can kiss me, a soft, short kiss. "So yours."

My lips curve and she opens her mouth to speak, but before she can, shouts reach us from the open door. We pop up right as her friends burst into the room.

"The cops are out front!" Delta, she said her name is, shouts. "My grandfather will murder me. Probably literally if it avoids a scandal."

"Yeah, we can't talk our way out of being inside this house," Bronx shouts. "So get your ho ass up!"

Rocklin is already at the window by the time she's done, and Bronx yells down the hall. "This way!"

One by one, they rush in, jumping out the window with panicked hisses.

I look to Hayze, and we both laugh, shaking our heads. "The others split. It's just us and the cast of *Clueless*."

Damiano's glare snaps over his shoulder before he climbs through, his eyes flying to the satin I peel off the floor, watching as I slide it into my pocket.

He shakes his head and climbs out, the two of us the last through.

The girls run through the grass, giggling and whispering as they sneak out the side gate to the back lot of the house—we wouldn't have used this house if it wasn't an easy escape route. We're poor, not ignorant.

Once we reach their car, they climb in, all waiting for Rocklin, but she comes to me first, glancing behind me, hesitant to leave.

"Go," I whisper. "I'll come to you."

"When?"

"Soon." I hold in my smirk. "Good luck with the third degree, make sure you include all the dirty details."

"A little secret?" She smiles, and I bend so she can meet my ear. "I rank higher."

Chuckling, I swat her ass, and off she fucking goes.

Into a car with a dude who's had her.

Back to a life where another one wants her.

In a world where I'm not allowed to have her because she's her and I'm me and we don't match. Yet our bodies disagree, and our souls have stretched, those thin little threads reaching out, the tips touching, trying to grab on.

Not sure how long I stare after the car, but it's not until there's a flashlight beam on the back of my head and a voice shouting, "Stay right there," that I move, Hayze on my heels.

We run, jumping two fences and popping the lock on a shed, and slip inside. We curve to the back, dropping down next to a bag of fucking manure.

I scrunch my nose, looking away.

I'm down in the dirt, surrounded by bags of shit.

If this ain't an omen, I don't know what it is.

Hayze must read my mind because his hand clamps on my shoulder, aligning my eyes to his.

A silent promise passes between us.

We will get out of the dirt.

We will bury our shit.

We *will* come out on top.

The two of us might not have been able to control our pasts, but the future is ours to find.

And we'll take it if we have to.

God help a motherfucker who stands in the way . . .

Chapter 17

Rocklin

"I don't understand what you're thinking." Damiano follows me down the hall, his words from two nights ago annoyingly on repeat yet again.

"I don't need you to."

"This affects all of us."

"Keep your voice down, or Sai will hear you."

Damiano glances around until he spots my guardian several feet away. "I'm just saying it's not just you in this. You have to see that."

"It's not a marriage proposal, Damiano."

"I would hope not! Your father would—"

I'm done.

I whip around and his mouth clamps shut. "I know what my father would do. I know I'm lucky I wasn't killed, and I'm lucky the people at The Enterprise are under contract and I'm lucky the employees are our people, not our parents'. I know I put the girls at risk, and I know you don't like it, but here's something *you* should know." I step closer to him. "I am going to do it again, and about something you might be questioning . . . I still need you on my side. We are what comes next in this world. I will take my father's seat one day, you yours, and we will need each other, so stop acting like a hurt puppy when you're not. You literally fucked Jess Morgan three days ago. You're taking Mia Calder to the Gala, and you're going on a little trip this summer overseas to meet with a man about his daughter and her possible place beside you."

Damiano's eyes are sharp, his nostrils flaring, but as my words set in, his shoulders ease and he blows out a long breath, scrubbing his hands down his face. "I'm worried, all right?"

"I know."

"You have been groomed for your role all your life, and you've never stepped out of it. Not like this."

Anger builds in my gut. "I am aware of my father's hooks and how deep they are in me, thank you."

"I don't want you to get hurt, that's all."

"He wouldn't hurt me."

"You don't know—"

"He will *not* hurt me, Damiano."

"Maybe not on purpose," he relents. "But this is dangerous, and you know it. Especially for him, and with the Enzo issue? They could come for any of you at any time."

"Still no movement from him?"

He shakes his head, glancing around, but we're the only ones in the hall. "It makes no sense. Bronx showed me what she found, and it seems he's content in Costa Rica. No sign he has any idea his fiancée is gone."

"Boston is lying about something, I'm just not sure what it is. Sai has the car locked and loaded with weapons and all these new escape plans he told me not to tell anyone about, not even my dad, just in case. Yet my dad says nothing is happening. I need to talk to him again."

"Speaking of your dad." Damiano veers us right back when I thought I slid us past, but I should have known it was too easy. "What are you going to do when he finds out about the . . . about Bass?"

Sighing, I look to him. "The only thing I can do."

If my dad finds out about Bastian, I have to cut him loose, show my dad he means nothing and he's no one. That, in an instant, I can release him, and I wouldn't care in the slightest.

It's the only way my father won't tie a brick to Bass's ankles and throw him over the side of his yacht.

214

Dom gauges me, his expression growing as soft as his question. "You sure you'll be able to do that?"

"Of course I will."

I knew we'd get to that point eventually, as it's the only place the road leads, so I've prepared for it. Expect it.

It'll be easy.

Right?

I look up at Damiano, and suddenly I'm not so sure. "What?"

He gives a sad smile. "I said you misunderstand."

"Misunderstand what?"

"I know you will do as you must, no matter how hard that might be for you, but I don't think it's that simple."

When I frown, shaking my head, he dips down a little. "You will walk away if you must. I know that, but . . ."

But Bastian won't.

He won't let go.

He won't allow me to let him go.

He said it more than once now. I am his.

Shit.

I force a smile as I have many, many times, and lift a single shoulder. "Well, then I'll simply have to make sure they steer clear of one another. It shouldn't be too hard."

Dom nods.

I nod.

And then we both straighten our spines when the man himself steps around the corner.

He tips his chin at Dom, his focus shifting to me. "What shouldn't be too hard, daughter?"

Double shit.

I worried my dad had overheard too much earlier, and now I'm sitting here, dumbfounded as I stare at him, wondering if it would have been better that he had, but that's ridiculous and would solve nothing as he'd still be here, in Greyson Manor, laying down the law.

"Absolutely not!" I shout, jumping to my feet.

215

"You will watch your tone."

"Dad."

"*Daughter*."

I turn to Calvin. "Help me out here! The students at Greyson Prep are your responsibility. You can't possibly be okay with Boston coming back to class."

Calvin clenches his jaw but nods. "It's not the worst idea," he treads carefully, and I scoff before I can stop myself.

"Rocklin," my father scolds.

I force my head to bow like a pathetic little princess would. "Sorry."

When no one says anything for several moments, I peek at my dad, who watches me far too closely.

It's clear enough Calvin isn't happy about this, but it's above him.

It's above us all, way the fuck up there with Rayo Revenaw in his damn tower of terror.

"My sister signed a contract alongside both of you, *giving herself* to a man who wants to see the Greyson union fall so he can take our family down."

"You mean to a man who *thought* to take me down and then thought better of it."

"Right . . . because you gave him your daughter as a bartering tool, she was the white flag, and now that flag flew away. It's here. *She* is here, and you want to put her in the school with the sons and daughters of people who would come at this place with everything they have if something happened to their kin in a zone they are promised it will not?"

"Like with Greyson Manor, we know Enzo won't risk what would follow should he show up. You have just said it yourself. They will come with all they have, joining together for the first time under the same cause. He is an arrogant bastard, not an ignorant one."

My father almost looks sure, smug. It's as if he's excited by the idea should Enzo do exactly the opposite of what he's saying.

216

My eyes narrow before I can stop them and he raises a dark brow at me, daring me to voice my thoughts aloud when he knows I won't. That's why he does it, for the short little win it warms him with.

God, what would he'd do if he knew his daughter was fucked like a goddess by a "street rat," as he would call him? The shock that would cover his face would taste so sweet.

No. Stop.

Family is everything. First.

I swallow. "Do you think Enzo will simply allow her to stay when he finds out? And while oddly delayed, he will find out."

My father sits back, his face a sharp mask. "I think he will come to realize she is not what he expected."

That is not an answer, and coming from him, it could mean so many things.

Does he mean in a good way or a bad one? That Boston is more than he thought or less than? Does he think he'll honestly change his mind when he has a bride in his hands and our name beside his? I'm betting on no.

My father pushes to his feet, smoothing his black hair back, even though not a strand has fallen out of place. "The girls are being informed of this decision as we speak, so there is no discussion for the three of you to have. The Greyson Society and The Enterprise are yours, so of course, you three have the final say where that is concerned. I don't expect you to allow her back into the folds."

"I would certainly hope not."

He moves to stand before me, and I straighten my spine like a good little soldier. "The anniversary of your mother's death is three days from now."

I wince despite myself. I hate his use of the word "anniversary," as if unknowingly consuming poison is something to celebrate. She was murdered, not that he'll admit to that, being no one could prove it.

"It is." I nod once, the reminder an unnecessary one.

"Boston won't be able to join us outside the walls, of course, but I expect you to be available." He scowls, warning me not to question him. "Wear something red. It will bring out your eyes."

"If you insist."

This time, it's my dad who scoffs, kissing my head as he says, "Sai will be ready at seven sharp. Do not make him wait."

He walks out the door, once again stopping by simply so he can give my leash a little tug, a leash I've only recently come to realize I was wearing.

Be strong, be dominant, be the best, and don't forget to smile. Those were the words I heard often and held close. They were an assignment I was to ace, and so I did. Do.

I was to earn the right to the north wing, the wing with my family's name on it, and so I did.

Find my place within the manor and a way to leave my legacy.

Earn the respect of the others at Greyson Elite by being all the things a leader should.

My father had been thrilled about the waves I'd made, yet slowly, the nudge behind the knees, encouraging me forward, stopped, and now the one against my chest, pushing me back, has taken its place.

Why?

I'm no fool. I know being dickless in my world is a negative where most are concerned, but I'm no Southern belle, as many of my peers were raised to be, though sometimes I play the part of one at my father's orders. For the outsiders.

For the sake of the school and its reputation.

For the world outside our own.

But I have proven my place is in one of leadership.

I can handle the head seat of the school, and once my father is older and grayer, I will do my duty, *do as I must*, transitioning into the chair in which he sits.

I've made a mark, and I'm still mid-studies.

My father said bloodshed is necessary, always, and I took his words and gently washed them down his throat, proving we could eliminate threats against him without bloodshed and avoid the headache, not to mention the cost of a "cleanup crew" that follows. Jacobi Randolph was the latest example of this and the scheme we pulled was child's play. Too damn easy, as most are.

I, with the help of my girls, increased our bankroll tenfold, simultaneously growing my own, while smoothing over business relationships that were on a kill-or-be-killed level, creating new ones at the same time.

Me.

I did that.

You would think I would be allowed to deny my father when his "ask" could potentially affect the school I'm supposed to speak for, let alone make my own decision about who and where I eat dinner, but no. Boston is coming back to Greyson Elite, and in three days, I'll be ready at seven sharp, wearing a red dress, accompanying him to a dinner I'd rather not attend. I'll smile and walk with pride and power as my sister parades around my fucking zone as if she isn't a cow at risk of being corralled at any moment.

Boston gets yet another free pass she doesn't deserve and will not be forced to sit and fake laugh and chat, drink bourbon or champagne, depending on what my father chooses to order for his nineteen-year-old daughter on this little dinner date to "celebrate" our mother's death. Not that he'll mention her name a single time during . . . or permit me to do so either.

No, we don't speak of Mother. We "enjoy" our meal, grateful for the family we do have because family is everything. It's the be-all and end-all—blood before all.

We might work with and worship the Greyson union, but we live and breathe for our name.

I am sworn to be a Greyson first, to think and act with consideration of the girls I stand beside, but according to my father, I am a Revenaw above all else.

What sense does that even make?

My mind and body are ticking time bombs, begging for some sort of release while also warning me against it. The sensation leaves my limbs heavy, and it takes real effort to force myself to the dining hall for dinner.

There is a seat for all who live in the house at the dining room table, and shockingly enough, most days, we're all here together, if only long enough to finish our meals, but this evening the Greco brothers, Delta, Alto, and Ander are feeling chatty. Bronx chimes in and Damiano laughs with them, Boston having excused herself early on—probably to throw her food up before it has time to settle too long—but I don't feel like talking, numbly pushing the braised cherry duck that I'm sure is divine, but tastes like nothing on my tongue, around on my plate.

Suddenly, I want barbeque. Chicken with a bone in it I can eat with my hands.

I want Bastian, but not the way I should.

I want to sit with him and do nothing, talk about things that don't matter, invite him for dinner and laugh when he tries something for the first time and hates it. I want to wear his headphones and listen to what he likes while he pushes my hair over my shoulder, feel his rough hands holding me still if only so my heart will stop pounding against my ribs.

Goddamn it, it is pounding.

I excuse myself, ignoring the glances I get from around the table, and make my way down to the pool. I change into a suit and ease into the temperature-controlled water, slowly swimming from one end to the other. I do this until my body takes control and my heart rate demands I concede.

Dragging myself up two steps, I sit, stretching my torso back and placing my head on the brick, wishing the dizziness away. When this first started happening a little over a year ago, I thought it was a panic attack, which is the last thing someone like me needed. I could hear my father's voice in my head the moment I was sure I had figured out what was wrong.

If you cannot be composed, you cannot be what is needed. You must be in control at all times, aware of your surroundings, and able to lead a conversation or situation the way that you wish it to go.

What use would I be if every time things grew tricky, I turned into a shaky, fuzzy-headed mess?

I thought that was the worst I could get, but I was wrong.

Asthma. Late asthma onset caused by overexposure to chemicals.

From diving.

I had always been told my dedication to the water showed strength and resilience. It turns out that what my father claims is wrong. There is such a thing as overexertion. As too much practice, training too hard, but he was also right—love does kill, and mine for the water nearly claimed my lungs as payment.

It's not a huge issue outside the water. Muggy air, such as a sauna, can sometimes tighten my rib cage, but other than that, the punishment only comes when I step inside this space.

No one knows, not even the girls. I have an emergency inhaler hidden in several places, but I've yet to use them. People assume I reached the top and therefore had no need to continue, but a musician doesn't stop making music simply because she earns a Grammy, and an artist doesn't stop creating a national metal. The same goes for a diver, but I don't dwell on the loss. It would do me no good.

I don't bother changing from my suit but wrap a robe around me and head for my room.

The girls and I have a job to set up, this time to send a warning to someone who rubbed Bronx's dad the wrong way, and we're told it's for us to handle, not something to use as training for any Greyson or Greyson prospects. So it will be a long night of planning after Delta's rehearsal and Bronx's studio session. Thank God for that. I need the distraction.

As I step into my closet, tossing the robe into the hamper, my body stills.

Footsteps and the low trickle of water reaches my ears, and I tear through the space, throwing open my bathroom door.

Kylo whips around, throwing his hands up, a grin spread across his lips.

I look from him to the bath, bubbles spreading before my eyes, and I snap them back to his. "What the hell are you doing in my wing?"

"I have permission," he rushes to add.

My head yanks back, a humorless laugh leaving me. "Excuse me?"

"Took the words right out of my mouth," comes from behind, and I spin as Kenex steps around me, wine bottle and glass in his hand.

My mouth opens, but nothing comes out at first. I stand there, watching as the two prepare a bath, and then Saylor is there.

"Excuse me," she says quietly.

All I can do is step aside and glare at them and the plate of cheeses and fruits Saylor sets on the glass shelf designed specifically for this use.

She dips her head, walking out, and then the boys follow.

I blink and blink again, and then my phone beeps from my room.

With backward steps, I go to retrieve it, a text from Bastian waiting on the screen.

Bastian: nothing a hot bath can't fix.

Frowning, I reread those words with a wave of confusion.

"Bad day?"

"Nothing a steaming bath won't fix."

My memory clicks, remembering the conversation, if you can call it that, we had that first day. My brows crash, eyes darting over every inch of the space.

My bathroom is a thing of beauty, a personal escape meant solely for me.

Black marble floors with a floating countertop and large golden bowl sinks rising above them, a fountain-style spout and black mirror that only allows for your reflection when you're directly before it, a warm, golden tone light reflects around its surface, fanning out over the walls into a soft glow. The walls are the same black marble as the floor but gold-dusted.

222

Though that's not what my gaze is frozen on.

It's the golden candles on the three-tier corner shelves, each one's flame flicking, when I've yet to light the new set. Same as the ones at the head of the jet bath, which sit angled in the same corner. The deep, arched chromotherapy tub is full and mountained with bubbles, my bottle of melatonin and marijuana-infused soap at the foot of the steps. A bottle of some wine I've never heard of the twins left sitting at its edge, the glass from my room decanter set beside it.

My pulse jumps up, but only by a single beat as I step into the private zone.

The closer I get, the deeper my frown grows. Steam rises through the soapy suds, and I dip my fingers inside. It's as hot as it can get.

Just the way I like it.

This is exactly what I needed right now, water to swallow me whole without repercussion.

But how does he know this?

Slowly, I start to strip until I'm completely naked, and climb the three small stairs, stepping down into the oversized bath.

Sighing, I drop my head back on the embedded pillow and kick the jets on, but a few minutes in and one of my eyes pops open, staring at the wine bottle.

I reach over, grab it, and search for the opener, but it's not there.

Rolling my eyes, I go to set it back down, but then the top catches my attention.

No cork.

A twist-top wine?

I fumble with the plastic seal a bit but get it opened easily enough and take a slow sniff.

Cinnamon and maybe . . . clover?

Pouring a small taste in the glass, I let it settle over my tongue. Black cherry.

"Hmm." My brows lift, and I pour a decent glass, lowering into the water once more.

My phone beeps again, and I reach for it, having almost forgotten how I got here.

Bastian: like the wine?

A small smile pulls at my lips and I lie back against the bath pillow.

Me: I do.

Bastian: good 'cause it took me way too fucking long to pick it out. The labels don't say shit about what they taste like.

Something in my chest warms and I lower my lips beneath the water.

Me: you bought this wine for me?

Bastian: don't get too excited. It was only five bucks.

Really?! I look to my glass, swirling it and taking another small sip, the flavor even more soothing this time, but then I remember how the boys were in my room along with the wine Bastian claims he purchased.

Me: what am I missing?

Rather than a text, my phone rings with an incoming video call. I accept, toes folding in the water when his rugged face comes into view, black hair falling in his eyes as he looks down into the camera.

His smirk is slow, and he lifts his eyes over the screen a moment as he shuffles away from something. "Rich Girl."

"Bass."

He frowns instantly and a low laugh leaves me as I tip my head to the side.

"*Bastian.*"

His eyes spark with satisfaction. "You didn't think a couple of scrapes and bruises would be enough, did you?"

I catch on fast. "You're trying to turn the troubled two?"

"No turning. We're on the same side, me and them Greco brothers."

"Are we now?" I hold in my smirk but keep my gaze stern, Kylo's words circling back to me. "They said they had *permission* to be in *my* space."

"They did. Mine, and I gotta say . . . not happy to learn you live with all of them, including Damiano. He is not allowed in your wing, Little Thief. No exceptions."

I ignore his Damiano comment. "You cannot have my men, Bastian."

"*I* am your man, Rich Girl, so watch your words."

My tongue rolls along the backs of my teeth. That line shouldn't send little flutters through my rib cage, yet here I am, suddenly victim to girly shit I wasn't sure I'd ever like the feeling of.

It's not enough to distract me from the purpose of this conversation, though. "The boys choose to pledge themselves to us, so this is where their efforts and loyalty must be, even if I'm still unsure I want them here. If they lose focus, they will be gone, and the Grecos have nowhere else to go. Their mother is dead, and they worked for another prominent family, which is how we found them."

Bastian frowns, leaning forward. "What the fuck does that mean? You're unsure you want them there?" He latches on to one part of what I said. "Then why are they? What did they do?"

"They haven't exactly done anything," I start honestly but think better of it. "Well, you and the counterfeit money are a big fucking deal Dom's working through, but other than that, it's been nothing more than boys being boys. Pranks and things that cause no real harm but take time to amend."

He sits on that a moment, his tongue flicking his lip ring in thought. "So you don't want them there 'cause they're different? Not robotic and Ken doll dull?"

"That's not what I said." I frown.

225

"Then why? I see the way you like being around me outside all that shit, so you not likin' those two for being a little rebellious like you crave to do makes no sense to me."

Call me out, why don't you?

My muscles clench a little as his words fall into me, all true, as much as I hate to admit as much, and sharing this next part isn't exactly going to paint me any different than the judgy bitch he describes.

"My dad doesn't trust them. He didn't want them here; he can't stand the sight of them actually, says they will bring chaos we can't control, and he's never wrong. Ever."

My words hang like a weight between us, and slowly, Bastian nods, looking away.

After a moment, his crystally eyes come back. "If I wanted to take the Greco brothers, I would do exactly that, and they wouldn't be able to tell me no, but for now, I will use them when I need to."

Anger flares in my stomach at his very Rayo Revenaw-like statement, but it doesn't spread. It's a softer heat settling in my bones. "What's the matter, can't sneak your way to me anymore?"

He eyes me a moment, and I grow anxious, which is irritating, but I know he's seeing what I'm not saying, his next words confirming as much, shocking me in the process.

"Wanna see you too, baby."

An instant fluttering races through my abdomen like bees fleeing their hive. My fingers tighten around my phone, chin subconsciously dipping, eyes still locked on his, but through a shadow of my lashes.

Baby.

Not Rich Girl.

Not Little Thief or Rocklin.

Baby, and he misses me. He misses me, and he hardly knows me, and he wants nothing from me *but* me. My teeth sink into my lower lip, and his gaze flashes to my mouth.

"Stop," he rasps. "Don't treat my lips like that."

226

Now it's heat that spreads, and I shift beneath the water.

Bastian's eyes narrow knowingly. "I can't get to you tonight."

"Why not?"

He licks his lower lip. "Some shit happening over here."

"Tell me."

He looks off a moment and then starts walking. "Guys I work for are brothers going through some shit, and my homegirl has been living with them a minute now. They got some family stuff going on, and since I'm on their payroll, they're keeping me busy. Which reminds me, I need to give my sister a call."

"Sounds boring, aside from the sister part."

He chuckles, eyes falling to the bubbles begging to separate near my chest. "I can definitely think of something a lot more fun."

His expression gives him away, as does the flick of his lip ring and low rumble that muffles through the microphone.

He wants to demand I show him more, and I want that even more, but it would lead to something else. We both know it. Suddenly, he glares, eyes flicking up to mine. "Damiano stays out of your wing. I will know if he doesn't."

The line goes dead, and I wait for the anger of his little rule to come, but it doesn't.

Desire does instead, heat pooling between my legs and tugging low in my belly.

Closing my eyes, my hand drifts deep into the water, thoughts of my tattooed tyrant at the front of my mind, where he stays long after the girls go to bed, and I collapse into mine.

I have an inkling he may never leave.

The thought should terrify me, but it doesn't.

And that . . . is terrifying.

Chapter 18
Rocklin

It's Thursday morning when we pull up at school to find my sister already there, donning the uniform she gave up, pleated skirt rolled high at her hips, and for a moment, I wonder how many people look at her, assuming she is me.

"And so she has arrived," Bronx muses. "Straight back to breaking the rules."

I look her over from her silky blonde hair to her knee-high socks. "She is a fool."

"And bold to stand there with the boys as if she deserves to walk alongside us." Bronx leans forward.

"As if we are going to allow her to." Delta grabs her bag.

Tension wraps around my ribs at their words, a small, teeny-tiny hint of me wanting to defend my sister, but that's simply the last thread of loyalty, fringed and frayed, that won't break, no matter how badly I want it to.

I'm not angry at the girls' words. The sentiment is the same. I'm angry that we feel them.

Bronx and Delta might be my best friends, but Boston was a part of us too, albeit later and then not at all, though a part nonetheless.

I don't wait for Sai to open the door but do it myself the moment the car rolls to a complete stop. Instantly, my sister's eyes fly my way. She keeps her smile in place, I will give her that, but that's all I will give. The girls and I step from the car, making our way to the stairs as we do every other day, smiling politely, spine straight, and uniforms worn as instructed. When we reach the point where the boys wait, I turn my back to Boston, facing the others as they look to me, sparing her no glance. They slip behind us, and, of course, she chooses to ride our tail all the way into the building but gets lucky when a familiar face realizes she's not just seeing double, calling out her name. Boston pivots so fast I can't help but laugh. Her need to be recognized as disgusting as her presence back in school is. She knows, as well as everyone else here, that to be a Greyson, you must complete your education regardless of the role you'll take in life.

Future princesses don't get a pass because their throne awaits them, and sons of the cartel aren't permitted to leave for bigger, better, or whatever the hell it is their fathers put them on.

To wear the seal of a Greyson on your jacket, or earn the golden pin of a secret society member, and in turn, obtain access to The Enterprise later in life, should your family need it, you have to commit, show you're capable of holding to the word you agreed to. It's a test, just like everything else in this world.

Accepting a place in our school, which takes a spot from another, is a binding contract . . . as is the one my sister signed herself away in.

Her being back goes against everything we demand from the rest of the attendees. It's a show of prejudice to allow a pass for my own bloodline.

Of course, as my father made sure to mention, the contractual marriage between my sister and Enzo Fikile had yet to go public. As far as we're aware, no one knows about it.

I guess that's still to be seen, but a lie is a lie, even if no one figures it out.

As expected, the whispers begin shortly after the first class bell rings. No one asks the direct question, but it is in the eyes of everyone around, all wondering where Boston disappeared to these last three months and why she's back.

Once lunch break rolls around, the girls and I separate, going up to the Greyson den. The rest of the day is much the same, the three of us avoiding as many people as possible, just in case questions are asked.

Unfortunately for me, on my way to meet Sai, none other than Oliver Henshaw steps up beside me.

"Princess."

"I am no more a princess than you are a prince."

He smirks, flashing his ridiculously expensive watch, and that means a lot coming from a girl with handbags that rival the cost of a sports car, loaded with the earth's rarest diamonds, the Argyle, the family heirloom he never lets anyone forget about. He makes a point to run his hand along his hair to be sure I don't miss his pompous little treasure.

"I like to believe I'm pretty equal, without the crown of course, but I can commission whatever is needed. Shall I order you a matching one?" he teases.

Ignoring his not-at-all-subtle intent, my eyes slide to his. "What can I do for you?"

"Just making sure my father isn't telling me lies yet again."

"I'm supposed to know what you mean?"

"Dinner on the yacht this evening . . . you, me, and our power-hungry fathers. Does any of this ring a bell?"

Lead fills my veins, and I jerk to a stop, my head snapping toward him, giving myself away.

So my dad is setting me up for what? Courtship now?

"Ah, yes, of course." Oliver nods, creases forming along his temples. "You've been ordered to attend."

Obviously not a question, so I don't bother answering but start walking again.

"You should head back down to the hall," I tell him. "If I recall, you have archery practice this afternoon and if you delay any longer, you will be late. I happen to know your captain will not be happy with that."

"You mean you won't put in a good word to Ander for me?" He smiles.

"Please." I flick my eyes to the sky as I step out the double doors to where Sai is waiting, as always. "And I will not be making dinner tonight, but have a good time."

Despite my recommendation for him to get lost, Oliver follows me out the door with a nod, glancing at my driver slash guard with a look I can't decipher. "Saw your friend the other night," he says lowly, and my eyes fly his way once more. Slowly, he moves them from Sai to me. "He was new."

Bastian.

Of course people saw him. I knew this, but no one questioned me. And no one but the girls and Damiano knows who the people we allow into The Game Room actually are. For all they know, their own father's money man could be the one eye-fucking them each night.

I manage to keep my expression masked as he's watching me closely, the urge to jab my fingers into his big blue eyes is hard fought, his nerve almost as shocking as the smile on his face. The heir's words are as carefully chosen as they are spoken, but there's only one conclusion to be drawn from them, and he's a bold son of a bitch to dare let them slip through his lips. But words are only words until they're not, and he's betting they are ones I don't wish to gamble with.

"Careful. I know where you sleep at night." It was the wrong thing to say, and I realize that as my threat evaporates into nothing when his smirk turns up ten notches.

Oliver is far from unattractive if you're into the—as Bastian puts it—Ken Doll variety, wavy brown locks, big blue eyes, silken skin that's sun-kissed all over, dimples, and a perfect pearly smile to go along with it.

Clearly, I'm not into that clean-cut type, and *clearly*, he wishes I were.

"So, no need to text you my room number, or will you simply follow me after we feast for a bit of dessert?"

"Go away."

This comes from Dom, and Oliver frowns instantly. My smile spreads wide, and I cock my head. Everyone knows to be dismissed by Dom is to be scraped across the floor in training.

Oliver doesn't test our best fighter's patience, the two of us watching his retreat until he's back in the building and heading toward the tunnel that will return him to the dorms.

"What was that about?" Damiano asks as we head for our waiting cars.

"Oliver being Oliver."

"I don't like him. Remind me why we invited him into the fold?" He glares in the direction the heir disappears in.

"Because he's a fucking genius with connections, passed all our tests, aces his courses, and has shown nothing but loyalty since day one, even if he is a slimy bastard."

Dom's expression doesn't change, and he's yet to look away.

"Don't worry too much about him. It's nothing but harmless bullshit," I tell him, and it's the truth.

Oliver is using risky words to guarantee he's not the only one who must suffer through a dinner with our fathers, but he would never speak of anything he saw inside The Enterprise.

He would owe his tongue if he did. Literally, and being his family has made their fortune in anonymity, I would say he values his speech. That, and he knows what I know, as he's in the same boat as me.

What Daddy says goes.

All his little comments, truly made for teasing purposes only, did was keep me from calling my dad for a quick fight that would end with me in a red dress, just as planned.

Which is why when seven o'clock rolls around, I'm stepping out the double doors to meet Sai.

His features are pulled tight, drawing a frown from me in return.

He gives a slow shake of his head, so I slip inside, waiting for him to take his seat behind the wheel.

He doesn't speak until we're rolling down the path toward the front gate, his eyes meeting mine in the mirror. "I don't like that he's insisting on a public dinner the day your sister

232

was thrust back into society. It's risky, and I'm to drop you off and leave."

"Why would you leave?"

Sai shakes his head, taking a left onto the long, winding road. "I didn't question him."

Right. Of course not, Father's orders, but why would he make such a demand?

"I want you to be careful, Rocklin. Watch everyone around you from the corner of your eye. You have been on the yacht, had meals with the Henshaws. If you spot men you don't recognize, tell me. He won't leave the peninsula, but you will be moving. Stay away from the edge and don't—"

"I know what to do, Sai, and my father will be there. No one will dare make a move, but thank you."

His hands tighten on the wheel as he faces forward.

After a few silent minutes, his eyes pop up several times, and finally the fourth or fifth try, I lift mine to meet his through the mirror. He doesn't waste the moment. "Can I ask you something?"

"Since when do you request permission to ask me things?" I gauge him.

"This is personal."

Curious, I sit back, nodding slightly.

"If you had a choice, and it came down to leading your family name or taking the head chancellor seat at Greyson Manor, what would you choose?"

My mouth waters instantly, a tingling sensation sweeping across my arms, goose bumps rising. I look away from his prying eyes, unable to speak the words, but my hesitation, my delay in response, is answer enough. So, when I give one, we both know that while the words leave me, it's my father's voice that's heard.

"I would do as I must, no matter what." My eyes slice up and hold his. "Like a good daughter would."

Silence stretches, understanding passing between us, though on what, it isn't completely clear. We're speaking in riddles,

233

ones that cannot be solved as the question hasn't been established. What's worrisome is Sai and his knack for anticipating trouble. Like a Doppler before a storm, he can sense when something is coming. For weeks now, he's been acting odd, leaving his post and slipping away. He's never done that and I'm not sure what to make of it. All I know is something has changed.

"Sai, tell me what you're thinking."

"I can't do that, but I can tell you this." He spins to face me, so he can look at me head-on, "You are doing exactly what I hoped you would, and without the guidance I had planned to offer."

The car door opens, and he faces forward, so I wash away my frown, accept my father's hand and climb out.

Chapter 19
Rocklin

I can count on one hand how many times I've seen my father intoxicated, drunk to the point of flushed cheeks and incessant laughter, and I wouldn't be holding a single finger in the air.

Not when he faced new threats or after the loss of soldiers.

Not even when my mother died eleven years ago today.

He would never allow himself the reprieve, never weaken for the enemy and paint himself as prey, so sitting across from him and Mr. Henshaw with Oliver at my side, I have no idea what to think.

My father is relaxed, one leg up, ankle balanced against his knee, with his arm thrown across the back of the bucket seats. The glass in his hand, his fourth of the evening, half-empty.

He's drunk outside, in the open, and with only one of his guards on board, the rest left behind on the dock with Mr. Henshaw's men, who is also accompanied by a single soldier. I've counted no less than six other faces, all staff brought on deck to serve us the over-the-top meal of caviar and roasted lamb, and all I can think about is the conversation or lack thereof, I had with Sai in the car.

I'm dumbfounded. This makes no sense.

My dad is relaxed, and yes, Mr. Henshaw is someone who has been around since I was young, though I wouldn't call him a friend. My father has none of those, not even Sai as that drifted away when Sai's allegiance shifted to me—something my father was deeply grateful for. At the end of the day, Mr.

Henshaw is a colleague at best, someone my father works with sometimes when in need of his particular forte.

Whether any of that is true or false doesn't matter, though, as either way, this is so unlike the man I know.

My sister was seen today in the open by eyes who may or may not share the news, assuming it's harmless, and we would have no idea who to blame should the word get out—*when* the word gets out. Not that anyone knows why she left in the first place, but word travels fast, especially when it comes to the man other men must seek approval from in order to cross our borders.

I've replayed a million ideas in my head and have come up empty every time, doing it all over again with each glass filled, so when Oliver holds a pipe before my lips, I part them, pulling in a long hit of hash-dusted weed.

I wait for the man across from me to scold me, to make it clear he's unhappy with my decision to alter my mind, but he glances over with nothing more than a smile, returning to his conversation a second later.

It makes no sense.

"I think our fathers are drunk," Oliver whispers.

Resisting the urge to shake my head, I take a second drag when offered before pushing his hand away. "I think you're right."

"I bet if we unloaded the Jet Skiis and hit the water right now, they wouldn't say a word or even notice." He looks my way, grinning. "Honestly, they may encourage it."

"Doubtful." I chuckle, making a point to look down at my dress. "And does it look like I am Jet Ski ready?"

"I'd be happy with whatever you have on underneath, but you already know that much."

He shifts where he sits, turning slightly, his thigh near my thigh, his arm resting on the back of the curved booth behind my shoulders, and then his fingers dare to touch my skin.

I narrow my eyes at the brazen move. "Watch yourself, Oliver. I would hate to break your trigger finger."

236

"You wouldn't because Daddy would be really upset if you did."

I face forward, lifting my glass to my lips, knowing where his focus will fall, while my left dips into the slit of my skirt. I raise and slide my blade across his finger.

He's bleeding without having seen it coming.

He jolts but bites his tongue when our fathers easily shift this way at the sudden movement.

Oliver yanks his hand back, inspecting the clean slice across his knuckles.

"You were saying?" I lift a brow, wiping his blood from the blade along my red dress. I didn't want to wear this thing anyway. It's only fair I add my favorite shade to it.

Oliver's eyes narrow, anger clear as day, but he blinks it away. "We should talk about my family's offer."

"Let's not."

"You'd be wise to accept, Rocklin."

My hackles rise and I shift, my body facing his fully. "You would be wise to remember your place before I strip it from beneath your feet, and I won't be subtle about it. Don't make us regret offering you a place and don't forget nothing is permanent."

"Go ahead, princess. Try and kick me and see how fast Daddy steps in."

My brows snap together and I open my mouth to clap back, but then our fathers approach.

"We're on our way back to the docks," mine announces, a loose smile on his face as his palm pats his stomach.

Frowning, I stare at him, but he only meets my eyes for the briefest of moments and then speaks to Mr. Henshaw once more.

Oliver's eyes slide my way, and he leans close, whispering, "We don't have to fight like this, you know. It's best to accept me on your own terms."

I "accidentally" nudge my elbow, sending my glass into his lap.

He jumps up with a curse, stomping away, and thankfully, we're docking before he comes back.

I move to stand, and Oliver rushes forward, offering me his hand that I have every intention of slapping away, but Mr. Henshaw's eyes burn into the side of my head, so I accept, allowing his heir to pull me to my feet.

My jaw clenches as I force a smile, whispering for only him to hear. "If you aren't careful, you will no longer be a member of the Greyson society."

He smiles, leaning in, his lips brushing my cheek. "If you're smart, you will accept my hand in marriage. I can protect you."

I swallow my scoff, nodding at the pair as I step off the yacht, silent as I slide into the car with Sai.

"I don't like him." He glares at the side mirror.

"That makes three of us." I recall my conversation with Dom.

Maybe it is time to reconsider his position in our society. He's always been a pushy flirt with open intentions as to what he wants from me, but he's never stepped over a line. Tonight, he jumped it. That's a problem.

On the way back to Greyson Manor, Sai doesn't speak and neither do I, leaving me at the mercy of the thoughts I succeeded in pushing away until now.

As usual, not one word was spoken about my mother at dinner, the woman we were to 'celebrate' today. It's been a long time since I've found myself sad over her death. It was so long ago. I was young, and she preferred the company of Boston over me. What mother wouldn't?

I wanted to shoot guns, throw punches, and swim for hours. Boston wanted to dance in fluffy costumes, and god forbid she ruined her nails with water.

I am my father's daughter through and through, but I loved my mom, and I know she loved me. It's almost as if the universe knew what it was doing when it gave my mother, the woman who was thought to be infertile after four years of marriage went by without a single hint of an heir on its way—the sole purpose of the bride of Rayo Revenaw, even though he did love her in his own way—two babies instead of one, one for her and one for my father, or at least that's the way I see it.

He would have left my mother if my sister and I didn't come along when we did—a man with such a legacy to leave behind couldn't possibly fall without an heir waiting to take his place at the top. It just so happens I became what he was waiting for, and Boston . . . didn't.

As we pull up to Greyson Manor, coming to a stop, Sai steps out, but rather than the right door opening for me to step out, the left one opens, and my dad slides onto the seat beside me.

He's silent for a moment, studying me with a tilt of his head. Finally, he says, "You understand that there are roles we sometimes must play, yes?"

"I understand." I eye him with curiosity and then realization. "You're not drunk." I attempt to read his blank expression but come up short. "Dad, what's going on?"

"We are being watched. By whom, the answer is not yet clear."

"Enzo's men?"

"I don't think so, no, but perhaps. I have a few trusted men looking into it, quietly, of course, but so far, nothing concrete has come back to me. We're dealing with a shadow, it seems."

I mull over his words in my head a few times, coming to a conclusion. My eyes widen, and I shift, my body facing his. "You're creating bait."

He tips his head back and forth. "Not so much bait as misconception."

"You know someone is watching, and you chose to put me on that yacht. To put us both on that yacht, right there in the open for dozens along the shore to see."

"I had men every four hundred feet, darling. I am no fool and I would have protected you with my life, but whoever it is paying such close attention to our family needs to see what I wish for them to. Weaknesses and flaws in our system that do not exist."

He's wrong. There are flaws in our system, big ones, but how can I tell him this without giving Bastian up in the process?

"Such as being on a yacht without security and allowing yourself to be intoxicated?"

239

"Precisely."

"Are you hoping someone mistakes me for Boston?"

"No." He pulls a gun from beneath his coat and wipes the handle clean with his pocket square. "What I need is to see if they're smart or easily set up for failure. If they believe us to be weak or flawed, they will come at us, and we will be ready."

He holds the weapon out, offering it to me, so I open my palm, and he sets the lightweight metal in my hands.

A small frown builds along my brow as I draw it close, a small golden Greyson crest etched into the bottom of the handle.

"It's a Staccato XL. Custom built."

I nod, admiring the work. "It's lighter than my clutch."

"I imagine it is." I look to my father, catching the slight tip of his lips.

His eyes lift to mine, dark and heavy. Suddenly he looks so tired, aged, but in a steely, strong sort of way.

Worry works its way into my veins. "Dad?"

"I cannot leave you in this world unprotected. You know this, yes?"

My pulse spikes. "I am not unprotected. That is what the Greyson society is for."

"The Greyson society is full of young, impressionable students."

"They're essentially trained soldiers."

"Who wear pleated skirts and gowns or suits purchased with their parents' money."

I say nothing, leaving the Greyson's fast-growing accounts where they belong, in the dark.

"What you're doing is a good thing, smart and beyond what I would have assumed we'd reach in strides in my lifetime, but those students will graduate. It would be foolish of you to assume the allies made today will be there for every tomorrow."

"I am no fool, Father."

He nods, watching me for a moment, and then his face is a mask once more, his spine straight, as he repeats himself, "I cannot leave you in this world unprotected."

Before I can open my mouth, he kisses my temple and climbs out, my door opening moments later, allowing me to do the same.

My steps are slow as I enter the foyer, and Jasper approaches instantly, offering to take my coat and bag, not bothering to ask for the gun hanging in my right hand. He follows behind me up the stairs. As we reach my door, he rushes ahead, opening it for me and trailing me inside.

I sit on the chaise at the end of my bed, pulling off my heels, and he returns from the closet, hands empty.

"You look just like her, you know."

My head snaps up to Jasper, finding a soft smile on his lips. "She was strong, like you. Soft. Same hair. Same eyes."

It's true. Boston and I are replicas of her, opposite of my father in every visible way.

He has dark hair and dark eyes, whereas we're blonde with green eyes.

I swallow beyond the unexpected lump in my throat. "I am not soft, Jasper," is all I can say.

Jasper winks, bowing once more. "Of course, Ms. Revenaw."

He moves for the door but pauses as he grips the handle, preparing to close me inside. "Let me know if you'd like me to prepare a few things for you. I'll be up and waiting, just in case."

My brows pull, and he walks out.

Sighing, I drop back on my bed, lifting the gun above my face and inspecting the engraving once more.

"A Staccato."

My body doesn't jolt, panic doesn't set in, and I don't point the weapon in the direction of the voice. My muscles ease, and slowly, I lower it to my chest, and then his face is in sight, hovering over mine from where he stands at the foot of my bed.

"It's a good choice. Lots of power, little weight." He presses one knee into the mattress and leans over, his giant, calloused hands planting firmly beside my head. He tips his head, taking me in, and then he whispers, "Hi."

Everything in me melts. The tension disappears, jumbled thoughts vanish.

My muscles turn to mush, and I couldn't stop the smile spreading across my lips if I tried, but I don't try.

"Hi." My voice is light and airy, and I might be embarrassed at such a girly, giddy sound if anyone else were here.

But there's not. It's just him.

No embarrassment comes, and I'm rewarded with a gentle nip of my lips, but it doesn't stop there. He dips down, taking my mouth more firmly, his tongue thrusting inside and reclaiming its place there. My hands find their way into his hair and he groans, shrugging out of his leather jacket one arm at a time. His shirt is peeled off next, and I work his jeans open, my legs falling wide as he drops between them.

"Your mind is heavy." His cock pushes at the cloth keeping the neediest part of me from him, and he shifts, using the head to nudge it aside, sliding all the way in with a single thrust. "Let's fix that."

I moan into his mouth, my legs wrapping around him, and he sits back on his knees, bringing me into his lap.

My chest smashes against his, our mouths crashing once more until he pulls back, eyes a glacier blue tonight. His legs stretch out beneath me, and I fall deeper into his lap, farther onto his length.

"Perfect fit." He groans, nose trailing along my collarbone and neck. "Slither like a snake, baby. Make your man feel good."

My lips part, my head falling back, offering him more. Everything. He digs in, his lips sucking on my skin, tongue flicking and licking as I roll my body like a worm, ass pushing back and sliding in, his cock straining against my walls, the pressure alone causing my toes to curl.

I move a little faster, still swaying the way he asked me to, and his hands find my ass, fingertips digging into the skin there. I gasp into the air, so he does it again. Harder.

He tugs my dress over my head, his giant hand wrapping around the back of my neck as he leans away a little.

242

My eyes fall to his stomach, his abs flexing from the position and I drag my nails down his skin, smiling as he shivers.

A low chuckle leaves him, and then he reaches beside us, coming back with the gun, my new gun, in his hand.

His eyes are locked on mine, holding, his movements slow as he brings it higher and higher. "Mine?" he teases, and I'm not sure if he's talking about me or the gun.

Still, I say "yours," and he groans in satisfaction.

My pulse quickens, heart pounding, but my hips keep rolling, my hand lowering, dipping between us in an awkward position, so I can grip his balls.

His chest rumbles, and then the barrel is pressed to my chest.

I jerk from the cool steel, shuddering, and he drags it lower, using it to tug my lace bra down and circle my nipples.

"Rock hard," he muses, dipping to take one between his teeth, the gun now pressed low to my stomach, and it only goes farther south as he moves to my right breast, biting, sucking.

The tip of the weapon, the muzzle where the bullet releases from, presses over my clit, circling it, and I clench around him, my palm squeezing him in my grasp, and when he starts to make small loops over it, I cry out, tearing my hand free and gripping the sides of his face.

My pace picks up, sweat beading, orgasm cresting.

"Come for me, baby," he whispers. "Come all over my cock."

"You first," I beg. "I like the way it feels right after you do."

He groans, his head flying up and then my back hits the mattress, the gun still between my legs as he pumps into me.

My muscles lock as his do and then he bites my chest hard, and I whimper, pleasure and pain meeting in the middle as his hips jerk.

He comes, his lips meeting my ear. "Okay, Rich Girl. Give it to me."

The harsh click of the gun, bullet now in the chamber, has me jolting, shaking, and when he licks my throat, I come with a loud moan, his lips spreading into a smile against my neck before he collapses at my side.

He lifts the gun into the air, licking over the tip, and in less than four seconds, he has the clip out, hammer pulled back and separated in three pieces, tossing them beside me.

I look to him, chest heaving, and he smirks.

"Just in case you got any ideas to use it on me."

Rolling my eyes, I drag myself to my side, and his knuckles come up, gliding over my breast as it falls farther from my bra. I stare at him for a minute or two, waiting for my breath to even out before speaking, but what comes out isn't what I expect.

"My mother is dead." It comes out in a rush as if delivered as a single word.

Bastian doesn't stiffen at my outburst, and no frown pulls over his brows.

He simply stares, hand coming up so his knuckles can glide along my jawline, encouraging me to say more.

"She died when I was eight. Poison, but my dad refuses to admit it was by someone else's hand." My eyes snap between his. "Want to know why?"

"Yeah, baby, I do," he murmurs, still touching. Always touching.

"Because it means someone moved against his family, that she died because she loved him. Someone probably thought it would bring him to his knees, take him away for a while so they could swoop in and sweep us out." I swallow, voice lowering. "They were wrong. He didn't even cry, at least not that I saw, but he did take time off so he could stay home with us for a while. After a few days, we started being able to sleep again, but I would always wake in the middle of the night, and he wouldn't be in the room anymore. He'd be in his study most mornings, still wearing what he did the night before. He gave up sleep and time away to be there for us, but no one ever made it past the gates if they did try. I was back here nine days after my sister found her, and eventually, it was like she never existed to begin with."

"What do you mean back here?" he wonders.

"What?"

He pulls back a little. "You said you were back here, but she died when you were eight."

My lips tug to the side, and for some reason, I move my gaze from his. "I've lived here a long time. I was only here a few weeks before she passed."

"But you like it here?"

I smile now, my tone darkening. "Yes, I love it here, but what's not to love, right?"

I fall onto my back, glancing around the space, and he drops and does the same, staring up at the crystal chandelier and beautiful crown molding.

"Pretty things don't mean shit, Rich Girl." His hand finds mine on the comforter, his fingers threading through mine. "But you know that already."

Because the good things aren't pretty, they're dark and messy and confusing and wear leather jackets.

A sharp breath races through my nostrils, and he gives a little squeeze.

My heart feels the tiny tug, and worry wrapped in *what the fuck am I doing* whirls in my head. The feeling is foreign, dangerous.

Love kills . . . not that I love him, but I might like him too much, and while this, whatever this is, might be free, it will still cost.

What if I do love him, though?

Needing a distraction, I ask, "Do you go to school?"

"When I feel like it." His lips curve, and when mine don't, he jerks a shoulder. "Missed a lot my freshman year when my dad lost his job and took it out on me, so I should have been done last year, but it doesn't matter. Took the exit exams not long after I got to Brayshaw."

"So you're a smart badass then?"

The corner of his mouth hooks up. "I am. I only go now so it doesn't raise questions. Social workers come by the group home from time to time, dropping off or picking up kids, and

245

couldn't have them wondering who I am and all that. Best everything seems in place, so I deal."

"And I imagine it's good for . . . business?"

He nods. "It's great for business. Just like a secret little club for gangsters and the mob."

Every muscle in my body stiffens and Bastian laughs, his free hand gliding over his chest. "Come on now, girl, you already knew I knew."

He's right, I did, and he's still here. Still breaking into places he shouldn't.

Still calling me his.

"My dad would kick my ass if I even thought about not showing up to my classes when I felt like it."

"He could try."

My eyes snap up to Bastian's.

He lifts a dark brow, daring me to question him, and a low laugh leaves me. His rough palm falls to the curve of my hip, tugging me closer, so I lay my head on his chest, my fingers drawing along his heated skin. "Good thing I enjoy my classes then, huh?"

"Such a good girl," he teases, his lips sliding along my temple.

"Always." I close my eyes, but as soon as my body settles, the sex haze officially fading, my mind is back on high alert. "I need to clean up."

Climbing to my feet, I lock myself inside the lavatory and quickly clean myself up, allowing my head to clear a little more as I wash my hands, gazing at myself in the mirror.

My skin is flushed, my neck and chest marked too many times to count, and I smile as I towel my hands dry. Of course the man who's marked all over would want to leave his all over me.

As I step out of the room, I find him glaring at the wall ahead, his eyes slowly moving to mine as I lift one leg, slowly sitting near his hip.

I trace the tattoo just over his left peck, a small scowl building. "You know if the Grecos let you in here, they have to be punished, right? We can't allow them to put the manor or our operations at risk, no matter the reason."

"Good thing they didn't then, huh?" His tone is detached, but I keep my attention on his body.

"No?"

His gaze burns into my cheek. "Nope."

"Then how?"

"Doesn't matter."

My hand stills at his words and curt response, my eyes snapping up to meet his. "Yes, it does. Did they let you in or not?"

His eyes narrow, searching. "No one let me in, Rich Girl."

"This isn't a game, Bastian." I shake my head, my father's words from earlier filling my ear. "If security is at risk here, I need to know."

"I told you I would come to you, and I did." He studies me for a long moment. "What aren't you telling me?"

"I asked you a question first."

"Rich Girl."

"Don't."

"*Rocklin*," he barks.

I attempt to yank away, but his grip tightens.

I draw my legs up as if to kick off him, and he shifts to wrap me up, as I knew he would, so before he's able to flatten, I spin. My bedside dagger is in my hand, my arm flinging around and coming straight to his neck as he flips us, putting him back on top, but I press my ankles into his shoulder blades. When he tucks the slightest bit, I flip him.

Bastian has my shoulders in his grip, his ankles now locked behind my back.

"Tell me how you got in." I hold the blade firm, my thumb pressed to the dual sides.

He stretches up, pressing farther into the blade, and I hold still, calling his bluff, but he keeps coming, and red droplets appear, slowly running over the side of his neck.

"I told you not to hide from me," he speaks through clenched teeth.

"*How* did you get in?"

"Don't worry about it. No one else will."

"Bastian! This isn't a bad boys' club. This is real-life shit here. We don't beat people up in a ring as punishment!"

The moment I say it, I want to take it back, but I know that I can't, and now it's out there. It's not exactly what I meant . . .

Okay, honestly, it's exactly what I meant, but I wasn't aiming to insult him; I don't *want* to insult him. I'm making the situation clear because I must. Things are different here.

A gap in security is a potential loss of life. Probably mine.

Unless it was my father's doing?

Did he lower security here too, as another fake show of weakness?

No. He wouldn't put me at real risk like that.

Right?

"That right?" he rasps, his expression clear as he pops up on his elbow, hand wrapping around my wrist and pressing at my pressure point. The bloody blade falls beside us and he drags his fingers higher until they link with mine from behind.

"You peel their nails from their fingertips?" He drags my hand across his left pec, right over a burning phoenix, a small groove hidden under it. "Cut the tips off their nipples?" My skin meets a harsh dark line, a jagged heartbeat along his shoulder blade, a long slash pebbled against my touch. "Maybe a tongue?" We're tracing his throat now, random size welt-like scars decorated with the Eye of Horus. "A limb?"

We trail his breastbone, and I tear my hand away, glaring at him. "I get it."

"I don't think you do." His tone is impatient, disapproving. Bastian quickly flips me, crawling over me and stretching high on all fours above me, the blood from the new cut on his skin threatening to drip onto me. "Your security is airtight. If it wasn't, I would be the first to fucking say it, got me?" he hisses, continuing without a breath. "I told you. You. Are. Mine. I might seem tame to you but don't fucking test me, baby, 'cause I'm on a leash right now, same as you. The difference is mine can be cut, and I'll let you in on a little secret, my little secret keeper. I've already got the knife picked out." His eyes flash. "But know this. No one will keep me away. I'm invisible. Told you that too. No one sees me coming until it's too late. Not even you."

He jumps up, his shit in his hands, my new gun in the other, back flexing in all its tattooed glory as he walks straight out my bedroom door.

"What does that even mean?"

His head snaps over his shoulder, eyes cold and daring. "Fuck around and find out."

And then he's gone.

I throw myself back on the bed, a low growl leaving me as I punch my fist against the mattress. My phone vibrates a moment later and I pick it up, quicker than I'd like to admit, ready to read whatever words he decided to send, but it's not from him.

It's from Oliver.

"What the hell does he want?"

I open the thread, finding three messages rather than one.

Oliver Henshaw: I can't stop thinking about the dress you wore tonight.

Oliver: Red looks good on you, and it would look better with me on your arm, so be sure to keep your little tat-tooed toy away from now on, sweet Rocklin.

Oliver Henshaw: I want you in the same color at the gala.

"Ugh." My face scrunches in disgust and I toss my phone to the side. "Is he fucking serious?"

He's out of his damn mind if he thinks I'll be going with him, and if my dad made such a promise, that mistake is on him.

There is no way in hell I will be putting myself on his arm on a night like that. Everyone who is anyone in our world will be there, every member of the dynasty and all allied gangs and Mafia families.

249

And to boldly speak about Bastian like that? I should have his fucking tongue for even thinking he could drop threats on me. His attempt at subtle playfulness was a huge failure.

That was no less than a warning from a boy afraid of his own father.

Why Oliver Henshaw assumes he has a chance with me and that he's somehow an exception to the rules here, I don't know, but I will find out.

Chapter 20
Rocklin

Ms. Milano's soft knock has me turning from the gaping window with an audible sigh just as Bronx invites her in.

She smiles, her wrinkles deepening as she does, a true gentleness in her gaze not many in this world hold—probably because she's on the outside of it. "Students have arrived."

"Thank you, Ms. Milano." Delta floats to her feet, facing me, worry in her gaze as it meets mine, though she doesn't pry, being I've yet to offer my thoughts to my best friends. "Ready?"

"Always," I deadpan, tracing my fingers along the folded cashmere around my neck as I round the desk, following the girls out the door.

Today is one of the few I dread at Greyson Elite when we're forced to open our doors for potential students, only one or two of them having the slightest chance of securing a spot in a few short months when invitations go out. It's yet another way to appease the masses and curb the minds of those curious about the private academy tucked away at the highest peak of the valley hills.

The shooting range is obviously disguised today, as is the detonation room—last thing we need is someone to ask why we teach our students how to create and defuse explosives.

The double doors are opened as we reach the entrance, and as one, Delta, Bronx, and I ease out onto the brick steps to find the eager, wide-eyed group waiting.

Their attention moves to us immediately, gazes raking over each of us, from our crisp blazers to the matching pastel-pink pleated skirts. Their attention snaps over our shoulders and I know Damiano and Alto have joined us, the boys wearing our black-and-blue uniform option today.

I take a step forward, and all eyes fall on me.

I smile bright, big and fake and exhausted as I hold my hands out. "Welcome to—"

The door to the giant charter bus opens once more, my gaze lifting, locking onto a pair of icy gray ones, and my words freeze on the tip of my tongue.

No . . .

All heads turn, and he takes one step, then another, and I swear the group below parts for him to slip through, to push forward. He doesn't stop but keeps coming until the tips of his tattered shoes are pressed to the brick.

Eyes locked on mine, he cocks his head. "You were saying?"

Fuck.

Bass

"My, my, the color shock paints your skin is a pretty sort of pink," I whisper in her ear. "One might even call it . . . *red*."

Rocklin shoots me a glance over her shoulder, promising her deepest wrath, and I, for one, am looking forward to it.

It doesn't take her long to come out of her little moment of surprise. She recovers quickly enough, but the smile she pastes on is even faker than the first one.

She's pissed.

That makes two of us.

Damiano's eyes snag mine as he turns, one hand behind his back, the other ushering a group of giddy girls through the double doors leading into the fancy-ass building. Just before I can slide on through, his body shifts, now facing mine.

I step in closer, bringing me and Pretty Boy toe to fucking toe. "Go on. Your chivalry means shit to me."

High blond brows dip, nostrils flaring. "I don't know what you think you're doing here, but this is not a place for any more of your games."

"Didn't Rocklin tell you, pretty boy?" My chin dips. "This is no game."

"You cannot be here."

"I am. What are you gonna do about it?"

His jaw flexes, that little pulse line running through it tic, tic, ticing away and a slow smirk grows across my face.

"Yeah." I nod, shouldering past him. "That's what I fuckin' thought."

The dude isn't scared of me yet, so I know he'd come at me

253

if we were anywhere but on the front steps of their precious little rich prick academy.

"This place looks like it was built for the queen," Chloe, the contract girl the Grecos mentioned and a chick from my hometown, mutters as she falls in line beside me.

"Maybe it was." I look around from one golden beam to the next. "Bet they think real high of themselves here. Higher than you think of yourself, in fact."

Chloe scoffs a low laugh, and what do you know, Rocklin's head snaps around, eyes tightening as she sets hers on the brunette at my side.

My cock twitches at the sight of her not-so-well-hidden glare.

"Suddenly it all makes sense," Chloe whispers, lifting her chin as if to appear half as superior as all the eyes roaming over our little tour group seem to believe they are.

"What does?"

"Why you blackmailed me into getting you on the tour."

"If you didn't want people to know how much you liked sucking dick, maybe don't get on your knees so much."

She whips her body toward mine, hissing. "You came onto me!"

"Never said I didn't." I was a dumbass last year when it came to women.

She huffs, shakes her head and moves as far away from me as she can.

Thank fucking god.

She and I were a twenty-minute drunken night of fun we both pretended never happened . . . until those brothers dropped her name and I knew I'd need to call on her at some point.

Rich bitches will do about anything to hide their dirty little secrets from the rest of the world. Including wearing a fucking full-on bodysuit that covers every inch of one's throat.

My attention zeroes in on Rocklin, but I don't have to wait for hers.

I've already got it, but the second Chloe steps away, she focuses forward once more.

The girls take turns, spitting out lines straight from the brochure and adding some background bullshit to make it all sound pretty, knowing damn well that all these wannabe crew members are eating up are the perfect plastic people all around.

It's like a walking, talking wax museum in this bitch.

My girl isn't playing, it's privileged perfection all around. "Boring, right?"

My thoughts are mirrored when the porcelain princess slows to walk beside me, the two of us trailing the group now, her white harried boy toy keeping one eye on her from where he walks five feet away.

"Nah, it's just my style."

"Sure, it is." Delta smiles, looping her arm into mine, and my eyes slide her way. She winks and leans a little closer, pausing a few feet back from the group as Rocklin goes into some speech of founders and whatnot. "Let me give you the real tour." She speaks low, turning us the slightest bit. "The brunette by the wall, she's the daughter of a crooked congressman, and see the guy across from her? His father is the underboss of the eastern Chicago district. He's only here because his daddy wants him to spy on her, report back with all sorts of naughty details to help get the backing he needs to move product in the city. But he'll be sure to leave out how he feels the need to run off every guy who has tried to get with her." She turns us to the left.

"Over here, it gets really interesting," she whispers. "See the dark-haired guy leaning on the wall with his arms crossed? His father . . . well, eliminated the father of the guy beside him. They act like they're best friends but must be planning vengeance on one another, each secretly pretending that is not the case. Then there's the orange-haired girl with the big lips. She's a royal, the actual crown-wearing kind, and the guy holding her hand is the son of a duchess. They were betrothed at birth, supposed to marry after graduation." She lifts her chin, so I lower mine, giving her my ear. "Little does she know, he's sneaking into her brother's room at night."

My brows jump and I pull back, looking at her.

"Why you sound so excited by all that?"

"Forbidden love, a sexual scandal, and a murder plot leading to the potential fall of a powerful empire that, in turn, creates openings for someone else to step in as the white knight? Gee, I haven't the faintest idea." Her smile is too damn wide.

"You girls are twisted."

"Hmm." She hums in agreement as she glances around. "That's not the worst of it. All of the staff are banned beings."

"Say what now?"

I follow her attention to the back corner of the room, where a woman wipes down already shiny as fuck photos on the wall, then to a man wearing a tool belt and carrying a drill as he hustles, eyes on the floor, down the hall. "Exiled people, scummy and disloyal and unwelcome where they come from. They're dropped here. Transported in and out on a bus each day, dropped back into their jail cell of an apartment each night. Wash and repeat."

Unease works its way into me, and I shake my head, eyes tailing the man as he disappears into a door marked Staff Only. "That's dumb as fuck, having people like that around you."

"It's punishment. They can't look or speak to any of us. Eat only what they're allowed, and they don't get paid. Besides, they're not hard-timers, just ignorant people who made the wrong choice or stayed quiet when they shouldn't have. The woman against the wall is the sister of a Mafia wife, and she knew the wife hired someone to kill her secret lover, a man who worked for her husband. The husband found out . . . *dealt with* the wife and lover and spared her." The woman climbs off the step stool, moving it to the next image.

Okay, that changes things, but still. "Isn't that mercy?"

"No. It's a message to everyone else. Why do you think they're here now? So you and everyone else can see what the

256

future holds for those who make poor decisions or sit on things they shouldn't. Most places have cleanup crews come in after hours. Ours are only here when we are. It's more humiliating this way, depending on their task of the day, anyway."

Can't argue with that.

"Every soul in this place has a reason or ulterior motive for being here, some worse than others, but they have one nonetheless." Finally, she releases my arm, facing me fully. "What's yours?"

"If you're asking me if I came here today for a reason, the answer is yes."

"That's not exactly what I asked."

"Isn't it?"

She studies me, dropping her head onto her man's—one of her men—shoulder when he steps up behind her, pressing into her back. "You're here to make a point."

I say nothing and she smiles, whispering, "It better be a big one."

"Don't encourage him any more than I'm sure he already is," the guy, I forget his name, tells her before offering me a hand. "I know we met briefly, but again, I'm Alto."

The dude is pretty, which is kind of odd to think, but it's what he is, like some sort of preppy version of a mortal combat doll. "Bass."

"I'm sure telling you this will make no difference, but I'm going to anyway. This isn't the place for bold moves. Think of this campus as you would a moving train. If one cart comes loose, the whole thing derails, but the crash wouldn't be the biggest threat. The cleanup crew would."

"Where I come from, I am the cleanup crew."

Alto smirks, steering his woman away. "I believe it."

I want to say I don't need you to, don't care if you do, but no point in making an enemy I don't need. Out of the corner of my eye, I catch something I do not expect. At all.

Not even a little fucking bit, and to be real, I'm almost kind of mad about it.

I spot a girl leaning against the door, staring right at me. Her skirt is shorter than everyone else's and her headband stands out in her blue-and-black uniform. She tips her head, and my eyes narrow as do hers, a curious glint in her green eyes.

But it's the wrong shade of green, as is the blonde, not to mention shorter.

Her gaze starts at the top of my head and works its way down, slowly rising to meet mine once more.

"That is a snake you don't want to let too close. If she doesn't bite, the more poisonous one will," Delta warns.

"The sister."

"The *twin*," she says, and I'm not sure if she's correcting me or simply stating, because yeah, she's my girl's mirror, only less than, at least in my eyes.

A fucking twin.

"Boston Revenaw," she continues. "Secretly engaged to a big bad man, yet here she is."

My eyes narrow. So she ran back home.

"What's the damage?"

Delta chuckles darkly. "Catastrophic."

"Enough," Ander murmurs, steering her away.

I stare at the girl, and across her face, a slow smirk starts. She shakes her head, taking a half step forward, but freezes in place when a pretty, shinier blonde slips in front of me, attempting to block me from view.

The sister laughs, turns, and walks away.

Mine spins once she's gone, teeth clenched and eyes full of wrath.

She opens her mouth to speak, but I cut her off.

"You didn't tell me the bitchy sister fucked over a deal or that you had a fucking twin. So much makes sense now."

She scoffs in pissy awe. "Do not even start. Follow me," she forces past clenched teeth. "Now."

Maybe before, if only for a minute, but now? I'm doubly mad.

"I think I'll stay with the group. We're headed for the archery room next, right?"

Her face falls, her hand coming up, but before it latches on to me, she thinks better of it, lowering it back to her side.

I don't like that and she knows it, her lips pursing.

"You are supposed to be a ghost, remember?" she whispers, almost pleading. "Don't do anything stupid that makes you a real one."

Rage bubbles beneath my skin, clawing and scratching its way to the surface, but her eyes. There's fear, something I've never seen on her before, and now all I want to do is take it away.

I want her to fear me in a lot of ways, none of which would hurt a single hair on her perfect little head, but fear me nonetheless. What I don't want is for her to fear anyone else and I sure as fuck don't want her afraid *for* me.

I step in close, and while she tenses a tiny bit, she doesn't move away. My fingers itch to trace along her skin, to erase the worry lines deepening the corners of her eyes, but I don't. I don't know why, but I don't. "Ain't nobody going to hurt me, Rich Girl."

"I told you," she whispers. "This is real-life shit here. There is no forgiveness, no looking the other way. If you want something, I know you are going to get it, but I need you to get it somewhere else."

Her brows lift the slightest bit, and she stares into my eyes. So she knows what I'm here for and what I want, realizing now that I saw that rich prick's message to her last night, but she's asking me to wait. I'm not a patient man. When it comes to her, I don't know that I ever will be, but this isn't about that.

This is worry and concern from a girl for her man. There might be a lot of things that I can't do for her yet, but I can do this. Not that she deserves it.

I push closer, and I keep going, forcing her to shuffle back, little by little, until her shoulder blades reach the locker and I'm caging her in, in a tiny little alcove in the hall, the group now four steps ahead.

"I'm here when you don't think I am, I see when you don't think I can, and that ain't gonna stop. But there are times when my back has to be turned and it just so happens last night was one of them." Reaching up, I run the back of my finger from the edge of her jaw down to her chin, then right beneath it. "Let me find out he touched you and you didn't tell me, and stirring things up at your little school will be the last of your problems. His too."

Her jaw flexes defiantly, and she lifts her chin a bit. "It's not me I'm worried about."

"Oh, believe me, I know." Leaning in, I bring my lips to her ear, flicking my tongue along the lobe. "That is the only reason you'll be getting what you want today, but if you think you're getting off that easy, baby, you haven't been paying attention."

Gripping her shoulders, I whip her around before she has time to stop me, and she never sees the blade in my hand. I cut it straight across her chest, gripping the fabric in my palms and twisting before slicing the left side and then the right until the soft material droops in my hand.

She gasps, spinning around, her hand flying to her chest, her turtleneck now cut into a deep *U*.

Heat builds in my groin as my eyes lock on my marks across her skin, one, two, three, four, too many to count. Hickeys and teeth marks and tiny little scratches, all left behind by me in moments where she begged, moaning and writhing beneath me, my dick buried deep inside a body that belongs to me.

Her eyes flash, looking like my own little cheetah, and she's even got the claws out, cheeks growing red with anger, those little hands making fists at her side. She opens her mouth to speak, but I shake my head, and what do you know, she snaps it right shut.

"Go on, Rich Girl. People are waiting for you, and I, for one, am *dying* to meet this nationally recognized archery team."

She knows what I mean. She will show proof of me on her skin, or I'll filet that heir's right off. Today. Now. In this very school.

And she can't claim the dress code shit on me. I saw shirts some of the other preps were wearing under their jackets. Rocklin's cleavage isn't even showing, just her marked-up chest, neck, and throat, but so what? She and all the girls wear kink clothes to that gambling room, so it's not like Little Miss Perfect has to pretend to be the Virgin Mary. No, her covering them up is her preference. Well, too fucking bad, 'cause showing them off is mine.

Jaw clenched, she shakes her head, but I swear I detect a hint of humor hidden in those pretty green eyes. She steps closer, voice a raspy little whisper when she says, "Behave, Bastian."

"Yes, mama."

This time *I know* I see a bit of laughter, but I don't call her out on it.

I follow behind like a good fucking boy.

Oliver Henshaw.

Tall. Tan. Brown hair, blue eyes, and basic as fuck.

Son of Otto Henshaw, American businessman and entrepreneur, twice accused of usury and illegal immigration trafficking. Twice cleared of all charges.

The article I found on him said he calls himself a philanthropist, and it makes sense. Throw your money all around so people praise you for your efforts, and just maybe, if you "donate" to the right cause, it'll help you out. He sure as fuck lucked out after the green-thumbed DEA, who picked up his last case, was found tied up and tongueless on Treasure Island last summer, some kind of plant killer thick in his bloodstream . . . or so the internet says.

I imagine his work in the world they live in is much different than what court records state.

His son, though, has made no waves. He's nothing but a boy in the background, but maybe that's why he's here. Maybe . . . that's why he's chasing what has already been caught.

I track his every move as he laughs and bumps his elbow into Delta's second man's arm, but the guy doesn't join in, his jaw clenches, and he looks away. Not that this pompous fool notices. He just turns to the next dude, but as our group makes their way in, his attention snaps to the doorway.

He's yet to spot me, but I keep him in my peripheral as I curve along at the back of the group, coming around the long way. He searches and searches, and then he finds his target.

He stands tall, a smirk pulling at his lips when he sees her.

Rocklin reaches the head of the group, and that chin of hers is held oh so fucking high. Too high, in fact, even for the queen bee.

My brows pull slightly, but then I see it. The quick flick of her eyes toward the brunette at the front of the pack, to Chloe.

My teeth sink into my bottom lip, satisfaction building in my gut.

Jealous, baby?

Show her them love bites . . .

Oliver's attention falls to her exposed skin, and man, don't I wish I was recording. His face falls so fast it's comical, and the dude is far from being as well trained as the rest of these people are.

He can't hide the frown that follows, and he can't take his eyes off her, but that's enough looking for him.

I come around the front, standing at the edge of the group here for a demonstration. They face forward, I face him, and it only takes him ten seconds to realize it.

His eyes widen in surprise, brows snapping together a second later and then, finally, the anger comes. His teeth clench tight, but when I cock my head, my face a mask of fucking calm when it feels like I'm about to hulk the fuck out, he makes a wise choice.

He looks away, turns away, and then he walks away, but not far. He stays in the room but tucks himself in the back corner, where the weapons are hung over giant racks, pretending to busy himself while he tries to figure out what the fuck I'm doing here as if it's not a blinding light blinking in the back of his mind. At least it should be.

Ander steps forward, bow in one hand, arrow in the other, and starts going over some basics. He gives a few demonstrations, adding in some jokes that have all the girls giggling, and Delta takes a possessive step forward in response.

Then he looks around the room. "Does anyone want to give it a shot?"

Some dude with a man bun and a Rolex steps up, firing the thing off with ease. "My boarding school has a team. I'm captain." Big Boy's chest puffs out, but Ander doesn't acknowledge his unwanted information.

Next, a couple of girls give it a shot, probably only hoping he'll step up behind them and help them out, but he doesn't. When the third one does the same thing, he takes the bow from her hand and jerks his chin toward us. "Next time, pay attention. Do not waste my time. Anyone else?"

I step forward and he lifts a single brow, eyes flicking to his left, where Rocklin stands, stiff and straight.

He holds the bow out for me to take, but I stride right by the guy, meeting Rocklin's gaze for a quick second, long enough for me to read the panicked warning she throws at me. I step straight up to the equipment holder in the back corner, eyes on little Oliver the entire time as I blindly choose a weapon and lift it off the steel stick it hangs from. I grab the arrow next, noting the few steps closer both Rocklin and Damiano have taken in my peripheral.

I check the ties as Ander said to, inspecting the arrow as he instructed, and load it exactly as he taught. Oliver stands taller, shuffling from one foot to the next, and I twist my upper body, looking over my shoulder at Ander as I pull back on the nock. "Which target?"

He smirks, eyes narrowed knowingly. "Hit the one you want."

I nod, turning my body, and with the arrow still pointed toward the ground in the waiting position, I let it fly.

"Fuck!" Pretty Boy shouts instantly and gasps fill the room like music to my fucking ears.

We're not at some weak-ass school where people come rushing to his aid to make sure he's okay. Well, a couple of the girls on the tour do take a few steps forward but pause when they realize no one else has.

Angry blue eyes flash to mine, face tight with pain. "You shot my fucking foot!"

"My bad," I say a little loudly, bending swiftly before he can, gripping the wood near the tip.

"Wait, no!" he pants, but it's too late.

I'm already yanking the quartz from his flesh, but not before giving it a quick twist no one can see. Like a little bitch, he grunts, unable to cover his pain, and still bent, my eyes flick up to his. They hold as I slowly rise to my feet, the bloodied arrow now lifted between our faces. "Thought you liked the color red."

His lip curls but flattens oh so fast as some of the color drains from his face. The arrow falls between us, hitting the floor with a soft clank, and I turn to the group as I hang the bow back where it belongs.

Yeah, motherfucker. I know.

Try me . . .

I walk on back, this time placing myself in the crowd at Rocklin's side.

I fight a smirk and say, "Should have been more careful."

Bronx covers a laugh with a cough and Ander openly grins from me to Rocklin.

The archery room pit stop ends there, and the tour moves on to the next, the three chancellors in training taking the lead, but I'm blocked from my exit when Damiano places himself in my way.

His eyes narrow, searching, and I stand tall, lifting a black brow. The dude doesn't like me, I know this. I've taken his toy and rich people like him aren't much for sharing, but that toy was made to be mine. I know it. She knows it.

He will know it too, if he doesn't yet.

I expect him to feed me some line about not the place or the time or to serve me a reminder I don't belong in these halls, a fact I know as much as he does, so color me curious when instead, he dips his chin and says, "I'm watching him, too."

He doesn't explain, doesn't offer a single thing else, he just walks away, and as I go to follow, my eyes spot something shiny on the wall. A giant, blinking banner, the fancy imprinted kind held in place by what I'm sure are white gold clips.

The Greyson Gala, it reads, next Saturday at eight p.m.

Interesting.

I follow along the crowd, my mind spinning, and two uneventful hours later, we're loaded on the bus, ready to head back to where we came from.

Never did I feel the difference between me and my rich girl more than I do right now, seated on stained bus seats, surrounded by people I know will never call the walls within these giant gates home but are leaving here today wishing they would.

Praying all their hard work pays off and the school sees their perfect GPA for what it's worth.

They won't.

No, you don't get into the Greyson Elite Scholar program unless your daddy has something someone else can gain from.

The only thing gainable from the man who shared my blood was freedom, but not even my rich girl has that.

My eyes find hers as she stands on the brick steps, her privileged posse at her sides.

Invisible leash around her fucking neck.

I'm gonna find the lock fastening it to her and cut that bitch at the bone.

Free her, and then I'm gonna add my own.

It's another two hours before we're pulling into town, and I pop up, moving down the aisle until I'm dropping beside Chloe on the bench seat.

She huffs, tugging her earbuds from her ears. "Can I help you?"

"I need one more thing."

"You said to get you on this bus. We're even."

"One more thing."

She eyes me, her curiosity far too potent to say no. "What is it?"

Frowning, I face forward, forcing the words from my lips.

Chloe laughs, her hand coming up to cover it, but when my head is slow to turn, eyes meeting hers, the humor slowly fades. Her brows jump into her hairline. "You're serious."

Again, I say nothing.

She tips her head, gauging me. "Okay. Sure, but purely out of morbid curiosity, and you can't tell anyone."

As if I fucking would.

The bus pulls into the parking lot, and I'm the first to jump up when the doors open.

I look to her. "Tomorrow."

She nods. "I'll call you."

I feel like a little bitch waiting for my phone to ring.

Chapter 21
Bass

"Where are we?" Rocklin looks around, nothing in our line of sight but a tagged-up fence and a row of overflowing dumpsters.

"This is the south side of town." I keep heading down the rock alleyway, taking a sharp right into the parking lot just before the end. The line of concrete cubes is as good as empty this time of day, so I pick the one at the farthest end, roll into it, and kill the engine.

She frowns at the cement walls, leaning forward to look at the hook bolted there, and follows the stretch of the hose. She glances behind us, then back to me with a raised brow.

I simply stare at her, my little blonde badass. I watched her shoot this morning, forty-five rounds, only a single missed target, and even it was by less than an inch.

She looks wrong in this car.

It's too old, too dirty, and too beat down, unworthy of her presence.

Just like I am . . .

"Bastian," she says quietly, and I snap out of it, finding a soft smile on her lips.

"What, Rich Girl's never been to a car wash before?"

Her head tugs back and she looks around again. ". . . car wash?"

"Yeah, car wash." I dig around in the center cup holder, pulling out some change and she frowns, following me as I climb out.

Arms folded across her chest, she steps near the hood, glancing around, spotting a couple chain fast-food joints and a liquor store.

I put the coins in and the old thing rumbles. I give it a little squeeze and water shoots out.

She swiftly looks my way, eyes comically moving from me to the hose and then the car. "So you're just going to . . . wash your car?"

Taking the soap sprayer in my free hand, I let it loose over the driver's side and the hood, and she lifts one foot as if some splashes her way. "So you've never been to a car wash, then?"

She pulls her lips between her teeth and a low chuckle leaves me.

"Go on, say it," I tease.

With a playful roll of her eyes, she says, "My car is always clean."

"So someone washes it for you."

She stares off a moment as if she has to think about it and then lifts a shoulder.

It's an honest answer. She has no clue 'cause when she needs it . . . it's always ready and waiting for her.

I cock my head, spraying the hood once, then again, a little harder.

Her eyes narrow, and I grin.

Her hands shoot out and now I'm laughing 'cause my girl knows what's comin'.

"Bastian . . . no. Don't even—" She squeals, arms flying up, mouth forming a pretty little *o* as I spray her from head to toe. She freezes for a solid three seconds, but she doesn't get mad. Doesn't whine or throw a fit, doesn't complain that I ruined her perfect curls.

Nah, she rushes me, wrestling for the hose, but then discovers the second one and now I'm the one who jerks.

"That one's for tires!" I warn, taking backward steps.

She tests the trigger, getting a feel for its weight, so she can calculate the trajectory, like a true sharpshooter.

268

"So what you're saying is it might hurt?" she teases, but before I can respond, the jet is aimed at me, and she doesn't go easy, spraying in a long, hard, steady stream. A full fucking blast.

I drop to my stomach on the wet ground, drenching her legs from under the car and she hops on the hood, heels and all, tugging herself forward, and when I look up, her smiling, wet face is right above me.

"First rule of combat, recognize your opponent's strengths and weaknesses and spoiler alert . . . I don't have any." She blasts me in the mouth, and I run away, laughing as the water beats against my skull, and drop my water weapon.

I jump up, spinning, and stretch beyond her, tugging the end of the hose that's buried beneath her body. It spins her, and she yelps, trying to hold on, but the slippery surface won't allow it, so she flips onto her back, nozzle pointed my way in a playful warning.

But I tug on her ankle, drawing her closer, and pry it from her grip. She slips forward, catching herself with her hands on my shoulders as she laughs, long and loud, her head falling back and I wrap my arms around her lower back, her heels propped up on the tire.

My eyes are glued to the girl, fucking fused to her, and slowly, her laughter fades as she looks up, a few straggling chuckles following.

She licks her lips with a smile, her hands grabbing on to my soaked jacket for a loose hold.

Her hair's a sloppy mess. Gone are the perfectly laid waves and little bits of black are smeared beneath her eyes. Her uniform is dripping and sticking to her skin, one knee-high sock halfway down, while the other holds strong. Silky wet strands stick to her cheek and lips, but she doesn't seem to mind, if she even notices them at all.

Like me, her entire attention is focused on the person in front of her, on me, and it's a new kind of fucking feeling, one that leaves me with a primal pull toward her, but the tug comes from deep in my chest.

My head tips slightly, left hand coming up so my knuckle can push her blonde hair from her face and forehead, curving along her temple until I can tuck the small tangles behind her ear, the pad of my thumb blindly brushing over the shiny diamond sittin' pretty there.

My touch travels down her jawline, skating lightly along her skin. My eyes find her lips, and I trace the fullness of them before sinking my hand deep in her hair. My need for her is insatiable. Been that way since the first day, as dumb as that sounds.

"Such a pretty little thief . . . stealing my time, my thoughts . . . my fantasies . . ."

She tugs me closer, eyes changing shade, the green deepening, wild and anxious, a little heavy, like a tropical rainstorm.

"Pretty, hmm?" she rasps just to have something to say.

My full attention, without the playfulness she loves, is too much for her right now 'cause my little gold medal diver didn't choose to make this move. She didn't climb a ladder prepared to send herself sailing down. No, my girl didn't have a say, and here she is, free-falling right into my filthy fucking arms.

Into that black, torn organ I'm shocked still beats in my chest.

"Beautiful. Gorgeous. Fucking stunning."

Look at that, a blush . . .

"Compared to what?" Her arms loop around my middle, head dipped back to keep those eyes on mine.

"Nothing," I answer instantly. "No one. You're in a league of your own, ma. A fucking beacon, bright and blinding, and mine."

She pinches her lips together to keep from smiling, but it breaks free regardless.

I lean forward, forcing her to drop back against the soapy hood. "You mine, baby?"

My lips hover over hers, her palms sliding under my shirt. "It doesn't seem I have a choice."

"You don't."

Her eyes flick back and forth between my own, and slowly, she nods.

"Say it."

Her tongue comes out to play, flicking my lip ring before tugging it between her lips for a sweet little tug and releasing it with a slow pop. "Yes, Bastian. I am yours."

"Good," I whisper. "Now show me."

Her eyes bulge, desire flares with her surprise, her need, and like I thought she might, she morphs right before me. The wildfire in her gaze, now a pot of molten lava that must be stirred, the possessive grip around my body nothing more than a feeble feathering touch, and then those teeth sink into her puffy bottom lip.

My girl waits for instruction. Waits to be bossed around by her favorite dictator.

By the only one she's ever chosen 'cause while she might not have made the conscious decision to fall for the punk that is me, she does choose this.

"Belt," I snap.

Her hands fly between us so fast my dick jumps with excitement, and the soft clink sounds seconds later. Her eyes fly to mine, waiting for what I want next.

"All the way off."

She tugs it free.

"Drop it."

She does.

"Take me out, nice and slow."

Her breath shakes, her body trembling as she follows my instructions.

A car door slams somewhere around us, but she doesn't look and neither do I.

The heat of her palm has my balls drawing up tight when she wraps her long fingers around my shaft.

Gripping her ass, I tug her to the very edge of the hood, heels still dug into the tire, and flip the front of her skirt up.

Her thick swimmer thighs press against mine, barricading us in our own little bubble.

Neon-green panties this time, little pink hearts trailing down the center, my knuckle tracing the path. I move them aside, and she whimpers as I stare down at her needy cunt. "You're wet."

I press my knuckles between her folds, sliding up and down, back up and then all the way down, nudging at the tight ring there. She gasps, her hips lifting greedily.

"You want me here?" I add the lightest pressure and her lips part with her nod. Groaning, I move my hand, squeezing her thighs. "That's too bad, baby, 'cause your pussy needs me right now." Without warning, I dip two fingers inside her, swiftly pulling them out as she tries to lock me inside. "Look how much she's crying, begging me to fuck her." I lift my glossy fingers between us, separating them into a *V* as I grip the back of her neck and haul her up by it, her eyes begging for more.

I dip my chin, open my mouth, and she knows what to do.

She mimics my movement, slowly, just in case—wouldn't want to do something she wasn't supposed to, my good fucking girl.

Slowly, I cover my pointer finger with my mouth, hers in perfect sync, doing the same with my middle, and when I close my lips around the base of it, she does the same. Her nostrils flare at the taste of me covered in her, and as I drag my mouth back, sucking my finger clean, she does the same, a small cry escaping her as she frees the tip.

"Please," she whispers. "Please," she begs, shuddering in my arms, and I've barely fucking touched her.

"Lead my cock home, my little thief."

Her hands fumble a few times, her need peaked, her body desperate to feel me sink inside, and she doesn't have to wait long.

Her throat bobs against my palm and I lick her cheek, hissing as she covers me in silken heat.

"Fuck, you feel so good. Already squeezing." I rock into her, pumping slowly. "Such a good little slut your cunt is."

She moans loudly, and my free hand comes up to cover her mouth, a dark brow rising as I use my grip on her neck to lay her back flat on the hood.

My thrusts are slow fucking torture, but the toe-curling kind. I pump and pump.

"There're people all around. Can't let them hear my girl." Pushing her skirt up a little more, I smack at the side of her ass. It's light, but the slapping sound has her back arching.

She looks so fucking good like this.

I cover her ass cheeks once more, gripping her hips as I drive into her faster, our clothes hiding the fact that we're fucking right here in broad daylight, even if the way she's positioned suggests we are.

"I want to rip your shirt apart. Shake those tits free, my tits, and watch 'em bounce. I want em' in my mouth, between my teeth."

Her muffled cry heats my palm, and I spread my fingers a little, her tongue poking through, fucking my hand like it's my mouth.

Her eyes close, her pussy pulsing.

"Yeah, you like that idea, don't you? I might bite you, too. Make you bleed for me, but only a little."

More whimpers, and she's close.

Thank fuck, 'cause so am I.

Reaching between us, my eyes quickly click around, just in case.

My cock takes control then, and I pull out, damn near to the tip and slam back in, over and over, her body bouncing on the hood, slipping and sliding, sweat mixing with the water dripping from our skin, soap bubbling up beneath her hair.

"Give me what I earned, baby. Take what's yours."

I yank her up, pushing in deep, and she grinds down onto me, her moan loud and shrill, so I bury her head in my neck, groaning when her teeth sink into my shoulder.

She pierces flesh and I jerk, hissing, spilling deep inside her.

We stay like that, connected, looking like nothing more than a close hug to anyone watching.

273

I run my hands through her tangled hair, smoothing it as best I can, waiting for our labored breathing to calm.

Slowly, her head rises, eyes dazed as they meet mine, and then she grins, showing off the hint of red coloring the tips of her teeth.

A low chuckle leaves me, and I kiss the corner of her mouth. "My submissive little masochist." I tap her thigh, easing her down to the ground, then tuck myself in. "Come on. We need to wash this bitch, and I need to get you back."

She pouts but steps aside while I dig more coins out and put them into the machine.

A few minutes pass and I'm soaping the last side of the car when she asks, "Will you come to me tonight?"

"My *cum* is still dripping down your thighs and you're already planning for next time?"

Her tongue slips beneath her teeth as she smiles, and she turns, showing me her ass as she bends down while keeping her knees locked, and snatches my belt off the ground.

She spins, sending her skirt sprawling around in the air, and loops it behind her head, the buckle in one hand, tip in the other. Then she shrugs, taking backward steps.

A groan leaves me, a million fucking ideas running through my head just as she knew would happen, just like the girl wanted, and she chuckles.

"Maybe I want you to stay the night this time . . ." She trails off, going for sassy, but it's more than that. The question is there in the back of her mind.

My brows snap together, and I look away, focusing on the hood of the car. That ain't gonna happen. I've crept into her room almost every night this week, but there's a reason I leave before she wakes. I know she's wanted to ask, but this is the closest she's come to doing so. My skin prickles, thinking about accidentally falling asleep in her bed, and I turn away from her. "We'll see, Rich Girl. Got fights to run tonight."

Her phone rings, stealing her attention, and thank fuck for that.

She settles herself in the front seat, so I quickly start scrubbing along the hood and bumper before hosing it down once more.

Her door opens and she darts out, expression tense as it finds mine.

I drop the hose, moving toward her. "What is it?"

"My dad. He found my car. I left my cuff on the front seat and he tracked it."

"I thought he didn't know about the tracker?"

"He didn't." She holds up her screen, showing me a picture of the back of the head of a buff dude in a suit, his hand wrapped around Damiano's neck.

My lips curve up to one side.

"Bastian!" she shouts.

"What?" My head tugs back, a low chuckle leaving me.

"Of for fuck's sake, get in the car. I need to get home and fast."

Huffing, I toss the damn hose and slide into the front seat. "Will your little gang tell him where you're at?"

"They don't know where I'm at," she says, typing away. "But no."

"You sure?"

"I trust them, Bastian. All of them."

Her words bring a bitter taste to my mouth, but I get it. She's had them in her corner most of her life. Of course, there's trust there.

But would they take a bullet for her?

A knife to the chest?

Would they kill for her?

Bet not . . .

"Shit, okay, take me to The Enterprise. Sai will pick me up there."

"Who the fuck is Sai and what makes you think your dad doesn't already have people there looking or isn't already on his way himself? Not that I care."

"Don't start," she cuts me off, the conversation a repetitive one. "And I'm sure he does, but Sai is keeping watch and he's parked outside the gates waiting. He's my driver and guard and has been since I was little. I think I told you about him."

"You didn't. Why was your dad looking for you? Why go searching instead of calling?"

When she says nothing, my eyes slice her way expectantly.

I slam the brakes, her hands shooting out to keep herself from eating the plastic of the dash.

"What the fuck?!" she shouts.

"Tell me."

"Drive."

I pull the keys out, roll the window down and wind my arm back.

Her hand locks around my wrist, halting me. "Wait, stop! Shit."

Sitting back, I give her a blank expression. "Why you still keeping shit from me? If something is wrong, I need to know."

"The less you know, the safer you are."

I grip the back of her neck, yanking her face to mine, my brows snapping low in the center. "Never try to protect me. Do you understand me? That is my job. Whether you're aware of it or not, I am your first line of defense."

She frowns, questioning me silently, but I give her a squeeze, and finally, she nods.

Sticking the keys back in the ignition, I put the car back in drive and start moving.

"My sister—"

"Is supposed to marry someone and bailed?"

She gapes at me. "How do you know that?"

"Put a few things together." With the help of Delta, but I don't tell her that. "What's this got to do with you? He comin' for her?"

"He should. It's the ultimate disrespect to the Fikile name to make a deal and back out of it."

Fikile, need to remember that.

"My dad says he has no idea she's gone, but it's been *weeks* since she came home, and we can't find any movement on him.

Bronx said he's in Costa Rica, so my dad must know this, but it doesn't make sense. Enzo's people would have called and told him. He would have come. The only reason she's back at Greyson Manor is that my dad thinks he won't step onto the grounds. And now he's got her back at Greyson Elite with every other asshole who probably already told their parents all about her returning. And now people are wondering what the hell's going on being the gala is two days from now, and that's probably why he's here looking for me right now unless something else happened he hasn't told me and—"

"Whoa, whoa, whoa, chill, baby." I reach over, squeezing her thigh. "Slow down. So you think this Enzo Fikile wants to send a message, show no one can fuck him and get away with it?"

"That's exactly what he will want," she says, so fucking sure.

"What if he just wants his girl back?"

She gapes at me, her expression clearly saying, *Did you seriously just say that right now?*

Popping a shoulder, I face the road. "That's all I'd want. I'd want you and I'd come fucking find you."

She's quiet, so I take a quick glance.

"Keep talking," I tell her.

She rolls her eyes. "It just doesn't make sense."

"So you think your dad's hiding something from you? Am I getting that right?"

"He has to be."

"What reason would he have to do that?"

"I don't know." She drops her head back with a huff. "I have gone over it a thousand times in my head, with the girls, with—" she cuts herself off, eyes snapping my way briefly. "Dom and the others. My sister won't say anything other than she was ignored by his staff, and supposedly, no one even looked at her, so she's fully convinced no one would notice—foolish girl is convinced she's invisible and not worth other's time or something." She mumbles the last part, more to herself than me. "She says they brought her food, but she had a fully stocked kitchen in the wing where he put her, so she thinks because of that, it covers those being left untouched. Who knows." She lifts one shoulder, looking out the side window, her tone betraying the words that leave her next. "Maybe she's right."

We're both left to our own thoughts the last couple minutes of the drive and then she's telling me to pull up behind a black town car. Kylo hops out, running back this way, his dark hair flopping all over the place.

"Your guard." My mind is running. "Do you trust him, too?"

Rocklin nods, reaching up to touch my face as Kylo waits outside the door, eyes bouncing around like a good guard dog. "He's the only reason I am able to be here. He trusts me and my judgment."

"Why you whispering, Rich Girl?" My tone is sharp, something clawing at my chest.

The corner of her mouth lifts, but it's not a smile I want to see. "I might not see you . . . for a while, depending on what's going on. He'll have me on lockdown."

"He can't keep you from me."

"Security will be insane."

I don't say anything. I let her say what she feels the need to say and when the lights of the town car turn on, Kylo opens the door.

Her thumb strokes my cheek once, and then she climbs out, sliding in the back seat of the car in front of us, a guy that ain't me sliding in beside her because he's part of whatever's going on and I'm not.

I glare at the road as I peel out, the fucking canyon between our worlds getting real fucking old, real fucking fast.

My eyes flash to the driver, but the windows are so black I can't see anything beyond the ratty reflection of my rusty Cutlass, worth less than the cost of the paint job of the mirrored car.

If he's her guard, the man who swore to protect her and keep her safe . . . why haven't I ever seen him? Where is he when I'm creeping at night or checking up on her from a distance?

Where was he when she ran out of the school to come to me and where was he today?

That's not a real dedicated employee if you ask me.

Tension tugs inside me and I put a pre-roll between my lips, flicking my Zippo open and pulling in a long drag.

Rocklin said this man's the only reason she could be with me.

Like he could keep her from me.

Like any of them could.

She let me inside her, came to me when she was feelin' heavy.

She wanted me, then needed me, and that makes her mine.

I need to bridge the gap, and I know exactly where to start.

She's going to be one pissed-off prep, but she'll get over it.

She'll have no choice.

Rocklin

Sia pulls into the curved driveway, forced to slam on the brakes, when my dad more or less throws himself in the front of the car. He bangs his fists on the hood, the expression in his eyes manic as they catch mine . . . Even though he can't see me through the windshield, the man knows where I sit.

"Oh shit," I whisper.

"Yeah." Kylo grimaces. "It's bad."

"Could have warned me."

"Was coming to get you not warning enough?" He chuckles. "Besides, I only heard his rant from afar. The asshole is in rare form tonight, even for him. He came in guns blazing, bitching and moaning, and the second he saw me, he went stone cold, turned around and stormed off. The others had to chase him, just to get their heads ripped off."

Okay, yeah. That sounds about right.

Blowing out a long breath, I glance at my uniform with a wince, then follow Kylo out the door.

My dad grips my elbow, drags me inside, and slams the door in Sai's face. The staff is nowhere to be seen, but all my friends and Boston are here, and as soon as my dad sees Kylo walk in, Kenex stepping from around the corner, his brows snap together. He gives them his back, and the others use that moment to offer apologetic smiles, their frowns bouncing from my dad to me.

My dad releases me, voice booming through the wide space as he gets in my face. "Where the hell were you?!"

"Out."

"Where, daughter?" he demands.

280

"I went for a swim," I tell him.

His eyes narrow. "In your uniform? Off campus? In a pool where they don't use special chemicals you require when you have one that does in this house?!"

My muscles tense, but I don't show it, avoiding looking over his shoulder toward the others. "I dipped into the lake."

"You are lying. You weren't with your car . . . that I told you not to be driving around in. And you better give me a damn good reason Sai would leave you unattended before I go out there and put a fucking bullet in his head," my father seethes, tension deepening the wrinkles at the edges of his eyes.

Shit.

Fuck.

Why did Sai let me go? He didn't even put up a fight, and while I told Bastian he's the only reason I get to go see him, it's not as clear-cut as it sounds. Sai allows me my escapes, understanding the need I had to break out when I started to feel caged in, but it's not like we sat down and had a conversation about the guy I'm . . . more than fucking. We haven't spoken about why I've been going out more and more with a smile on my face in place of a frown. But it's like I said before, Sai?

He knows everything.

And *I* know my father isn't bluffing, so something has got to give.

I spin a few things in my head, use my training, and act as calm as ever, without a care in the fucking world—my go-to response.

"You wanted it to look like we had weak spots, right?" I lift a single shoulder, sweeping a hand out as if to add a bratty *duh*.

Wrong thing to say.

My father's eyes flash, flicking to the side where the others hover without letting them know he is looking. He doesn't want them to know he's baiting a bull.

"Leave us," he forces through clenched teeth, and everyone moves at once.

You don't deny Rayo Revenaw, and surely not when it concerns his daughters.

The only one who stays behind is my sister, but apparently, he doesn't even want her to overhear as the moment he realizes, he snaps his head over his shoulder. "You brought this to our feet. Now, go."

Tears well in my sister's eyes and I frown but wipe it away when my father looks at me.

"What's going on?" I ask once she's gone.

"I received a copy of a manifest this morning. Enzo's name was on it."

My blood pumps a little faster. "So, he's coming then?"

"I expect he is."

"And why were we not warned this morning?" I push. "Did you tell the girls? Boston? She needs to know."

"She has done her part."

Done her part?

Confusion has my gaze narrowing, but his hardens.

"Dad?"

He clenches his jaw, presses his lips together and then spins, raking his hands through his hair, the first true sign of distress he's shown when it comes to Enzo.

When he turns back to me, his features are crestfallen.

Unease trickles along my spine, weighing me down. "Dad . . ."

His shoulders fall, and then he's gripping mine, his hold *too* gentle.

"I am not the man I was twenty years ago. I'm getting older, and with that, I will become weaker than the young. I cannot leave you in this world unprotected," he repeats for the third time, his voice nothing but a tragic whisper.

"I'm not unprotected." I expect to sound strong and sure because I don't doubt what I'm saying in the slightest, yet my words are meek.

"Rocco," he murmurs, stepping closer. "You are the daughter I wished for. I gave away . . . much in life to lead you to where you are, and you did not disappoint. You are everything I meant for you to be and more. Strong. Determined. Smart. Everything a partner would wish for, and as my successor, all the enemy would need to end us, so we must do what we can to prevent such a thing from happening. A woman as powerful as you will have a man of equal power at her side."

My face falls and I take a step away.

My father eyes me for several unnerving moments, and before I can question him, he stands tall.

Gone are the deep wrinkle lines of worry and the haze of concern in his gaze. His shoulders widen, as does his stance, the no-bullshit kingpin of the north now before me, my father long gone.

"The gala is two nights from now."

I think of how easily Bastian slipped in. How he continues to do so. "Is it really smart to move forward with the event, knowing Enzo might be on his way back to the States?"

My father rolls on as if I haven't spoken. "You will not leave the house until then, and to make sure, I will be placing a guard outside your door. On top of that, I will be the one who picks you up. You will wear what I send over for you, and you will not fight me. You may be in charge when it comes to matters of a Greyson, but you are in charge nowhere else."

"What aren't you telling me?"

"Focus on what I have told you." He gives a single curt nod and moves for the door. He tugs it open, eyes finding mine over his shoulder. "The enemy is coming, daughter. Be ready to do as you must."

With that, he leaves, the door swinging right back open as not one but four of his guards step through.

Fuck my life.

Chapter 22
Rocklin

Many times my father shocked me when it came to Boston, like when he didn't send her to a convent after she shared how she approached Enzo Fikile alone on Alcatraz Island to propose a union between the two. Or when she agreed to the contractual marriage that ended before it began for the most recent examples. He had to know this would happen, that she would bail and choose herself over her responsibilities.

It isn't new for her.

Boston always had a knack for doing the opposite of what she was told. It's an odd dynamic really, because she's seen as the weak one. The "lesser" twin, and while I'm pissed at her decisions lately, I also admire my sister. She's blinding in an effortless way, even when she sinks into herself with episodes of depression or doubt. She's my mother and I'm my father. She's nurturing and I'm . . . hard. There have been times when I envied her lack of fucks when it came to training or topping the chart in academia. She never fought for our father's approval, whereas most of my life has been one move after another, reaching for it because he continuously set a new goal in front of me, waiting for me to reach it.

In his eyes, she was the goose, I was the swan, and it had nothing to do with appearances but everything to do with her lack of devotion. He's more or less loosened his reins on her while tightening mine, when it should be the opposite.

So yes, I've been shocked many times by his lack of action or overall decision-making regarding Boston. Though nothing comes close to when I slide inside my father's car to find my sister already seated inside, golden ball gown poufed up all around her, blonde hair in an elegant twist.

Her eyes flick to mine, but she says not a word, turning to fill the champagne glass in her hand.

"I guess tonight will be an eventful one," I comment, my attention pointed at my father.

He knows what I'm thinking, so I don't have to say a word. Why he would bring her with us, away from the protection of the grounds, when his entire reasoning for her being here was his lack of concern or assumption that Enzo wouldn't dare enter.

But The Enterprise?

Enzo holds a suite there, so should he wish to enter, enter he may.

Two nights ago, after my dad left, I didn't even make it to my stairs before the girls came down from their wings, sleepwear in hand. They stayed in my room and we didn't leave it once over the last forty-eight hours. We had no idea who could be listening in, so we didn't trust the phone, and we had some digging to do but came up short. My father claims he was given a manifest, but Bronx could find proof of no such thing. That's not to say it doesn't exist, it might. Probably does . . . but what if it doesn't?

What if he lied?

Why would he lie?

That's the question that won't leave my mind. Why would he lie if he did, and if he didn't, tonight is going to be one hell of a party for all in our world to witness.

It won't be just Greyson Elite Academy alumni and their families in attendance tonight, but other Mafia families, local and traveling gangs, corrupt royals and more. The richest of the rich, the elite from all around, will come together in one place as we do once a year in recognition of the relationships we've forged in the last few. It's a risky move on the best day, so when the head honcho takes a contract and spits on it, then flaunts the fawn before the faux?

It's no wonder the dress my father sent hides what must be carried underneath it.

But if he's expecting trouble, why are his only heirs on the way to step right in the middle of it?

"Dad, did you hear about Rocklin's new recruit?" Boston asks after several minutes of silence.

He looks to me. "I did not . . ."

"He's brilliant, a quick thinker, and quite striking in a nonconventional sort of way."

My eyes slice to hers, and she lifts a blonde brow, swirling rather than drinking her champagne.

"So you took my advice." My father nods, half listening, half paying attention to his phone. "You've considered adding more males?"

I open my mouth to speak, but my sister beats me to it.

"Oh, this one is quite persistent. In fact, you might say he's determined to get his way."

At that, my father's gaze does lift, and he sets his phone in his lap. "Is that right? And who is this new recruit?"

"Your daughter is telling lies again." I look to her in warning. "Not that that's any surprise. She's bitter Miss Giano has refused to allow her a spot in the showcase next month."

Boston purses her lips. "I have never not had a solo, let alone been a part of the showcase."

My father nods along with Boston's words, a small frown building. "Why would Miss Giano deny her?"

"Because I told her to."

His gaze sharpens and I hold it unwaveringly. He said I am only in control of my world, and *this* is a my-world problem.

Checkmate, Daddy Dearest.

Besides, who is to say Boston will be here in a month's time?

At this rate, who is to say any of us will be?

After what feels like the longest drive of my life, our dad looks out the window, realizing we're pulling around the front of The Enterprise. He gives us his full attention, face serious, and tone just as stern.

286

"There will be no surprises from the two of you tonight. You will smile, you will laugh, you will praise, and you will be gracious when you yourselves are praised. You will accept any hand offered to you, no matter who it belongs to. You will stay on the floor where I can see you and you will not return to the Revenaw or the Greyson Suite at any point or anytime under any circumstances. Most importantly, you will drop the attitude between the two of you and remember you are sisters, twins, that you love each other, and how, before the arrangement that was made that brought us to this next stage occurred, you would do anything for one another."

Next stage?

"You girls have been close all of your lives," he continues. "Do not allow anything to come between that. Not a man and not me. The decisions I make, I make with the two of you in mind, so if you don't like what I have to say or what I must do, you may speak your mind when no one else is there to hear it. But no matter the call I must make, you will not turn your back on each other, as when I am gone, the one and only person you will ever be able to count on as deeply as you can count on me to protect you, is the person beside you. Blood over all. Always, no matter what. Family? It comes first. Do I make myself clear?"

Forcing myself not to swallow past the sudden dryness of my throat, I look to my sister, to the girl who was once my best friend, who I could never hate, but can't help feeling betrayed by.

She made a mistake, and she didn't own up to it, and then she made it worse. She made a commitment, and she bailed. She took our family name and did the one thing we were raised never to do.

She placed the power of it in someone else's hands.

The car pulls up to the red carpet set out for tonight's event, and my dad's driver makes his way around the hood, pulling the door open.

"Where is Sai tonight?" I ask. Tonight of all nights, my guard should be my shadow.

"Around" is all I get in response. Dad steps out first, and one by one, at his offered hand, my sister and I follow.

He holds his arms out, and we link ours through his and head inside the building. Suddenly, Sai appears, standing just to the left, then falls in line beside me; Boston's old guard before he was reassigned when she left, at hers, and my father's guards create a wall at our backs.

Once inside, we're forced to pause to say hello to the over-eager men after my father's attention and it's not until after another twenty minutes of mundane conversation that we are released. Boston, of course, prevents my escape, looping her arm through mine, and steers us both toward the bar.

"What the hell were you thinking bringing that up in front of Dad?"

She tugs me closer. "Now, sister, we're supposed to be getting along, remember?"

"Cut the shit, Boston. What am I missing here? What is going on in Dad's head and what are you hiding?"

"Oh, you want to know what I'm hiding, yet you're the one running off to sleep with some tattooed biker bad boy or whatever he is."

"Not everyone who wears a leather jacket rides a motor-cycle, Boston."

"How am I supposed to know that? I'm nothing but a shel-tered brat." She grins. "I'm just saying, do you even know who he is? He popped up out of nowhere, and all of a sudden, you're sneaking off to go meet him, leaving campus, lying to Dad? Leaving your tracker!" Her eyes grow wide, a small laugh leaving her. "I mean, girl, that's so unlike perfect little Rocklin."

"Please." Rolling my eyes, I accept the glass of champagne the waiter hands to me, eyeing the two guns strapped across his chest in open view. "I can hear it in your voice. You're proud and it's disgusting."

My sister laughs, and I can't help but join in with her.

Shaking my head, I look her way, and after a moment, she sighs.

"Maybe I'm mad you didn't tell me about him," she admits, lifting a shoulder. "Yet Bronx and Delta seem to know all about the mystery boy from campus. And don't say it's Greyson business. It's not. I'm your sister. Don't cut me out because I'm foolish. You knew that already, so what's really changed?" she mocks herself, offering a smile, but it's fake and full of self-loathing.

"You're emotional and rash, not foolish."

She scoffs a laugh, but again, it's directed at herself. "Are they not the same thing?" she muses, eyes falling to the bubbles in her drink. "For the record, if I knew it was going to end this way, I never would have asked Enzo to meet me."

Shifting slightly, I give her my full attention. "Why did you really leave, Beeks? Tell me the truth and not the one Dad wants you to."

The corner of her mouth lifts into a sad smile and she looks toward where he stands. Sadness clouds her features as she returns her gaze to mine, and she tips her head as she reaches out to smooth a loose hair near my temple.

"I knew I wasn't the queen," she whispers softly. "But I didn't know I was the pawn until it was too late."

I open my mouth to ask her what she means, to demand an explanation, because the ideas running through my mind can't possibly be anything close to what she means, but then goose bumps rise along the back of my neck, and my eyes are drawn to the entryway.

Silently compelled by some invisible force buried within me, so deep I know there is no removing it.

No . . . .

My face falls instantly, a sick, twisted feeling rolls over in my stomach as a pulsing knot grows thick in my throat, blocking my airway.

My blood turns to ice and then stone, and I must begin to shake as my sister steps in close, the warmth of her palms jolting me as they wrap around my biceps.

"Oh my god, Rocklin." Her hands move up and down my forearms. "Stop."

My throat stretches and stretches, the veins in my neck bulging but with no relief.

My heart beats wildly until I feel it heavy at my temples.

"You're not even breathing! Get your shit together," she hisses.

My head snaps to hers and I glare, but my sister glares right back.

She nods, my teeth grind together, and I force air into my lungs in short, harsh gasps. After a few seconds, the tightness in my chest settles.

"Hold your chin up and knock this shit off right now because Dad is coming." She rushes the last part, dipping her fingers into her drink and swiping them along my neck for shock factor.

It works. I jerk, practically gasping as air pushes its way into my lungs and I throw my glass back in one go.

My body heats and I know his eyes are on me, that he found me, but, of course, he did. I'm the reason he's here.

As I think that, I realize while it is true . . . it also isn't, and before I can stop myself before my father reaches me, I spin on my heels, marching right for the boy in black.

His face is sharp lines, soft scars, and utterly unreadable, but the brunette on his arm isn't.

She smirks and smiles and bats her fake lashes at everyone she walks past, oblivious to what's coming toward her, but he sees me. I'd argue I'm all he sees, even with the beautiful bitch at his side. Holding on to him. Touching him.

Anger licks across my spine, begging me to unstrap the knife at my hip and send it sailing straight into her chest, but I manage to refrain, pressing forward.

The closer I get, the more those crystal eyes flare, a deep dark dare gleaming within them, wishing me to do whatever the hell it is I'm about to do. Waiting for me to approach him, to come to him.

To claim him for all to see.

Wait, what?!

I jerk to a stop, freezing in the center of the room, and his eyes narrow.

What the *hell* am I doing?!

His chin lowers in warning, and he takes urgent, giant steps toward me.

My eyes fly wide as he grows closer, but my feet won't move.

No, no, no . . . not here. Don't do it. What the fuck is wrong with me?

He's but ten feet away when my hands are caught. I'm spun and dragged halfway across the room, muscles tense, jaw clenched, Bronx and Delta whispering shit in my ears I can't hear. As quickly as they come to me, we're locked in the lavatory. They whirl me around and push me onto the tufted, round couch, glaring down at me.

"Do not even think about it," Bronx warns. "Not tonight."

"I can't believe he's here." Delta looks between us. "He must be crazy."

"He's fucking insane!" I bury my face in my hands, snatching a pillow, and scream into it, keeping my face buried there while I count to fucking ten. Finally, I pull in a deep breath and I look up at my girls.

"What the fuck, I mean, right? What the fuck? He's here, like seriously? All the deleting we did of the freaking surveillance, as stealth as I've been, hiding him away, and he shows up here? Of all places?"

"Girl, please. He was in The Game Room, in the school, and in the *manor*. He isn't worried about being any kind of stealthy. The boy gives no fucks."

"Maybe he'll lie low, just watch?" Delta, the voice of reason. "People might think he's simply her plus-one."

Her plus-freaking-one? He's not *her* anything!

My face must give me away, as Delta yelps when Bronx elbows her in the ribs.

I jump to my feet, remembering why my heels clicked in his direction in the first place. "How the fuck did Chloe Carpo get a ticket?"

"Her dad runs security for that Brayshaw family Bass works for. A trio of fine-ass brothers, from what I heard." Bronx moves to the mirror, fluffing her curls. "Calvin said he extended the invite as a business courtesy, something about his daughter royally fucking up with the Brays and in need of an escape."

"Those brothers have been keeping him really busy." I share. "Is Chloe one of theirs?"

She raises a dark brow. "Do you really think she'd be here with the help if she were?"

The help. Right.

Because Bastian Bishop is an enforcer in his world. A soldier, as we call them. One of the lowest-ranking males who never so much as see the man on top, let alone become him. And technically speaking, he isn't even that.

Sighing, I look to the girls. "What do I do?"

"Ignore him," they say in unison. "It's the only thing you can do."

I look at them like they're crazy, and they only nod because they don't get it.

No one does.

I have tried to let this go, to convince myself it's a rare bit of fun and the fun must end, but it won't work. It's impossible.

Bastian Bishop cannot be ignored or forgotten.

He won't allow it any more than my mind will.

He's a fucking tornado in dead lands—all eyes called to the chaos without realization.

Again . . .

Fuck. My. Life.

He's wearing a suit.

A nice suit and it looks . . . wrong.

Draped in well-fitted black from head to toe, he's what wicked dreams are made of. Hair as black as a panther, eyes as majestic as one, with beautiful ink sprawling up his neck, down his hands, and across those scarred knuckles. The air of dominance in which he walks is of the effortless kind. The *envious* kind. He's devastatingly, devilishly handsome. Tempting in the best and worst ways, yet still, he looks . . . off.

That is not his suit and he is missing his jacket.

It's all wrong.

Not like my Bastian.

Not like my tattooed tyrant, my public school punk, my sort-of, kind-of stalker.

"Stop staring," Bronx says through a tight smile as we approach her father. "Dad!"

Mr. Bandoni beams, wrapping her in a hug and stealing his only child so he can show her off to the men before him, but not before offering me a simple squeeze and nod hello.

Free at last, I move toward the bar for something to do, and Kylo and Kenex are quick to join me.

"My new guard dogs?" I guess, going for a water first this time.

"Considering Sai ran off like his ass was on fire, yes. Yes, we are."

My head snaps their way. "Why would he run off?"

"I'm sure he's lurking somewhere or checking in with security or something, but he took off after you went all zombie Barbie and froze." Kylo's eyes fall to my gown. "You look nice, by the way."

That grabs Kenex's attention, and he nods in agreement, his focus quickly falling back to his phone. "Bishop probably hates your dress."

The way he says his last name so casually is irritating. "How would you know what Bastian hates?"

"He's like us. I know."

I consider his words a moment, remembering what Bastian said about how they're different than us, and I won't deny it's true. It is. It's why my father hates them.

It's interesting though, as the more I'm around them, the less like outsiders they feel. They're more like us than I gave them credit for. They're strong and resilient and hardworking. They never give up and always push for more, for better. They don't place blame on others but take responsibility for their actions and don't fret when punishment is given.

I meet both Kylo and Kenex's dark eyes, and when I offer a small smile, a real one, both boys nod their chins in acknowledgment. Maybe it's time I lower the wall I allowed my father to build between us, if only by a few inches because if Bastian believes there is something trustworthy within them, as odd as it sounds, something tells me I can too.

Maybe I always sort of knew that. I wouldn't stay in a home they lived in if I didn't, right?

Suddenly Kylo grins and when the waiter lowers a fruity glass of champagne, he shakes his head. "No, she needs something stronger tonight."

Chuckling, I turn to face them in my seat, accepting the scotch he passes me. "That's more like it," I tell him. "And keep them coming."

It's going to be a long fucking night.

Chapter 23
Bass

Burgundy. That's a little too close to red for me. That's what that little Henshaw fucker said he wanted, right? To see her in red.

The bastard is here like I knew he would be, but he hasn't dared step through the center of the room yet, and not a single foot toward her. I caught him in my peripheral, the way his head snapped to the side and body tensed when he spotted me was damn near comical, but I didn't give him the satisfaction of letting him know I knew he was there, watching. He's still watching, tucked in the back corner, probably trying to come up with a plan that gets him from where he is to where she is without me stepping in.

I have every intention of stepping in, but I have no reason to look his way, not when the person I want to see is right ahead, looking all kinds of pretty and pissed off. Straight-up miserable. She says she loves this world, yet it's obvious this is the last place she wants to be. The smile on her face is fake as fuck, but it's not like it doesn't match every other person in this room.

They laugh and joke and make plans to meet up after tonight to discuss some kind of business that no one says out loud, but all seem to understand, depending on who the words come from and who they're going to. The wives, if they've earned such a right, stand around and smile, seemingly worthless in their position, but it doesn't look like they mind. They get to play dress-up, all glitter and shiny shit women like them kill for. Maybe even literally, but who knows.

Maybe her misery has nothing to do with where she is and everything to do with who she has to be on nights like this. This world of back-alley criminal organization shit is supposed to be hers one day, or at least a part of it. According to her, she's the heir that will take over when her dad's time ends, but if that's the case, then I'm having a really hard time figuring out why he makes her wear a mask of perfection when he should show them the chaos that creeps inside her. Those little manic moments she gives glimpses of? That's what he should want the world to see. A viper with a poisonous bite, not a princess with a preening smile.

Logically, that's exactly what he would do.

So why doesn't he?

There's no doubt in my mind there's a reason. People like him in places like this don't make moves on a whim.

From the left, golden fucking hair catches my attention, but I don't bother looking, and he doesn't need to step in front of me to announce his arrival.

Damiano places himself at my side with his hands in his pockets, attempting to stand taller and stretching out his chest as he does it. "You shouldn't be here."

"You should fuck off."

He looks around the room, shaking his head slowly. "You're putting her in a bad spot by coming."

"You're putting me in a bad fucking mood tryin' to tell me what's what with a girl who ain't yours." My eyes slide his way.

He shifts so his body is facing mine slightly, but I keep mine pointed toward the bar. "She would come to you if she could."

"I know."

"She's kept you away with good reason."

"I've been in her bed every night for the last week, with the exception of the last two." Raising a brow, I look to him. "That sound like she's keeping me away."

If he's shocked by my announcement, he doesn't say it. "You know what I mean."

This time, I do face him. "No. I don't 'cause there is no *keeping me away*. You should have plenty of proof of that by now. I go where I want, and if she's there, chances are I'm not far."

"So you *have* been watching . . ." He trails off, but he's gonna have to do better than that. "Do you not have a life back in Brayshaw?"

Okay, he wants to pussyfoot around. Got it.

"No."

He waits for more, but it ain't coming. Do I have shit to handle? Yes, more than normal since Raven Carver showed up in town and flipped the Brayshaw family on their ass, but that ain't my life. That's work. That's doing what I can for a friend and what I'm paid for.

My sister isn't there, and if my mother was, I would know.

So, again, no, I don't have a life there. There's no trust fund sitting around with my name on it, so I have to work my way out of the gutter.

Sighing, Damiano faces forward as I do and finally says something real that's on his mind. "You've seen him watching her."

I press my tongue to the back of my teeth to keep my jaw from clenching. "I have."

"It's not about his proposal."

My head whips around so quick I can't fucking stop it. "Say what now?"

Damiano's brows jump, and then he scoffs a laugh. "Yeah. He thinks he's got a shot at a union between them."

A union, he said.

"That all relationships here are agreements between two people who ain't even the ones stuck together?"

Damiano tips his head, smiling as if to say *pretty much*. He eyes me a minute, and when he speaks again, it's with a watchful tone, almost as if he's attempting to reassure me. "She's not interested."

I can't help the laugh that leaves me, and my eyes snap forward as Rocklin's spine shoots straight, the sound reaching her from across the giant room.

Yes, baby, I'm still here, but you knew that.

I don't bother with a reply to his little informative note that I did not need. I know she's not interested, just like I know some things aren't her choice, and from what she's said, I'm betting whose ring ends up on her finger falls into that category.

That ain't gonna work for me and it sure as fuck isn't all that's happening here.

I lick my lips. "Why would a man who has everything Rayo Revenaw does entertain the idea of giving his overachieving heir to the son of a dude who makes his fortune off fucking over and enslaving immigrants?" I throw the question out there, not foolish enough to believe I'm the only one who knows about her little red dress dinner date with this punk, waiting to see how he chooses to respond.

Sliding my eyes his way, I catch the slight dip of his brows and then the slow rise of them that follows.

"You have a theory," he says more to himself before standing tall and slipping in front of me, expression straight business all of a sudden. "You have a theory," he repeats himself, this time sure.

Good. Not a complete waste of muscles.

Rocklin starts to fidget, her restraint running out, the need to know who I'm talking to officially winning out, and finally, my girl peeks over her shoulder.

Our eyes lock and she sucks in a breath, yet her muscles seem to settle, even if she does keep her perfect little posture.

She's so fucking gorgeous, so damn beautiful, my ribs grow tight. It's unreal, what the sight of this girl does to me, and I know it's the same for her. It's written in her big green eyes and the blanket of softness that falls over her when I'm within range.

I feel no logic when it comes to this girl, just a pull deep on the inside that tells me she's it.

She's what I've been blindly searching for and she knows it.

"Tell me what it is." Damiano regains my attention. "Your theory."

"That sounds a lot like a demand." I move my eyes his way. "I don't answer to you, and I don't share a working theory that might not mean shit. If I'm wrong, you'd call me a fool. If I told you what I'm thinking, you'd *definitely* call me crazy."

"I think they have something on Mr. Revenaw," he speaks in a rush. "I've been quietly looking into it, but so far, I haven't found a link. The Henshaw family, they offer . . . services that leave them with many secrets."

I simply stare at him.

His frustration doubles. "I just want to make sure she's safe."

"That ain't your job no more, pretty boy."

He grinds his jaw, stretching his shoulders out wide, not realizing he had already pulled that move tonight. It has the same effect as it did the first time—none.

Still, he keeps on rolling. "Despite what you claim, you won't always be around, and there might be a million reasons why that is, but it's a simple fact. Why not have someone else she trusts in the loop, so I can be there for her if she needs it?"

"What makes you think I want you anywhere near her?" What makes him think I don't already have someone doing exactly what he's suggesting?

"My point is, I *am* near her. I live in the same home she does. I go to the same school she goes to. Chances are, if you aren't there, I am."

My blood heats, his words as irritating as they are true. "None of that means a damn thing to me. I don't trust a blond hair on your head."

"I need to know what's going on if it involves the girls," he snaps, face heating as he pisses himself off more and more with each attempt to get in my head. "Part of my role is to help lead security at the Greyson Manor, Greyson Elite, and at The Enterprise."

A low whistle leaves me, and the implication isn't missed.

Boy's doing a piss-poor job at that. I got into all three.

"I can only do so much," he forces past clenched teeth. "I'm not in the security room, simply the one they call when they find something."

"So it was your call to send Kylo after me that day?" The day we took him straight off their property.

His lips smash together, but after a moment, he sighs. "Look, I know we aren't exactly . . . fuck," he mutters, then stands straight, stepping back a little to allow a blonde to slip between us.

The wrong blonde.

Damiano slides his hands in his pockets and nods his chin toward the uninvited incomer. "Bass Bishop, meet Boston Revenaw."

Rocklin's twin sister smirks, playing coy and sucking at it. "Are you going to ask me to dance, Mr. Bishop?"

"I'm no mister, and you're trouble. She's got problems with you, so no. I'm not." I shrug. "Not that I would have either way."

Boston stares, and then a wide smile spreads. "Oh man, this is going to be so good. You're right, she is mad at me, but it's surface level. I'm blood."

"Blood means nothing."

"She knows where I stand at the end of the day."

"Words mean nothing."

Boston's smile is slow, and she nods. "You're right, Bass. They don't. I look forward to you changing your mind about me, and while I understand, maybe even appreciate, your decision to be loyal to my sister, I was simply attempting to smooth this over for you to help avoid the inevitable, but now I retract my invitation." She looks to Damiano, raising a brow.

He swallows his annoyance, looking to me as he accepts her arm, but not before she steps in, rising onto her toes to whisper in my ear, "She's on strict orders to turn down *zero* offers for her hand tonight."

She pulls back, sending me a wink, and then the two walk off, joining the others in the center of the dance floor.

My eyes zone in on my girl. I watch her for a minute, talking with the Greco boys and a couple other girls who made their way toward her, wondering what girls like that have to say at a place like this.

Coming here was a plan I made, even if the reasons for it shifted a bit here and there, but an opportunity is an opportunity.

One song shifts to the next and I realize I'm being a little bitch, delaying, and for what?

I don't feel unsure, and I'm not worried about much, so I pick one foot up and then the other, headed right for her.

The Grecos spot me first, standing in the protective mode I've noticed they always hold around her, more so than the others, even if she doesn't see it. I'm betting they all expect me to stand back, to watch from the shadows like I've been, but that was never the plan for tonight. So tell me why the closer I get, the tighter this fucking collar feels around my neck?

It's prickly and unfamiliar, that's all.

No other reason.

I clench my teeth, the pressure erasing the scratchy feeling along my skin.

She realizes I'm coming now, slowly shifting in her seat and climbing into those pretty, pointy heels until she's standing. She's facing me, long fingers wrapped around the back of her chair, digging into the leather of it as if it will keep me from her.

You know better than that, baby.

I step closer, gaze straight shackled to hers, and she follows, keeping two feet between us, green eyes tight with worry but shining with something else. Something deeper.

"Bastian . . ." she whispers, voice thick.

"Dance with me, Rich Girl."

She's shaking her head before I even finish the sentence.

"You can't tell me no, baby." My words are teasing, but I'm not sure why. I'm not nervous. I don't get nervous. "The way I hear it, you're not allowed to say no. Daddy's orders, right?"

"Don't do this," she murmurs, hands folding in front of her. "My dad is staring."

"I saw him."

He's the first thing I saw when I walked in the door. Tall as fuck, big and broad, filling out a suit like no one I've ever seen before. Not that I've seen many men in suits, but this dude, he's solid, not overly bulky, but full, thick, every bit the boss she says he is. Even if I hadn't found his picture online, I'd have known he was the man worth mentioning.

There's a lot of men in this room right now, a bunch of big strong, no-neck fuckers, but they carry themselves like they want others to know. Slow and thought-out steps, elbows bowed a bit to keep their chests out and chins up. Even blank faces and simple nods while they sip on some kind of golden liquor.

Not Rayo Revenaw, real estate mogul by name, kingpin by might.

"Just bow your head and walk away. Please," she begs.

I move closer and her chest lifts with a full breath. "Tell him I'm Chloe's man, just looking for a dance partner 'cause I've misplaced mine."

Her glare is instant and too fucking adorable.

My little thief is jealous.

"I will find you later," she says. "I promise, but this is not the time for a power play."

My lips press together with irritation, and I cock my head. "Tempting . . . but no." I take another step and her jaw tightens. When I speak this time, my voice comes out softer than I expected.

"Dance with me, baby." I swallow after the last word. What is meant as a demand almost sounds like a fucking plea, but I shouldn't have to beg my girl to take my hand, yet here we fucking are.

"Fine." I feel the frown take over before I realize I'm showing it. "One song and I'm out."

Her eyes narrow a little and she considers me. She doesn't believe me, that's for sure. She thinks I'm just looking for a way to get my way, and I am, but I mean what I say. One song and I'm out.

Out of this room, anyway.

Another step, the tips of our shoes now touching. "So, what do you say . . . you gonna give me what I'm askin' for?" My knuckles skate along the backs of hers, and her hand turns, soft fingers tracing over my tattoos.

Slowly, her muscles ease, the left corner of her plump-ass lips lifting the slightest bit, painted a pretty plum-pink color. Her hair is left long and draped to one side, the other part pinned back with a golden clip, jewels matching the shade of the dress her curves are wrapped in.

Come on, baby, take my hand . . .

Her fingers fold over mine and fuck me if my chest doesn't rattle with something unnamable. Something—

"Rocklin."

Her spine shoots straight and she jumps a foot back, both our heads whipping toward the motherfucker who dared.

"Oliver," she shoots for calm, but there's a bit of a shake in there, "I'm—"

"Back the fuck up."

His eyes snap to mine, and the little bitch tries hard to hold on to his tough-boy bravado, but I recognize fear when I see it, and he's right to be on edge.

But all these men think the same. Just like her dad assumes Enzo Fikile won't cause problems on the Greyson Estate because of what it stands for, this dude thinks I'll back down because of where we are. Because of who he is and who I am not.

What sets me apart in all this?

I ain't got shit to lose, no face to save, no bond at risk of breaking.

I'm a lone wolf in the middle of a dangerous-ass pack, yet I've still got no fucks to give, 'cause at the end of the day, what happens here means nothing.

The girl is mine, regardless.

There's a difference between being taught and being forced to learn, and that's adaptation. That's understanding shit changes in the blink of an eye and knowing how to get out of it. You can plan ahead all you like, having a backup plan from *A* to *Z*, and I bet they do for most situations. But it makes no difference when influence and money are the keys that unlock the door, giving them what they want, when the guy who has no key can find his way in regardless. Street smarts win every fucking time.

Oliver grins, and it's too wide. Too fucking sure, sending a prickle of awareness down my spine. "It wasn't my intention to interrupt . . . well, to be honest, it was. So why don't you head back to the other side of the room. We are already gaining attention and you wouldn't want to find out what happens when Rayo gets curious."

"I said back the fuck up."

"Bastian—"

Oliver reaches for her hand, but I catch it, twisting until his back bows, his face scrunching with pain like the weak bitch he is.

"Touch her again and—"

"Bastian, stop!" she hisses.

"—this will end so much worse for you."

"Fuck you," he seethes.

I toss his ass and he stumbles, bumping into a waiter, the tray crashing to the floor.

Rocklin gasps, people look, and this dumb fuck's ego is burning. He comes back, cheeks red with rage, but I meet his one step forward with two of my own.

"I fucking dare you, pretty boy."

"What the hell is going on here?"

Rocklin jerks and Oliver stands taller, masking his expression.

My eyes are glued to his, muscles tense to the fucking max, rage blistering.

Oliver starts to smile, a perfect pretty-boy smile and he smooths his arms down his jacket. "Just a misunderstanding, sir. All is good now." His grin is smug, triumphant, as if his savior just stepped up with a golden ticket to the prize that is not up for grabs. "Rocklin and I are about to have that dance she promised me."

"Fuck if you are."

Rocklin might have squeaked, can't say for sure, but I don't miss the way Oliver's eyes widen, flicking from me to the shadow at my side. He laughs, and he's the only fucking one.

That shadow shifts, and suddenly, Rayo Revenaw is in front of me, blocking Oliver from my line of sight, so I lift my gaze to the man my girl never wanted me to meet.

His dark eyes are sharp, expression a mask of indifference, but I see the demand there. He wants me to submit, to step back, to stand down. He wants to know who the fuck I am, why I'm here, and why I'm standing so close to his daughter.

Most of the people in the room are back to their own little worlds, the spilled tray a momentary issue, a sound shock having snagged their attention, and not that I give a shit either way, but we lost it when the pretty boy started laughing.

When I say nothing, Rayo's eyes narrow and he shifts his stance, chin lifting a bit as he tips his head.

"Oliver," he speaks slowly. "Why don't you and Rocklin go on and have that dance."

"Dad—"

"Go," he cuts her off.

After two more seconds of hesitation, Rocklin steps around her father, eyes tight and flicking toward me as she moves toward another man.

Oliver reaches out.

Rocklin offers her hand.

I grab her around the fucking wrist, and then Rayo Revenaw is in my face, four guards fanning out around him.

"Get your hand off my daughter before I show you what happens to people who touch things that don't belong to them."

"If he puts one hand on her, I'll be giving a demonstration of my own and I won't wait until no one's watching to do it."

Small gasps fill the air, but the only people who can hear us through the wall his men made are Rocklin and her girls, who slowly shift this way.

The man's nostrils flare, the dude on his left taking a step forward, but Rayo gives the smallest shake of his head and steps closer.

"Your name, boy. Now." His tone is low, lethal, and promises pain, but that's alright.

Dealt with plenty of that in my lifetime.

Bring it on.

He steps closer.

I stand tall.

Rocklin throws herself between us. "Enough!" she hisses in her dad's face before spinning to me. "We don't want to disturb our guests for no reason, even if they might find a bullet to his head entertaining."

She's shaking, biting down on her pretty lip, eyes twitching as her brows dip low and then lower. But then they smooth out, her wretched expression clearing, the turmoil in her pretty green eyes evaporating before my own.

My rich girl is gone and in her place is a plastic prep.

"Who is he, daughter?" Rayo demands, voice rumbling.

Rocklin's lip curls and not in a good way. Disgust stares back at me, and then she says, "He's no one. A wannabe interested in joining our school, but like I told him, we don't hang with the help."

My temple tics, pulse ready to pound through my skin and leap at her.

I'm overflowing with rage, ready to raise hell and the devil him fucking self, right here, right now, but unlike all these assholes, mine doesn't show.

I'm stoic as fuck. Straight-faced.

Not a care in the fucking world.

And so I raise a brow and the little brat raises her fucking chin.

"Get out of here and do not come back," she spits, gaze flicking over me from head to toe. "And return the suit to whomever you stole it from, as clearly, you could never afford something so nice."

My phone vibrates in my pocket, but I don't pull it out, instead rubbing my lips together to keep my limbs from shaking, working my peripheral.

Chloe is near now, Damiano too.

Turns out Rocklin ain't done. "Leave, lackey. Run back to where you came from and stay there. We don't want your kind around here, and as you can see, we're trying to enjoy the evening with the people who were actually invited, so unless you plan on taking your last breath tonight, I suggest you get the fuck out." She blinks once. Twice. "*Now.*"

When I take a step toward her, her brows jump into her hairline, and her dad flings himself in front of her. He darts for me, catching me around the neck in a tight grip.

Triumph shines in his brown eyes, but when I merely lift my chin, offering him an even better grip, something flickers in his gaze.

"Leave him, Dad." Rocklin shrugs, stepping toward Oliver, who dares to fucking smirk. She wraps her arm through his and my fingers slip under my sleeve to meet cool steel.

"Why should I let him walk out the door?" Rayo growls, fingers twitching against my skin.

I refuse to swallow or show a single sign of a struggle, even though the air in my lungs is all used up.

"Because he's no one. Not worth the trouble he rode in on." She levels her glare, doubling down. "He's nothing but a poor punk with mommy . . . and daddy issues."

Reluctantly, her father releases me, but his eyes stay glued to mine, even though mine flash to hers, narrowing, and goddamn if there isn't a fucked-up pressure now falling on my chest. My gut twists and I take a step back.

Her lips smash together, but her nose holds high. "You don't belong here. Now go."

The vein in my cheek starts to throb and they see it.

They laugh.

Look down on me.

Shake their fucking heads.

The stiffness in their muscles eases, and every single one aside from Rayo fucking Revenaw takes a step back, no longer seeing me as a threat.

My colors are showing now, so fucking bright it blinds.

Dirt brown.

Worthless white.

Blunted black.

They can't see the red haze of rage clouding my eyes or the promise of retribution aimed right at them.

I'm just a broken boy, mad at the world 'cause Mommy and fucking Daddy didn't love me.

I told her that shit in confidence and have no fucking idea why.

I should have known better.

She wasn't ready for it.

One day she will be. I'll make fucking sure of it.

As for them, I'll shred their dignity one layer at a time. They'll see and learn if only the hard way.

Effort I haven't called on in a long fucking time is needed to move my feet and carry them out across the floor, then out the side doors leading to the garden—the easiest route for a clean break from what I've found.

I'm not halfway across the floor when I hear Rayo's attention called elsewhere, and mere seconds pass before Oliver's protests follow.

Next, it's the soft click of heels, and then Dom to the rescue, but I don't look back. I keep fucking walking, and what do you fucking know?

Rocklin follows.

I make it two steps down when her urgent voice breaks through the air.

"Wait!" she shouts.

I don't wait.

"Would you hold on a minute!" she screams.

I keep moving.

"Goddamn you! This is why you're so bossy in bed, right? Because you can't handle anyone else telling you what to do because you spend every other day taking orders from someone else!"

She's gasping. My feet spin and face hers before the last word leaves her.

I spot Dom at the door, not far, but he doesn't come closer.

Her mouth is clamped tight while she waits for me to speak, but I'm so fucking pissed all I can do is look at her until even the sight of her pisses me off.

"That's right, Rich Girl. I'm a bottom feeder. Nothing but a poor punk who rides for someone else at someone else's call. That's the life I live 'cause that's the hand I was dealt. No ace was slipped in my pocket at birth, but you better fucking believe when I die"—I bend so we're at eye level and that lower lip of hers trembles—"I'll have the entire fucking deck in the palm of my hands, *including* the queen, *my fucking queen*. So have your fake fun tonight, do Daddy's good deeds, but watch yourself. Watch your world real fucking close, 'cause you never know who might come in and turn it upside down. And what a scandal that would be, Miss Greyson."

Her entire body droops. "Bastian . . ."

I hear the plea, the silent cry only I could detect because I am the *only* one who knows her well enough to hear it. She's begging me to understand, to take this at face value and assure her we'll fight and make up later.

Instead, I stand tall, looking down my nose at her, as if she's the leech and I'm the leopard.

"My name is Bass and don't fucking forget it." Shaking my head, I take backward steps away. A mocking laugh that's bitter on my tongue and a smirk I don't feel curve my lips. "Not that you could."

She takes another urgent step toward me, but I give her my back, making sure to move fast 'cause no one here is going to watch it for me.

And I disappear into the shadows.

Rocklin

He walks away, disappearing into the safety of the dark gardens, not even his shadow in sight. I run down the last few steps but stop short, my chest heaving as I replay every word I had said over and over.

"You know he sent people to follow him," Dom's voice comes from behind me, but I don't turn around.

I know he's not wrong. There is no way my dad allowed Bastian to walk out of here after that.

"Should we . . . help him?" Damiano asks hesitantly.

His loyalty to me adds to the war of emotions already raging in my chest, but this is Bastian.

I shake my head no. "They won't find him."

"Rocklin . . ." he disagrees, tone asking me to use reason, but I am.

My world is dark and daunting, but his is too, and he adapts in ways he can. Ways that work and help him in his personal pain. Our people are vicious, but I see that same shadow in Bastian's eyes.

He isn't a nobody.

He's so much more.

Forcing my shoulders straight, I shake my head again, eyes still scanning over the darkness before me. "They won't find him, Damiano. He's . . . invisible."

I got into that little club, ma, 'cause my pops beat silence into me, and those beatings taught me how to be invisible. You can't touch what you can't see, and you can't find what you can't hear.

His words replay in my head and with them comes a throbbing sense of regret.

"You should come inside." Damiano's hesitant voice comes from a little closer this time.

I whip around, eyes locking with his, and he simply pauses his advance, a small nod following as he turns, heading back into the building.

Frustration I've never felt before forms and knots in my throat and I grip my hair, glaring up at the stupid arch above me. I spin, shoving over a giant stone pot full of pink roses. The pot shatters, dirt spilling over into the grass as loose petals filter across the cement steps. The wind picks up right then, blowing them across the tip of my shoe, and I scream, but when an airy laugh sounds behind me, I swallow it halfway, anger threatening to explode from my chest as I face the person it came from.

Chloe fucking Carpo.

My jaw clenches so tight I can't seem to open it to yell and scream at her like I want to. Why the fuck would she bring him here? She had to know what would happen.

Then she shakes her head at me as if she's disappointed in my actions. As if she can't believe what she's seeing. As if she fucking knows me, and then she starts to speak.

"He took a risk coming here." She states the obvious. "For you."

My mouth opens, but when she shakes her head, it closes without permission.

"He had a hard life."

"I know all about his life," I spit out, annoyed that she knows anything about it. She can't possibly know more than me.

"Did you know he had no idea how to dance?"

When my brows crash, she nods.

"I mean, he can dance like anyone else. To the beat of the music, to whatever feels right in the moment. But this?" She hooks her thumb over her shoulder and my eyes flick into the ballroom, swiftly raking over the couples in the center, midwaltz. "He didn't know how to do that."

She watches me, and for a long moment, I'm stuck staring until I catch exactly what she said.

Didn't.

He *didn't* know how to do that.

Icy despair fills my veins, battling for dominance over the heat of jealousy burning through my blood.

"Shame, really." She tips her head, wrapping her shawl tighter around her glitter-covered shoulders. "He never even got the dance he practiced so hard for." She leaves me with that and walks away.

My lips begin to tremble before I can stop them, eyelids fluttering as I will myself not to be weak. Not to be sucked in by this . . . I don't know what it is.

I growl, shouting into the night around me before bending at the knee and burying my face in my hands. Then, something I forgot the feeling of happens.

I start to cry.

I fall back onto my ass, elbows on my knees, and it only gets worse.

My palms are soaked, my cheeks warm and sticky, and then two slender hands wrap around my middle, and my sister's soft scent makes its way into my system.

She presses my head into her shoulder, and I lean into her.

"I'm sorry," she whispers. "That was rough. I know you . . . more than like him."

I do.

"I can tell," she continues.

She can?

I sniffle, hating the sound, and look away.

"He learned how to dance for me, and I just . . ." I groan, angrily swiping at my tears as I pull the item from my dress's hidden pocket.

Trailing my fingers over the switchblade, I flick it open and trace the tip. On a normal day, he would grin when he got home, dig into his pocket and realize it was missing. I don't think he'll find it so entertaining that I took even more from him tonight. "He's pissed."

"He'll get over it."

I scoff, looking out into the night, but it's no use. He's gone. "I don't know."

"Well, if he doesn't, he'll at least come back for that, won't he? I mean, if he's broke, he's going to need his handy little knife."

I chuckle despite myself, smiling sadly at the blade. "Yeah, maybe. He did come back for his phone and his wallet when I took those."

My sister starts laughing then, and I join in, allowing her to pull me to my feet and lead me through the double doors, where our father awaits, angry as ever.

Maybe she's right.

Maybe I didn't ruin everything.

Maybe I'm being dramatic, and tomorrow, everything will be fine.

But then again, maybe it won't be . . .

Chapter 24

Bastian

"Wait."

I jolt, digging into the back of my slacks and coming up with the gun the girl who did her best to gut me gave me.

Doesn't she know all she did was piss me off?

When he comes round the dark corner, I don't lower the weapon but put one in the fucking chamber. I was drowning in my fucking anger so much I didn't hear him coming up on me.

He could have put a bullet in my head like Rocklin made sure to mention, and I would have never seen it coming.

Rocklin would be left to the wolves.

"Don't come closer. I will fucking shoot you."

He lifts his hands. "I want to help."

"Help what?"

"Protect her . . . from him."

I press forward, jamming the muzzle into his chest. "From *who*?"

He eyes me a long moment, and then he says, "From my father."

My eyes narrow, mind spinning when suddenly, it all makes sense.

Well, I'll be fucking damned.

I put the gun away.

Chapter 25

Rocklin

My dad's a fucking liar and my sister's optimism can suck a dick.

It's been two weeks since the gala and things have gone to shit.

My dad pretended he was unfazed for the remainder of the party, but the minute we got back into his car, he laid into me, demanding to know every little thing about the *boy in black*, as he called him. I didn't give him much outside of his chosen name, keeping his real, full one to myself as he intended it.

Yeah, you're really loyal, Rocco.

Stupid.

For four hours, I sat across from him while he treated me like a ten-year-old who talked to a stranger, and after that, he ran down every possible scenario of who he could really be and where he might really come from and what his true intentions are. Then, one of his minions walked in and delivered the bad news . . . there was an "issue" with the security the day of the school tour, and the surveillance from the tour was "accidentally" destroyed—Oliver's snake ass must have given me up, but at least he didn't mention his appearance at The Enterprise.

My dad's eyes grew murderous and speculative and poor Damiano would hear about it, but he won't rat me out. He'll take the heat in stride. I'm going to owe him one now.

The entire time my dad was in detective badass boss mode, all I could do was sit there and take it because the only other option would have been to correct him on all of his *incorrect* yet understandable concerns.

I did the same thing when I met Bastian and continued to play the what-if guessing game the weeks following before I realized he wasn't some hired hand out to get me.

I'm the one who found him, after all.

Found him, stole from him, and then fucked him.

The last thing I expected was for him to show up at The Enterprise that night, but even more shocking was the fact that after I shamelessly let him play with my body, he came back for more.

And I'm not talking about sex.

He wanted that too, of course, we both did, but the boy who'd been burned in his own personal hell for almost fifteen years didn't need me to keep his cock wet.

He needed me for more.

Something in his broken-down soul recognized the tears in my own and little by little, he peeled them back, revealing things about me that even I didn't know. Or maybe it's that I didn't want to know.

Like how I loathe being forced to do what other people demand of me, yet apparently crave to be commanded when it's my choice and coming from the man my mind considers mine.

How twisted is that?

I hate to be controlled, but I want to be controlled.

I'm a rich girl through and through. I was born into money, and I'll die with more of it. I have everything and the means for more. There isn't a person in my world who wouldn't jump at the chance to befriend me, to crawl into my inner circle, or be the very center of it.

People respect me, love me, and yes, some fear me. A few may want to secretly drive a knife through my back, but they wouldn't dare do it, at least not yet anyway.

I have two of the best friends a girl could ask for, both of whom would literally die for me if it came down to it. A sister I love who, despite her many flaws, would stand beside me no matter what. A father who protects me at all costs, quite literally.

I have all these things people can only dream of.

A dark, fairy tale life full of glitter and glam. Gold and silver, diamonds and fucking pearls. Galas and art shows and musical theater, where I'm the future queen, my throne warm and waiting, my people supportive and loyal to a fault.

But beneath the smile and strong, assured words is a crack that runs deep down into the darkest part of my soul, the part Bastion Bishop bled into, filling the hole that hid there with his own brand of bad. Of good.

Of him.

He didn't look at me and judge me or call me pathetic for feeling like a princess in a caged castle I dutifully pretended I was in charge of when, at the end of the day, it wasn't true. Like everything else in my life, for as long as I can remember, the decisions that mattered didn't come from me or the girls. They came from the men who latched our leashes into place.

If I was in charge of my life, I would have taken the hand he offered and pressed my body into his waiting one, melting into his warmth, while his entire focus remained solely on me and me alone.

Every single eye in the place would have been glued to him, desperate to know who the man of the moment was, curious beyond reason about the uninhibited power leaking from his very being, demanding their attention without their permission, but he wouldn't spare them a single glance. He would have known in the back of his mind they were watching because he's alert like that, but he wouldn't have spared them a single second of his time, reserving it for me and me alone.

Always me.

He cooked for me, fought for me, learned how to freaking dance for me, and I couldn't even give him five minutes to show me how quick of a learner he was. I bet he picked it up fast; I bet he had perfect form and unmatched rhythm.

Dance with me, baby . . .

317

A true, physical ache stirs in my chest as his rasped words replay in my head for the hundredth time. When he spoke them, I didn't catch the hint of nerves or the tiny bit of shyness that was woven within them. He stood there strong with sharp, crystal-colored eyes and a small smile as he asked me to take his hand.

I almost did, my mind so overtaken by his closeness in the calm that comes with his presence alone that I almost forgot where I was. All that mattered was where I wanted to be, and that was in his arms.

What's more disgusting is if I could go back in time and do the evening over, I'm not so sure I would have done much differently.

My father cannot get his hands on Bastian.

He'll take him from me and I . . .

I what?

I don't fucking know, that's what!

Huffing, I kick off the bathroom wall, only to drop my shoulders against the other one.

I want to rage. To walk into enemy lines, all so I can fight with someone, stab them with the stupid blade Bastian didn't come back for and watch them bleed all over the floor.

It would slice skin so easily now that I sharpened it.

Goddammit, I'm going fucking crazy and it's all Bastian's fault!

My dad has me on complete and total lockdown. I'm not allowed to leave the manor unless it's to skip over to campus and that's it. The Enterprise has been taken off the table for me, my own fucking creation, and I'm not even allowed there. He keeps telling everyone it's a security measure, but it's not.

It's his arrogant asshole way of doing all he can to keep me away from the boy he doesn't want me near, the boy who could never meet his impossible standards. Sure, okay, he still thinks I'm sneaking away to meet some assassin who's going to snipe me in my sleep or something equally ridiculous, but hey, his wife was murdered in the room they shared, so I guess I can't blame him. Not that he'll admit it.

And then there's the Enzo issue and the fact that there doesn't seem to be one.

There has been no sign of Enzo whatsoever. Zero movement at his estate, no record of his plane returning to the States as my dad claimed, nothing. From what Bronx gathered, he's still sitting tight in Costa Rica, drinking mimosas for breakfast with a bunch of bougie businessmen. Or mass murderers who dress like businessmen, it really could be either and the latter is more likely.

The point is, he's not here, and my sister still is, and there hasn't been a single hint of trouble he claimed was coming, so what the fuck?

My leg starts to bounce and I flip my hair one way, only to flip it the other before counting down from ten.

It doesn't work and I pull up the message threads again, rereading our last meaningless conversation that now means more than it should. I had told him I tried some sort of chili chocolate our dessert chef prepared, and it tasted like shit. He said he'd bring me one from a local market in his neighborhood because he was sure the two-dollar bar would change my mind. I didn't tell him the chocolate the chef used was imported and cost a hundred times that, but I'm pretty sure he gathered as much. The cost part of it anyway.

And then I do what I told myself I wouldn't, what Delta's little ten-second exercise was supposed to keep me from doing.

I reread all twelve texts I've sent him since he disappeared that night, all left unanswered, wincing as I get to the last one . . .

Me: if you don't respond, I'm going to assume this is done and the ban on keeping Dom out of my bed is void.

Yeah, not my proudest of moments, but the thought of Chloe consoling him brought literal vomit up my throat and the message was the result.

I fully realize there's no way in hell that happened. He used her and she let him, which means he pulled something dirty to get his way. Blackmail, if I had my guess, but something sly nonetheless. She's not his type. She's weak and childish and brunette—

I cut off my own thoughts, closing my eyes and dropping my head against the wall. God, I'm so pathetic.

I send another message.

Me: I have to tell you something.

It's a lie, sort of. I have lots of things I could tell him if he were to call, but nothing pressing . . . if you discount the pressure *pressing* in my fucking chest.

I wait. One minute, then two, and then ten.

Shoving my phone in my uniform jacket pocket, I slap the wall, gripping the edge of the sink, and squeeze my eyes shut. The cluster of emotions I don't want to sort through swirling and merging, settling into the one I can live with, anger, because fuck him, right?!

I didn't ask him to come back that first night, nor the second, nor the third, but he did! Despite my false act of indifference toward him, he kept pushing, kept coming, and now he thinks he can just disappear?! Just leave me on read, if he's even fucking reading the messages at all!

After he made me crave him?

Made me trust him?

Made me fucking need him?

Huffing, I push to stand, glaring at my reflection.

Stupid, perfect hair and makeup and uniform.

Pathetic little "rich girl," feeling bad for herself.

"Fuck you, Bastian."

"Bastian . . ."

I whip around, glaring at the empty-eyed janitor I didn't even hear come in.

"I've always liked that name," she mumbles to herself as she moves toward the mirror beside me.

She's not supposed to speak to us, it's all a part of the punishment of working here, yet she doesn't seem to care.

320

Is everyone just losing their damn minds?

"Bastian," she repeats it, and I want to lash at her for daring to speak what only I'm allowed—*was* allowed—to call him. Pulling the rag from her pocket, she rubs circles into the glass in the same spot, over and over again, staring at herself in the mirror. "It's nice, don't you think?"

"No, I don't. I hate it," I lie, turning for the door. "It's a horrible fucking name."

I walk the hell out.

Professor Johnson looks up as I turn my test in, a slight frown building along his forehead. "Done already, Miss Revenaw?" he whispers so as not to interrupt the class.

Pressing my lips together, I offer a tight smile as I nod and the suspicion on his face only grows.

Okay, so maybe I should have been more stealthy. Class started a total of fifteen minutes ago and this is a fifty-question exam.

Not my brightest idea.

I've had way too many of those lately.

"I am free to leave, yes?" I ask.

He hesitates for a moment, but the second he nods, his eyes falling to my absolute tank of a test, I speed walk out of there, down the long hall and slip through the men's locker room door.

There is no training during first class, so I weave through the building with ease, but as I push through the second set of double doors leading toward the gym, the clink of weights and soft conversation reach me. I push forward, looking straight ahead as I stay close to the wall on my way to the side exit.

My pulse kicks up and I walk faster, swiftly swinging open the door, breaking into a run as soon as I'm through it.

The wind hits my face and I smile . . . two seconds before Hue Benson steps around the corner, hands folded together in front of him and cocks his head, bringing me to a swift halt.

Hue is somewhere in the top fifteen on my dad's security detail and is as tall as an ox, as in not at all, but he's fast and nimble and would definitely catch me if I tried to break past him. He says nothing, just stares, and I stare right back.

And then I look to the sky and scream like a fucking brat before adjusting my jacket, spinning on my heels and walking back into my daytime jail cell.

I need to get the hell out of here.

I need to see Bastian just for a minute.

I need to talk to him, yell at him.

I want to fucking scream at him.

My breath grows shallow and my nostrils flare.

I breathe in my nose and out my mouth and I don't go into the Greyson lounge to wait for next period to arrive but walk right out the front door.

What do you fucking know? Sai is there, apparently now ordered to keep himself parked in the same spot for eight fucking hours.

He offers a small smile, but I stare straight ahead, climbing in the door that's held open for me like the spoiled rich girl I am.

I close my eyes and will my lungs to open, some deeper, darker part of me hoping they don't.

I'm fucked in the head, and I know it.

It's all Bastian's fault.

I'm going to get to him. I just need a little help, and I know just where to find it.

"Hell no." Kenex frowns.

"No way." Kylo shakes his head.

The girls laugh, grinning as they look between me and the Greco brothers.

"Oh, come on! What's the worst that could happen?"

"Are you joking? Your dad wants to murder us on the best day." Kenex lifts a brow.

"I'm convinced he's waiting for a reason, not that anyone would question him if he did," Kylo adds.

"We can't," they say at the same time.

"I'm not asking you to go near him. Just . . . you know, pull some shit on his guards. Make a scene, cook up a scheme, whatever you want. We only need four minutes to get off the property."

"And when it gets back to Rayo we helped?" Kenex drops into the seat with a huff, already resigned to helping me, even if he hasn't said it out loud yet.

"You're not going to do something obvious. You're both smarter than that."

Their brows jump at my sort-of compliment and Bronx chuckles.

"Be real, Rocco." She looks my way. "The Grecos pop off and suddenly you're nowhere to be seen? They will put two and two together."

I want to scream *I don't care*. I'm getting out of this magnificent fucking prison if I have to drug every fucking guard in this place.

Wait, that's a fantastic idea.

Well, okay, it's a *bad* idea, but a great backup.

I sit back, crossing my arms and instead say something more sane. "Why do you think you are all coming with me? I won't be alone, so what can anyone really say?"

Everyone pins me with that "really?" kind of stare, but I hold strong.

Damiano is the first to speak, his expression closed off. "This is reckless, Rocklin. Someone could follow us. Enzo could be waiting for one of you to step outside the walls to make his move."

I want to remind him we're on *Team Enzo Isn't Fucking Here* but don't.

"We will be careful and quick."

"And armed." Delta reaches over, squeezing Alto's thigh, likely sensing his displeasure.

Damiano holds my gaze a moment. "What happens if he's not impressed with our arrival?"

My stomach flips, but I ignore it, lifting a single shoulder and looking back to Kenex and Kylo. "We're offering a free pass for trouble. Are you going to take it or not?"

The boys look to one another. Slowly and perfectly in sync, their smirks spread, telling me all I need to know.

They're in.

One way or another, I'm getting out of here tonight.

Let's hope no one gets their asses kicked in the process.

Chapter 26
Rocklin

Someone does get their ass kicked, but dear Delilah had it coming.

I warned her of the boys' little games the day she took my deal to break their one rule and fuck one on the other's assigned day, but, of course, the little deviants were far too enticing for her to remember my warning.

She knew exactly what was in the contract she signed that made her theirs for that week, and the big, bold line that gets them all to agree—as if the mere fact that they get to play with both isn't enough—reads "during the dates listed approve, Kenex and Kylo are the sole property of the above-mentioned name."

The boys have themselves a new girl this week, and she's a feisty one. The daughter of an arms trafficker, raised in a house with four brothers. She's tough as shit and right now?

She's pissed.

Delilah fell for the shirtless thirst trap of the boys skinny-dipping in the property pond. "All alone," the caption read.

"They knew someone would show, just as they knew this week's flavor would." Alto shakes his head.

Bronx smirks at the security footage, all of us huddled in the back of Dom's town car, watching the grounds team rush over as a wave of students dashes that way to catch a glimpse of the livestreaming fun.

"Sexual sadists, I swear." She shakes her head with a grin as Damiano hauls ass out the gate and zooms down the long, winding road. "That's ending in a giant orgy in the dorm pool."

"Why do you think they did it?" Delta grins, leaning into Ander while crossing her legs over Alto's lap. "People are shredding clothes as they run."

"And that is where the orgy shall be born."

Everyone chuckles, but I'm hardly hearing them anymore.

We're on the road with no lights behind us, and our phones have yet to ring. Granted, it's been a total of five minutes, but that's better than I've managed on my own.

What should be a two-hour drive is just a little over one with Dom behind the wheel, eager to get us there and back as fast as possible, yet to me, it feels like five, maybe even ten, long sets of sixty minutes.

At one point, I even closed my eyes to count them but grew distracted each time, and then suddenly, we were in Brayshaw.

As we pull up to the old warehouses Kenex had led us to last time though, the place is a graveyard, nothing but empty, busted bottles littering the ground and dried bloody dirt mid-ring.

I step up to it, gripping the rope as a wave of emotion rolls over me, causing me to shake.

Where the fuck is he?

I pull my phone out, but Delta plucks it from my fingertips, and I press my middle fingers to the corners of my eyes.

We've been out here for a good twenty minutes and have seen nothing but a cat jump across the busted crates lining the edges. I walk over to the large warehouse building, yanking on the locked chain, but there's no light peeking through anywhere, and it's not like anyone could be inside with the door bolted down.

The thought sends a shudder down my spine.

Oh my god, what if my dad *does* have him?

What if he's locked in Dad's soundproof "business," a.k.a. torture room in our family home's basement?

Panic flares and I whip around, eyes wide.

Damiano darts toward me, gaze flying from right to left in search of the threat, but then Bronx jumps off the crate she climbed up on in her four-inch platforms. "Found it!"

All heads snap to hers, but she says nothing as she moves toward Dom's car, so we follow at a quickened pace, climbing in.

"What did you find exactly?" he asks as he puts the car in drive and looks to the navigation screen as she types in the location.

"His car. It's been parked for about an hour at this address." Her gaze locks with mine in warning. "It's a house on the nicer side of town."

My pulse leaps in my chest. A house.

Chloe's house?

No. Stop.

I will literally burn it down.

Bronx smirks as if reading my thoughts and I check my bra for the Zippo I stuffed inside it, just in case, but as we pull onto the street, a second small stroke of . . . rightness, the mere possibility of going to him soothing part of me. I hold on to the feeling as we make the small trip to the house Bronx believes Bastian might be.

The street is semi-deserted as far as the homes go, most still under construction or with For Sale signs in the front yards, like the place he took us the night he met my friends.

Only this time, the court is filled with cars, most blocking each other in. The only vehicles with a clear path out are two identical black SUVs, the kind my father's men barricade him between when he's out on "business."

"That's . . . worrisome," Delta notes what I just have.

"It's probably just the Brayshaw heirs."

"And all these other cars?" Alto edges, unloading, then reloading his Ruger.

Damiano pulls up behind the last black SUV right as a handful of people stumble out onto the lawn. A couple drunk frat-looking boys begin wrestling as the girls giggle and cheer. He turns to me. "I don't think this is a good idea."

"Oh, please. They're drunk trust-fund kids, not Mafia heirs."

I climb over Ander and push out of the car without another word, the others moving to follow.

As we make our way up the path, a few people glance at us from the lawn, and I wonder for a moment if they'll say something, but they do no more than size us up before turning back to their entertainment for the evening.

We don't appear completely out of place, all young enough to blend in for the most part, but if you look close enough, there is a stark difference between us and them.

Their biggest problem is what to wear to prom, while ours is, well, unexpected death.

We reach the door and Dom pushes himself in front of me, Ander moving to the back of us while Alto stays firmly at Delta's side. Bronx loops her arm through mine and as one, we move inside.

The music is heavy, the chatter loud, and the place is full of more people than I expected to see.

A hand slaps out in front of us, blocking our path, and a tall, attractive male meets each of our gazes.

"This is invite only."

I scoff, and he raises a brow.

My head tugs back. Okay, so maybe they aren't basic teenagers.

"Seriously?"

His eyes narrow and he settles his gaze on Damiano, deciding the biggest of us all is the boss. "I don't recognize you, but that doesn't mean you're one of them."

"One of who?" Dom asks, attempting to keep his tone nonchalant, but his hand has already disappeared into his pocket. No telling what kind of weapon he has hidden inside it.

"A Graven."

Graven. Not Greyson.

Then I remember the tour we did last semester; there was one senior from a school called Graven Prep. It doesn't click for the others though, and suddenly, Ander and Alto are in front of us, shuffling us back. Then I see her.

Brown hair and pretty pink smile.

Bitch.

"Chloe!" I shout.

She's laughing, her eyes moving toward where she hears her name, and she freezes, a small frown taking over.

The guy at the door, his muscles lock as he snaps his head over his shoulder, narrowing his eyes at her.

Chloe blushes but clears her throat, now walking this way . . . with a little too much sway in her hips, in my opinion.

Her gaze slides my way, and I hold it.

One way or another, I'm getting into this fucking party.

Slowly, she nods, facing the guy once more. "I see you've met my new friends. Guys, this is Mac."

Mac doesn't look at us but keeps frowning at her. "Who said you could bring people?"

They stare at one another, and finally, he shakes his head, walking away, so we step farther into the house.

Chloe frowns. "If anyone else asks, I didn't get you in here. My name doesn't hold a lot of weight right now, so you'll be on your ass fast. I suggest you stay out of trouble."

"Move."

She glares, eyes calculating. "I hope you approach him," she snaps, not bothering to say who "him" is. We already know. "And take the boys with you. See how fast they end you if they go near her."

Her.

Her who?

Chloe stomps away and we let her, despite how easy it would be to knock her out without so much as a sound.

We weave through one living room and move into another.

That's when I spot him sitting in a chair with a beer bottle in hand, one I'm sure is still full to the brim. One I want to take from his fingers and smash over the girl's head who's beside him.

That's the "her" Chloe spoke of and she's leaning closer than I want her to. They're talking quietly. Comfortably.

"Okay, so . . . he's alive," Bronx eases, grip tightening on my arm as if she's afraid I might charge over.

Honestly, I'm not sure why I'm still standing here.

So, yeah. He's not in my dad's basement and he's not fucking dead.

I should be relieved.

I'm abso-fucking-lutely *not*.

Bass

My homegirl Rae shakes her head, eyes moving to Maddoc Brayshaw, who watches our every move from where he stands, trying to pick up on our conversation, but the place is too loud for that.

She tries to avoid my gaze, but I keep myself in front of her, wanting her to hear what I'm saying. She's good for this place, for the Brayshaw brothers and the world they've built.

People like us come from shit and when you find a spot you belong, you don't let anyone take it from you. I know I won't.

So, yeah. She needs to hear it from someone like her, who wasn't born with a silver fucking spoon, but a broken, plastic one. She needs to understand what she's found here, the power they're giving her, and the girl needs to take it.

When she stays quiet, I ask, "What, you thought not?"

She presses her lips together. "I'm tired of people saying that like it's what I was looking for here. I mean, who fucking cares—"

"I care," I cut her off. "I care because you doubt your power over this place, and I want you to find it." A frown forms over my brows instantly because I know I opened a door, but I want to see what she knows. If she's heard about my life before or my sister, maybe she's heard about my mom.

Like I knew she would, she asks for more. "Why do you want that for me? Why's it so important?"

"Fuck," I mumble, running a hand over my face. My mind is busy lately. Too busy.

I'm ready to leave. Got shit going on and half a foot out the door already, most of my time spent elsewhere, but Brielle will have to stay where she is, at least for now.

I can't tell my sister when I cut out; she'll want to come with me, but it would be more dangerous for her to follow than it would be to have her here in Brayshaw, and I didn't keep her away for no reason.

It's a fucked-up mess.

This place has its dangers too, and things are only getting stickier by the day, not that it has much to do with me, but working here, I'm in it.

It's like every part of my life is deciding to start the fucking timer at the same exact moment, and all bombs are about to go off.

I need to find a way to delay one while the other detonates.

I keep talking. "Because I need to know a girl who lived like me, fucked-up mentally and cut off emotionally—to most, anyway—can fight her way from the bottom and come out with sharper claws, not broken ones."

Rae slowly drops against the cushion. "Who is she?"

"Who?"

"Don't play dumb." She grunts. "Who's the girl you're worried about making it or not?"

And there it fucking is. She doesn't know about Brielle, so she can't possibly know anything about what happened to my mom.

"They didn't tell you . . ." I realize. "I almost thought they'd brag."

"They're not the type." She defends her crew. "Well, maybe Royce, but . . ." she jokes of the hotheaded brother.

A small grin forms on my lips and I look away a minute, coming back with a squint. Fuck it. She's good people.

"My sister."

"Sister."

"Yup. Your boys, they stepped in when the people around us failed." Or some suit-wearing fucker did on their behalf. "Got us out before worse could happen." I trace the tattoo on my left fist.

Like before, I could come to and point the smoking barrel at my mother's head and pull the trigger for a third time.

332

"Got you out . . ." she trails off, glancing at Maddoc once more. "Like they saved you?"

I saved me, saved my sister, so I don't say anything. This isn't a shit-talking chat, and it's starting to sound like too much of a therapy session for me.

Maybe I smoked too much tonight.

Maybe I know my time here is almost up 'cause there's somewhere else I'd rather be. And that selfish part of me I never knew I had is burning a bigger pit with each passing day, melting the single-minded side that has only ever wanted one thing, my sister happy and safe in a life she chooses.

I want more now.

I want for me.

And I want to fucking stab myself for it.

"So where is she? One of the girls in the home?" she asks of the group home, wondering if she's met my sister without realizing it.

"Nah." I shake my head. "She's away from here, as she should be."

"Bass—"

I serve her with a pointed look. Nope. Not doing this shit.

I said what needed to be said to find out what I needed to know—the Brayshaws didn't tell their new queen anything about me, so chances are they don't know more than I do. We were only kids when I was brought here, so why the fuck would they?

If there's someone I'm going to ask about the woman who brought me into this world, it's becoming clearer it ain't them . . . but maybe their dad can help if I can get him to accept my visit.

The hairs on my neck stand in the next moment, my muscles growing stiff, and I know.

I'm about to jump up, but Raven's words make me pause, confirming what I already figured out.

My rich girl is here.

"And, uh . . ." I can hear her fucking grin without looking at her. "How about the chick who looks ready to castrate you while also looking like someone pissed in her Pradas?"

I scoff, keeping my face blank and forcing myself to joke with her. "You even know what Prada is?"

"Fancy shit, Collins told me all about it." She grins.

A low, forced laugh leaves me, and I wait several seconds before slowly looking the way she did.

There she fucking is, Damiano at her side like a good little soldier. This time, I allow my features to harden. Downing the beer because I know she doesn't expect me to, and small creases form along her temples.

Letting my head fall back lazily, I eye Rocklin while speaking to Rae, so she can read my lips clearly from where she's standing. "She is the opposite of you—a follower. A rich bitch who only dates rich boys."

She's not a follower, I know this, but she did follow her daddy's rules out of fear, and she needs to get past that. She'll never have what she wants, what she's worth if she doesn't.

It's not something anyone can do for her. The girl's gotta figure out how her damn self, to spot the crack she keeps missing, holding on to that *family before all* bullshit he ingrained in her.

I scoff at the thought.

Damn, she looks good, pissed off and a little tortured, but good.

Her big green eyes beg me to come to her while her sharpened features dare me to deny her.

Cute, Rich Girl. Still pretending you're in charge when you never have been, not when it comes to you and me.

After a moment, I move my eyes back to Raven.

"Wanna make her jealous?" she jokes, and an instant laugh breaks free.

In my peripheral, Rocklin jerks, but someone keeps her in place.

"Nah, I'm not in the mood to fight your boy tonight."

"Ah, come on, you can hold your own." She smiles. "I mean, at first."

I smirk at her as I push to my feet, letting her keep her little opinion of her man. No need to ruin it for her.

334

"You're good people, Bass Bishop." She offers me her fist, so I push mine into it.

I pull a pre-roll from my pocket and slide my headphones over my ears as I nod goodbye.

I don't look at Rocklin once, heading in the opposite direction she's standing, but I know she's coming.

Pulling my phone out to send a quick message to Hayze, I find he's already sent one my way.

Hayze: your girl's here. Six total.

Me: Leave.

Rocklin needs to do the same. She's got no business being here.

And lookee, lookee . . . no fucking guard on her tail.

Again.

Rocklin

"Do you want to go to The Enterprise? Maybe wind down and—"

"No," I cut Dom off, moving toward my wing without a single look back.

I'm fuming, on the verge of shaking or screaming or throwing myself down the fucking stairs, but I make it no more than five steps up when the front door bursts open and my dad flies in.

"What did I say?!" he booms.

But I'm not given a chance to answer, as no less than two dozen men file in behind him, half head toward me, the other half breaking toward the right.

"What the f—" My arms are gripped on both sides, and I yank away, but then each limb is in someone's grasp and I'm carried out the door. "Dad, what the hell! What is going on?"

I'm literally tossed into the car. The door slammed in my face.

Growling, I dart forward, reaching for the handle, but then it's thrown open and my sister is tossed in, dressed in nothing but a long shirt that is definitely not hers.

She looks from me to the men surrounding the cars and back. "He's here, isn't he? Enzo? This is it? The trade?"

"Trade? What *trade*?"

"The clause in my contract."

"What clause?"

She hiccups, and my eyes narrow.

"Are you drunk?"

"If only." Her smile is sloppy and sad.

I shake my head, focusing once more. "Boston, what clause?"

"The one about me being a failure."

My heart pounds in my chest and she opens her mouth to say more, but movement out the window catches my eye, so I slap my hand over it in perfect time for our father to slip into the vehicle.

He's shaking, absolutely livid, as he glares from me to my hand over my sister's mouth, but he doesn't say a word.

He sits back and glares some more.

"Dad—"

"Don't. I told you to stay put. You're being followed. Everywhere you go. Everything you do. You are being followed. I have no idea by who, but they want me to know for a reason." His frown deepens, and he clenches his jaw.

My brows snap together. "How do you know?"

"They've been sending me shots of you, both of you. Images and videos. It's been going on for a while now. I don't think they can tell you two apart, and that's the only reason no move has been made."

"What?!" I snap, glancing at Boston when she jerks, well on her way to passing out again. "How could you not tell me?!"

"I am telling you now." He scowls. "I had added security in place all this time, and I've told you to behave. You were aware of the risks we were taking here, so I don't know why you're surprised."

"Are you joking?!" My eyes snap toward the driver when he rolls up the privacy window. "You're telling me someone has been watching me. That's pretty fucking surprising!"

His eyes narrow at my tone, but he doesn't comment on it. "Does Damiano know?"

"He's being debriefed now."

"This is messed up." I shake my head. "You should have warned me."

"And you would have what . . . listened?"

I press my lips together, and he lifts a knowing brow.

Huffing, I focus on what's important. "What do we know and don't tell me nothing."

337

He tips his head slightly, an irritated sigh leaving him. "That's the problem and exactly what we have. Nothing." His eyes meet mine. "I can find nothing. I can trace these back to no one." A fierce form of rage flashes in his gaze. "It's your mother's case all over again."

My inhale is sharp, his words catching me off guard. My mother's case.

He has *never* spoken to me about her case before . . . or lack thereof, really.

We stare at each other for a long moment, his gaze constantly shifting as his mind runs a mile a minute. When I don't break under his watchful eye, he sits back, and the anger slowly fades into a curious sort of pride.

He pulls his phone from his suit jacket, looking at the screen. "There are things we must discuss. We will speak on it soon," he dismisses me.

As the silence stretches, it doesn't take long for me to fall back into my endless thoughts. Bastian won't speak to me, won't return my calls, and tonight, I went into his world as he came into mine, desperate for a conversation, at the very least. The man gave me nothing, pretended I was just some girl with eyes for the bad boy, while he gave all his words to someone else.

A girl who fit beside him in ways I never will. He sat there enjoying his night, all carefree and grinning at a girl I had vivid images of stabbing when she smiled back at him.

My ribs constrict and I breathe through the tension.

Fuck him.

He's clearly not interested in what I have to say, doing just fine and not sitting around wondering what I've been up to or who has been in my bed when he was so quick to demand *no one* be. So, yeah. Fuck him.

He can go fuck himself for all I care.

I don't need him.

I don't.

I do fucking *not*.

Chapter 27
Rocklin

"So how was school?" my father asks as he cuts into his steak with ease.

Boston bounces in her seat. "Since I can't be on the dance team anymore, I convinced Miss Giano to allow me to choreograph for the showcase."

"That's excellent news. It will look good on your application to Juilliard next term."

My eyes snap up, flicking between my father and Boston, the tension in Boston's shoulders obvious, while my father appears as lax as ever.

She pushes another bite of food around on her plate, none yet making it into her mouth, though she keeps cutting small pieces and shuffling them around.

"Maybe we could even get you an internship with Hass Morgan. You know he's on Broadway now."

My sister clears her throat, her voice coming up lower. "I had heard, yes."

"I could put in a call, see about—"

"Are we fucking kidding?" I snap.

My sister's head slices my way while our father, ever the methodical one, slowly drags his eyes to mine.

He chews his steak, taking a sip of water before he speaks again. "Something wrong, daughter?"

A humorless laugh bubbles out of me, and then a second one as I push my chair back.

"Yeah. Something is wrong. Something is really fucking

wrong!" The air hisses from my lungs. "We're sitting around a fucking dinner table we haven't sat at in almost twelve years, having a little family chat about classes and admissions like we're normal. We are not normal. This is not normal. I'm spending half my day locked in a house that is no longer my home, in a room that was mine when I was seven before I was shipped away like a trading card and dropped into the mansion *alone*. And now you want to sit and chat about school and college as if it fucking matters when it doesn't! We literally run our own academy because we're a bunch of fucking psychopaths with murder tendencies." My eyes slice to Boston and back to my dad. "Stop talking to her about a dance school she can never go to. I know it, she knows it, and you know it. She'll either be dead by fall or locked in a basement somewhere south."

"Rocklin!" he booms.

"It's true! If not her, then me, or maybe even all of us, since you thought it was a bright idea to put us all in one place. Might as well offer to light the fuse yourself."

"Watch your tone, daughter."

I should, but I can't. Anger and so much more are boiling inside me, stewing and stirring and I'm going fucking crazy.

"I have been locked in this house for *weeks,* only 'allowed' out for classes I shouldn't even have to take because I'm a fucking Revenaw. Because someone is watching us all like a hawk and you can't figure out who it is, but you won't allow me to help."

"It's not your concern."

"It is my life! My work is being handled by other people. I'm putting my members out into the world, chewing them out from a room with a pink princess canopy over my bed!"

His eyes narrow, and he speaks slowly. "I am taking care of things. This is not forever. It's a temporary hiccup we are dealing with."

"I want to go home. I want my life back. This is bullshit and you know it."

"What is *bullshit,* dear daughter, is that you do not listen." Warning flashes across his features, his anger deepening the wrinkles along his forehead, making him appear older. "You sneak off to go god knows where to do god knows what, with god knows who. I will not have it, not while your safety is at risk."

"Our entire world is a risk. If you wanted to avoid risk and trouble for your children, maybe you shouldn't have had any. Or better yet, maybe you should have just kept trying until you had a son because a man could protect himself better, right?!"

Our father flies from his seat, the table shaking, his chair soaring back and crashing to the cold marble floors. His eyes are thunderous, his voice roaring, rattling the dishes between us.

His body shakes, hands tense and clenched at his sides as he glares down at me.

His jaw is locked so hard I'm sure his gums will bleed.

For the first time in maybe ever, a hint of fear flickers down my spine.

I've never been afraid of my father. Nervous of his actions, yes, because duh.

He kills people and if he doesn't, he has someone do it for him.

But right now?

The dead, dislodged void in his eyes as he stares at me from across the table makes me want to shrink, just as my lungs have.

"Go . . . to your room." His voice is low and gravelly.

I begin to nod, but he doesn't stay around to witness it.

He stalks off, a harsh slam echoing moments later.

I feel Boston's eyes on me, but I ignore her, flying toward my room as quickly as I can without running.

My lungs fight me, demanding dominance, ceasing control beyond my own, and I know it's too late to breathe through it. I lift my hands over my head, breathing in through my nose and out my mouth.

I hate this. I hate . . . everything!

I feel weak and pathetic and it's disgusting.

My life was in control before . . . before what?

Before I was eight and moved into a mansion without my family because the manor had gone two decades without holding an heir and my father wanted me to be the first of the first females, even though heirs weren't required to arrive until the age of ten.

Before my mom went to bed and never woke up, just two weeks after I left?

Before Bronx showed up two years later?

Delta a few months after that?

Before I dominated the Olympics, went to Greyson, climbing every fucking ladder put forth just for another to appear at the top?

Before my body decided to fuck me over and weaken me?

When was it *ever* in control?

Yes, I love what I do.

I love the Greyson society we've formed and love creating schemes to fuck those who try and fuck us, who break the rules and step over the very thin line painted in the sand.

I've made grown-ass men weep. Destroyed them from the ground up with little effort and minimal blood. I love that too. I love my girls and the mansion, and I want that head Greyson seat Calvin is keeping warm, but I'm Rayo Revenaw's daughter. My duty first is to my family, to my name.

Family, above all, always, no matter what. That's what he says.

But what the hell does that even mean anymore?

My sister fucked us and here she is, planning a fucking dance routine and eating imported salmon. I want to fucking scream.

To fight.

I want to fucking cry.

Apparently, I am because when I pick up my phone, unlock it with the stupid, immature password I updated it with, a wet drop falls onto the screen.

I swipe it away, go straight to the favorite tab and type out a message.

Me: don't make me fucking beg, Bastian.

I don't know why I sent that. He loves it when I beg.

Or he did.

I glare at my phone, tucking it back into my skirt as I grab my jacket and pull it over my shoulders.

I refused to "get dressed" for dinner about a week ago, and it feels like the most minimal of wins, but a rebellious one nonetheless.

Every night, my father forces these family meals on us. One might think it's sweet that he's using a shitty situation to try to make up for lost time, having all the dinners we never got the chance to have together, but a smart person knows the difference.

I know the fucking difference.

He's not making up for lost time. He's giving himself more. Facing the truth that at any moment, there may never be another chance for one.

Anyway, I've stopped changing into my dinner attire and don my Greyson uniform all day, every day, which is why I'm still wearing it now at midnight.

It's been a few hours since my father sent me to my room, and I've paced around it for just as long. Waiting.

Sure enough, the moment he assumes we're asleep, he slips into his car with his driver and down the long driveway they go, off to handle boss shit I'm not allowed to know about, even though I'm supposed to take his place someday.

I slip into the hall, using the secret escape staircase in the lavatory, and take it all the way down to the floor-level garage.

I'm not stupid enough to think there aren't guards everywhere. Even if I hadn't tried to escape a total of five times already, I would know.

This is why sweet little Delta brought a gift to campus for me today, and I'm ready to use it.

I slip into the hall, and sure enough, Hue is standing guard against the door.

His eyes flick up, hand lifting to his earpiece, but he only has enough time for his eyes to widen, and then he's slumped against the wall, the arrow having shot into his leg before he felt the sting.

I smile at him and slip into the garage, sending a second and then third dart toward Victor and Franky, more freaking guards. Thankfully Franky has his back to me, or he might have gotten a jump on me and called for backup.

He falls to the side, hitting his head on an armchair, and I wince.

"That's going to hurt later."

I whip around, holding the gun up to my sister, but she only smiles, coming down the few steps to stand before me.

"Where are we going?"

"No."

"Rocklin, please—" I shoot her in the thigh.

"Bitch," she whispers, and I catch her as she falls, easing her to the ground.

I run through my dad's car collection, choosing his Aston Martin, five years older and a lighter shade of blue than mine, and slip inside.

The fob is in the console, as always, and I start the engine, speeding toward the garage door in seconds. It's motion censored, my leg bouncing over and over as I wait for it to open up a few more feet. I only need it halfway to get this baby out.

Few more inches . . .

I grip the wheel, and then legs come into view and my gut plummets.

Sai stands there with his arms crossed, glare heavy over his brow.

I could shoot him. I would just have to stick my hand out the door after I got it opened and shoot. He would slump to the ground, of course, and at about, I don't know, two-hundred-sixty-five pounds of solid muscle, I *might* be able to drag his dead weight to the side enough to pull out.

"Don't even think about it," he warns, and then he slides into the passenger seat, eyes hard on me. "I thought I told you, no more sneaking off until I—"

His brows crash, and then he looks down at his arm. "Goddammit, girl."

"Sorry," I mumble, hitting the button to close the door, but only after I drag his big-ass legs inside the car and shut it.

I need out of here.

I need freedom.

I know what I fucking need.

The drive is slightly different from my family's estate, with a few more twists and turns, but my memory knows where to take me, even if my mind has yet to catch up.

When I was young, my sister and I would look around at the other kids in our world and pick out our future husbands the way our mother had told us hers was picked.

Her father wanted the strongest man for her, the biggest, baddest, and most brilliant one. The one no other could rival. That no one could reach, no matter how hard they tried. The most handsome and loving man, as she told it.

So Boston and I would look for that. Whatever we saw as "the best" little boy. The toughest or coolest or whatever other word we might have used back then.

She always picked bullies, while I always picked the quiet ones. She would make fun of me, saying how I would be kidnapped and she would be safe because she chose the strongest one, just like Mom. Weird shit for two little girls to fight about, who were more likely to get kidnapped, but that was our world. It was a normal threat we were all aware of, even if we didn't fully understand what it meant outside of being taken from our parents. We would make our picks and then we'd fight about why we chose them, and then Mom would step in with a laugh.

She told hers and our dad's story as a fairy tale, but as I got older, I realized it wasn't. Their love was real, from what I know, but it didn't begin that way.

It was a transaction between families, much like Enzo and my sister. A power play and one my mother refused to allow us to fall into. Having daughters in our world is tough, and

345

the most common practice if you do birth a female heir is to find the man she'll stand beside one day. Or, you know . . . stand behind.

She was adamant about never allowing such a thing. It had to be our choice. We had to choose if we wanted the man that was offering us his hand. It was the only demand she made of my father, and as I've heard from many over the years, one she made known widely. Men would come to our home with their children when we were only five years old, offering their fortunes for promises of the future, but my father turned them all away. As my mother told it, he prayed for daughters, but I think he just prayed—the devil maybe 'cause no one else would listen to a murderous man—my mother wouldn't turn out infertile so he didn't have to divorce or step out on her to get himself the heir he needed. Then once she got pregnant with us and it was learned that *all* the wives of the Greyson Union families were pregnant with girls, he was thrilled. Because, as always, fate shined on my father and proved, yet again, he was superior.

The other families were having girls . . . he was having two.

He wanted strong, independent girls. Girls who would rise up and take over and be the first of our kind.

A new wave. Generation setters.

He got one in me, but Boston was different.

She wanted what my mother had. The pretty home and nice things and a love she couldn't possibly hold on to. And I mean, who knows, maybe she would have found that one day, but she rushed into the future. Boston chose Enzo, and so my father gave her him, but only because he is who he is. There is no love there, no relationship. There isn't even a conversation they've shared from what Boston has said.

But there is the most important of things.

There's power.

Money.

There's possibility.

There is no love.

346

I blink, my eyes flicking around, realizing I'm in a familiar parking lot, the area as dark and desolate as always, nothing to be seen but the soft-yellow light from inside the small store for miles. I don't know how long I sit here, but it's a long fucking time. Long enough for my ass to go numb and my mind to go crazy.

When I can't take it any longer, I tear from the car and stomp my way across the dark space, straight inside it. The little old man behind the counter knows I'm coming before I've even set foot inside the door. He doesn't have to say a word, the small smile he gives answer enough.

He called Bastian.

He called him, and he's not coming.

He's leaving me here to rot.

I want to fucking scream. I want to fight.

I want him to regret this.

Storming out of the building, I pull my phone from my pocket, slipping my card from the back.

I swipe it through the pump and then the one behind it.

My eyes grow foggy, and I refuse to acknowledge why as I lift the handles and squeeze. I watch the golden liquid puddle all around, pouring from both spouts until they grow heavy in my hands, and then I let them fall.

I move back to the car, put it in neutral and roll forward several feet, and then I take the Zippo from the center console and flick it open.

The man opens the door as I straighten once more, the flame bright in my hand.

His face falls, and he goes back inside, swiftly disappearing from sight.

I set the lighter down and get back inside the car, pulling out into the middle of the road.

I wait for the gasoline to roll its way down the uneven pavement until it catches.

And then it blows like a fucking bomb, a giant fireball spanning out like a balloon, before a billow of smoke lifts into the air.

Warm, hot streaks stain my cheeks as I watch the fire burn, turning the place into ash.

Into nothing.

Just like we are. Nothing.

I sit there, staring for a long time, vaguely aware of the sirens in the distance.

"Feel better now?" Sai's voice is groggy, and when I look at him, his mouth curves into a small, sorrowful smile like he knows. Like he's aware I'm unwanted and unworthy and royally fucked up.

Like the man inside the building who just lost his livelihood at my hand, I could argue it's Bastian's fault, but that isn't really true.

What is, is that messing with people in our world leads to destruction, and now he knows.

His good deeds done here will be no more. He no longer has a reason to come back this way now. No reason to cross my path again.

"No," I rasp, facing forward and heading back to my prison cell.

Fuck him.

Fuck *everyone*.

Chapter 28
Rocklin

Spinning on my feet, I place my heels at the edge and close my eyes. I take a deep, calming breath to clear my mind and prepare myself, but it doesn't work. It never works anymore. Nothing does, which is why I'm here, fifty feet above the water, ready to throw myself into it, half hoping my lungs decide to seize and take me since no one else will. Or, at the very least, knock me out for a while, if only to give me a fucking break from the chaos inside my own mind.

Slowly arching my back, I push myself off the board, my body a straight line, toes pointed in the air above. The world whips past my eyes as I sail toward the water, my head in a neutral position.

The indescribable rush fills me all at once, and though I'm midair, time going by too fast to process, it's as if I can breathe for the first time in months. My palms flatten just before I break into the water and then I'm deep within its depth, floating back to the surface before I'm ready. I don't wait or take a breath, but swim to the edge, climb out and make my way back up the stairs. Then I do it again, and again, and again, until my lungs are heaving, the muscles in my neck straining, desperate for air my stupid, broken body refuses to allow.

This time, I left my inhaler in my locker on purpose. I don't want it. I don't want the help to breathe. I just want to erase him from my memory, but he won't fucking go away. It's been months, and still, every time I close my eyes, I see him.

Every time I open them, I look for him. Every phone call I get or incoming text.

It's disgusting and pathetic, and I hate him.

I may even hate my father more at the moment though, which is saying something. Here at school, it's the only time I have for myself. He's still obsessed with whoever the hell is following us and it doesn't seem to be something that will end anytime soon. I don't get to see my girls unless they're here because he refuses to allow them to come over. He's held a meeting without me, explaining to everyone why a Greyson isn't at Greyson Manor where she belongs.

Shaking and tight-chested, I climb the ladder once more, but this time, only to the middle plank with no bounce. I move up to the edge and bend, placing my palms on its base, and kick my feet into the air, toes pointed until I'm in a handstand. I close my eyes, taking a deep breath.

"Look who's back in the water."

My concentration slips, and I tumble over the side, skilled enough to tuck my body halfway, but my left hip still slaps into the water with a small sting. It's nothing I can't handle and nothing I haven't felt before, but I'm a perfect fucking diver. I shouldn't have felt it at all.

I fly up to the surface, whipping around until my eyes connect with the person who interrupted, Oliver fucking Henshaw.

His eyes travel over my face. "I haven't seen you in here in a long time."

"I don't come in here when other people are around," I snap, kicking so I float in place.

"You don't come in here at all." He smirks, hands sliding into his uniform pockets as he makes his way closer.

I force my eyes not to narrow, and as if he senses it, his smile only spreads. It's a little calculating but not unnerving.

The only reason this guy is still here is that it's easier for the others to keep an eye on him here than it would be if he were sent home.

"Or at least you haven't in months, maybe even longer than that?" He pretends to guess, but there's a sureness in his tone that has my eyes narrowing.

How would he know that if he wasn't watching?

He comes to stand by the pool's edge, mere feet from where the ladder is located. "I assumed you've been using the pool at the manor? I hear it's nice." He nods to himself. "I'm sure it's better than the one we have at the dorms, but everything is better at the manor, right? Better food, better company . . . maybe even better security?"

His words are like a trigger, causing my gut to stir, but I mask my facial expression as I swim toward the stairs, gripping the right handle, leaving my left beneath the water.

"Shouldn't you be, I don't know, anywhere but here?"

He lifts one shoulder, eyes bouncing around the space, and I can't help but think he's checking to see if we are alone. He should know better. There's no such thing as being alone on the Greyson Estate. There are eyes everywhere. More so nowadays.

Then again, not enough to stop a certain someone from sneaking in wherever he wanted . . .

A small pain hits my chest, and I ignore it, tearing myself from the pool, accepting the outstretched towel Oliver hands me from the bench he swiped it off of.

"I'm going to a fundraiser this weekend. Some big investors my father is looking to sweet-talk, and he wants you there, at my side."

I scoff, swiping at my legs and then wringing my hair out as I lift a brow at him. "And I'm supposed to care why?"

"Because you're bored and locked away like a bad princess." He cocks his head.

I have to work hard not to react. As I said, my father had to have a meeting with the rest of the union families, explaining to Bronx's father and Delta's grandfather why I wasn't with the girls and why he didn't feel they were at risk as he does me. The Henshaws aren't exactly in the know, but it's no secret I haven't been involved physically in any of the schemes we've been running. I haven't been seen at The Enterprise or anywhere else for that matter.

That doesn't make it any less humiliating.

"What did you do, anyway?" His eyes are locked on mine, and he does nothing to hide the humorless glint within them.

"Just get to the point already," I tell him. "I don't have time for this."

"Oh, but you have all the time in the world, don't you?" His tone is teasing, but he's mocking me, and we both know it.

I stare at him in silence, and he gives a small nod.

"Your father will let you go with me. All you have to do is agree."

"You clearly underestimate my father."

"And you clearly underestimate the dealings of his and my father's relationship." There's an edge to his voice that I don't like, but I don't call him on it. "Agree to come and you'll have a night out."

"I don't want a night out."

"Of course you do." He grins.

Okay, correction. "I don't want a night out with you."

His eyes narrow. Very slowly, Oliver licks his lips, stepping toward me, so I straighten my spine and do the same, beating him to the punch.

"Before you decide to say something you will regret, and you will regret it one way or another, I suggest you back the fuck up."

"And I suggest," he whispers, "that you get on board a little faster because, eventually, you will be . . . *one way or another*." He throws my words right back at me, a shadow building over his brow.

"How is your foot feeling?"

"Better than your heart, I would guess."

My brows snap together before I can stop them and he chuckles in my face, leaning even closer until I can smell the mint on his breath.

"There are a lot of ways that I could bring you to your knees, sweet Greyson, but I'm trying to give you a chance to stay on your feet. I might not be able to force your hand, but your father can, and he will."

"My father thinks your family is beneath us because they are."

He nods, not denying the common fact. "We might be, yes, but not so low he was against coming to my father for a little help way back when. The kind my father specializes in."

I'm not exactly shocked. My father uses all resources available to him. Who wouldn't? But the way Oliver says this, as if using the information to get me in line, isn't missed. "What good is a lackey if he can't be used from time to time?"

"You have firsthand experience with that now, don't you? How is your little lackey boy, hmm? Or did Daddy run him off too? Or maybe, just maybe, he got exactly what he wanted from the little *rich girl* and he has no use for her anymore."

Rage bubbles inside me. How dare he speak of him or mutter that nickname, but I channel the rage.

Forcing a low laugh, I shift the smallest bit, stepping closer until my chest is pressing to his and his pupils dilate, the pathetic boy he is. And he is a boy. He might be strong and smart, we wouldn't have pulled him into the Greyson Society if he wasn't, but he's no wicked man worth running from.

His gaze holds hard on mine, waiting for me to relent, to give him exactly what he came for. Me.

I do give him me, but the version I choose.

I grip his biceps, giving a small squeeze, and his lips twitch as if he's won, but then I'm throwing us both into the water, his shout cut off by a mouthful of water.

He grabs my waist as I kick him beneath it, spinning quickly to put him in a headlock and wrap my legs around his middle until my feet lock into his inner thighs, preventing him from meeting the pool's bottom.

We begin to sink, and he struggles, his stubby fingernails digging into my forearm until the water grows discolored with little bits of blood, but I don't feel it and I can hold my breath for a really, really long time.

Oliver, on the other hand, never did take swimming in school, opting for double training instead, and he wasn't prepared, so he didn't get to take a single breath, whereas my lungs are nice and full.

Or as full as they can be after being beaten up for an hour or so.

I hold him until he grows frantic, reaching back and gripping my hair, tugging at every part of me he can reach, and then I hold him for ten seconds longer.

Only then do I release him, kicking close to his spine as I dart away, flying up and climbing the stairs before he has a chance to poke his head above the water.

He gasps and chokes and sends murderous looks my way before he points a horrified look at the precious family heirloom around his wrist. I hope I fucking destroyed it.

"Double the training didn't seem to teach you much about the element of surprise, did it?"

Oliver spits into the water, slowly making his way back to the stairs, his backpack floating above the water while still stuck to his back. "You will be going with me to that fundraiser, and if I have to take things into my own hands and away from your father's and mine, I will."

Smirking, I bend down, bringing myself closer to show him there is no fear here. "And if I have to destroy you for threatening me or my father, then I will do it with a smile on my face and an audience to watch. Don't forget your place, Little Henshaw, because I can erase it with the snap of a finger, and there won't be a damn thing you can do about it."

His sneer is venomous, his eyes darkening. "That's where you're wrong, sweet princess. We've made things disappear before and that little bit of pride and family devotion you're holding on to? I will wipe it right off your pretty face if you test me. I would suggest that you don't."

He pulls himself from the water and I stand as he does, and then we're nose to nose.

"I'll be sure to give my father the message." I go to walk past him, but his arm darts out, gripping mine and yanking me back.

I could easily break free. Break his fucking face and dreams and everything else in between, but I don't. I want to see how far he'll go, how far he dares to push because it will tell me more than any word he whispers will, so when his grip tightens and twists in a way that's sure to leave a mark, I make no move.

"Perfect," he breathes, eyes growing dark. "Then I will be picking you up at eight."

A smile breaks across his face, one so wide and sure I almost falter, and if he could hear the rapid increase of my pulse, he would know that he got me, that he roped me right in and now my mind is reeling. Running with a million different thoughts, none of which lead me anywhere.

Only one thing becomes sure in this moment.

The Henshaw family has something on my dad, which is the only reason why I say, "I'll be sure to wear red."

Bass

I lower into the cheap hospital seat for what feels like the millionth time this week, wincing as my ribs fight back. Bruised but not broken, from what I can tell, and I know the fucking difference. My left eye's a little blurry, temples pounding heavily, but I ignore it and the tiny shards of glass still embedded in my neck.

An ice pack lands on the seat beside me and Maddoc Brayshaw, one of my three bosses, drops down, looking in about as bad of shape as me, but for entirely different reasons.

"Where'd you run off to?" he asks, kicking a leg out. "Where you *always* running off to?"

"And you know I run off how?" I lift a brow, ignoring the ice pack he offers. "You been back, what? Half a day?"

His eyes narrow, but he nods, facing forward, eyes glued to his girl's hospital room door. "Thanks for watching her."

"Told you I would."

"'Cause it's your job or 'cause you want to?" he asks.

I don't answer. There's no point. I want her safe; she's good people and more like me than they'll ever be. I'd even say I care, want what's best for her, but I'd be lying if I said I'm fully committed here.

It's like I said, I've got one foot out the door, and the second the path is clear for me, I'm out. Until then, I'll do my job and do it well.

He asked me to guard her when he couldn't, so I did. I'd have done what I could for Rae even if he hadn't because I know what it's like to need and not have.

If it weren't for Hayze and his loyalty to me, I would have

356

had to walk away from my responsibilities like an asshole, but it didn't come to that. I've had a few hours to myself here and there and I used them wisely. Still, I owe that man and I owe him big.

I can still feel Maddoc's eyes on me, so I finally look his way.

"If you've got questions for me, now's the time to ask 'em," he says the second our eyes lock.

When I ask nothing, he calls me out. "Heard you went to the Greyson Gala couple months back."

He doesn't have to say Chloe told Mac, who told him. That shit's obvious, but what's it to him? Slowly, I nod, waiting for more.

"You know the Greysons are allies in our world, right?"

My eyes narrow instantly, and he chuckles, though it's almost hollow, his world too heavy right now for a real one.

"Man, do you pay attention to shit around here?"

"I don't get in your business unless I have to."

He lifts a dark brow, and I scoff at him.

"Rae's different. She needed my help. You told me to give it to her."

He stares at me a minute. "You see your sister in her, don't you?"

My eyes harden, yet my expression goes blank. This is the first time any of them have ever mentioned my sister. Not once was she brought up in the last four fucking years. Not. Once. When I don't allow that door to open the way he's trying to, he nods. I'd argue the dude owes me for gluing my ass to his family's side the last few months, but I doubt he sees it that way. Still, I ask for more, "So you know Rayo Revenaw?"

His eyes narrow, but he shakes his head. "I met Calvin, he's the dude who sits on the council for the Greysons, but that's it. The council we have is made up of five families, one top dog from each, but how they function in their towns has nothing to do with us. Here, Brayshaws rule, but there are a lot of families that fall under the Brayshaw name." He shrugs. "Guessing it's the same over there."

I nod, thinking over all the shit I do know about the girls of Greyson.

It's true. Rocklin and all her mansion friends come from different bloodlines, but all consider themselves "Greyson." Sort of like here. The Brayshaw brothers aren't real brothers but were adopted and raised as siblings. Three families under one name, functioning as one.

Same shit, but the worlds are night and day, the biggest difference being the Greysons have Greyson Elite, and that brings in all sorts of fuckers.

"Right now," Maddoc continues, "it's our battle for one seat, and the others who have it are the Riveras, Greysons, Haciendas, and the Henshaws."

My brows snap low, my anger from earlier bubbling right back up in my chest, not that it ever went away. I glance down at my screen to make sure Hayze hasn't messaged as I draw the name out. "Henshaw . . . as in Otto Henshaw?"

Maddoc watches me closely. "Fuck you been up to, Bishop?"

"A lot. The Henshaws are a problem. Mine, not yours. What do you know about them?"

He shrugs. "That he's a good dude to have in your corner when things go south and need correcting. He was my dad's go-to guy for years until we took over and started handling shit on our own."

"What kind of shit?"

"The kind that makes people disappear."

"Way I heard it, that family makes people appear. Fake papers and shit."

Maddoc nods, holding my eyes for a long, pointed moment I'm intended to read into. "Yeah, but papers and passports go both ways, fake or not. It's the same shit."

Very fucking true . . .

"Ever heard of Enzo Fikile?" I try my luck.

"No, but we stay out of that shit. They ain't like us. We might be fucked up over here, but we do it to keep our town clean. We don't want all that extra shit here. We have the council's support in an emergency, but we don't mix."

No, they don't. My work here is child's play compared to what's waiting on me, not that I've got time to deal with it quite yet, but with Rae passed out in the hospital bed, maybe I can slip away for a few more minutes.

Royce, one of the other brothers, comes over, angry and tense. Ready to tear my head off 'cause the dude's always hated me, threatened to "get me back" for having Rae's while his brother was gone. I know it comes from concern for her, but he's got to give that shit up. She's safe and I know that means a lot to him. His issues run deeper than me and we both know that. Still, I'll watch my words in front of him. Never know what he'll pull to piss me off for sport. I'd put nothing past the guy.

"We need to deal with Leo." He speaks to his brother but glares at me.

I bite the inside of my cheek to hold in a grimace and climb to my feet. "I already did."

Both heads snap my way.

"We could have fucking dealt with him," Royce spits.

I only nod. "I know, but you were busy with Rae."

"Man, you're fucking limping. He just slammed into and totaled your car with your bitch ass in it. How'd you handle him?"

"Pent-up shit I was dying to let out."

He eyes me. "How'd you do it?"

I think back to Rocklin, a small smirk pulling at my lips. "I was inspired."

He scoffs and stomps off, so I turn back to Maddoc. "This council . . . they fuck up, they get booted?"

His gaze is questioning, but he only nods, and I walk off.

As I turn the corner, Royce slams his fist into my chest, and I groan, eyes flashing to his, but then I feel the poke of the metal there, looking down to find a pair of keys.

He glares. "I'm not about to tell you what these go to and I'm only giving you them so you get the fuck out."

I nod and he steps back, and when I step into the elevator, glancing at the keys in my palm, I can't help but grin. I know exactly what these go to; I've picked it out of their little secret car lot for jobs a couple times.

It ain't pretty, but it is a Mustang.

Perfect for a hunt.

Or two . . .

Chapter 29
Rocklin

Dom and I are in our talent for treachery class when the soft sound of the speaker clicks on. The low ding that follows demands silence across the campus.

Our professor closes his lips and not a moment later, Calvin's voice fills the air.

"Good afternoon, Greyson Elite." Dom and I look to each other, keeping our expressions masked. "It's your chancellor speaking. At this time, I need you to pack up your materials and file into the gym as smoothly and quietly as possible. We will have a meeting fifteen minutes from now. I expect every student and staff member to be in attendance."

The speaker clicks off and my phone vibrates in my lap.

"Prepare yourself for anything," Dom whispers as he turns, easing his items into his backpack as he leans toward me.

Nodding, I look at my screen, our group thread lighting up.

Bronx: Bitch, you take off again?

Delta: Location shows she's still here.

I roll my eyes.

Me: I am, assholes. This isn't me.

Bronx: Boring! I thought this was about to get exciting. It's been too dead lately. I'm bored.

Alto: Do not jinx us, B. For once I've had my girl in my bed all week.

Ander: Our girl. In our bed.

Dom: You boys sharing a bed now?

Alto: Fuck off.

I look to Dom with a small grin. "You're an ass."

He smirks, having already packed my bag for me, and hangs it over his shoulder.

"Thanks."

He nods, face once again unreadable as we step into the hall.

"Calvin hasn't shown for an announcement since Claire Walter was exposed for selling information to the Russian Mafia three terms ago."

Dom nods but doesn't say a word. He never does when there're this many ears around.

As we curve right into the main hall, Ander and Bronx come from the left, falling in line beside us, and the four of us walk toward its end, where, in perfect timing, Delta and Alto come into view.

Heads held high and faces carefree, we strut our way across the room, listening to the whispers of those around us as they try and guess what we're about to walk into.

Here, you just never know.

We make our way through the heavy double doors held open by staff members and descend the stairs. The auditorium is set deep below, like a giant, rectangular bowl. The highest level of seating is the first row you pass, and we continue down the steps until we reach the box seats at the bottom, reserved especially for us.

Single file, we slide, Damiano on one side of me, Bronx on the other.

The room echoes as everyone enters, the chatter loud as people laugh and joke, enjoying the few minutes free from class, an extreme rarity. In fact, it almost never happens.

362

Classes are interrupted for nothing here at Greyson Elite.

Even when the spy was uncovered, a student Calvin and our fathers had overridden us on, thank you very much, he waited and stole our free lunchtime to deliver the news.

Exactly fifteen minutes later, Calvin walks into the room from the far east door. He's perfectly poised, his suit pressed, and he walks with his chin held high, an approachable smile across his handsome face. The Greyson Elite crest is etched proudly on his left pec and he waves to a few students as he makes his way to the podium that's been placed in the center.

The room instantly falls silent, so when the door on the west side of the room opens with a small creak, all eyes are called to that location.

My muscles tense as my father walks in, his face blank and unreadable, but my heart doesn't start pounding until Bronx's father comes into view, and right behind him Senator DeLeon, Delta's grandfather. The senator *never* comes here. Ever.

I know this has nothing to do with my little outing and pyro moment of weakness four nights ago. I was high-strung after everything with Oliver and thoughts of he who shall not be named, and after I told Sai what happened with Oliver, he covered for me, somehow got the guards on his side when he made up a lie, saying he knew I was struggling and just needed a little moment to breathe, so he took me out in the souped-up sports car and sat there silently in the passenger seat while I sped around the hillside lost in my own thoughts. I did speed around the hillside and he did lie there silently, but that's because he was knocked out cold from the horse tranquilizer I shot him with. And my dad never did find out about the destroyed gas station.

Guilt works its way through my stomach, turning it, but it goes away quickly enough. The old man woke the next day, likely devastated and at a loss of what to do, only to find an obscene amount of money funneled into his bank account with no explanation, but I'm sure he put two and two together. He no longer has to worry about his bad knees or needing anyone to help him stock his shelves or clean his dumpster or use his yard as a body dumping ground just to get that little extra help.

Glacier eyes and gorgeous tattoos flash through my mind, bringing with it an ache I can't shake, but I stomp the photo out as quickly as possible and refocus. Only then realizing our family members are not the only ones who have joined us. None other than Otto freaking Henshaw is following on their heels.

Damiano pulls in a long, steadying breath beside me, and when I flick my eyes his way while remaining facing forward, I catch the sharpness of his clenched jaw.

Using my peripheral, I peek at the girls, knowing that they're doing the same.

The only time our parents have been in this place at the same time was the first day of our term here at Greyson Elite and never again after that, and that day, Delta's shit for a mom was here to stand for her, not the senator. My father and Bronx's do come, making their random visits as if to show support and to appear as devoted members of our union. They also show their faces to remind people of who they are, maybe how big and strong and influential others need to see them as. Because that's exactly what they are.

But Mr. Henshaw? He doesn't belong at their side. He may be on the council with Calvin, but he's not a part of our core that makes up the Greyson Union, and this is Greyson Elite. So again, he does not belong at their side while they stand strong in front of all of our students and staff.

Calvin clears his throat and I wait with bated breath for him to begin to speak.

"Again, good afternoon, everyone. Thank you for making your way in here as quickly as I asked. We won't keep you away from your studies any longer than we must, so we're going to get right to it." He glances around the room, and I watch as his chest rises with a calculated inhale. "It has come to our attention that four nights ago, a student of ours went missing."

The whispers begin instantly, but the second Calvin raises his palm, absolute silence falls once again.

364

"A little after six p.m. on Thursday evening, Oliver Henshaw was seen leaving the male locker room with his gym bag slung over his shoulder. He returned to the dorms, using the underground tunnel as required, and was spotted entering the shower before returning to his room. What happened after he stepped into his assigned dorm that night, we do not yet know."

Those whispers return, but louder and louder as the smallest hint of panic works its way through the auditorium. My eyes flash to my father's and he's looking directly at me, face blank and eyes pointed but not on me.

Damiano speaks without so much as moving his lips. "What he's saying is there's no footage to be found."

I give a curt, nearly unnoticeable nod and his chest inflates.

Someone tapped into security and erased any proof of where he might be. A gap in surveillance.

From four days ago, the day he interrupted my moment of self-destruction.

There's no doubt in my mind the entire day's footage has been reviewed, the little incident in the pool not missed.

Subconsciously, my palm wraps around my arm, the skin still sensitive there from the bruise Oliver left behind. This time when I look up, my father's eyes have narrowed, and his chin lifts the slightest bit. So little that if I wasn't staring directly at him, I wouldn't have noticed, but he's not the only one who's staring. So is Otto Henshaw and he doesn't look happy.

Did they see him put his hands on me?

Did they watch as I forced panic into his mind, waiting until the last bit of air left in his lungs was useless to him before allowing his head to breach the surface?

I don't realize my lips have curled until Otto's hardens.

Yes, I believe they might have. If not, he most definitely made a call home to Daddy afterward. Perhaps to brag that I agreed to his little date night after his hint of blackmail.

But missing?

365

That's as bold as it gets and I can't help but wonder if my own father is to blame for the disappearance of his "friend's" only heir.

I didn't speak a word of it to him, but this might be one of those situations where my and Sai's agreement to keep my father out of things is trumped by his need to keep me safe. Putting hands on the daughter of Rayo Revenaw is the furthest thing from allowed, but if Sai was there and did see, why is my father looking at me with keen eyes, trying to decide if I know what he doesn't? When really, I have no idea what he does or does not know or what he assumes that I do.

He's probably just pissed I didn't tell him and wondering what else I could be hiding since I seem to be accidentally revealing all sorts of hidden shit lately.

"Some of you may be wondering why we're only now notifying you, and that is because we've only just been notified ourselves. Mr. Larry, Oliver Henshaw's roommate, assumed Oliver had spent the evening in another's dorm, and when he didn't return the next day, it was assumed he made a trip home, but as the weekend passed and Monday's classes rolled around, he realized perhaps it was something more. We were notified immediately, called his family, and now we're here with all of you. As we speak, a notification is being sent to your families or guardians back home, so be prepared to be bombarded once this meeting concludes, as the second I dismiss you, that email will be sent through." He looks around the room before focusing on the six of us for a split moment.

"There is nothing we're asking you to do at this time. You will continue with your classes as instructed; we have already added more guards, and I myself will be overseeing security until further notice. If you believe you know something that we do not in regard to Mr. Henshaw's disappearance, we ask that you come to the chancellor's office directly. If you do not wish to be seen doing so, you may email me, and I will arrange different conditions. This is not a rat or snitch or any other term you may choose to call this situation. If you know something, this is duty. Your loyalty lies within these walls while you are here, as says the contract you signed when you entered and all of your families are aware of such, so if we find that you're hiding something, you will be dealt with as if you are the enemy. Enemies fall, so remember that, and if you think you will get away with something, think again."

Slowly, Calvin steps back from the podium, looking to our family representatives, three of the cardinal compass that makes up the Greyson Union, one still not ready to show their face to complete the core four, and the fourth man beside them, a man unworthy of the place he stands. Yet, he is the one who steps forward to take the mic. Not entirely shocking, is as he does, his focus is solely on me.

He's quiet at first, using the moment as a silent warning meant to intimidate—too bad for him, that's shit we teach in Treachery 101.

Finally, he speaks. "I will find my son, who I am certain is unharmed, and when I do, the person responsible will wish they made a different choice."

A small smile forms on my lips, one of pure spite, while on the inside, I'm working through every possibility of what could have happened to him.

Finally, Mr. Henshaw looks out over the room, eyes calculating and searching as they sweep the students and staff, settling and hardening on his archery teammates, being they are the ones he interacts with most.

"I'm happy to have the help of my colleagues behind me in retrieving my son."

"What if he ran off?" someone from archery shouts.

I hear Bronx's stifled laugh because, yeah, fucking right.

Oliver, his daddy's personal ass wiper and oddly also his whipping boy, disappearing on his very own? Negative.

"I assure you that is not the case, and I won't allow such rumors to spread throughout the community." Otto steps away and my father eases forward.

With his every step, a harsher silence falls over the room, little inklings of fear filling the space as the real power of our community prepares to speak.

He knows his role and what must be said.

"As your fine chancellor has pointed out." His voice is even as ever and the pride I feel for my father swells within me. Rattled or raging, it doesn't matter. He's always poised and in control, his very few moments of weakness only witnessed by the eyes of his daughters. "When here, your loyalty lies with your peers. The men and women on your right, left, front, and behind. Those are the people you represent until the day you graduate from this fine institution. As a community, as one, we will do what we must to find the answers we need." My smile spreads at his cryptic words, the true meaning behind them holding countless possibilities that will later drive Mr. Henshaw insane trying to decipher them as was intended.

"Before you leave this room, you will read the email that will be sent to your family as it will be sent to you the second I'm done speaking. Nothing outside of what is mentioned within it will you discuss with your families. You may converse as much as you wish among the people in this room, but that is all. We are hiding nothing, but the more outside influence, the less chance we will find ourselves with in locating Oliver Henshaw, and we will not rest until he is safe and back on the Greyson grounds."

Ever the loyal leader, his promise is wide and far, as I knew it would be.

As Otto Henshaw, Mr. Bandoni, and Mr. DeLeon knew it would be.

The question was never if we were on his side. The question is, is the very reason that we're here today my father's doing, and if so, is Oliver chained in his basement as we speak?

I, for one, am dying to find out.

My father steps away, and in unison, dozens of phone alerts go off, my own vibrating in my skirt.

None of us bother to pull our phones out but quickly stand, being the first to exit. We keep our eyes locked forward, ignoring the many heads that swivel our way as we head up the stairs and into the main hall. We don't speak as we walk through and around the corridor until we reach the elevator that leads to the Greyson Suite.

As we step inside, my phone beeps again, and I look at the screen to find a text from my sister. The door begins to close, and with a reluctant sigh, I stretch my heel out to stop it. Damiano raises a brow at me but settles as Boston whips around the corner, squeezing herself inside. Still, no one says a word and it's not until we're locked behind the soundproof walls that we do.

Of course, Boston is the first to do so. "Do you think it's Enzo? Do you think he found out about Dad pushing you on him and now he's here to make sure you don't create a union between us and that family and give him the lead on our name before Enzo could have it for himself?"

"Enzo will never be head of this family."

Her lips slam shut, and she gives a tight nod before moving to sit in the chair in front of the window.

Damiano eyes her before flicking his attention to me and I only shake my head.

"I wouldn't completely rule out Boston's concern, but I'm tempted to," Bronx says.

Delta nods in agreement. "Considering the timing, me too. It has to do with the other day, don't you think?"

My spine steels, but it's too late, and she mouths her sorry. Sighing, I pull myself up on the desk and cross my legs. "There's no point in hiding it, especially if the footage is already there and all the dads, including Oliver's, have watched."

"What are you talking about?" Alto questions, flicking accusatory eyes toward Delta, even though he knows this is the way it goes.

"Oliver showed up in the poolroom when I was there on Thursday."

"Thursday," Ander deadpans. "The day he disappeared?"

"Seems that way, yes." I drop my head back a moment, shaking it as I face forward again. "He made some shitty remarks, and I sort of . . . pretended I was going to drown him."

"How exactly does one pretend to drown someone?" Ander grins, crossing his arms over his chest.

My eyes fall to the tattoos on his hands. The only person I know who has any outside of my—

No.

"I pushed him under water and held him there until he couldn't breathe, and I only let him up at the very last second before panic took over."

"So you literally almost drowned him?" Ander lifts a brow, his grin even wider now.

"Not almost. I knew what I was doing."

"Okay, can we get to the part that tells us why you did that?" This comes from Alto.

I look to Damiano, surprised he's silent at the moment, but he simply glares out the window, slowly moving closer to it as his mind runs. He's always silent when he's thinking, so it's nothing to be too concerned about.

I tell them what he said, and the consensus is the same across the room, especially when my father chooses that moment to demand entrance inside. Boston shoots from the chair she settled in, the others standing to attention, but Damiano doesn't move from the window.

The door is opened and my father stalks in, closing and locking it behind him. He knows what we're up here discussing, and he knows we have no secrets between us, so he steps right up to me, wasting no time.

"Take the jacket off," he demands.

A pinch of embarrassment heats my chest. I might not have mentioned this exact part to my friends, not for any reason other than it was unnecessary. So, as I undo the three buttons of my blazer and allow it to slide down over my shoulders, Alto stepping up behind me to ease it off my arms to keep it from falling to the floor, I try not to stiffen or cringe or to have any other reaction. Especially not when my father grips my sleeve at the hem near the shoulder and shreds it all the way down to my wrist.

His eyes lock on the hand-shaped bruise there and his nostrils flare. It's momentary, the smallest sign of a break in his ever-present armor, and then his eyes snap over my head. I can only assume he looks to Damiano, perhaps putting the blame on him, but he isn't my guard. I'm not his responsibility. My father likely sees it as otherwise since the man was bold enough to ask for my hand, knowing he would be turned down exactly as he was. This only cements my father's decision to deny his request further.

I know instantly Sai will be reamed for this, but it's my father's own fault he wasn't there watching in the wings. He's been pulling him from what Sai has said.

My every step has been watched; my dad is the one who told me this. That's how Otto knew where I was going and when I was leaving that night in time to stop me.

The others quietly slip from the room, the air inside it shifting, and then it's only Revenaws left. My father, my sister, and me.

Our father wastes not a moment of our time.

"The boy will die," he promises.

Uncertainty washes over me. "Dad—"

"The boy," he booms, cutting me off, attention still locked on my skin. "Will die."

I swallow the words locked in my throat because a warning of what that could start isn't one he needs. He knows good and well what killing the son of a council member could cause. In his mind though, it wouldn't be murder.

It would be a reprimand, the only kind he's capable of.

Finally, his eyes come up to meet mine, a scary kind of hardness within them, and he gives the smallest of nods. "Finish today's classes, find your sister, and together, walk to my car. I will be parked where Sai is normally parked, and we will head home as one."

I know instantly that his comment from the night he forced us to move back into his mansion is now finally coming full circle. He said we would speak, and he held off on what he had to say for as long as he could. He can't anymore.

Which means that I was right.

Otto Henshaw has something on my father, something his son was well aware of, and with him missing, it's bound to come to light.

Mr. Henshaw undoubtedly believes we're responsible for his son going missing.

And I think maybe we are . . .

Bass

My phone beeps in my pocket, so I pull it out, waiting till the very last second to move my eyes to the screen to find the third Brayshaw brother's name there.

Captain: Raven's ready to end this. Get here.

My insides fucking flip as I hold my screen up for Hayze to see, eyes sliding right back to the high glass windows.

"So, this is it, huh?" he asks.

I nod, eyes narrowing on the blond head that appears.

For the last four years, I've given my loyalty to the town and family that took me in, even if it was for their own benefit more than mine.

Nah, that ain't true. It benefited the shit out of me, got me out of trouble, kept me out of juvenile hall, maybe even straight-up prison based on how I maniacally laughed and added a second bullet to a dead man right there for all the cops and firemen and shit to see. But then again, they did bring me because they needed hands, and they like to use the rough street rat ones in Brayshaw. But the puzzle pieces are falling together in this place, so it's time to make the jump, especially knowing what I do now.

I waited a long fucking time for this.

Maddoc has no idea about the bomb he dropped on me, but then again, maybe he does. Maybe that's why he told me in the first place about this *council* and the men who sit on it, about what Mr. Henshaw does. It makes sense now. Unexpected, that's for damn sure, but a circle is a circle, so I shouldn't be too surprised.

There're still some gaps, but I'll get those filled in . . . *one way or another.*

A smirk pulls out my lips, and when I tap the dash, Hayes pulls out and back onto the road, heading back to Brayshaw for what will be the last time as one of theirs.

Things are about to change. The minute I release myself from the family I work for, nothing will be the same.

I'm cutting the fucking leash wrapped around my neck. There will be no strings left to be pulled. No person to answer to. No cliff I can't climb.

For the first time in a long fucking time, maybe even ever, I'm going to walk under the shadow of the night as Bass fucking Bishop.

I know better than most that nothing worth having is given to you, so I will take what I want. I'll become the thief in this story. The pieces are already in position, just waiting to be played and play them I will. After that, all that's left is to capture the king and claim the queen.

Should be easy enough for a shadow.

A nobody.

A no-good punk *no one* saw coming.

That's what I am, but I'll be damned if that's what I stay, so watch your world, Rich Girl.

Or better yet . . . *don't.*

Chapter 30
Rocklin

"I made a mistake."

That's the sentence my father decides to start with as he stares my sister and me down from his seat across the coffee table.

"A big one," he says. "I don't believe I have to spell it out for you, but I will tell you what I can. The Henshaw family was involved in the mistake I made. Otto, to be exact, but I'm assuming, given recent events, he was foolish enough to pass this information on to his son."

My father waits for me to confirm, so I give a slight nod. "I already told you how he acted and what he said. The insinuation is there."

"And you fought back against it rather than heed his warning," he accuses.

"Is that why you kidnapped him?"

My father's eyes hold steady on mine, and it's as if he's searching for something. "You should not have pushed the boy. You should have held on to your grace and you should have come to me, so I could deal with this."

It's been the same 'conversation' for the last thirty-one days, and it never gets us anywhere because he clams up or gets called away every single time. I'm sick of it.

Things are getting tense on campus and people are starting to look at each other as if we're all the enemy. If it keeps up, we'll crumble within our own walls.

"Do not blame me for whatever it is you've done that's falling on our shoulders."

Boston gasps, looking from me to my dad, but she doesn't say a word.

"I will never allow anything to fall onto you girls that you cannot handle," he fires back, neither confirming nor denying. "But this is different. This is something with the potential to rock the foundation the Greyson Union sits on. This could mess everything up, especially for you, Rocklin, including the society you've built. I can't say I regret it, at least not the way I should, and that might be the worst part."

His words mean nothing without the knowledge of what he's hiding, so I force myself not to dwell on the anger they bring and speak on what we know. "Mr. Henshaw watched the surveillance from the pool the day Oliver disappeared. He saw Oliver approach me, saw what followed, so there is no way he believes you're not involved after seeing him grab me the way he did."

My father watches me too closely, but I'm not sure why. Slowly, he nods. "Yes, I would agree Otto believes his son is at the mercy of my hands."

"So if only Otto knows and he's gone, the secret is safe, right?" Boston wonders. "We can stop worrying about some giant shitstorm coming out of nowhere?"

My father cocks his head, eyes narrowing on mine slightly before moving to hers. "I imagine it might be for now, yes, but this is his legacy we're talking about. His only heir. He will come for me if the boy does not show up. He has grown edgy. Our team is sure he's about to break, and the moment he does, he will cross a line he can't come back from."

"You sound like that's exactly what you want, so you can keep this secret of yours buried."

He lifts his hands as if to say *if I can be so lucky, I won't complain.*

"Otto must have a lot of enemies," Boston offers.

"He does, and he's about torn through them all now, to no avail." My father shakes his head. "Make no mistake, he will be coming for us."

"There's no way he would dare come at you without help and he wouldn't get it without proof, if even then," she pushes on.

Father looks to me. "His son put his hands on my daughter and then disappeared."

"Coincidence." Boston shrugs.

"The daughter he was trying to blackmail me into selling to him."

My head snaps back, hearing this for the first time. "What?"

"Yes. You are what they were after." He finally shares something new. "They've been after one of you for years. It was his plan all along. I didn't realize this until after I used his services. From that moment on, I was locked in without knowing it. He wasn't deep in our world at the time. He was just a man with a skill I required, nothing but another gang out there who was no threat to my organization that I used for a job. He was on the council with the Greysons, so I knew his work would be efficient and, more importantly, discreet.

"The Henshaws sit on the council alongside Calvin, but they are nothing but a name to the Greyson Union, but where we have four powerful families united under one name, the Henshaws do not."

Curious, I sit back and wait for more.

"Power and greed led Otto down a different road, one that wiped out the people beneath him, to who he was supposed to give his loyalty as we do the Bandonis, the DeLeons, the Henleys. He decided he no longer liked the idea of being equal with the names tied to the Henshaw empire, and so he picked them off one by one until he and his heir were the only ones left. The problem with this is the times changed as the new generation came and took over and he realized we were outgrowing and outpowering him in every way possible. He knew eventually someone would come for his seat on the council and his family would be done, so when someone tied to a second member of that council, me, came requiring his services, he hatched his own plan."

377

"To blackmail you later into giving him one of your daughters so he would have the power and influence of the Revenaw name," Boston nearly whispers.

"Not only that but the Greyson Union as a whole," I add. "But Mom never would have agreed. She was adamant, and from what I remember and what I have been told, everyone knew the 'Revenaw daughters' wouldn't be pawns to be used later. We were stronger than everyone else, so people knew there would never be a need for it. We were raised against contractual marriages."

Our dad's face hardens, and he glares at nothing, the vein in his jaw ticcing. He doesn't touch the comment about our mother but says, "As I had mentioned before, none of this even remotely would have made sense to me, but then you girls . . ." He pauses, looking at me. "You, Bronx, and Delta took your places and we founded Greyson Elite, the first school of its kind, bringing families from outside districts and criminal organizations into one place. If I had thought about it then, I would have advocated against Oliver Henshaw joining the program, but I was a fool. That was his way into the community, into our lives. It wasn't until after orientation, the very first day, he approached me again, and I knew. I knew then he'd be a problem in the future. I remembered a comment he made in passing after that. He had said something along the lines of the possibilities being endless for me with two heiresses instead of one. I realize now that was his way of letting me know he would be back and with an expectation I would be expected to meet."

Frustration builds and I scowl at my father. "Why didn't you warn us then? Why not let us know to watch out for him? I could have kept him out of the society so he was nothing but a student like the others."

Guilty, my father nods, finally admitting to something. "A part of me wondered if maybe he would be good for one of you. I saw no reason to instantly object to his offer, and he knew not to throw it out as a demand at that time, knowing the moment he mentioned it, I would consider all sides before I came to a decision, just as he knew a decision wouldn't be made in any sort of hasty matter. He did what he planned, came to me early and before anyone else could, knowing you'd be meeting a lot of powerful people on campus. I didn't know the Henshaws were slimy at the time and I was impressed with Oliver, just as you were." I open my mouth to speak, but he gives a light shake of his head. "Don't deny it. You never would have accepted him into the society if he were not, and as I said, I had two daughters to think about, so he had more than one chance to get the yes he was after."

"Are you going to tell us what the Henshaws have over you?"

"I will, but I haven't decided when. Right now, I'm struggling because I have to make a decision, and it is not an easy one."

Unease weaves its way into my gut. "What decision?"

"A criminal is after blood. My blood. I cannot allow this."

"We're all criminals in some way," Boston states the obvious. "We're stronger, and like you said, we have more on our side if it comes to that."

"True, but the Henshaws are of the poisonous kind. His loyalty is to himself, and he gets away with what he does because of the secrets he can use against others to make sure it happens. It's how he killed the DA. How he killed others without retaliation or punishment." My father's jaw hardens. "We must remember he has many people at his disposal he can blackmail. It's his forte. Erase problems for a price, but the real price paid is the debt never settled. This is why you never trust a criminal."

"What decision?" I repeat, a little harsher.

His eyes move to Boston, holding a long moment before making their way to me.

Slowly, he lifts his phone, pressing a button before bringing it to his ear. His eyes stay glued to mine as the line presumably rings, though I can't hear a sound.

"It is," he drawls deliberately, his expression growing dark and determined.

I sneak a glance at Boston, who curls her legs up in the chair, refusing to meet my eyes, then quickly looks back to my dad right as he says, "She has changed her mind. The clause will now kick in."

His eyes flash in the next moment, and I can't even begin to guess who is on the other line or what is being said. And then he hangs up, staring directly into my eyes.

It feels like a lifetime before he speaks again. "As I told you before. You are being followed. I'm being followed as well. I have been since before I brought Boston back."

"It was Oliver, he—"

Wait.

Wait, wait, wait . . .

I lick my lips, speaking slowly. "*Brought* . . . Boston back?" My head snaps from her to him. "What do you mean, you *brought* Boston back?" I study him a moment as I try and make sense of some of this. "You knew all along he wasn't on his way, but you wanted to draw him out. That's what the yacht dinner was about, kill two birds with one stone. Give the Henshaws a little to hold on to and hope someone runs back to Enzo, mistaking me for her. When that didn't get him here, you tried again by bringing Boston to the gala. That way, we would both be seen and there was no question one of us was her." I shake my head again. "Dad, what the hell?! What's the point of any of that if he knew she was here anyway?"

"He knew she was here, yes." He nods. "Permission was granted from him, as reluctant as it might have been, and only because he had a business situation come up that called him away."

"A business situation?" I snap, my eyes narrowing. "What did you do?"

"It doesn't matter. The why is irrelevant."

My breath comes in short puffs and all I can do is hope he keeps talking, but hope has been a real bitch to me lately, so I hold my breath instead.

He's silent for a long time, and when he speaks again, his voice is void of emotion, his expression completely blank. "Something you must understand, Rocklin, is it was never my intention to marry Boston off to Enzo Fikile."

I blink at him. "I don't get it."

"Your sister is not strong enough and she will not be taking over Revenaw dealings." He speaks as if she's not right here.

She's tucked into herself, not speaking, but she *is* here.

And even though I've claimed otherwise myself, she is strong. Her strength is just . . . different.

My eyes cut her way quickly, but I focus on him. "Why are we talking about this now when we have a separate issue to deal with? And what does her not taking over, which we openly discussed years ago, have to do with merging our families and growing our reach, doubling our strength in allies with the Fikile empire?"

"It leaves an opening."

A humorless laugh leaves me; this conversation is a whole lot of info, yet *no* info at all. "What opening? Stop talking in senseless riddles and tell me what's going on! What *opening*?!"

"The one at your side."

I suck in a sharp breath, distress shooting through me like it was injected into my veins.

"Who was that on the phone, Dad?" I ask, but he acts as if I haven't spoken.

He watches me closely, and then he says, "Enzo is the boss in his world. If he marries Boston, he becomes the king of ours."

No, he doesn't.

No, he does not.

Does he?

Beads of sweat build along my neck and I'm frozen in place, unable to move.

My father leans into my space, bringing us eye to eye. "A king requires a queen."

I knew I wasn't the queen, but I didn't know I was the pawn until it was too late . . .

The pawn for the queen . . .

I cannot leave you in this world unprotected . . .

When the time comes, you will do as you must . . .

The Henshaw threat, our family being watched, and this mysterious secret that hangs over us. My dad feels he's being backed into a corner and he thinks he's found the perfect way out.

"Dad . . . who was on the phone?"

"When he comes for her, he will have to come to me. When he comes to me . . . I will give him you instead."

What.

The.

Fuck.

"This is bullshit!" I jump from my chair, whipping around to glare at my sister, but she doesn't even look my way as she shoots from her seat and hustles from the room without glancing back.

My eyes fly to my father, narrowing. "Why send her there just to do this? I don't fucking get it."

"He made the deal with her, so it only makes sense."

Bastian's words come back to me and I throw them at my father. "What if all he wants is to get her back?"

My father pours a small sip of liquor into a glass and brings it to his lips. "Don't be a fool." He lets the golden liquor coat his throat before facing me once more. "With Boston, he gains a wife and a tie to our name, nothing more."

"Don't talk about her as if she's not worth more than a name on a contract."

"She will be to someone, yes, but Enzo is not that someone. He is power, and when he realizes what he stands to gain with you at his side instead, he will have no quarrel. He will come, and once the agreement is made, he will end the Henshaws himself."

I couldn't possibly form a harsher expression than the one I'm wearing now.

My father shakes his head, his chin tipping. "I told you. I will not leave you in this world unprotected. He is your best chance at success."

"I do not need a man to be strong and successful," I force past clenched teeth.

"No, you need one to keep you in line so you don't go sneaking around like a brainwashed, lovesick puppy who shacks up with scum who only sees an opportunity to gain something."

I jerk back as if slapped, the hatred in his tone heavy and unmistakable. "You don't even know him."

"Neither do you," he says coolly. "Tell me something, did he bring you into his world? Take you around his people? Did you meet his closest friends? Or did he only chase after yours?"

My throat runs dry, my mind trying to refuse the words he's saying, but the truth of them has the embers in my gut returning to a flame. He didn't bring me to his world. He did slip into mine. And he left it like it was nothing, like I was nothing, the moment I denied him the entrance he silently sought at the gala.

Regardless of the war waging in my head, I force myself to say, "You know nothing. Not everyone is out for blood and money."

"Don't forget power," he says indifferently. "And yes, daughter, in this world, they are. Another man touched you and where is this brave boy, hmm? Not here, so as I said, you can trust no one. Maybe not even your closest friends. I will be the one to make this go away. You can only trust the word of your family. *Blood. Before. All.*"

"Says the man who swore he would never give his daughters away without their consent."

He doesn't even wince. "Decisions must be made and I will carry no regret."

"If you think I will go along with this, you're wrong."

"If you think you or anyone else can stop this," he says, his tone growing gentle. "Then you, daughter, are very, very wrong. I have said it a hundred times, so I will say it once more." He steps closer, ignoring the water threatening to spill from my eyes. "I will not leave you in this world unprotected."

"We're not unprotected. We have you."

A shadow falls over his eyes, and then he whispers his final words for the evening, "the way things are looking, you won't have me for long."

And then he walks out, leaving me alone with too many bombs to count and no idea how to keep them from blowing up in my fucking face.

Chapter 31
Rocklin

My eyes flash open, locking onto the hideous pink netting above my bed, my mind still frozen halfway in a nightmare state, last night's conversation heavy in my head. I'm not even sure if I slept or not, but when a loud boom sounds once more, I realize it's not a dream or the hundred scenarios playing out in my head while I lie here fighting for sleep.

I fly from the sheets, my bare feet no sooner hitting the plush carpet beneath them, when my door is thrown open, my dad's wide and panicked eyes staring back at me. I quickly clap my hands and the light turns on, my panic flickering to life within me as I take him in.

Still wearing his clothes from last night, his suit jacket the only thing missing, but the white button-up is wrinkled and half-untucked, small blotches of red splattered across it.

"Let's go. Use the private back exit down to the garage and get into the car. Sai is down there getting the car ready; I just need to grab your sister."

I've already got my robe over my shoulders, feet in my slippers, and bag thrown over my shoulder before he's done speaking.

"What the hell is going on?" I ask, dashing back to my bed to grab my phone as I meet him in the hallway.

He's half running toward Boston's door, two guards at my back and four ahead of me as I follow him instead.

"Rocklin, go. I'll explain in the car!"

When three more guards come around the corner, I decide to leave him as he commanded and make my way down into the garage. I dash across the concrete space, my father and sister jogging through the door before I've even reached Sai's side.

I turned to Sai. "What happened?" I demand, my eyes flying over his face to try and get a read on him, but he's nothing but a stone wall in front of me.

Even his eyes are blank as he stares into mine, the coolness setting me further on edge. This is how he gets when he's in full-on mission mode. "In the car. Your father will explain, but we need to go."

My dad's hand reaches my back in that moment, and I quickly duck into the car, Boston shuffling in beside me, and then the door closes behind us. Sai takes the driver's seat as a second guard climbs into the passenger seat, and we head out, two cars leading ours, and when I glance back, two more behind.

I look at my father expectantly and he slowly moves to the opposite seat so he can keep watching behind us, his eyes darting around, but dawn hasn't quite reached us yet, so there's nothing out there but darkness.

"The Henshaw mansion was attacked, and as of an hour ago, no one has been able to reach Otto Henshaw. His wife was left unharmed, but they lost several guards, and from the trail of blood found, she's assuming the worst."

Instantly, my focus falls to my father's shirt, to the bloodstains that weren't there last night, and when I look up again, his eyes are on me.

"I don't understand." Boston shakes her head. "First Oliver, and now his father?" Her tone isn't exactly guarded, the accusation clear as she, too, stares at our father in his state of disarray. "The only two people who happen to know whatever secret it is that you're keeping?"

It takes effort, but I manage to hide my shock. My sister is never one to snap or question our father, but it seems last night's little conversation, or should I say secret sharing, has changed that.

Of course, my father doesn't acknowledge what she's saying. "I thought home would be the safest place for you, but not

386

five minutes after I received the call about Otto, we had a total blackout. Complete loss of communication with our security team. Our home is now at risk of breach, so you're no longer safe there. I've already contacted Calvin and he's letting the others know we're on our way back to the manor."

I don't allow the sense of ease his words bring me to show. Sure, he has a bunch of security, each of them armed to the nines with unlimited resources at their fingertips, but soldiers are always at risk of being turned now more than ever. Money talks and anyone daring enough to cross my father is sure to have means.

That's not something I have to worry about in Greyson Manor. On the housing grounds and at the school? Perhaps, but not in the manor. Not with my girls, Dom, Delta's men and the Grecos, because yes, I've come to trust them. Kylo and Kennex have checked in on me so much since I've been forced to stay with my father. It's almost annoying if some lonely part of me didn't find it sort of sweet.

Bastian flashes before my eyes, never too far from my mind, and I know if he were here, that sense of security would no longer be as simple as a "sense." It would be factual.

Complete and total confidence.

It doesn't completely add up as to why, but it doesn't have to. A deeper part of myself knows it, regardless. That he would protect me at all costs.

Not that he cares to.

I fucked him over and he forgot me.

A knot forms in my stomach, twisting and tightening, but as the gates of the Greyson Estate come into view, it lessens some. They open and the first two cars slip through.

Sai keeps forward to follow, and I breathe a sigh of relief, but then my father's eyes widen. His attention is pointed toward the vehicles at our rear, but before I can whip around to see what he's looking at, my own freezes as the giant iron gate flies closed faster than I've ever seen it move, cutting off the back bumper of the second SUV with its force. They're trapped on the inside and us on the outside.

"Fuck!" my father curses, his gun already in his hand as he bends, flipping up the carpet and opening the safe in the floorboard.

I take the moment to look behind us. Steady streams of fire from a flamethrower illuminate the night. Our men scream and shout, blindly shooting as they throw themselves onto the ground and begin to roll around frantically. The entire inside of the SUV is engulfed now, the raging inferno and smoke billowing out open doors.

The moment I spin back, my father's entire form goes rigid, his eyes snapping to ours.

"This isn't . . . possible," he nearly whispers, denying whatever thought has dug into his mind.

We look at the steel box in the flooring and my heart rate spikes.

It's empty. It is *never* empty. It's checked every day, the guns taken out once a week, temporaries put in their place as the others are shot, cleaned, and then replaced.

It is never fucking empty.

"What the hell?" Boston gasps, pulling a small shuriken, a Japanese throwing star, from somewhere and gripping it between her fingers.

I dig the silver switchblade from my bag, flicking it open.

My father's eyes fall to it, narrowing at the cheap, dime-a-dozen weapon that's worth more to me than any other I own.

When he looks up, his expression is sure and strong, concealed, but he can't hide the hint of fear in his gaze. Fear for us in this moment. It's unnerving, seeing the epitome of strength afraid.

"Dad."

"Run through the side gate, go into the school if you have to. Any cover you can find, take it until the grounds guards and the others get here. They should be seconds away."

My chest inflates with a heavy breath. "Dad—"

"You will leave me here and you will not look back," he orders, dipping his chin. "You have to, my darling girls—"

The door is yanked open and smoke floods the vehicle.

Boston tumbles over me, reaching toward the opposite side, but I grab her, yanking her back in. She really needs to get back to training. They are pushing us one way, proven when my father does the same, but on purpose, so he is the one they focus on. His instant, harsh grunt follows, letting me know I was right. They were waiting.

With no other choice and nothing but a knife, I drag Boston out the door the smoke bomb was tossed through, and we drop to our knees, crawling as fast as we can across the concrete until we can tuck behind a stone beam.

I can't see my father, but I watch as a man in all black takes a bullet to the chest and no more than jerks at the impact. His hand darts out, wrapping around and snapping the wrist of my father's guard until he crumbles. The guard's screams fill the air and then he's jabbed in the neck, falling to his feet, his skull cracking against the cement, and Boston's nails dig into my forearm.

Sai is out the door, throwing his body across the hood, and I breathe an instant sigh of relief.

The soon-to-be-dead man spots him immediately, steps over the possibly lifeless guard's body and charges him like a bull, but Sai is built like one. He manages to knock the hit man to the ground, and while my heart beats faster in my chest, my mind knows that he's got this. He's a fucking savage and my sworn guard for a reason.

Together, they crash to the concrete, rolling a few times, the momentum shifting between the two of them, and then, to my horror, the man twists, flipping his body until he's at Sai's back. He pulls something from his pocket, a gun from what I can tell, but my vision is shit at the moment, the air around us still thick with the smoke bomb and the dark of the early morning doing nothing to help.

But the flames have grown, spread to our car, and suddenly, the hood erupts with a thunderous boom, but neither flinches nor allows themselves a moment's distraction.

"Where the hell is Dad?!" Boston panics.

"Shhh!" I hiss with a glare, keeping my eyes focused.

The man lifts his weapon right as Sai turns, and I suck in a harsh breath as he presses it against the underside of Sai's neck.

No!

And then both men freeze, Sai and the fool who dared to come at us.

It's momentary, literally no more than the blink of a second, and then Sai's arm twists and bends, his hand shooting out, gripping the back of the man's head and I wait for him to end his life. To snap his fucking neck and send him to hell, but he doesn't. Sai throws his right arm back, and my eyes widen as it falls into the flames, and I swear he holds it there a moment before swinging it back around at the masked man.

They shuffle backward a bit, and then with my next breath, ice shoots through my veins, cold and fucking staggering. The man in the mask lowers the gun.

He lowers his fucking gun, darts away, and Sai . . . lets him.

I hear the others coming now, the shouts and then the gunfire, but they're careful because they have no idea where we are. Fire blocks any clear line of sight they might have had, so it's likely their bullets are being shot straight into the air and not in any actual direction.

Still, the man runs, and I can't see where he goes, but the taillights shine back the way we came, the getaway car having been parked behind the second SUV, hidden from sight.

The gates squeal loudly as they are wrenched open and man after man runs into the street, searching each of the vehicles, weapons held high, fingers on the triggers.

"Rocklin!" Damiano shouts.

"It's safe!" Kylo screams. "Come on, girl, come out!"

It takes me a moment to find my voice, my limbs shaking slightly as my mind tries to process what I just saw. If I saw anything. When I look to Boston and her eyes slowly reach mine, I know I'm not crazy. The same dread shines within hers and when she goes to open her mouth, I give a curt shake of my head. Smartly, she closes her lips, straightens her spine and as we've been taught a hundred times over, my sister and I put on a blank face and slip out of the shadows.

Instantly, we're rushed and surrounded, completely barricaded and hidden behind no less than a dozen guards.

The Grecos, Ander, and Damiano lead us back into the property, all of us at a slight jog until we reach the bulletproof Hummer forty feet ahead. We jump inside, and just before the door can close fully, a large hand, charred with blood beneath its fingernails, catches it.

My sister folds her hand in mine, and I clench it as Sai climbs in with us.

Blood leaks down his left temple, but it's as if he doesn't feel it, his face a mask of nothingness as he quickly glances our way, eyes flying over us as if to check if we're all right.

When they meet mine, I feel my sister wince, and I know I'm drawing blood from her, but she only covers our joined hands with her free one. He gives a small nod, waiting.

This has always been his way of letting me know it's okay, that he'll deal with it, handle anything that needs handling, and I need not worry. So I give him the response he's after, a single nod back, and just like that, he faces forward.

Nobody speaks a word as we haul ass back to the manor, and just as we were led into the SUV, we're led into the safety of my home, cocooned by the others.

The girls rush me the moment the barricade reveals us, security, with semiautomatic weapons surrounding them, having stayed behind to guard the girls. The heavy doors slam behind us as a number of team members double down. Metal bars descend from where they are hidden in the walls, locking and latching and twisting.

Calvin rushes from his office then. "I just finished watching the footage. You were ambushed. They knew you would be coming here, and they knew your father would see to it that you arrived safely."

"Wait." I dart forward, panic licking across my spine. "What are you saying?" My eyes fly around. "Wait, where's my dad?"

Calvin's lips thin. "They took him."

My face falls, and I have to bite into the side of my cheek to keep myself from shaking like a leaf in the wind because, holy shit, the tsunami washing over me right now. It threatens to knock me off my feet, right onto my ass, until I'm drowning in the ocean. I know he went out first, I know he went down, but I thought . . . I don't know that I had time to think anything.

I look to my sister, hoping she understands what I'm trying to tell her without words, and when her lips remain sealed, her eyes blank and her face expressionless, I know she does.

From the corner of my eye, I find Sai. He's moving quickly, looking around every corner you can see from here, his body movements jerky and putting me off-kilter even more.

He tears at the curtains, shredding them with his teeth and I watch as he lowers it to the melted skin of his right hand, but before he can wrap the silk around it, my eyes zone in on his ring finger. His *bare* ring finger.

His guardian token, the one that represents his dying devotion to me. It's . . . gone. Removed. Acid, heavy and hot boils beneath my skin as sweat breaks out all over me.

I track his every step, cementing the spaces he looks and touches to memory so I can ask someone else to retrace them, but who? Who can be trusted if not the man I've trusted with my life more than anyone, my own father included? Horror and bitter betrayal threaten to spew from my mouth, but I swallow beyond the vomit.

"We need to get you guys in the panic room," he calls over his shoulder. "I'll take you and—"

"No," I cut him off, a little too fast perhaps, but my voice remains steady. But seriously. No fucking way. There is one way in and one way out of the panic room. We are not delivering ourselves on a platter.

"We're going to the basement." I leave no room for argument. "The training room and the bunker down there should be enough, and the largest of our weapon inventory is there. Damiano will lead us down and the boys will stay with us."

While Sai grows silent, the slightest of creases forming in the corners of his eyes, that's the only hint of disagreement or surprise he shows. I'm not exactly sure what he's thinking, but I know he disapproves of my decision, just as he knows he can't exactly override it. He could follow us down there and demand to stay with us, but I could argue he's needed more here and it would be never-ending.

Thankfully, Calvin agrees, calling Sai and a few of the other guards into the chancellor's suite for a quick debrief. "We'll go over the footage and circle the grounds as one," Calvin shares.

The second they start walking, we do as well.

Worry weighs heavy in the girls' eyes, but I offer them the smallest of smiles I can and excuse myself the second we've reached the last step. Desperate for a few minutes alone, I lock myself in the lavatory so I don't freak the fuck out and go crazy.

I take deep breaths, blowing in and out, but it doesn't help, and when I look up in the mirror, I crumble.

My face caving, my lips trembling as I drop, my hands gripping the cool granite as my knees hit the floor. My head falls forward, and I weep silently.

Trust.

My father always said it's both the best and worst thing in our world. I thought I understood what he meant.

I was so fucking wrong.

Chapter 32
Bass

My phone rings and a harsh thump drums deep in my chest, my fingers twitching when I look at it to find "My Rich Girl" lighting up the screen, but at the same time, something inside me settles for the first time in far too fucking long.

Been a hot minute since she's called, texted, begged and pleaded, all to turn around and cuss me out. It's a vicious little cycle my girl puts herself through every time she loses the battle of restraint she tries to pretend she possesses, but we both know the truth. She has none when it comes to me, same as I have none when it comes to her.

I knew the messages would start to fade, come fewer and further between, but I'd be lyin' if I said a small part of me didn't hate it, maybe even become worried, once they did. If I hadn't had one eye on her at all times from the day I left till now, I might even have thrown a fit about it, given in and gone to her. I might have felt compelled to let her know that this whole time she thought I was walking away, I was simply preparing for our ending while at the same time using her bad move as a light form of punishment.

I wanted her to stress over me, to sit there and wonder if I had just up and walked away, and I know she sat there many times, calling me a bitch in her head. What kind of dude can't handle some bullshit talk about his past in front of other people? Yeah, I bet she asked herself that a couple times at least, the man she knew me to be unbothered by words, but it served a purpose.

That shit did piss me off, which is one of the reasons why I decided to let her believe I cut her out completely and it led to my going about things the way I have. But it was also because I had to tie up loose ends where I was living before I could take the spot I wanted.

So yeah, seeing her name on the screen now, it does something to me.

So fucking close now, baby.

The phone stops ringing, and not fifteen seconds later, the notification pops up that a voice mail came through. My skin itches with eager anticipation, damn near desperate to hear her voice when her words are meant to be mine and not a conversation I'm listening in on. I can almost guess what she is calling to say, but as I put the phone on speaker and press play, I realize I am not prepared.

"Basti—" She swallows her own whisper and starts again, "Bass . . ."

My name, or what people call me, the one I never wanted her to use but demanded she did last time she saw me, is no more than an exhale past her lips and it takes a lot of work to keep mine firmly together. It sounds so fucking wrong coming from her lips.

The unmistakable desperation, dripping in uncertain fear, both new and foreign feelings for this girl, is like an electric bolt through my system, a painful shock that has my heart rate skipping. I'm completely fucked up on the inside, angrier for too many reasons to count while making sure there's not a single sign of it on the outside.

It takes her a few silent seconds to decide what she wants to say in her voice mail, and I wait for her shaky tone to, once again, suck the air from the room.

"Please," she whispers. "Bass, I need you. Someone has my father, and I . . . I can't trust who I thought I could, but I know I can trust you. Something's going on and I don't want to talk about it over the phone, but please just . . ." Her voice travels further away now as if she's preparing to hang up and her last words are an afterthought not necessarily meant for me, but I hear them loud and clear. "Come back to me."

The line goes dead, the silence heavy and thick and damn near suffocating, but I ignore it, tossing my phone on the small desk as I kick my feet up on top of it and lean back as casually as ever.

Slowly, my eyes lift, connecting with a familiar pair. It's damn near comical, the resemblance so fucking obvious now.

This is 'bout to get real fun, real fucking fast . . .

Rocklin

My mind is running crazy, my thoughts nearly incoherent they're so all over the place. Nothing makes sense, no thought leading into a moment of clarity. I literally feel blind inside my own mind and I have no idea what I need to do or what I even can do to help me "see."

My dad is missing, and my guardian might be at fault.

Why else would the man spare his life if they weren't working together? He wouldn't.

Or maybe that's the wrong way to look at it since there were no actual casualties on our team tonight, serious and life-threatening injuries, yes, but no death, at least not yet. The doctors on our payroll are only updating us as their conditions change.

So why did the man leave Sai completely unharmed? He had a gun to his throat, and he lowered it and left him there. It might not seem so odd if he would have at least knocked him over the head with it, left him with a gaping wound like so many of the others, but he didn't.

He literally let him live, and Sai let him walk away.

God. I run my hands over my hair. I don't even know how to bring this up to the girls; it seems so unreal, even to my own ears. I've seen the man murder in the blink of an eye to keep me safe. He doesn't even pause but pulls the trigger, sometimes before I even realize there's a threat. A body would fall and he'd use it as a training lesson, break down what I missed, and teach me what not to do the next time because there was always a next time. I was young the last time I watched him kill a man. Men are less inclined to come at my family nowadays.

This is a man who took an oath in blood, sacrificing a life of his own, family or any relationship whatsoever in exchange for the "honor" of being my guard. He's the man who took me to all of my diving practices and swim meets and training sessions. The only person around to witness the pains and struggles that come along with this life, the ones we're forced to hide to save face. The man who is sometimes more like a father to me than my actual one, if only because he was consistently glued to my side in ways my father couldn't be. That's essentially what a guard is, a protective figure you're forever supposed to depend on.

But he's been missing lately, not at my side or my back or within eyesight. He's been doing other things while I've been left in my father's care, tucked in the car with his driver rather than my own. I tear through my mind, trying to remember if a conversation existed where my father told me Sai would be busy with other things or if it just happened on its own. I want to call him and ask him, but I can't. He's gone and again . . . what if it was Sai who set him up to be taken?

A blanket falls over my shoulders, and I close my eyes as I wrap my fingers around it, pulling it closer, taking one more moment for myself. Finally, I force a small smile, my eyes opening and landing on Damiano.

His body faces forward, but his eyes flick to mine for a single second as he gives a curt nod, an acknowledgment of my gratitude. I can tell his thoughts are heavy as well, as he focuses straight ahead at the property behind the manor, and slowly, I do the same.

The soft glow of a light in the distance catches my attention, and my eyes narrow slightly. I shake my head, finally seeing out into the dusk for the first time rather than looking or focusing on my inner thoughts. As if sensing my surprise, he nods in my peripheral.

"When did that happen?" I wonder out loud.

"A little over a month ago. Bronx was the first to notice when the garden fountain suddenly flicked on."

"Someone purchased the property? I thought the deed was missing. Wasn't that why no one could prove it belonged to the Greysons?"

It takes him a moment, but he lifts a single shoulder and then casts a quick glance over it before I even hear their footsteps.

Bronx and Delta rejoin us, fresh cappuccinos in their hands, and they offer one to me.

"We figured you needed this." Delta's smile doesn't quite reach her eyes.

I pull it to my lips, cupping my hands over the warm glass and breathing in the roasted almonds and woodsy scent. I take a second sip, and then a long sigh escapes.

"I've combed through everything there is to comb through, and I can't find anything on the surveillance for your house or for outside the gate that's helpful, but Damiano already said he's going to go over it again just in case," Bronx shares.

"It has to be Enzo, doesn't it?" Delta says as she lowers onto the patio seating.

"It's not Enzo." We all look to Boston, who leans against the open doors, her arms crossed over herself.

I hold her eyes a long moment, watching as a clear gloss coats them. I nod, agreeing. "It's not Enzo. If it were, he wouldn't have gone after my dad."

He would have taken . . . damn, I have no idea who he would have taken: the girl he agreed to marry or the "better one" my father said he could have instead.

Anger threatens to consume me, but I wash it away because my father isn't here, and God only knows what's happening to him. The last thing I need is for him to take his final breath while I'm standing here, pissed off at what he's done. Or, more accurately, threatened to do before everything went to shit for the second time in twenty-four hours.

Behind Boston, the Grecos step in, Ander and Alto behind them.

Kenex and Kylo join us on the balcony as well, looking first to Damiano and then to me.

"Do you think they'll hurt him?" Kylo worries, and Kenex nudges him in the ribs. "Your dad, I mean?"

I lift a shoulder, giving him a small smile. It's sweet of him to care when my father has shown him not an ounce of humanity.

Everyone nods, looking to me, waiting for instruction I'm expected to give. Waiting for an answer that I'm supposed to have.

I have nothing. Well, maybe the smallest of insights. "I would say it was Otto finally coming after him in search of Oliver, but our dad said Otto was attacked just before our security went out. That's why we were coming home."

Dom nods. "Calvin told us about what happened at the Henshaw mansion."

"What if Otto and his family faked the attack to cover for himself, so he could come after Dad without repercussions?" Boston asks.

My eyes widen. "Holy shit."

"That has to be it," Dom agrees.

It does. "The Henshaws had to—"

Sai's giant form breaks into the room and my words die on my lips, my muscles tightening as he makes his way toward us, his suit still perfectly in place, no sign of an attack made on the name he's sworn to protect.

To everyone else in the room, his face likely looks calm and unreadable, but as I said, I've spent more time around this man than anyone in my family or friend group. I see the strain at the edges he tries to hide but can't. Lines of guilt?

His eyes connect with mine and my throat runs dry.

"Do you need anything?" he asks, his gaze pointed and searching.

I can't find my voice, so I simply shake my head, and while it takes him a minute, he finally accepts it as an answer and moves back into the hall.

The second he's out of sight, Boston's eyes narrow, and she quietly runs toward the door, closing it as softly as possible as she flicks the lock in place before rushing back my way.

"What is it?" she asks and then it's all eyes on me.

I take a deep breath, telling them everything that I chose to skip over earlier because I needed a moment to try and make sense of it to myself. I do acknowledge the fact that I should have mentioned it from the very beginning, especially since he was within these walls with us, but nobody faults me for it.

Bronx busts out her computer, and she and Damiano hover over it on my bed as she hacks her way into Sai's phone. Surprisingly, it only takes her three minutes to get in with her father's newest software. She divvies up the content and prints small batches, passing them to all the boys, and they hunker down, reading over all of Sai's private conversations.

He has no family, no woman, though I'm sure he finds a way to spend time with some, so there's nothing there but communication with my father and the other members of our team. Some from Calvin and house members, Jasper included. Each message relayed prominent information in regard to us girls and our safety. Or more me and my safety, since I was his responsibility, but none were out of the ordinary or raised cause for concern.

Another forty-five minutes go by before they begin to come up for air, and Saylor delivers my third cappuccino.

"There's nothing here. Nothing at all that raises any red flags," Bronx says, looking to the boys, who nod in agreement.

"The only thing I paused at was the arguments between him and your dad, but he was arguing against being placed away from you," Kylo adds. "But maybe that's how he kept Rayo off his tracks?"

Their words should be comforting, but they're not in the slightest. I can't shake the unease knotting within me. "What about—"

Bronx's laptop dings and her head snaps my way as all of ours point toward her. As one, we scramble, rushing for her computer, all of us hovering over her, seeing nothing but crazy coding across the screen that we have to wait for her to explain.

"He got a message, but the number isn't saved," she rushes. "Holy shit, it says he's all yours." Her eyes dart my way, corners creased. "What could that mean? Who is all his?"

I open my mouth to speak, but Damiano beats me to it.

"Wait! Look!" He's drawing closer.

"There's an attachment coming through," Bronx realizes, her fingers flying across the keyboard in rapid succession, small boxes popping up where she types in numbers before they disappear and another appears, followed by a loading screen.

"He's opening it."

And then a photo reveals itself.

Warm liquid splashes up my legs, a cup having slipped from my sister's hands as an image of my father chained to a concrete wall comes across.

Another ping.

Bronx works her magic, and then her words leave her in a low, cautious whisper. "You know where he is . . ."

My heart beats erratically, my fingers wrapping around Boston's as hers find their way into mine and we look to each other, glancing all around the room, and I'm unsure of what to say, how to say it, or what to do next.

And then I release her and suddenly, I'm booking it out my door, around the corridor, and down the spiral staircase, everyone else hot on my heels as we dash into the foyer.

Jasper's eyes widen as he sees us grow closer and he stands to attention, waiting for instruction should we give any.

"Calvin?"

"On the back patio, Ms. Revenaw." We're already on our way there before he's finished speaking, so we missed the bow I know he gives on our exit.

Damiano makes his way in front of me, shoving the double doors open and holding them for the rest of us to shuffle through. We run through the row of roses, curving around the fountains until we get to the main seating area, where we come to an abrupt stop.

Calvin and a few other guards' eyes jerk our way, and slowly, they push to their feet, but my attention is glued on the man standing ten feet to the side, alone and shadowed in the darkness.

Sai stands there, eyes and frown glued to his phone as he types away and I'm half tempted to run back upstairs just to see what he said.

As one, we mask our expressions, going completely blank and using every bit of our training to make sure we stay that way when finally, his head snaps our way.

I can't control the harsh inhale I take as his eyes meet mine, and it's as if acid is poured down my throat. The sting of betrayal is almost too harsh to stomach as worry fills his dreadful eyes and he rushes his way toward me.

His hands wrap around my biceps in the way they've done a hundred times before, but this time feels suffocating. "I have to handle something, but I'll be back. I'll make it quick and return swiftly."

He'll make it quick.

He'll kill my father quickly and rush back to my side to pretend as if he has no idea what's going on.

Before I know what I'm doing, before I can even pause long enough to breathe, the switchblade is pulled out, flipped open and dug deep into his gut.

A mumbled groan bubbles past his lips and his grip on me tightens for a split second before he stumbles back a step.

Tears fall, pouring down my cheeks in steady streams as I look down to where the blade sticks in his belly, a block of red slowly spanning out into a deep-crimson circle that only spreads wider.

Calvin and the others realize what I've done, screaming and shouting, darting over to where we are, but rather than rush to his aid, they shield us, unsure of what's going on as they stare at me and Sai in disbelief.

I cry, my feet starting toward him as if to take it back, to comfort him, as little sense as it makes. I watch as his hand wraps around the handle, a frown taking over his features as he pulls it out, only to fall to his knees a moment later.

I don't know why, but I fall with him, dropping before him, my hands shaking, my subconscious telling me to cover his wound. To apply pressure to the spot and save his life, even though I'm the one that just threatened to take it.

Slowly, his eyes come up to mine, and the softness within them, the love and commitment and devotion that shines back, rattles me to my core, and a bubbled cry escapes. My vision is completely blurred now as his bloody hands move up, gently covering my cheeks and the softest of touches.

He nods and I grip his wrists.

"Sai—" I choke, but he only shakes his head.

"It's okay. It's okay," he whispers, his touch growing colder by the second. His words are a plea, begging me to understand that he understands. That he knows me well and he knows exactly what I've done and why I've done it.

I don't understand it.

"I . . ."

"It's okay," he repeats yet again, his tone somehow managing to grow even gentler. "It's time. My job is done now. My oath is complete. The safe. Everything he searches for is in the safe," he stresses and then a ghost of a smile curves his lips as he says, "tell him I won the bet and that I had no doubt."

Confusion whirls in my head, and when he falls back, I fall with him, flicking open his jacket as I inspect the damage I've done. His riddles make no sense. His words mean nothing to me in this moment, and I'm torn between stabbing him a second time and begging someone to try and save him.

"I didn't even have to bring him to you . . ." His voice trails off into a mumbled whisper as his hands fall to his sides, and with his very last breath, he shares, "You found him on your own."

And then he's gone.

A choked cry escapes, and everyone huddles around, but I don't even have time to process what I've done, what has happened, and what he has said because, in the next moment, a loud rumble fills the air, and everyone shoots to their feet.

Our eyes dart around every surface as the ground shakes, guns are pulled from wherever they are hidden, the soft clicks and barrels sound as a bullet is released into the chamber, and then the loudest of crashes.

We gasp, standing back as the hundred-year-old wall crumbles at the back of the property line, a giant tank rolling right over the archery zone, crumbling into nothing beneath its giant tires.

Guns are pointed.

The door is thrown open.

A man steps out.

I gasp and then I hear the first shot fired, fire and panic flooding my ears as I dart forward on instinct, a bullet scraping along the edge of my thigh before I hear the demand for a cease-fire.

I pant, planted between my people and the giant shadow that's slowly making its way toward us. Toward me.

It's tall, trim and nearly invisible beneath the dark night sky. I shield my eyes as he steps in front of the blinding lights of the tank, my pulse hammering in my chest.

And then the lights click off.

I blink in to focus, and then I fall to my knees for the second or maybe third time tonight, but this time, in pure relief.

Finally . . .

Chapter 33
Bass

Two Hours Earlier

Slowly, I climb to my feet, making my way over to the man strapped up like a sacrifice but loose enough not to cause any damage unless I decide I want it to. That's not why we're here though.

His muscles constrict, the veins in his neck throbbing alongside the one on his temple as he growls around the gag, the heavy yank of the chains clanking around the room and echoing off the high ceiling.

My smirk only grows and I don't pause until I'm right in front of him and slowly remove the gag from over his mouth.

As expected, the threats start instantly.

"I will fucking destroy you, boy. You have no idea what you've done. I'll have you in pieces and sent back to whoever it is that paid you to come here. I can promise you no amount of money would ever be worth what I'm going to do to you when this is over."

I smile, jerking my head to the side when he spits, just as I knew he would.

Making a show of looking all around, I slowly bring my eyes back to his. "Not sure what you're seein', old man, but it looks to me like I'm the one running the show."

He scoffs an obnoxious sound but clamps his teeth shut into a snarl when the basement door clanks open, simultaneously slamming shut with a loud thud, alerting us both to a new arrival.

His eyes are alert, keen and flicking around every single inch of the place as he waits for who I'm assuming he believes is the boss, the big bad man who "paid me" to bring him here. So, when it's only my boy Hayze who walks through, his eyes narrow, more of that confusion filtering across his face, but he tries to keep himself as guarded as possible. I'd say he's doing pretty well, but over the last few months, I've become familiar with his many expressions, so it's easy for me to see when his mask slips over his face.

Hayze gets one look at the dark-haired man and lets out a little whistle. "Goddamn, my boy. You weren't playing."

"This is Hayze."

"You're both dead."

"Says the man with chains attached to his every limb." Hayze grins.

When Hayze looks to me, I give a jerk of my head, and without asking, he moves to grab the small table, bringing it closer, and sets it at my side, placing the small stool right behind me.

I reach into the back of my waistband, eyes trained on the man before me as I pull the small, lightweight custom toy out. With my last three fingers wrapped around the handle, my pointer resting along the barrel, I draw the weapon up between us, my eyes flicking from it to him.

Rage causes him to shake, the chains rattling with the movement as he focuses on the small golden crest carved into the handle.

"Thief," he spits the word with pure disdain, so sure the only answer is a sticky-fingered me.

Nodding, I bring my other hand up, and I don't miss the way his muscles tense, but I don't call him out on it as I slowly remove the empty clip, pull back the hammer and pop the final bullet waiting in the chamber out.

I set the gun and clip beside me before lowering onto the stool and lifting my hands, giving my fingers a little wiggle for spite.

He keeps his expression blank, waiting for me to speak.

"I'm sure you're wondering why you're here—"

"I know why I'm here."

"Oh yeah? So let's hear it then."

"Because someone hired you to take me out, too weak and fearful to dare do it themselves, so they sent a boy in place of a man to do their dirty work." He yanks on the chain for sport and an attempt to show some form of dominance while being completely dominated in his current state. "Well, let me let you in on a little secret to how this world works. The grunts who do the big boys' bidding? They don't live to breathe another day. I guarantee the second you step out of this room, there will be someone waiting for you in the next one, and I will relish in the screams that follow."

My chuckle is low, and I give a small nod as my tongue sweeps along my lip ring. "You got one thing right. There is someone waiting for me on the other side of this room, and don't worry, I have every intention of showing you who that is, but not until we're done here. Not until I've got what I want from you."

He holds for several moments, I'll give him that, but then he asks the question I've been waiting for. "What is it that you want?"

"Easy, and only one single thing." Cocking my head, I grin and say, "Your daughter."

Silence.

Rayo Revenaw stares at me in dead fucking silence, and then a scoffed laugh leaves him, quickly growing into a deep manic one. He drops his head back and all, so I wait for his little show to be over. "You, boy, are clearly even more of an amateur than I suspected you to be."

He doesn't ask me a question, so there's no need to respond, but when I push to my feet, his eyes narrow the slightest bit. So little if I hadn't been watching, I might have missed it. I pull my eyes from his as I step up to the giant stone wall to the right of him, and I don't have to look at him to know he's tracking my every move. I don't need to keep our gazes locked to know a hint of uncertainty makes its way down his spine when one of the stones slides downward as my palm settles over it, and a neat little pin code pad reveals itself.

The shit money gets you, I swear.

I punch in the password and his chains give a little shake as the wall disappears, tucking into itself as a second set of chains begins to rattle, and what do you know, the man of the hour goes stone silent.

Still, I don't turn back to him as my other guest is revealed.

I wink at the murderous eyes that find mine only seconds before spotting Rayo behind me. His gaze flicks back and forth, likely zeroing in on me when I keep moving to the next wall. Again, I expose the little pin pad, and get ready for the funniest part, the one I've been waiting way too long for. I should get a fucking medal for the restraint I've shown.

In what feels like slow motion, the next wall folds into itself and I stand there as the third member of our party comes into view, this one not faring as well as the others.

His head bounces around a couple times before he manages to lift it. He attempts to glare, but then his attention is called to his left when he catches a glimpse in his peripheral. Momentary relief floods the bastard's body, but panic sets in just as fast, the sight creating a thrilling little twist in my gut.

And then two sets of chains go fucking wild.

Swear to god, it's the sweetest music I've heard in a long-ass time. Finally, I spin, looking back to the man who's the farthest from where I'm standing. The ever poised and unreadable Rayo Revenaw can't hide the utter shock that sweeps through him as his gaze flies across the room.

I stand there, watching every shade as it washes over him, the shock morphing into confusion and then uncertainty as he wonders if maybe this is a play or a ploy, but then, once again, his gaze settles on the final cell. All at once, pure and utter rage fills him to his core.

I couldn't keep the smirk in if I tried, not that I care to. I'm fucking pleased as shit.

I'm the master of this show, delivering the biggest delicacy to my most vicious pet. It's the meal of his dreams, at least right now anyway. 'Cause if there's anyone who wants to slit the throat of this motherfucker and watch him bleed out as much as I do, it's the father of the girl he dared to touch.

To bruise.

To leave his mark on as if he has some sort of claim when he abso-fucking-lutely does not. Even if she were to give him permission, it would mean nothing. Not that that matters because she didn't. He grabbed her, threatened her, turning her perfect creamy skin six shades darker and in the shape of his grimy fingers.

Fingers . . . that lie at his feet, a little fact his father's just now come to realize.

Otto Henshaw yanks on his restraints, palms wrapping around the thick steel, and he heaves, thrashing all around as he tries to scream around his gag, eyes wide and taking in every bloody inch of his one and only heir.

"Relax, my guy," Hayze fucks with him. "It was only the tips."

My gaze flicks over to Oliver, from bloody stubs of his clipped fingers on his dominant hand, the one that touched her, to the five marks starting on his left shoulder to the right—a fun twist of the five-finger bruise he gave her—and the red river path they created down his chest, making him look like he's in much worse shape than he is. Granted, he's in pretty bad fucking shape. I've only watered and fed the mutt enough to keep him alive, and the only shower he's had was the rubbing alcohol I poured over his chest for an added little sting. Actually, the wounds across his stubbed knuckles are bubbled with puss and the coloring of his hands isn't quite right, so maybe he is in as bad of shape as he looks after all.

Serves him right.

Otto struggles again, looking to Rayo for help, hoping to see a spark of a plan in his gaze, something that will give him a sense of security or hope that he will come to the rescue and get them out of this.

As expected, when my eyes return to Rayo's, he's managed to contain his anger, so his gaze is expressionless as it meets Otto's. It's as if he's unfazed, and Otto seems to eat that up. He doesn't exactly relax, but he stops wasting his strength on the struggle and goes back to trying to kill me with his eyes.

Pulling a knife from my pocket, a new one since my little thief is holding on to my favorite one for me, I thump it against Oliver's skull a couple times. Not hard, but enough to draw attention to him . . . and it elicits a small squeal from him to satisfy my inner fucking demon.

It serves its purpose, and Otto's attention is once again on me. Slowly, I head his way, rolling the knife between my fingers as I circle behind him, loving the way his muscles clench like a little bitch. Finally, I settle in front of him.

"Months. You spent months digging and digging for any tiny, little detail that could possibly lead you to the one and only conclusion you were *so sure* you would reach. So you planned for it. Planned for exactly what you were going to do to make sure you got your boy over there back."

Otto's muscles lock, tension and unease bleeding out of his pores as he slowly starts to shake in his silk pajamas, the outfit I found him in when I tore him from his bed early this morning.

"Yeah, you know what I'm talking about, don't you, you sly little fuck?" I take a few steps away, looking over at Rayo a moment before facing Otto once more. "Or are you sly?" I pretend to wonder when we all know I'm simply mocking the man. "Imma say no . . . but I'd bet you'd be interested in making a deal with me to get you off the hook and leave this guy on it, hmm? So long as I don't speak the words rolling around in here." I tap at my temple, holding his eyes a moment.

Suddenly, I dart forward, knife open, and he flails all around as I bring it to his face.

"Hold still, motherfucker, or you'll have no lips left when I'm done," I warn as I press the tip of the blade into what I *think* is the space between his lips.

He screams, veins in his neck bulging as little beads of red roll down his chin. I slide the blade right, spin it and go back left. He gasps, spitting blood, eyes clenching closed. All the while, Rayo remains silent but watchful.

"There. You can speak now." I look at the few layers of skin I skimmed from his lips as he tries to push them from his mouth so he doesn't swallow a piece of himself. "But before you say a word, I'll give you two . . ." He shakes with anger, waiting, so I make him wait a little longer before I say, "*Paraquat dichloride.*"

Instant.

Literally, in the span of a single nanosecond, all the color drains from Otto Henshaw's face. He grows ghostly white, an involuntary shudder making its way down his spine. It takes him a moment, but then his eyes dart toward his son and I'm betting right now he's regretting having ever shared what he thought was a simple truth, having never expected it to come right back around to him in a situation like this.

See, Rocklin gets pissy when her daddy doesn't tell her every little detail, but at the end of the day, he does it for a reason, and we're staring at the biggest one.

Otto is no Rayo and he didn't think that part through—what your kid knows *will* hurt them.

Otto's eyes fall to the concrete floor beneath his bare feet, and I cut a quick glance at Rayo, who narrows his in question, but when I wink at him, his lip curls, and I'm focused back on Otto before he has a chance to catch the interaction.

Like I knew he would be, Otto is willing to play the game. Most people are when their back's against the wall . . . or should I say when their limbs are locked in steel bracelets and bolted to a basement floor.

"What do you want?" he whispers, but everyone is waiting to find out what the guy will say next, so there's not a sound to drown out his words, leaving them heard by all.

412

"I want to know where you keep your records."

His brows furrow. "What records?"

"All the shady ones, the favors for friends or acquaintances."

He starts to shake his head, but I slowly shake mine, and he stops.

"Don't lie."

"I don't keep records of everything. There are some things I have but not all—"

He cuts off with a sharp groan of pain when a dart is shot straight into his groin.

Cutting a quick glance over my shoulder, I grin at Hayze.

He's lounging in the chair with a half-eaten sandwich in his hand and smiles around it. "Stole this from the curly-haired wet dream. Good to know it works."

Chuckling, I turn back to Otto.

"Sorry to break it to you, but your son's already been broken, and even if he didn't tell us you keep records for every little job done, I'd have known you did. A man capable of what you did?" The insinuation is clear, and the way he shrinks into himself is comical, as if tucking his shoulders up high will keep the man to his left from staring right at him.

"No way you wouldn't hold on to every little thing, just in case the perfect opportunity popped up for some good old-fashioned blackmail, but I'll go ahead and tell you, I'm not interested in what you've done in your lifetime. I give no fucks about all the things I don't know. All I'm looking for is one thing and one thing only. The rest means nothing to me. I'll even burn it right here in front of you to prove that."

"Why should I believe you? You have me tied up in a cell?" he spits angrily.

"True." I nod. "But what have you got to lose other than your life, the life of your son, and the end of your line? The way Hayze tells it, your right-hand man jumped right in and is doing a real good job of comforting your wife right now in your absence."

413

"His body wouldn't even be cold yet, and she's got another warm one on top of her." Hayze chuckles behind me, but I keep my eyes on Otto.

"What exactly is it you want to know?" he asks as if he's in a position to, but at least he's talking.

"Your front business is helping poor immigrants get on their feet, even though we know they get the shit end of the stick, but what I'm interested in is your back-end dealings. Way I hear it, and from what your boy over there has confirmed, you help people disappear, those with or without a desire to do so."

"I don't kill people to get rid of them." He frowns.

The left corner of my mouth lifts in a smirk and he starts fidgeting in place once more, his choice of words, not quite the truth, even if they are when it comes to his "business." He knows what I'm thinking, and he's waiting to see if I'll call him out. Not yet. Instead, I say, "Good thing the person I'm looking for is very much alive then, huh?"

I eye him a moment, running my tongue across my lip, flicking at my lip ring. "Little more than four years ago, someone came to you with a woman. A shit woman who was being forced out of the town she lives in for being the shit she is. I want to know where she went."

"Let me go and I can take you to my records and we can figure it out."

"Nah, it ain't going to work like that." Slowly, I step back, my eyes moving from one cell to the next and then the last, and I realize something.

"You know, I had a whole plan for how this was going to go. For what I was going to say to you, how I was going to say it and what I was willing to do to get the answers I want. In case you're wondering, it's just about anything, but tonight . . . something happened, and it's kind of fucking twisted, but now that I really think about it, everything makes sense." My smile grows, a low laugh leaving me. "I'm not so sure I need you anymore to figure out where this woman is, not when I'm suddenly damn sure someone else does." I clap, rubbing my palms together. "So let's skip to the fun part."

Pulling open the small drawer on the tiny table Hayze placed not far from where Rayo hangs, I take out the file I stuck inside.

"This right here"—I hold up the manila folder, my face blank as I look from Rayo to Otto—"this is the coroner's file for a case closed eleven years ago. The man who signed off on it was a piece of work . . . allegedly, of course. Rumor has it he fucked his stepdaughter while she was underage, but when said stepdaughter disappeared in the middle of the night one night, so did his case, but no one knew that 'cause it happened a decade before." Rayo adjusts his stance, and Otto does all he can to keep his attention pointed forward. "Turned out the last place she was seen was leaving a restaurant on the east side. Imagine my surprise when Hayze here did some digging and found it was owned but later sold by none other than . . . Otto fucking Henshaw."

"And so blackmail was born." Hayze is enjoying this shit as much as me.

"You know what it is?"

Otto's skin grows a nasty shade of green, his cheeks puffing out as if he's holding back vomit from spewing out his mouth.

"Yeah, you know what it is." I drop the file onto the small table and move back into Otto's cell, stepping in front of him. So close he could reach out and try to choke me, but he's too much of a bitch for that.

Okay, Rayo, let's see what you're made of.

"Tell me what you have on Mr. Revenaw that has forced him to play nice with a weak fucker like you," I demand of Otto.

He attempts to snap his head left to make eye contact with his "friend," but my hand darts up, fingers wrapping around his chin in a crushing grip that has him squealing. I squeeze harder, so hard I can feel his teeth shift, veneers probably, and watch as a little bit of blood pools in the creases of his mouth.

"Tell me what you have against this man."

415

"I will fucking kill you!" Rayo shouts, yanking against his chains.

Honestly, he could be talking to either of us, but that doesn't matter. The man in front of me figures he's dead either way, so he's only got one option, and that's to play my game, hoping that if he wins, he gets let out at the end.

"I hid something for him," he says.

I pause, giving Rayo a chance, but when he says nothing, I push further. "Hid what?"

"Don't say another word, Henshaw." Rayo damn near growls at the man.

Getting closer . . .

I apply more pressure, this time digging the tips of my fingers into the space between his teeth until the skin breaks against the bits of my nails. When he makes no move to speak, I add my other hand to his neck, squeezing against his pressure points just beneath the jawline, and he chokes.

Oliver starts shaking around in his shackles, but I don't look his way.

"Speak," I demand.

"He will kill me!" he hisses.

"You think I won't?" Both my brows jump. "Look around. Who's in charge here? Me or your cell buddy chained up just like you are?"

"Tell me what you hid."

He screams, "I hid—"

"My son," Rayo barks, officially shutting Otto up.

My head turns his way, and Rayo's sharp glare locks with mine. "He hid my son for me."

And there it fucking is, straight from the horse's mouth.

He lets go of his lie, saying it aloud for the first fucking time in his life, unwilling to let the roach rat on him, taking control the only way he can.

To think I almost lost hope.

Rayo watches me closely, head tipping slightly. "But you already knew that."

My smirk is slow, and I lift my arms out as if to say *surprise*. "I know a lot of things, dare I say . . . all the things you wish I didn't, and I think I know your reasons why too."

It makes perfect sense when you think about it. The dude preaches *family fucking first. Blood over all. Always, no matter what.* Blah fucking blah.

That's the biggest piece of bullshit I've ever heard.

My family beat the fuck out of me, tried to kill me and nearly did kill my sister.

Fuck blood and who you share it with. Fuck family. It means nothing.

But to the Revenaw twins? It meant more because it was drilled into them.

How would they feel if they knew Daddy stepped out on Mommy when she couldn't "do her duty" and give the man the heir he was entitled to? But more than that . . . he cast out his own, leaving him to the wolves when his wife finally gave him what he wanted. He abandoned his blood, so how could he preach the importance of it to his twins if they ever found out?

It's the thought of losing his girls or their respect or love or whatever the fuck it is that's most important to him, and only he knows what that is that kept him playing the Henshaws' game. He's a weird kind of selfish, selfless prick.

But it wasn't only that. It was the foundation the new generation of Greysons was expected to sit on. He already knew the others were expecting girls; they'd be the first of their kind, and suddenly, he had two coming. Twins. The Greyson girls were expected to do big things. To leave a legacy like no one's ever seen before, to bring to the table an entirely new way of thinking. Proof of that is already long past seven figures, thanks to The Enterprise.

To throw a boy in the mix would have changed everything for the girls. Automatically that boy would have taken the lead because he had a dick and they didn't. The power struggle between male and female wouldn't have died and should that male have claimed for himself one of the other Greyson girls, that would lead to the fall of the Greyson Union because the power would no longer be equal.

Again, what a selfish, selfless prick.

Shaking my head, I stuff my hands in my pockets. "You let this fool think he was in your back pocket, put your daughter through some shit, both of them really, just to keep Kylo Greco, or should I say *Revenaw*, a dark little secret." A chuckle leaves me. "I tell you, once I figured it out, it made fucking sense why you didn't want them on Greyson grounds because you knew who he was the minute they turned up. How could you not? The boy looks just fucking like you, man. Too bad he's sworn his loyalty to me now, hmm?"

Rayo's lip curls and I laugh again. "Kid's fucking smart. Quick and tough."

I walk over to Rayo, placing myself directly in front of him, close enough that he could headbutt me if he wanted to, maybe even do a little worse, depending on how flexible he is. His chains ain't that tight, but he doesn't flinch, doesn't move, and he's breathing steady as I bring myself nothing but a breath away.

We eye each other for a long moment, nothing but the nervous shifting and clatter of chains coming from the other side of the room filling the space.

Finally, I speak, keeping my voice low and only for him.

"Clearly, you've got a knack for giving things away, but this time? You're trying to give away something that doesn't belong to you," I tell him, shaking my head back and forth. "That's not going to work for me."

"You are delusional."

"And you're about to foam at the fucking mouth when I tell you what I know that you didn't. This *man,* the one you eat with on yachts and share laughs with and pretend to stand to save face . . . he didn't only plan to take from you, to destroy you"—I lean closer—"he already did. He took the woman who gave mine life right out from under your nose, and I have the proof you couldn't find. Me. The punk with not a soldier to his name."

Rayo turns fuckin' feral, his chest rumbling, before a deep, long rumble erupts from him and he tears at his fucking chains.

I step back, ready to speak to the three of them when my phone rings from the table, so I clamp my mouth shut, turning around to grab it.

Royce Brayshaw's name, one of my now former bosses, flashes across the screen. He's the one and only brother pissed off at me 'cause I helped out his brother's girl when she needed it at his brother's request. If he even knows that part of it, I don't know. He's the last motherfucker I would have expected to call, especially since the day I walked out of there, they knew I wouldn't be coming back and that I had no need to since the check their new queen sent me off with was more money I knew a person could have.

I bring my phone to my ear, and he doesn't wait for me to say a word.

"Hey, motherfucker," he slurs, clearly on a heavy dose of liquor. "Never wanted you back in this town, but I'm thinking you might want to be."

"Thought wrong. What do you want?" I look over to where Oliver is crawling on his forearms, trying to get closer to his dad, but his limbs are still too weak. "I'm kind of busy."

"Yeah, I've been busy too. Busy with a sweet little thing, soft short hair and a perfect round ass."

Tension crawls down my spine, and I grip the phone tighter.

"Aye, this girl?" He chuckles in my ear, the sound setting off a warning alarm in my head because while his next words shock the shit out of me, they're the exact ones I expect. "She's got a brother."

The line goes dead, and I swear to fucking God, he's about to be if he touched one finger on her head. Shoving my phone in my pocket, I whip the keys out of the other and step up to Rayo.

"I'm giving you a gift. Three, to be exact." I speak so low only he can hear as I press my chest against his and he lifts his chin, holding on to his pride, even though he's chained to my fucking basement floor. "And now I'm going to collect my reward. If you think I don't know what your exact next move will be, you're wrong, so I will warn you once. Do not fucking do it. You will regret it."

With one quick flick of my eyes to the other two, I shove the key into the lock around Rayo's right wrist, freeing it before I drop it into the pocket of his shirt, leaving him to do the rest.

Otto and Oliver scream and shout, their voices echoing off the walls as Hayze and I make our way to the door, up the stairs, and into the mansion.

My mansion.

We close the door behind us so their screams are sealed inside.

"Boss?" he draws.

"Royce Brayshaw has my sister."

"Oh shit."

Oh shit is right. I'm not their bitch boy anymore. I'm not their errands man.

I'd go as far as to say we're nothing to each other now, a little fact I hope he remembers because I'm coming for him. My sister is supposed to stay out of everything related to the life I lead and he just dragged her straight into it as if she's some sort of tool to be used against me for his own bullshit. She isn't. She's kind and good and deserves better. She deserves more.

I'm going to beat his fucking ass.

"You headed out now?" Hayze asks.

"Almost." Rather than head out to the front, where my car is parked, he follows my lead out the back door through the gardens. "Just gotta collect something first . . ."

Chapter 34
Bass

Chaos. Complete and utter chaos is what I've bulldozed my way into, not that I expected anything different.

No less than ten guns are pointed directly at me right now, but their queen stands between them and if anyone dares to hurt her, there's a nifty little gun attached to this new tank of mine that Hayze won't hesitate to let run free. I told him to take me out if he had to.

If she hurts, I hurt, and they fucking die. Plain and fucking simple.

We planned for that horrifying possibility, but I counted on her team being smart enough to know when to hold back.

What I did not plan for or anticipate was the fuckery of emotions and thoughts the sight of her would bring.

Goddamn if I don't want to run to her, pick her up and hold her, fucking rock her back and forth a while. I want to tell her everything's going to be all right and explain where we're at and what's going on.

Then there's this other part that wants to look down my nose at her, turn my back on her and make her beg, plead and cry at my feet for dismissing me the way she did and in front of a little bitch like Oliver when all she had to do was take my hand—that part of me is an even bigger asshole.

But I've got shit to do and I'm on a time line so when Damiano steps forward, holding one hand behind him to

421

further hold off the firing squad and one out in front of him as if to placate me, I keep on moving, but my eyes stay locked on his.

"Bass . . ." he eases. "You can't just fucking barge in here like this. There's a way to go about things."

"Just came to get something of mine, pretty boy."

That's when I see it, the shine of familiar silver gleaming off the moonlight right there in the grass, and beside it . . . a body. My eyes narrow, my pulse thumping harder with each step closer.

It's *him*. Dead.

Dead by my knife, the one thing that came with me from my past life into the new one.

The fucking irony . . .

I was so fucking close. My feet grow heavier, knowing if I turn back now, I might get back to the basement before Rayo "deals" with Otto for what he did, but then my eyes slide a little left.

To my girl, lying out on the wet grass in the middle of this mess with blood on her hands and nightgown. She hit the ground the moment she saw me, letting the defeat that threatened to consume her take over, trusting I'll take it from here. Trusting in me.

Pride trickles up my spine, sinking its claws into it and leaving me burning, 'cause fuck me, I did something right. Somewhere along the way, I made a move that led us here. To the gift of this fucking girl giving up and giving herself over to me 'cause she knows I got her. Hasn't heard from me in months, had my back turned to her among that, and still . . . she understands.

She is mine and I will always stand for her when she falls.

I close the gap between us, bend down, and scoop Rocklin into my arms.

The moment my hands touch her, everyone freaks the fuck out: threats and screams and shouts. Feet pound behind me, but I don't look. I don't listen. I don't stop.

They do. The second that hidden weapon on the giant tank pops out of the sides, spinning in circles. Every single sound halts outside of the crunch of broken concrete beneath my feet.

I stepped through it all, climbing over the crumbled chaos, careful not to drop her. She doesn't fight me, doesn't try to move or rearrange herself. She's silent and dead weight as I carry her through the rubble, past the gardens, into the house, and straight out through the front door.

I lower her inside the front seat of my new car, buckling her in before closing the door, and then I make my way to the driver's seat.

I climb behind the wheel and then we're off to beat a Brayshaw for touching my sister.

Rocklin

Gasping, my body lurches upward, panic seizing my lungs as my eyes desperately search for a sign of something in the darkness. My hands plant at my sides, and when my palms are met with thick plush cotton, I look down, realizing I'm tucked into a bed, one that isn't mine.

Finally, my eyes adjust, snapping to the sliver of light creeping through the cracked open door. Once again, I trace every corner of the space, realizing I'm in a hotel I don't remember arriving at.

For a moment, my concern doubles down, but then obsidian blue flashes in my mind, and while my muscles freeze one second, they grow lax in the next.

Bastian . . .

My eyes slice to the small opening of the door, and my heart beats a little faster.

He's just outside it. I know it.

He came to me.

No . . . he came *for* me.

Wait. He busted through the walls of the Greyson Estate with a fucking tank.

Oh my god, Dad!

My hands fly around the bed, searching for my phone. I crawl around, tangling my legs up in the blanket and nearly stumbling when I climb off.

Wincing, I drop my eyes to my thigh. A white bandage stares back and I touch the scratchy cloth. That's right. I was grazed by a bullet. I'm tempted to tear the gauze back and look at it, but there're bold black letters written on the edge.

Don't even think about it, they read, and a sad smile tugs at my lips.

Shit, Dad!

I whip around, but my things are nowhere in sight. There's nothing but a black leather duffel I've never seen on the nightstand. I need to call the girls and Boston. I need to talk to Sai—

I jerk, freezing in place.

Sai.

I killed Sai. My guardian. My sworn protector.

I killed a traitor.

I did to him what he trained me to do to others, should it come to that. My hands begin to tremble, and hesitantly, I look at them.

A frown builds along my brow at the clean skin, the blood that covered them nowhere in sight, and then my eyes shift to the soft silk sleeve along my wrist. I'm in a pajama set that isn't mine, but it's a perfect fit. Soft and the same shade of pink as the Greyson uniform.

I knew one day I would have to kill, just as I knew it would likely be sooner rather than later. Death and murder are simply a part of our world. To be a Revenaw, to be a Greyson, is to recognize the value of life isn't what all understand it to be.

You must value life, but yours above others, with the exception of a few, should you be lucky enough to have any for whom you would throw yourself in front of a knife for.

It's kill or be killed in the world of organized crime, and I was born into it. Where normal people welcomed their fathers home with dirt on his jeans or grease on his shirt, I ran into my father's open arms, completely unfazed by the blood I would press my cheek against when squeezing him back. To his credit, he would try to clean up before my sister and I realized he had returned, but it was rare for him to succeed. The minute we heard him coming down the drive, we typically ran out to greet him.

Sai was always the first out the door and the last back through it.

A shuddered breath escapes me and I close my eyes a moment, jumping when a soft thud sounds from outside the room.

My feet move quickly, a heavy sense of anticipation and longing melting down my spine, and then my fingers wrap around the frame, but the moment they do, my feet freeze. All of those sensations begin to twist together, oddly mixing with an equal amount of hesitation and uncertainty. I have no idea what I'm about to walk out on, but I know I feel no fear. Every other emotion I can think of, yes, but not fear.

Everything in my world is fucked up, but knowing he's right outside the door somehow makes it a little better.

Slowly, I peel it open, peeking with one eye into the living area of what I can now see is a suite. I can't see him, but I know he's out there, so I take a single step through the door.

My heart drops to my feet with relief and so much more.

There he is.

Somehow taller than I remember and just as breathtaking as he paces the space back and forth, back and forth, his long tattooed fingers diving into his dark locks and tugging until he's yanking his own head down, the heels of his hands pressing into his eyes as he shakes his head.

Something's wrong, I note instantly, but rather than interrupt, I take a moment to just . . . look at him, his presence alone melting some of the tension from my muscles.

The shoes on his feet are new, as are the jeans stretched perfectly over his thighs, but it's that same worn leather jacket wrapped around him that I like.

A broken exhale pushes past my lips and I have to catch myself on the frame of the door to keep myself from falling over.

Instantly, his head snaps my way.

The second his eyes lock on mine, my breath is stolen from my lungs, my feet begging to carry me to him, but I hesitate in the doorway.

Bastian's jaw snaps shut, the thick muscles there pulsing, as he grinds his teeth back and forth, gorgeous eyes red from lack of sleep, the left one black from something else, and laser-focused as they fly across my features, taking me in as I do him.

What he sees, I don't know. I don't have the slightest clue what I'm giving away. All I know is I don't have the energy to mask everything that's rallying inside me. I'm a mess and I'm sure it shows. Even if it didn't, he would know.

Slowly, his eyes narrow into harsh, accusing and angry points, but his body betrays his internal battle; the utter relief it shows is a complete contrast to the murky shadows of his gaze.

The stiffness in his shoulders disappears, his fingers no longer clench closed but open and hang loosely at his sides as he subconsciously shifts, his body now facing mine.

A knot forms in my throat, and it seems to braid its way down, down until it's threading around my organs, squeezing, tugging and pulling. I know exactly where it's trying to lead me, but I wait. I wait because he won't let me down.

He holds my stare as the seconds tick by in what feels like slow motion, but I see the moment his control slips. His chin lowers the slightest bit.

"Come." His chest rumbles with his command.

As if bewitched by the single word from his lips, my bare feet pad across the floor. The second I'm within reach, his long arm shoots out, his fist tangling in my top and yanking me into him.

I gasp but not in fright, my eyes slicing up and fastening to his.

His lips flatten into a harsh line, a heavy exhale pressing past his nostrils, making them flare and then his arms are around me, my feet off the floor, and his face buried in my neck.

He inhales deeply, and a shudder runs through me as my hands loop around his neck, bringing him closer, squeezing him tighter.

I don't know how long we stay like this, our limbs wrapped around each other, our hearts pressed against each other's, but when he pulls away, it still feels like too soon. My forehead falls to his chest, and I don't realize I'm crying until the tears

427

fall along my wrist, my palms flat against his pecs. If this were to happen months ago, I'd hastily wipe away the evidence of the turmoil within me, but we're past that and I don't have it in me to care. A part of me thinks that that's the only reason the tears came. Because he's here, against me. He's holding on to me, even if his touch is lighter now and even if the tension is returning to his muscles with each passing second. He's still here.

That reminds me . . .

"Where are we?" I whisper.

Bastian takes two steps back until he's nearly flush with the wall of windows behind him. His brows pull in and he looks away, so I glance around the space, realizing the suite we are in is no average suite.

It's lavish and littered with high-end design and crystal decanters.

"Brayshaw," he shares, his tone clipped, and finally, his eyes return. The hint of softness that slipped through is nowhere to be found, the color fading, nearly overtaken by black fury.

"What happened?"

A scoffed laugh leaves him, and he shakes his head, a little of that anger now pointed at me.

"When are we talking about here, Rich Girl? What happened the night you kicked me out of the gala when you should have said fuck the world? What happened the night after that? Week after that? Are we talking the last few months? Or you want to talk about yesterday when I grabbed you or why I brought you here? Be a little more specific for me, huh?"

"I want to know all of those things and everything in between. Is that specific enough?" If he wants to fight, we can fight. I'll take the anger from him. I'll take anything he gives and I'll ask for more.

His eyes narrow and he shakes his head a second time, turning and looking out the window at the small patio decorated with roses and vines. "I can tell you right now you won't like half the answers to those questions."

"I want them anyway." I need them. Desperately.

428

For the first time ever, I feel like an outsider in my world, clueless as to what's going on and unsure who to trust or what to do. I need to go home and find my dad and protect my sister and . . . deal with what happened to Sai, with what I did to Sai.

I can't do any of that in this moment, so yes, I want his answers, if only to keep from falling to my knees. I can't do that right now, not when it's clear Bastian might need someone to hold him up.

"Yeah?" He glances at me over his shoulder. "How's it feel to want and not get?"

I refuse to feel embarrassed, so I give him the honest answer because that's the only one he's interested in.

"Like shit. Like losing. Like lacking in every aspect of everything. It has felt like breathing with one lung in a room steamed with chlorine and acid, like walking on broken ankles and sleeping on spikes. That's what I've felt like," I tell him. "That's what *missing you* feels like."

I'm not exactly sure what he expected me to say, but I know that wasn't it.

He knew I missed him; he knew I was going out of my mind and couldn't do a thing about it because I told him so with fewer words. There are no less than twenty texts sitting in our message thread to prove it and we both know that. He knew and I'm almost positive that's exactly how he wanted it.

I take a step toward him, his eyes narrowed and flicking between mine. "And being denied or forgotten by you?" My brows lift. "That feels like a brand on my skin, over every inch of it. It's like burning flesh, painful and raw and without remedy. It's been like living with the spokes of a Taser buried in my skin, the button frozen in the on position and the battery everlasting. That's what being unwanted by you feels like. Literal torture, actual physical pain that won't go away and I didn't even want it to because I knew I deserved it.

"I don't want to make excuses for myself because, trust me, I'm well aware of what I could have done, even if I still believe the outcome would have been a really fucked-up one, but I warned you. I told you this would happen. I told you my world was unforgiving and unwelcoming, but I still wanted you. Having you was enough for me and a part of me believes I should hate you because having *me* wasn't enough for *you*."

He jerks forward then, gripping my chin and lifting it so I have to look up at him as he speaks through clenched teeth.

"Got that one right. It ain't. Never gonna be, 'cause to be mine means everyone needs to know what they can't have, can't touch, and most aren't even allowed to look at. It means everyone knows what's at risk if they dare. It means everyone who does learns a lesson so their mistake isn't repeated. There is no other option. Not when it comes to you. They can take anything of mine and burn it to the fucking ground and I will not bat a lash, but you?" His eyes flare with rage. "I told you from the gate. I warned you what would happen. This is the result."

The way the words leave him sends a sense of dread through me, his eyes flaring with a deeper meaning I can't decipher.

When I speak, I tread lightly. "I need you to understand I've had nothing for myself, not completely. You were the only thing I had that was only mine. My dad." My chest aches at the mention of him. "He . . . he's had his hands in every aspect of my life in one way or another."

He scoffs. "That right there is the understatement of the fucking year."

I frown, shaking my head. "It's true. You're the only thing I chose selfishly."

"But did you?" he fires back, getting in my space and backing me up until the back of my calves meets the side of the couch. "Did you choose me? Did you 'pick me' like I did you? Truly and completely." He presses closer. His body hard against mine. His hand slides down the underside of my throat. His eyes burn a trail along its path as he whispers, "Absolutely fucking psychotically?"

There's a reckless edge to his tone, a thread of warning that has me shivering.

430

My tongue pokes out to wet my lips and his eyes slice toward the contact, his teeth sinking into his own as a low groan escapes him.

"I warned you, Rich Girl. I told you you were mine and what that meant. Everyone had to know. Everyone had to understand."

My brows pull, unease weaving up my spine. "Understand what?"

"What happens to people who touch or dare to fuck with what's mine."

We stare at each other for a long minute, and while his words are clear, the meaning behind them is lost on me, but then I hear my phone ring in the room somewhere and reality slams back into me.

"Oh my god." I scurry away, eyes flicking around as I search for where the sound is coming from, panic forming a knot in my throat.

Please be good news, please be good news.

I freeze as it rings again, looking to Bass, who pulls it from his pocket and holds it out with a sharp glare. My sister's name flashes across the screen and my breathing grows short as I flash back to the call that came the day my mother died.

My twin, who I was separated from for the first time in my life, called to tell me our mother was dead and that she was all alone when she found the body.

My eyes burn, clouding over, but still, Bass holds my cell hostage.

"Bastian, I need to answer. It could be about what happened—".

"It's not," he cuts me off.

My mouth opens but closes quickly. "How do you know what I was going to say?"

"Lucky guess."

My eyes narrow, and his words from moments ago come back.

He said they had to know, that they had to understand, not that they need to or will.

431

Had. Past tense.

No. No.

He wouldn't . . . I mean, he couldn't . . . could he?

My eyes fall to the new shoes and jeans, to the gleaming diamond-encrusted watch around his wrist and my pulse pounds wildly in my ears.

I stare at him in horror, but his expression remains as unreadable as ever.

"Bastian . . . what did you do?"

His gaze hardens, but I can see beyond the anger, down deeper to the fractured soul inside, the one that speaks to mine. He says nothing, but when my phone rings again, this time, he answers, the device held between us as he puts it on speaker.

I can't find my voice, but I don't have to. The person on the line speaks for me.

"Sweetheart," my dad's cautious tone drawls.

My knees shake and I pull in a shuddered breath. Bastian's eyes tighten even more, never leaving mine, his fingers on the phone turning white because he's clutching it so hard.

"Dad?" I breathe.

"Are you okay?" he fires off, but his tone holds a gentle edge.

I nod, even though he can't see me, quickly swallowing and responding with a rasped, "Yes, I'm okay. Are you?" The question leaves me in the lowest of murmurs and for a moment, I wonder if he can even hear. I want to say I'm not sure why I fear that answer, but staring into Bastian's eyes, I'm not so sure that's true.

"Rocklin, I need you to tell me where you are," he says instead.

Bastian's lips press into a firm line, but he says nothing, demands nothing, and he doesn't hang up the line, not even as my father adds, "You're not safe. Tell me where you are."

My mouth opens and then closes and then it does the same thing again because, on the one hand, I want to tell him where I am, if only for peace of mind and because he's my father and he asked. I always do as I'm told. I have to.

432

On the other . . .

"Rocklin." My name is a demand this time, and Bastian's lip curls the slightest bit.

I don't know what's going on, but I know my dad is okay because I'm hearing it from his lips. He called from his line to mine and the words he's speaking aren't words a prisoner would be forced to in order to lure me away, and this is my father we're talking about. He would take a thousand slashes to the skin and beg for more before he'd ever even consider giving me up for anyone else in our family. Blood over all. Family is everything.

But mine has grown and I've known it for a long time now, so when my father, once again, demands an answer, I give him the only one necessary.

"I'm with Bastian."

"Where?" he snaps, already knowing that much.

"It doesn't matter where."

"You have no idea what the boy has done. Don't be a fool."

Bastian watches me closely as I step toward him so I don't have to speak loudly for my father to hear my words clearly. I hold my favorite blue eyes and say, "I *was* a fool when I turned him away and I've been trying to get to him ever since, but you know that. You kept me away."

"Your safety was threatened. I was protecting you from the enemy, who I now know was him all along. Rocklin—"

"He's not the enemy."

"He was stalking you for months!"

He was?

A small frown builds along my brow as my father's words settle in me, tugging gently on the loose threads behind my rib cage. Of course he was.

Of course he didn't walk away.

He's said time and time again.

I am his.

A pitiful little fight with spat words and judgment of others doesn't change that. Those things roll right off his shoulders. I pissed him off, and his supposed absence was my punishment, but he wasn't absent, was he?

He didn't simply "go."

He would never go . . .

"No," I whisper, another wave of tears clouding my eyes, but these are born of a different emotion. "No, he wasn't stalking me. He was watching over me." Bastian's jaw flexes, his muscles twitching. "He was protecting me." *Just in case.*

Based on this conversation, the *just in case* came into play, and suddenly, small things begin to make sense. All those images, the videos, they were from him. He was doing what he could to help keep me safe, to force my father's hand to do what Bastian thought needed to be done to make sure I was safe until he was ready to come back to me for real.

"Rocklin—"

I give the slightest shake of my head and Bastian ends the call, but neither of us moves.

He still holds my phone between us, our eyes are still locked and when my shaky hand reaches out, my palm flattening against his chest, it rises with a deep inhale.

His free hand darts out, tangling into the hair at the base of my neck and tugging.

His teeth clench, his eyes narrowing, but then his lips press together, his hold easing as he closes the distance. His forehead meets mine and he pulls my hair over one shoulder.

My eyes close as I breathe him in, my fingertips digging into his shirt, and slowly, I start to shake. Months. I've waited and missed him for months.

One of his hands disappears, then a soft, velvety touch drags along my collarbone and across the bend of my neck, sending a shiver down my spine. The rough skin of his fingers meets my skin next and I swallow, shuddering once more as his lips find my ear.

His breath is warm, goose bumps erupting across my body as he takes my hair in one hand. And just as a soft click sounds, he whispers, rough and final, "Mine."

And then he storms away, but the velvety softness remains.

My hand darts up to my throat, and I whip around to face the mirror on the wall.

There're a million things to discuss, a thousand questions on the tip of my tongue. Call me crazy, but I don't even care what the answers are. At least not right now.

Right now, one thing and one thing only has my full attention.

And it's a black band.

A delicate band nearly a half inch thick in size clasped around my throat, a small rose gold diamond sitting in the middle, a matching *B* dangling from its center. It's a choker.

A collar.

It's his claim.

Chapter 35
Rocklin

The whats and whys and whatevers we left in Greyson are put on the back burner; Bastian's sole focus on the situation he faces now.

The sweet and perfect baby sister he spoke of is in town and he's livid. I remember him telling me she lived with a family member far away, and apparently, that's where she was supposed to stay until his controlling ass decided otherwise, but it seems baby sister had other ideas.

Apparently, the night we arrived, I was in a state of shock. Bastian washed, dressed, and tucked me into the hotel bed, and then he took off, none of which I remember.

He found his sister, midargument with one of his former bosses at the warehouses he used to run, that *apparently*, he doesn't anymore . . . yet another thing we'll need to talk about as it seems a lot has changed in his world.

I wasn't even aware he left the Brayshaw family, but then again, how could I be? He's effectively ignored me . . . or at least wanted me to believe he had.

We spent all of yesterday in near silence, me texting quietly with the girls and my sister while he continued to pace the small space, calling his sister every five minutes. When that didn't work, we loaded up in his car, a new, customized car, by the way, that he completely pretends is a nonfactor compared to the last one I saw him with, so I don't bother asking just yet. We made our way to some ancient-looking house, a group home he had mumbled, I'm guessing she's now living in.

Bass knocked on the door no less than a handful of times, each attempt a failed one and irritating the kind yet stern woman who answered in the process. At some point, I passed out and when I woke at sunrise, the spot beside me was still empty, Bastian putting in overtime wearing down the soles of his new shoes.

Day two seemed like it would be no different; I should have known better by the angry anxiousness rolling off him. It didn't take long for him to announce we were headed out once more, and I knew, without him confirming, we weren't making our way to the sister this time around. No, Bastian wants the man responsible for bringing her here.

And what Bastian wants, Bastian gets.

My hand lifts, my touch trailing along the silky soft velvet locked tight around my throat, my newest accessory, and I gently grip the charm dangling dead center, fingertips tracing over the bold *B*.

In my peripheral, I see his head whip my way, his hands tightening along the black leather of the aftermarket steering wheel, and I know exactly where those hands wish they were.

I allow my lips to curve into a smirk but don't look over, and his attention snaps back to the road.

Mad at me or not, I'm what he wants. Dare I say *needs*.

He hasn't gotten to play with his new toy and he's eager to.

For a split second, I wonder if I'm reading the rage in his perfect blue eyes wrong when we pull onto the property, where that same group home sits, but then he blows past it, kicking up dust and dirt as he flies through a slim opening between the large orchards.

We continue down the path, curving slightly at the end, and there it is. The Brayshaw mansion, his once bosses' home. While modest when compared to Greyson Manor, much like everything is, the gorgeous custom mansion stretches wide across the space, but there's no time to admire the giant flower garden that rivals my own as the second we make our way down the drive, a tall guy with deep-brown hair and a tattoo climbing along his neck is headed right for us, unfazed by the fact that Bastian is coming at him full speed.

My pulse starts to jump, wondering if we're about to start a war with Calvin and the council because I'm not so sure Bastian isn't fully set on creating a bloody Brayshaw pancake. That *is* a Brayshaw. There is no doubt about that. I might not have seen one in the flesh, but there's a charge in the air and only eighty-five percent of it is rolling off the man seated beside me.

At the last second, the very last absolute second, Bastian slams on the brakes, quite possibly bumping against the guy's shins.

"Stay in your seat." His voice is deep and deadly and there is no pause or moment's hesitation. Bastian is out the door before the car has fully settled into park.

"Got a message for me, Brayshaw?" he spits at who must be Royce as he had mumbled about killing him a few times on the short drive. "I'm here. Serve it up."

His fists clench and unclench at his sides, shoulder stiff and ready, and when the Brayshaw offers him the first shot, Bastian takes it.

He clips him clean across the jaw and I pull my legs into the seat with a smile.

Royce spits to the side, coming back with a smile. "Bass fucking Bishop." He comes closer. "Welcome back, motherfucker."

Then it's on.

Right away, Bastian is knocked against the hood and I glare as he swiftly rights himself, his leg sweeping out to knock the man on his ass. Good.

If he dented this baby, I might join in on this. It's way too pretty to be touched.

Maybe I'll ask to drive her home.

Deep grunts and growls demand my attention and I watch Bastian's every move. The way his muscles flex and lock and the power he throws behind every punch. I know immediately he's not going full force. I've seen him hit to hurt with Kenex and Kylo. He's not fighting to ruin or destroy. He's fighting to let off steam. To temper his anger. I wonder if it's due to unspoken respect for the man he's going against or for the sake of his sister, *just in case*.

Either way, watching him work might be my new favorite pastime. I want to spar with the man, get sweaty and fight against his strong grip, roll around on the mats until we're panting from exhaustion and then from something else.

I can picture it now.

A loud thunk clears my head. Royce has Bastian in a headlock, and they both go down, Royce having expected Bastian to give him all his weight and keeping his hold tight.

Fuck this guy.

Rolling my window down, I sink my nails into his silky hair and yank.

His head darts up, eyes narrowing on me in surprise. "The fuck?!" he shouts, banging his head against the door to jerk himself free.

I dig my nails deeper.

Bad boy.

"I said stay in your fucking seat!" Bastian shouts.

"I'm in the *fucking seat*." I smirk at his blotchy red face. "You said nothing about the window." Bastian growls his warning, eyes flaring and promising punishment, but I don't even get to enjoy the heated glare. Royce opens his mouth again.

"Hey, Pamela Anderson's spawn, get your fucking hands off me, or you're gonna have problems," he spits.

I could almost laugh. Seriously.

"Oh." I push my bottom lip out. "I've got plenty of those. What's one more?"

"How 'bout one that ends with a knife in your side?"

The feminine voice reaches my ears, and all at once, the three of us look toward it.

Standing there on the pretty porch is the gorgeous, opposite of me in every way, dark-haired girl from the party. The one Bastian laughed and joked and spent time with, then denied

439

me even a second of his attention in my moment of desperation. Raven. Her name is Raven.

Yes, I dug a little.

I'm so focused on her I hardly notice the girl beside her or
the fact that the other Brayshaw brothers have joined our little
playdate in their driveway.

I keep my eyes locked on the dark-haired girls, tugging
even harder, but this time, Royce chooses not to let it be
known. I wonder why that is, but then Raven flips a knife
open, running it along her finger, her eyes jumping back to
mine. "Been a while since I've got to use this baby. Give me
a reason to."

A shocked laugh bubbles out of me, and then it breaks free
once more.

Is she for real? She wants to play?

My free hand slips inside the front pocket of my skirt,
wrapping around my own blade, but then I feel Bastian's
laser-sharp stare.

Reluctantly, I lock my gaze with his and it's all there, written
in his marbly blues.

He knows.

He *knows* I'm good for the challenge and will play to win.
The others might not see, likely don't catch it, but he gives
the slightest jerk of his chin. Letting me know he's well aware
of what an opponent I would be, almost like he's attempting
to stroke me like I'm a kitten, with his eyes alone, to make
me purr at his silent acknowledgment that I am better in his
eyes, yet still he says, "Cut it, Rich Girl. Let the bitch go."

My eyes narrow.

Is he worried about her or about what the others will try
in the aftermath?

His eyes narrow right back, a clear indication he knows
what I'm thinking and he pointedly drops them to my neck.
To the collar he locked around it.

I'm the one he claimed.

Something stirs in my chest and I relent, releasing the man.

They don't hesitate to continue their brawl, and I sigh as I watch them roll around, knowing full well Bastian has the stamina of a beast. He can go all day.

I watch as he takes the Brayshaw by the throat, squeezing until his face grows an unsettling shade of purple, considering we're outnumbered if this goes any further south. But just before the point of unconsciousness, he tosses Royce to the side.

They hop to their feet, and then a softer voice calls out.

"Are you guys done now?" We all look and my brows jump at the sight.

Okay, she's not what I expected, but it's clear by the way Bastian turns to stone she is, in fact, Brielle Bishop.

She's a foot shorter than him, if not more, and her hair is a shiny, silky white in color, the complete opposite of his six-foot-plus frame and ink-black hair.

There's a tender softness about her, which is so strange considering the world she was raised in. But it's there. She looks as angelic as he made her out to be.

However, my world has taught me looks can be deceiving, even if I'm not so sure that's the case this time around.

"You're in his house . . ." Bastian's voice is low and changing, awe and horror twisting together as he steps closer. "I know what this place means to them, to him. If you're inside this house, then you're . . ."

"Inside his heart?" Brielle responds, her tone soft and loving, even in her anger.

Good. He deserves that.

I can't see Bastian's face from here, but his shoulders begin to stiffen, refusing to accept what she's insinuating. "Brielle."

Bass slips between her and Royce, gripping his sister's arm and he dashes up the steps, takes her by the arm, and pulls.

But then, everyone outside of Brielle and Bastian shifts at once, blocking her.

Shit.

As I expected, he loses it, starts screaming and shouting in their faces.

"Are you for fucking real?! You want to guard her *from me*? That's my fucking sister!" My chest aches at what he's not saying, at what they don't understand.

He loves her with all the parts of her he can. She is his family. His *only* family and he's here right now, fighting, because he's worried. Afraid. He wants her away from danger and based on what he knows about this town, he doesn't feel like she has that here. This is torture for him and I want to fix it. Tranq everyone and take her wherever he wants her to go.

But then Brielle slips through the wall of muscles hiding her, slowly edging toward her brother, and I breathe a sigh of relief. She understands. She gets it. Knows him and how he's feeling inside.

Or I thought she did, but then she says, "Bass, please. Don't do this."

"Seriously?!" flies from my mouth before I can stop it and they look back to find me sitting on the edge of the window frame. "We drove ten fucking hours through the night to get to you, then you ignore him for days, and that's the first shit you say when he whoops ass in your name?!"

I mean, come on . . . *seriously?!*

"Shut up!" Bass shouts, not impressed with my lie or speaking out. So the drive was no more than a few hours, and I wasn't even conscious during them. That's not the point. We had a fucking *day* and we're here. "What, you know you're thinking the same thing!"

He jerks around then, warning in his gaze, letting me know I'm doing nothing to help here. "I said—"

"Yeah, yeah," I stop him before he starts again, dropping back in the seat and rolling up the window.

But I watch and strain my ears a few moments longer because I suspect I have the sister's attention.

"Who is that?" she wonders.

"Don't." He swiftly shuts her down. "Get in the car, Brielle. Now."

But she makes no move and the words that leave him next have my muscles stiffening. "You don't belong here, Brielle. Let's go."

There's a shift in his tone the moment the words leave him, and I swear I know exactly what he's thinking *and* feeling as it does.

They're words he's heard time and again, words he knew were true but never thought he cared about because "fuck the world." Then I spat them at him in a room full of people who thought they were bigger and better because their name claimed they were born to be.

They weren't—aren't.

As I knew it would, his gaze, as brief as it is, flicks to mine.

I was wrong, love. You were meant to be mine.

Bastian's brows crash and he faces forward, battling his own inner turmoil as his conscience forces him to consider if he, too . . . is wrong. If Brielle does belong here, in this place where she has clearly found a home.

My phone dings, alerting me of the call I missed from my sister amid the fun, so I tune them out, texting her back.

Me: I'm fine. He's dealing with family shit and then we'll be headed back to deal with ours. Dad okay?

She responds instantly.

Boston: I need to talk to you.

What the hell?

Me: Why? What's happened?

Boston: Are you alone?

My head pops up on reflex because, no, I'm not alone, and the moment I look toward the others, Brielle's eyes move this way, meeting mine for the first time. I offer a simple wink.

I'm not the bad guy here, girl.

She says something, though I'm not exactly sure what, and then Raven moves closer to where Bastian stands. Her eyes narrow as she speaks, and my hand darts out to wrap around the handle as my phone begins to vibrate in my other one. Then something softens in her gaze and I don't like it. Not when it's pointed at him. Like she knows or understands or is somewhat fond of him.

I yank on the handle, the door clicking open, but I hold still when, in the next second, she spins, heading back inside.

Once she's out of sight, I softly close the door and look back to my phone.

Fuck it. I call Boston back, but after half a ring, it goes to voice mail.

Frowning, I try again, but then the roar of an engine sounds, and I whip around to find a car flying up behind us.

I rush for my weapon, eyes flicking from the vehicle to Bastian to gauge his concern, to see if I need to hop in the driver's seat so we can make a quick getaway, but then his gaze locks with mine. He gives a small shake of his head and I let out a deep breath.

Sai would always—

The burn of betrayal boils in my gut and I close my eyes a moment, but when the door is yanked from the frame, they fly open to find Bastian sliding into the front seat, his face hard and calculating.

He gets one look at me, and his eyes narrow. "What's wrong?"

Something tightens in my chest and I look down, the other cars zooming past us and leaving us in a cloud of dust, but Bastian holds firm.

His fingers slide beneath my chin, lifting it, his frown deepening as he gets a closer look. "Tell me," he whispers, his words a soft demand.

God, I've missed him, but this isn't the time or the place for me to lose my shit again, so I offer a small smile and remove his hand. "Something is wrong," I remind him, even if I don't know what it is. "Focus."

He wants to argue, I can see it in the firm set of his jaw, but like me, he knows there'll be time for this later, so he whips us around and takes a right out of the driveway.

"So what happened? Did they hire you again or something?"

He scoffs at that, taking a right when we reach the street. After a moment, he adds, "They couldn't afford me anymore if they wanted to, Rich Girl."

I face him, and when he sneaks a quick peek, I lift a brow.

A hint of a grin twitches his lips, but the angry frustration quickly settles back into place as a giant brick sign that reads *Welcome to Brayshaw High* comes into view, the others pulling into the parking lot already.

He works the engine, hitting the throttle harder to clear the half-mile gap, and burns rubber with his sharp turn.

Smoke rolls into the air near the open field, and I don't have to ask.

"Someone I punished in the Brayshaw name showed up where my sister was living. I don't know how he found out where she was, but she was gone once he got there," he shares, skirting to a stop. "They think he's here now, two birds, one fucking stone, so we're looking into a fire that was started." He throws his seat belt off, reaching for his handle.

"If he hurts her, we can get rid of him very easily."

Bastian's eyes snap to mine, holding, and while it's only a split second, there's so much to see.

He's angry with me. Really angry. And he hates how he has to keep reminding himself of this because, at the end of the day, he misses me too.

All the boys—I could roll my eyes so hard right now at that—are out of the car in seconds, looking like a gang of, well, gangsters. The Brayshaws really don't live life like the Greysons.

They're like Bastian, rough around the edges, and they won't allow you to forget it.

"Stay in the car," Royce orders Brielle like a puppet.

A small smirk pulls at my lips, but then Bastian pins me with a warning glare that means the same thing, I'm to keep my ass where it sits.

And I do . . . until the second they disappear, and what do you know, I'm not the only one.

Little sister jumps out as fast as me, the two of us staring at the dark smoke billowing high in the sky. I walk up beside her with a small quirk of my lips, unsure of what part to play here, but I adopt one fairly quickly—the stereotype is always the easiest.

"Brielle Bishop, in the flesh." I look over her petite frame. "You don't look like the helpless little lamb he's made you out to be."

Her brows pull into a frown as her chest grows with a deep inhale. "Not to be rude, but I don't want to talk to you right now. I don't even know who you are."

"Really?" I pretend to be surprised when I'm not. No part of me expected her to know who I was. Bastian shielded her from nearly all aspects of his life. I'm not convinced she needed him to, but what do I know? I do like how she's not fishing for info on big brother, though. It's admirable and I am more than happy to give her the silence she's after. "Huh." I nod, walk back to Bastian's car, and slip inside. I know she's watching me, so I do everything I can to make sure she's clueless that I'm doing the same as I find a pair of headphones in the center console and tuck them in my ears, lowering my eyelids so she's sure I'm not paying her any mind.

It works, and she moves to stand beside the truck that showed at the mansion and led to us coming here. She's nervous, but I can't guess why. I imagine it's a lot of things at the moment. Honestly, the girl kind of sucks at hiding her emotions. Her brother is nearly a vault, as she should be if this place really does have dangers that hide in the shadows, as they do in our world. That reminds me.

With one eye on Brielle and the other on my phone, I try Boston once more, but she doesn't pick up. I try Delta and then Bronx and it's the same thing.

"What the fuck, people?"

I text Dom.

Me: someone better call me and quickly.

Headlights flash across the side mirror and I look to find a car pulling up next to the truck Brielle is standing by. Quietly, I quickly step out of the car, flipping the knife open at my side and dragging the blade across my thigh, but then Brielle smiles at the guy who pops his head out.

So he's not a murderous lunatic who found food under the parking lot lights.

A small smirk pulls at my lips and I shake my head, taking a photo as Brielle climbs into the passenger seat. Well, well. Maybe it won't be so hard to convince Brielle to come back with us after all. That is what he wants, right? To bring her back to Greyson?

A twisted knot forms in my chest, and I press against it.

What if he doesn't plan on going back to Greyson at all? What happens then?

Slowly, I lower into the seat and try and push the thoughts away, but it doesn't work. I dial his number to tell him his sister is making a getaway, but it rings in the seat beside me. The panic doesn't stop, and then my lungs are squeezing, fighting against the dewy night air.

Oh my god, what if I'm not understanding this right?

He was so fast to run here, to leave again . . . but what does that matter? I didn't even know he was back until I saw him. Busting down the wall behind the Greyson Estate . . .

What the fuck has he been doing the last few months?

They couldn't afford me if they wanted to . . .

They *so* could. The Brayshaws come from money. Big money. But Bastian was never about money.

My eyes fall to the interior of the car, the fresh blue interior, nearly the same vibrant shade as the paint on my car.

Or was he?

Since I met him, the only thing he ever talked about wanting was for his sister to have a good life. And me.

We are here, so that means one of those two things still rings true, but the other . . . I'm not so sure. He hasn't said it. Hasn't touched me. The anger in his eyes shines bright, the hurt heavy behind it, but he did pick me up. He came to me after I left him a voice mail and begged him to.

What if all he's trying to do is piss off my dad because he felt disrespected? What if this is a game and I'm a chess piece to be dominated on the way to check the king?

I blink, looking up to find Bastian and Royce. He spins to me, his face taut. Slowly, I sit up and step out.

"Where is she?" he demands.

My unwelcome, twisted thoughts get the best of me, and I smirk. "Where is who?"

"Fuck this. Let's head back, grab her on the way," Royce says, already moving toward the truck he rode in.

"Yeah, that won't work." I cock my head. "She didn't walk."

Bastian prowls toward me, soaking up all the air and forcing me to breathe in only him. "What are you talking about?"

"I was scrolling through Instagram and lost service," I lie. "So I hopped out and walked around a bit, within the five-foot span, so don't have an aneurysm."

His eyes narrow accusingly, reading deeper than the surface of my words. Always deeper, and it takes real work not to crack.

He doesn't call me out, but his disapproval is clear in his tone. "Keep talking."

"Imagine my surprise when I spotted the girl of the hour slipping into the night with a different knight." I look to the sky as an excuse to break eye contact. "Ah, the irony, right?"

The Brayshaw doesn't appreciate my callous, mocking tone. "Get to the fucking point, girl."

"Oh, an angry boy, nice."

"Cut it," Bastian snaps. "Where'd she go?"

"Hopped in a car."

"What fucking car?"

I force another smirk. "I could show you."

Royce jerks forward and I lift my chin, daring him to come closer. I won't hesitate to take out his left lung, but I don't have to as Bastian flips into protective mode in an instant, blocking him with a sharp glare before focusing on me.

My chest warms, but I push it away, forcing a clipped laugh and shitty attitude. "Ah, down, boy." I stare into his eyes, my facade beginning to crumble as he holds my gaze prisoner. I need an answer, confirmation of . . . something. He knows, senses it, and I swear, for the smallest of seconds, his features grow soft.

"First, I need your word that you'll—"

Suddenly, his lips are hard on mine, angry and punishing and longing and way too fucking quick. I want to fall into him, but he pulls back before I can.

He's still there, so close as he whispers in a tender, promising tone, "Quiet, Rich Girl."

My eyes close briefly, soaking in the sound, and he gently takes my phone from my grasp.

A mocking laugh comes from the asshole beside us, and my attention flicks his way.

"Damn, Bishop, girl's got a Brayshaw-size hard-on for you," he says.

Frustrated, I slip my mask back in place, ignoring whatever comes from Bastian's mouth until I hear him say, "Password?"

Ohhh.

Shit.

He sees it, my panic. I quickly look away when his eyes narrow, but he closes the gap between us.

"We don't have time for this junior high bullshit," Royce pops off again.

My lips curl, but Bastian wants all my attention, as eager to learn what I don't want to share as he is to get into my phone.

"I haven't changed it in a while . . ." Kind of a lie. I did change it. When I was pissed at him.

It was petty and childish, and it felt good in my petty, childish moment. Now? Not so much.

"Password," he snaps.

Fuck it. He made me think he didn't want me. Maybe he deserves to be a little pissy.

I straighten my spine and prepare for the rage he'll feel but won't show. "*D-O . . .*"

"*M*?" he growls.

I clear my suddenly dry throat, nodding. "And add an *S*."

"Who's Dom?" We ignore the Brayshaw.

Bass glares and I can't take it.

It's a low blow, considering. I know this, and so I slowly step away, leaving my phone with him, but no more than a minute passes, and then he's tugging my door open.

He squats beside me, the look in his eyes haunted as he drops my phone into my lap. "The dude I told you I punished? He has her."

Guilt falls heavy on my shoulders. "I tried to call you and tell you she was leaving."

He nods, shuffles closer and grips my thighs, his expression growing serious as he speaks for only me to hear. "This little role you're playin' here? Stop."

"I'm—" I almost lie but cut myself off.

"Ain't no scheme here. No roles, fake smiles, or flirty bullshit." He frowns, a hint of hurt in his gaze, though it's buried deep down. "When you're with me, you're you and no one else."

There's no malice or condemnation in his tone, simply a clear expression of his expectation. Delivered strong and clear, but . . .

"You don't get it." I don't mean to whisper, but that's how my voice leaves me and then his fingertips glide down my jaw. My eyes flutter closed a moment, but I shake my head. "This is how it has to be. It's why I had to do what I did at the gala."

Because love kills. If the outside world knows what he means to me, bad things could happen. I couldn't survive that. Not now that I know what life without him feels like.

I know he wants to argue, to fight, just like I know this isn't the time.

"If you never listen to me, Rich Girl, listen to me right now." His chin lowers, gaze fixed on mine. "You are my number one priority here." He taps his temple. "And here." He taps his left pec right over his heart. "You've been since I met you and that ain't changing. Like it or not, fight me or not, it doesn't matter. You're mine. Today, tomorrow, always. Even when I'm six feet under. Never question that. Never doubt it, but right now, I need to figure out what's going on with my sister and it ain't looking good, so I'm gonna say this to you once again, if you never listen to me again, listen now." A shadow falls over his eyes then, a darker Bastian Bishop now kneeling beside me.

His tone drops to a thick, rumbly rasp that sends a shiver down my spine. "I know you're a fucking badass, and I have no doubt you could take on anyone you put your mind to, but it ain't happening today. Today, you will be my sweet little submissive woman, and you will stay in this fucking car, no matter what you think you hear or see. Understood?"

Uncertainty scratches up my spine, and I squeeze my phone tighter.

His eyes flick toward Royce and back. "Say you understand."

Swallowing, I force myself to nod.

His thumb comes up, gliding along my lower lip, and I press a soft kiss to it, not realizing I close my eyes until the comfort of his rough touch disappears. My lids open, but he's already gone.

I track his every move back to where Royce stands and the two start rushing through a conversation, trying to work out what to do and where to look, when suddenly Bastian's spine shoots straight. His head snaps over his shoulder and he meets my gaze, terror flashing across his face, but it only lasts a single second.

Bastian takes off full speed, blowing past the vehicle and down the long cement path until he disappears around the building, Royce right behind him.

My knees begin to bounce, my head snapping from right to left, over and over again, before settling on the spot he vanished. I squint my eyes, trying to pick up anything in the distance, but come up with nothing but darkness.

The minutes tick by slowly, panic once again consuming me, so I drop the seat all the way back so I'm staring at nothing but the roof of the car. I put Bastian's headphones on, this time the big bulky ones, and press the button on the side. His phone is still beside me, so his playlist picks up instantly and I do my best to get lost in the music, hoping each song is at least three to five minutes long.

After four have played, I can't take it any longer. I can't. I can't listen. I can't sit around and wait. I have to—

I cut it off, jerking around in the seat when, yet again, lights catch the mirrors. One of the big, black SUVs from the Brayshaw mansion barrels down the street, and my heart drops into my stomach as I wait, convincing myself it's going to go right past, that nothing is actually happening here, but then it turns into the same parking lot that we are in, heading straight for where I'm parked.

I'm out of the car faster than it reaches the curb, dashing in the direction the others took off in. I run and run and run until, finally, something comes into view.

I gasp, my feet freezing in place when the loud pop of a gun goes off, and I watch someone fall to the ground.

No . . .

I stay low, darting forward on shaky legs until I reach the large iron gate of the school pool. My eyes shoot wide when I spot Brielle's still body in the water, and I start to scale the fence, but then she jerks up and I pause, making out Bastian flying over the fence on the other side, a guy with a gun inching toward the pool's edge.

Fuck!

I quickly dash a few feet left, tearing open the electrical box and flicking on the pool lights as I look on.

The gunman is blinded, and for a split second, Brielle catches my eye, but her focus moves back to the asshole.

Then the Brayshaws rush in as Brielle talks to the guy who is sure to die today.

I don't listen, running around the space until I'm near the door.

Just before I reach the other side, loud shouts and cries fill the air, and my heart beats double time, and then a bloodcurdling scream sounds and my heart ceases in my chest.

I spot the body on the ground first, blood darkening the cement beneath him and my legs threaten to give out when I spot the dark clothing, but then to his left, Bastian shoots to his feet, and everything in me settles, an unexpected sob bubbling from my lips.

Then, as if in slow motion, I watch as sheer panic turns his face white and he makes a run for the water.

Frowning, I look over in time to spot Brielle's body sinking beneath the surface.

There is no thought. I don't pause to consider the chemicals in the water, the ones that stole my perfectly working lungs and ripped away my water-filled dreams.

I beat him to the edge, diving in, arms and legs working at rapid speed to get to her. Her body is already dead weight, dragging her to the bottom of what must be a twelve-foot-deep pool. Using the bottom surface for momentum, I kick off, my arm locked around her chest as I push for the top.

Her head no sooner breaks through the water when arms reach for her, gripping and easing her out. I start to cough, gripping the pool's edge as my lungs spasm, and I press my forearms to the concrete, fighting for a full breath, and then two strong hands are lifting me.

Bastian tears me from the pool, his body stumbling and falling into the fencing as he yanks me down on top of him, but I crawl off, hands shaking as I position Brielle, tipping her head the slightest bit and pointing her chin to the sky. My breath is shallow, my lungs fighting back, and soon, they'll win out, but if I have to offer her the last decent breaths I have, I will.

For Bastian.

"Get the fuck off her!" someone shouts.

"Back the fuck up!" Bastian growls back, and then there's a scuffle of some sort, but I don't look.

Someone grips my arm, yanking me, but as I tear away, a loud crack follows.

"Touch her again and I'll fucking kill you right here," Bastian seethes. "Don't test me."

I ignore everything, deep into CPR that isn't working. I don't know if my breathing is too weak. The doubling pressure on my chest warns me it might be if it's worse than that, but then her body jerks. Everyone gasps, and Bass drops to his knees beside me.

"Come on, come on . . ." I rasp, trying to swallow, but the wheezing begins, and I grip my throat, my eyes flying up to meet Bastian's.

His eyes flare with a second wave of panic, then sirens sound, lights reach us and within seconds, EMTs are rushing toward us.

With shaky limbs, I start chest compressions again, and Brielle gurgles, water spilling from her blue lips, and my body gives in at that moment, my eyes flying to where the blond brother applies pressure to his unconscious brother's wound.

The EMTs rush in and panic erupts once again as everyone starts barking orders.

Bass hauls me onto his lap in one swoop. I wheeze against him, his arms wrapping around me so tight it's almost harder to get the little bit of air I can, but I don't care, and when he buries it in my neck, his limbs shaking as mine do, I press his head closer.

The first responders begin loading his sister and Royce onto gurneys, his body as stone still as hers and bleeding from somewhere, but Bastian doesn't look. I don't think he can handle the sight of his sister's lifeless body, something he likely feared he'd come home to find as a child now a reality. He grips me tighter and even after the screams and shouts of the others fade, he doesn't let go.

Neither do I.

Chapter 36
Bass

I can count on one hand the number of times I've cried in my life, and today, looking down at my baby sister's beautiful face, it's number four. When I think back on our lives, the pain we lived, the darkness we saw, the end result, as much as it hurts to admit, was inevitable, but the path toward it, I'd never have fucking guessed.

All my life, all I ever wanted was to protect my sister, to make sure she understood how important she was to me, as a good brother would, but somehow, with those thoughts constantly sitting in the back of my mind, I dropped the ball. And this is where it brought me. To the goodbye. I failed her in more ways than I can count, failed myself, and I'll never forget it. Never ever forgive myself for it. But I will be better for it. Because of it. The memory of what happened here will never leave me, and the nightmares will only get worse, but I'll find comfort in knowing my baby sister isn't alone. That she'll be loved no matter where she is. That she'll be safe and without fear. That no one can ever hurt her again. And if they tried, they'd have a hell of a fucking wall to get through to do it. Because my baby sister . . . she's no Bishop. She's Brayshaw. Through and fucking through.

She was meant for this place the same way I'm not.

Yeah, I got my start here, learned a lot, but I was held back, constantly itching for more. Never fulfilled and forever waiting for the answer of why to hit me in the face. I was under the thumb of someone else, and like my home girl Rae said to me the day she handed me a check with too many numbers to count, I don't belong behind anyone.

I know my place now. All it took was a taste of what the other side, the darker side, felt like, and I knew, without a doubt, where I wanted to be.

And that's in a town not far from here, beside the girl who took my valueless life and flipped that shit. The tempting little thief who slid out of the sweetest ride I'd ever seen and smirked at me from across the parking lot. Who stole my shit with zero fear when I had the body of a man on the ground at my feet. The girl who dragged my sister's dying body out of the water at the risk of her own.

I knew something was up with her and the water. Why else would an Olympic medalist up and quit diving in the blink of an eye? Now I know why.

The hospital we're in might be run and owned by the family of this town, the top floor dedicated to those of its blood and choosing only, but I've done a lot of good here. My sister's their family now, so when I demand Rocklin be treated in the same room so I don't have to be away from either of the two most important people in my life, there is no fight.

My sister lies unconscious in a bed, and across from her is my girl. She sits in a chair hooked up to masks and machines that do the breathing for her because the chemicals in the pool weakened and shriveled her lungs, stealing her ability to breathe easily and on her own.

She put herself at risk for me.

Gasping for three days, being stuffed with steroids the whole time, she didn't complain once. She didn't ask for her own space, even though this one is full of others, Royce's bed positioned right next to my sister's.

She's getting antsy, though. Fucked up over all the shit that went down at home and she still doesn't know the half of it. Has no idea what I've done and what I'm about to do the second we get back. This isn't a detour I anticipated when I took Oliver right out of the school and locked him in the basement, which surprisingly already existed on the property I threw a grip of money down on. Or when I grabbed his father and then hers. Thank fuck for Hayze.

A frown pulls at my brows at the thought of him. Shit, I haven't talked to him in days. Been so preoccupied with waiting for my sister to wake and making sure Rocklin didn't go and fucking die on me I haven't taken the time to touch my phone.

Where the fuck *is* my phone?

Rocklin sighs beside me, and I look to her.

Gripping her hand, I draw it to my lips, running her knuckles across my lip ring.

Her eyes lift to mine, her head dropping to the wall behind us, and for a minute, it's just us in this room.

I've known she was what I wanted for months now, but it's been molded and cemented deeper. Now more than ever, it's crystal fuckin' clear Rocklin Revenaw was meant to be mine.

My sister almost died in the water because she didn't know how to swim.

I don't know how to swim.

But my girl? She's an Olympic gold medalist.

The water is her second home.

I will be her first.

From the day I arrived in this town, to the moment I met her at her edge of hers, to this second right here, it was all in the cards for us. It was meant to lead us right fucking here, to bind her to me in a deeper way, through the only other person I love, before we go back to her home and do the same.

She's about to learn a lot of shit, but she can handle it. She's Rocklin fucking Revenaw, a queen in her own right.

And me?

I will be her king.

Even if I have to take out the current one . . .

Rocklin

As I push through the heavy hospital room door, Brielle's voice reaches me. It's thick and heavy with a rasp, having been out of practice with use. This morning marks day four. She's been coming in and out of consciousness. She's wide awake now, and something settles in my chest as I find Bastian is the one to whom she's speaking. He's at the edge of her bedside, looking down at her.

"You've been sitting beside me for four days," she says. "I can't imagine the new world you've found can run smoothly without you in it."

My lips twitch when Bastian responds with, "You have no idea."

"I object to that statement." All eyes look to me, and he sighs, narrowing his eyes a little, and I pause where I stand.

Something about this moment feels too intimate, I'm not really sure I should stick around for it, so I spin on my heels to leave, but just as I reach the door, it opens.

The head of the Brayshaw family steps in, and then I get the first glimpse of the man behind him. My eyes fly wide as I look into the deep-set, rage-filled ones of my father.

"Oh shit," I mutter, breath lodged in my throat.

His gaze slices past mine and I know exactly where they're focused, on the tattooed, black-haired boy behind me. I don't look, so I have no idea if Bastian stares this way or what expression he wears, but when he speaks, it's not a request.

"Take it outside," Bastian orders my father, the head honcho where we come from. The man who has killed more men than I could ever guess. Who makes cartel soldiers cry and weep at his feet. The whisperer behind my every move and the true controller behind my role as a Greyson. "Now."

And holy. Shit.

My father turns on his heels and walks out of the room.

It could be because we are out of our jurisdiction, so to speak, our word meaning nothing in this town as theirs means nothing in ours, but I can't be sure. It takes me a moment, but then I get myself together and quickly follow him out into the hall, but he's already curving to the waiting room, so I have to pick up the pace to meet him there.

I'm expecting a gang of guards to be standing around him, but it's only him, his anger, a freshly pressed suit, and two black eyes?

He knows I'm following, and as soon as we're out of ear and eyeshot, he turns with open arms and I readily throw myself into them, hugging him back as he does me, his chin pressing to the top of my head.

"You're okay?" he whispers instantly.

I nod, pulling back. "You're okay?" I worry, looking him over, but outside of a few red marks on his neck and the dark circles around his eyes, he looks unscathed, not exactly what I expected for a man who was kidnapped right in front of me.

He doesn't answer, and suspicion slowly grows within me as I release him, taking a step back.

"Dad, what happened?"

No sooner than the last word leaves my lips, he's gripping my wrist and tugging me down the hall toward the elevator, but we don't make it three feet before Bastian's clipped voice comes from behind.

"Bad fucking move."

I turn, looking toward him and then my dad's chest hits my back, his arm wrapping around me as he takes slow steps away. My eyes narrow, but Bastian isn't looking at me.

His chin is low, nearly touching his chest, as he eyes my father through the thick sweeps of his dark lashes.

He stands careless and calm, though his expression is anything but. I tug from my father's hold, my body pulled in the opposite direction on its own accord, and my dad's grip flies to my arm, tightening.

I see the second something slips into Bastian's mind. I don't have time to panic before he's flying this way. He has me released, spun and tucked behind him, my father by the throat and slammed against the wall before I can even breathe.

My dad's lip curls, his own arm shooting out to wrap around Bastian's neck just the same, but Bastian doesn't fight him. He lifts his chin, the same way he did at the gala, speaking beyond the powerful grip threatening to close off his airways.

"From now on, your hands don't touch her without permission. Keep it up, you won't see her without permission. Fight me on this, you won't see her at all," he tells my father.

My heart beats heavily as I look between the two, shocked and confused at the apparent change in power.

My dad doesn't respond, but it doesn't seem he was expected to as Bastian lets him go and steps back, reaching behind to wrap his arm around my waist. He pulls me into his side.

My dad's face is stone cold and unreadable as he stands silently in front of us.

Bastian reaches out, but my father doesn't flinch as his long arm moves past him to press the button on the elevator door, and when it dings, almost instantly, there's no argument from any of us as we all know any conversation that needs to be had cannot happen here. Bastian might trust these men, and Calvin may have some of that trust as well as part of the council, but our business is our own and nothing changes that.

Silently, we step into the elevator, the entire ride spent with the two men gauging one another. It's not until we're out in the parking lot all of us secretly canvas the area without being obvious about it. Watching for threats that might be hiding, both of them likely assuming the other has orchestrated some sort of attack against the other.

There's no one there, not a single guard waiting for my father, only his vehicle parked in the red zone, just in front of the private entrance meant only for the elite. Why he would travel without security, considering everything that's happened, I don't know. Then again, he must know what our most trusted guard did to us.

My father walks toward his vehicle and we follow, pausing when he pivots, his focus on me.

"We are going home," he announces.

"Agreed," Bastian says next.

The moment my father reaches back, tugging open his passenger door, I know there's going to be an issue.

"Let's go," he demands, stepping aside and sweeping his arm out expectantly. "There's much for us to discuss."

"Now that's an understatement." Bastian almost laughs, wrapping his arm around me. "We'll be at the mansion at eight a.m., ready to . . . *talk*."

My father holds my gaze. "You will come back now."

A small frown builds along my brow, and I look up at Bastian as he cocks his head at my dad and says, "Make that nine."

My father is doing all he can to control his rage, everything within him fighting against what's happening here. Honestly, I'm surprised he hasn't pulled a gun out and placed it to the temple of the man at my side. My muscles are stiff and waiting for it.

His eyes come back to mine, and he studies me for a long quiet moment as if he's trying to decide if a few more hours away from his grasp will leave me in a worse state than he thought I was in. His nostrils flare, his chest rising with a full breath.

Slowly, his attention moves to Bastian and he takes solid steps toward him, not stopping until they're nearly chest to chest.

"If my daughter isn't walking through the door of Greyson Manor by nine a.m. sharp . . ." He leaves the threat open, and when the only response he's given is a nod, he moves to climb into the driver's seat, but he doesn't leave.

He pulls forward, parking right in front of Bastian's car, and he waits.

With a clipped chuckle, Bastian gives my shoulder a slight squeeze before gripping my hand and leading me toward the vehicle. We climb inside, and then we're on the road heading home.

I have no idea what we will find when we get there, but it can't possibly be any worse than any of the other shit we've gone through.

I mean . . . right?

"I can feel you thinking," Bastian finally says, his shoulders heavy and voice less sharp than normal.

The last few days have done a lot of work on him in ways I likely can't imagine.

"My father is angry." I look to Bastian after I say this. "You are angry."

Bastian nods.

"What are we going home to, Bastian?"

His eyes leave the road for a fraction of a second to meet mine, his words, not the ones I want to hear. "A whole lot of fuckery, baby. Your world is shifting and you're not going to like a lot of it. The only thing I can promise you is that you're mine, and nothing will change that." He reaches over, pulling my hand to his lips, pressing a soft kiss to my knuckles before gently nipping at the tips. "Nothing."

That's the last word spoken and what a bold one it is.

Chapter 37
Bastian

At no point on the drive does she ask where we're going, just sitting back, trusting wherever it is I will lead her, but as we round the giant wall that protects the Greyson Estate from the outside world, she sits up in her seat, things coming back to her that the last few days have blocked out.

Slowly, her head swivels toward mine, but I don't look and just keep curving around for another mile or so until we reach the back of it, where a second estate sits.

The mansion is just as ridiculous as the one she calls home but less kept up. As far as I was told, the place hasn't been touched in decades, and I like it like that. There's a twisted, haunted appeal to the place that fits me perfectly. It's dark and gloomy and damn fitting of the shit I've used it for so far.

Hayze did have someone come in to fix some shit up though. Couldn't have us sleeping on moth-eaten mattresses. The whole fucking place was furnished, heavy sheets and shit lying over some fancy-ass furniture, like some shit out of evil times. The chairs that surround the giant table, which I'll never allow enough people in this house to fill, are straight-up thrones.

We had them pull everything out of the bedrooms, though, and I stayed on a dusty couch downstairs while a team came in and set the room up the way I wanted. All I told them was I don't like color and I like my privacy and they went to work.

As we roll up in the driveway, her mouth drops open, and she can't hold it in anymore.

"How in the . . ." she trails off, eyes slicing my way. "What the hell have I missed?"

My lip curves into a small smirk, but I don't pull my head off the seat, exhaustion sweeping in and quick.

"You do realize we've been trying to find documentation of this property for longer than I've been alive? Seriously. We were always led to believe that this was part of the Greyson Estate."

"It ain't," I tell her as I put the car in park. Reaching up, I push her hair over her shoulder. "Ain't, but can be." I leave the line hanging between us and climb out, my girl quick on my heels.

She practically dashes up the steps, fingers trailing over the giant stone posts carved out in the shape of a god, with snakes wrapped around his chest and neck.

"Exquisite," she whispers, rushing for the door, but before she can pull it open, it opens on its own.

She jerks back, eyes narrowing when Saylor, her lady's maid from the manor, stands there with a smile.

Her head snaps back and forth between the two of us.

"I wanted to make sure I had things set up for you the way you like. Saylor knows all that better than anyone."

A softness falls over her and Saylor dips her head, her cheeks pinking.

"Toiletries and your preference in most things are where you'd expect them to be in the north wing," Saylor tells her, eyes lifting to mine.

I give a small nod. "You can go back now."

She pauses a moment, looking to Rocklin, and then darts forward, wrapping her arms around her before rushing off in the opposite direction. Rocklin watches her go, only looking to me when I grab her hand and lead her into the house.

"She's going back to the manor?"

"She is."

"The wall you knocked down?"

"It's been rebuilt with a gate. The only way to open it is from this side, unless you have access on the other."

While there's a frown covering her forehead, she nods, and we head into the space. Her eyes dart and dash around every inch and I can tell she wants to explore. Hell, so do I. There're a shit ton of spots in this place I haven't even looked at. I didn't even step foot inside before I put the money down because all I needed was its location—right beside her was the only prerequisite.

There will be time for exploring later, and she seems to realize that, so when I lead her up the winding staircase to the floor above, she says not a word, just follows my steps with her hand clutched in mine.

I pull my phone from my pocket, texting Hayze to let him know that we're back but exhausted, and I'll catch up with him before we head to the manor in the morning.

When we reach my bedroom door, she doesn't wait for me to open it but pushes it herself, and a small smile spreads across her lips.

It's black on black. Black floors, black walls and drapes. Black bed and comforter and everything else in between. The bathroom is the same, which is where I lead her, straight to the giant-ass stone shower, the entire ceiling pouring like rainfall across every inch of the space. I let her go, and silently, we strip down into nothing.

When she goes to attempt to remove the collar around her neck, my hand darts out, halting her movements, and she slowly lowers them to her side.

Little does she know she can't take it off. It's a permanent fixture on her now. Waterproof, stain proof, fade proof, and equipped with a little hidden tracker just behind the rose gold diamond in the center.

She'll forever be in my back pocket now, a tiny dot on the app that follows her and her alone.

Rocklin gives me a soft, flirty little smile as she presses her lips to my shoulder and slips into the separate bathroom, so I chuck the rest of my clothes, looking at the burned flesh beneath my ear. I don't want her to spend the night beating herself up, and I've managed to hide it with a hoodie the last few days, not to mention we've kept our hands to ourselves. So, I throw some Vaseline on it and a quick bandage before stepping beneath the spray.

I let the heated water roll over me and take a deep fucking breath for what feels like the first time in a long-ass time. My sister is safe and she has a home. It might not be what I envisioned for her, but I realize now that's on me. Not her. She's too fucking strong to live a docile life. Too good not to shine some light on a little bad. They'll be good to her there, and she'll fucking blossom beside them.

It's crazy, the timing. How I only ever wanted two things in my life, until suddenly I wanted three, and here I am, at the cusp of having all three, all at once.

I run my hands through my hair, my shoulders sagging a little lower as I quickly wash myself before she gets in here.

Tomorrow is going to be rough on my baby, so tonight, I'll need to be good and gentle with her.

The glass door opens, and I smile when her soft hands wrap around me from behind, her palms pressing to my chest as hers meet my back. She hugs me, pressing her cheek to my spine with a long exhale, the last few weeks catching up to us both.

She was here alone, but not alone, hating life and missing me, and I was out there fighting motherfuckers for my old bosses, secretly coming to her when she didn't know it. I watched her sleep, then went back to Brayshaw for business.

It was the hardest shit I've ever done, leaving her each time I did. I had never needed someone before, but I needed to be near her. I had to have eyes on her, or I couldn't fucking think. Shit sounds weak, but it is what it is. She's a drug and I'm fucking addicted.

Keeping myself busy was the only thing that helped, and it wasn't for nothing. It paid off.

Literally, I never expected anything, but I won't lie and say it didn't change some things for me because it did.

Slowly, I ring her around my body, and she smiles up at me when I gently take her hair and tug so the water falls over her. Her eyes close and she lets out soft little mewls as I massage her scalp. I start washing her, beginning with her hair, and work my way down, leaving no part of her unwashed. When I reach between her legs, she squeezes her thighs together a little, clasping her hand on my bicep.

I look up from where I'm kneeling before her now and she lifts a shoulder, her lips pressing to one side.

"I'm sort of—"

"I know and I don't care."

A small frown pulls her brows and I rise to my feet, rinsing my hands under the spray behind her as I lean down to skim my lips over hers. "The nurse at the hospital told me."

She bites her lip, eyes growing hooded, just as fucking eager to have me again as I am her. "That's an invasion of privacy," she whispers, flicking her tongue over my lip ring.

I catch it between my teeth, closing my mouth around it and sucking slightly. As I pull back, I shake my head. "There is no wall between us, baby. I will know all. See all. Speak on all, and I expect you to do the same. And tonight . . ." I press her into the wall, "I fully expect you to coat my cock. Your period means nothing to me, ma. It's just a little extra lube, that's all."

Rocklin's chest heaves, her eyes low and needy . . . and waiting, like a good fucking girl.

"Kiss me, Rocklin Revenaw. Right fucking now," I whisper.

She pulls in a long breath and presses her lips to mine. It's not a hard crash but a leisurely fuck of her tongue. It's therapy for the deeper parts of ourselves and exactly what I want—her to take me how she wants me while still being what she needs me to be for her, the man calling the shots. It's a delicate little dance we'll do tonight.

"I'm so hard for you, baby." I kiss her jaw and then her neck, squeezing and kneading her ass. "Can you feel what you do to me?" I press into her abdomen and she nods, running her fingers through my hair. "Are you ready to make me feel good?"

"Dying to."

I groan, finding her lips once more, and she grips my shoulders. "Love that answer, Rich Girl. Now move that ass before we make an even bigger mess than we plan to."

I release her, spin and step out, and she's right behind me, tearing her towel from the rack beside mine, and we dry as we move into the room. I toss my towel onto the floor and she gently folds hers over the end of the bed, where we stand facing one another.

Her hair is dripping wet down her body, but she doesn't care, her eyes locked on mine.

Her nipples pebble to sharp points and I bring my knuckles up to run along them, watching as gooseflesh bursts across her skin. My cock twitches at the sight.

"Perfect body for the perfect girl," I murmur, skating my knuckles higher until they're gliding along her neck. I hook my pinkie in the little loop of the *B* hanging from her collar, my eyes popping up to meet hers.

Her pupils are blown wide, and when I give the tiniest of tugs, her lips part.

Slowly, I tug her to me, my lips meeting hers as we stare into one another's eyes, and already, she's panting, her harsh breaths fanning along my mouth and I sink my teeth into my lower lip.

Slowly, I lower my hand, keeping my finger hooked where it is and she understands, lowering until she's on her knees before me. I let her collar go with a nod of approval and she starts to shake.

She fucking shakes and I'm not even touching her.

Cupping her jaw, I rub small circles along her skin, simply staring at the beautiful thing before me. "So fucking perfect." I bend, pressing a small kiss to her cheek, my mouth moving to her ear. "You know what I want, so make me proud, baby."

She sucks in a sharp breath as I release her, slowly taking backward steps and not stopping until I'm lowered onto the small sofa against the wall.

Taking my cock in my hand, I give it a good squeeze, and her eyes zero in on the tip, already leaking with proof of how badly I fucking need her.

Slowly, her eyes find mine and I drop my head back onto the cushion, keeping my gaze locked on hers. I stroke myself lazily, my tongue running along my lower lip and my hand moves a little faster when she does exactly what I intended for her to do.

She drops onto her hands and fucking knees and crawls.

Chest heaving, mouth open and eager, she heads right for me.

My eyes fall to my initial locked around her perfectly slender fuckin' neck. It's dead center and fucking gleaming, leading her right fucking to me. When she reaches me, her hands find my skin first and my body jerks, drawing a small twitch from her lips.

She leans in, eyeing my dick like it's her favorite fucking flavor of ice pop, and those liquid huntress eyes flick to mine for permission. "Mine," she rasps.

"Yours."

She dives down, her tongue lappin' over my fingers and the head of my dick, where she whirls it, before sucking the head into her plump-ass lips for a better taste.

Her eyes close and she moans around me, but she needs more, and when her wild eyes meet mine, I nod.

She crawls up me, digging her knees into the cushion, lining her pretty pussy over my head.

"Slide on my dick, little thief. Take what's yours and give me what's mine."

She does exactly that, sucking me inside her in one slow swoop.

We moan in unison and our lips meet instantly, kissing and nipping, her hands holding my face, mine holding her ass as she slowly rocks on top of me.

It's exactly what we need, a leisurely kind of ride, the slow fucking painful kind.

Gripping her hips, I lift one leg and tip back more so we're half sitting, half lying and her hands fly to the back of the couch.

"It's so deep like this," she gasps, moaning the next second.

"Does it feel good, baby?" I urge her on, my eyes fucking glued to the sight of her above me, hair soaking fucking wet and sticking to her face. Her eyes are closed, and she switches between biting her lip and licking it, a small frown above her brow, the feeling too fucking good.

I'm a fuckin' rod inside her, too hard to comprehend, these last few months without the feel of her wrapped around me, I'll never go through again, but I don't take over.

She needs this and I'm close to coming just watching and feeling the way she fucks her worries from her body, using mine how she wants, chasing the angle that best suits her right now and every little move she makes is so fucking good.

"Bastian." She moans, blindly seeking out my lips, so I give them to her, kissing her long and hard and she cries into my mouth, her body trembling as her orgasm rolls through her. Slowly, her green eyes open, and she runs her hands through my hair, her forehead falling to mine. "More."

"Okay, baby," I murmur against her lips, pulling them between my own as I haul us to our feet, remaining locked inside her.

Her arms lock around my neck, burying her face in it and I carry us to the bed until we're in the center.

Her legs fall open and when I pull back, her fingers trail the bandage, worry in her gaze.

I kiss her wrist, threading my fingers with hers, and shake my head, and when I slowly rock in and out of her, she forgets all about it.

Our bodies are pressed together, completely smashed, and still, she presses closer.

"You need more than this, Rich Girl?" I lift one of her legs over my shoulder, pull back all the way and back in, deeper this time. Her back arches off the comforter. "You need . . . this too?"

I bring my hand under her leg, pressing my thumb to the tight ring of muscle there.

470

She gasps and moans at the same time, pressing into my hand.

"Yeah, you do, don't you?" I kiss her throat, just above and then below the jewelry there. "I'll stay right there. You take what you want, hear me?"

I nip at her collarbone and when she drives her ass down, the tip of my thumb pressing into her tight hole, my cock flexes.

"My greedy girl." I groan. My muscles stiffen as I drive into her. "I'm gonna come, baby. I'm gonna fill you up and then lie next to you and watch as I leak out of you."

She whimpers, and with two more strokes of my cock, my thumb still playing with her, she clenches, her body quaking, and I spill into her, taking her mouth as she digs her nails into my back. Her pussy convulses around me and we stay like that until we're nothing but dead weight.

Slowly, I roll off her and take her with me into the bathroom to clean up and she slips into the private restroom attached, coming out just as fast, just as naked. I lift her off her feet, carrying her back to bed.

We climb into the center, burying ourselves in the blanket and she wraps her arms around me with a yawn. "I thought you wanted to watch me leak all over."

A throaty chuckle leaves me, and I close my eyes, holding her tight. "I do, but I thought better of it, and I don't think you'd be all that comfortable bleeding all over the bed."

She hums, burying her face in my chest. "You thought right. Are you . . . will you stay in bed all night tonight?"

I grip her chin, tipping it up so she can look at me, her green eyes exhausted and content. "I'm not going anywhere."

She holds my gaze a moment before nodding and burying her head once more.

We lie there in silence for a long time, so long I'm sure she's asleep, but then her soft, sad little voice whispers into the darkness.

"I killed somebody."

"It's okay, baby," I whisper back. "I did, too."

Chapter 38
Rocklin

For the millionth time in a row, I wake from a dead sleep. My eyes fly open, and I hold perfectly still, unsure of what I heard if anything at all. I reach toward Bastian, prepared to shake him awake, but my hand hovers over an empty space, the spot he was in when I fell asleep now vacant.

A deep groan and muffled shout sound once more and I tense, jerking up in the bed.

Bastian . . .

I kick the comforters off and jump from the bed, tiptoeing across the thick plush carpet until I reach the black flooring, following the gurgling sounds as my heart beats double time.

A third mumble sounds and my head jerks left and I rush toward the closet, quietly easing it open as I peek inside the dark space. His bare feet come into view first, and I push the door open a little farther, frowning slightly when I spot him lying on the floor with nothing but a pillow, his chest rising and falling in rapid breaths.

Pausing there a moment, I watch him.

His body jerks violently in his sleep, his face contorting and thrashing from side to side, lip curling as his hands ball into fists over his chest before flattening on the floor beside him. His mouth moves, words coming out, but they're so jumbled I can't begin to guess what it is he says.

I go to him, lowering to my knees at his side and gently run my fingertips over the side of his face, he jerks at first and then his features settle as he turns his cheek into my palm.

472

Slowly his breathing evens out, his hands unclenching, but it only lasts a moment. Suddenly his eyelids twitch, and then he lurches. I'm flipped to my back, a gun digging between my ribs in a second.

I clench my teeth together to hide the wince as I stare up at him and he glares down at me, lip curled into a sneer. Then he blinks and blinks again and throws himself back, crawling on the palms of his hands as he looks from the gun on the floor to me.

His mouth opens, but he says nothing and then he glares.

We stare at each other a moment, and suddenly, it makes sense why he would never be in my bed in the mornings after he would stay the night. Why he wouldn't share a bed at the hotel.

Bastian has nightmares. Of course he does.

He was beaten by his father his entire life, alongside his sister, as his mother watched on, doing nothing. The one man on the planet he should have been able to trust, the one who was supposed to love him unconditionally, who he was supposed to love in return, he killed instead.

He was barely fifteen then and his problems weren't solved with the bullet—or two—he put in his head because then he was forced to make a choice, yanking himself away from the only person who ever did love him.

Slowly, I lean forward, planting my palms on the floor and working my way to him. I grip his hand in mine and stand. Reluctantly, he rises with me, allowing me to drag him back to the bed he tucked me into last night, and together, we dip under the covers. I wrap myself around him and he does the same, burying his nose in my hair.

A few moments pass, and he takes a heavy inhale. It's not long after that his chest rises and falls with full, deep breaths, and I know he's fallen back asleep, but I don't. I keep stroking down his bare stomach. Every handful of minutes or so, he jerks, but I just keep touching him at the same steady pace and eventually, just as the sun begins to rise outside the slightly open curtains, his body relaxes completely.

I lie there, replaying the last few months in an attempt to avoid the last few days, but I can't. I'm half tempted to crawl out of this bed and make my way back to Greyson Manor before he does, so I can speak to my father and the others alone. The only thing that's stopping me is the utter chaos that would follow if Bastian blew up and ran in there half-cocked. Or all the way cocked, if that's even a thing, because I'm not sure he does anything half-assed. My disappearing on him to run home definitely wouldn't be the situation where that happened.

The sound of the door opening catches my attention, and when Bastian doesn't stir in the slightest, I slip off the bed and out into the hall.

From the overlook at the top of the stairs, I spot Bastian's friend Hayze coming out of a large steel door with one of those giant wheel-style locks dead center. He doesn't close it, rather he leaves it hanging half-open as he stalks off in the opposite direction.

I make my way down, looking to where he disappeared before slipping through the door. No more than five steps down, it opens into a narrow walkway, creepy yellow-tinted lighting flickering along the path, almost as if it was intended to add to the serial killer vibe the place gives off.

It's freezing in here and I only need one guess as to why. My dad's "work" basement is same.

I carry myself off the last step and move the next few feet. From here, I can see four doors in total, So, when I ease the first one open, I expect to see a narrow space, but instead, find a wide open one, but that's not the shocking part.

Nor is it the giant chains hanging from steel bolted rings on the ceiling, three sets in total, all perfect distance from one another.

It's not even the thick smears of blood on the one farthest from me, the poor attempt to hide whatever happened here revealing it's not aged blood, but on the fresher spilled side.

No . . . it's the long wooden box at the edge of it with the lid off. Inside, bunched up, there are red-stained sheets sticking out that garner my full attention.

Suddenly I wish I had shoes on as I inch my way closer, crossing my arms over my chest as the chill gets more severe within the new set of walls. I glance at the small splatters of blood trailing from the first set of chains to the second, noting the softball-sized stain beneath the second set, but I keep moving toward the end, toward the home-crafted coffin that can only have one thing inside it.

I'm three feet from it when a golden gleam catches my eye, and I turn my head to see what it is.

I would recognize the custom shade of gold anywhere.

Pivoting, I bend, picking the small item up off the little ledge it sits on.

I stare at it in my open palm, running my thumb along the Greyson *G*, but it's not just the Greyson *G*. It's the golden double-walled *G* of the Greyson Society, only crafted when it's meant to be presented. The *G* that solidifies your spot in the Greyson Society.

My frown builds, doubling as I consider it, but it doesn't take long.

"I warned him," Bastian's rasp comes from behind me.

I glance over my shoulder to spot him leaning against the door, feet and chest still bare, black hair gloriously sticking up in all the wrong directions.

What a stupid thing to notice at a time like this, yet I can't look away, and he cocks his head, studying me with a blank expression.

I think about the day in the hotel when I first took him in and spotted his new additions, a diamond-encrusted one, to be exact.

"The watch . . ." I remember.

"No reason for it to go to waste."

Slowly, I push to my feet, jerking my head toward the casket.

Bastian's eyes narrow slightly, but then he gives a slow nod. "He's lucky the blood infection took him while we were gone. It would have been worse once I got back." He pauses, contemplating, before deciding to add, "If your dad didn't beat me to it."

My brows jump. "My dad," I said deadpan.

Another nod and when he looks to the first set of chains, the ones with nothing but teardrop-sized red stains littering the ground below them, I know.

"It was you . . . *you* attacked us that night. You took my dad."

Unapologetically, his crystal eyes hold mine. "I did."

"I . . ." My mind spins and I shake my head. "How?"

"Help. A warning from a . . . man of mutual interest."

I don't even know what to say to that. I don't know what to think or ask or feel.

My dad is fine, clearly. He didn't hurt or kill him. The blood on the floor isn't his. I know this. I've set eyes on him myself, so . . . "Why?"

Slowly, he pushes off the wall, and I stand, spinning to face him as he grows nearer. When He reaches me, he holds his hand out, and I set the golden pin in his palm. He brings it closer for inspection, blows a warm breath over it and then rubs it against the material of my pajama top, twisting and turning it until the solid gold catches the light and shines in greatness.

"I cleaned this up once already. Saved it for you, but not for reasons you might think." His eyes lift to mine. "I saved it to serve as a reminder of what will happen to anyone who hurts you. This is now my promise pin. He touched you. Hurt you."

"I could have drowned him easily."

Bastian's smirk pulls at his lips and he pushes my hair from my face. "I know, baby. I was inspired that day." A shadow flicks across his gaze, a small frown pulling instantly, and it all comes together.

"The guy who took Brielle . . ." I put it together. "You were there that day at Greyson Elite? You saw when I talked Oliver into the water?" He was inspired, he said, so that means he used the water against this guy.

He nods. "Hog-tied him to the disabled chair in that same pool. Left him to drown in it. Should have chained some bricks to his ass."

"Bastian."

He blinks as I speak, refocusing. "Why did you take my dad that night?"

"Because you're mine, and he wasn't going to understand that if I didn't. I'd waited and planned for months, finishing out my responsibilities in Brayshaw with you at the front of my mind the entire time. I wanted to make you sweat, to ache and regret and miss me, and you did, Rich Girl. You did exactly what I wanted while I was getting ready for you." He walks into me, backing me up and twisting me until my shoulder blades meet the cool stone wall. His knuckles come up under my chin, and he lifts it, his tongue flicking along his lip ring as he fixates on my lips.

"I was a boy who had no idea what he wanted but knew it wasn't what I had until I found you. Everything clicked. I didn't know how I was going to be what you deserved, but I knew I would be. The only thing I wasn't sure I'd be able to give you is what you needed most, and that's love, but I learned how to give that. It might be unconventional, it might not even be right, but it's real, my love for you." My lungs expand with a sharp inhale, and his eyes flick to mine, darkening. "I don't need your old man's acceptance. You are mine regardless . . . but I want it. For you, because I know you want it. You love him."

"I love you."

Bastian's eyes flash, his chest rising and falling in rapid succession, but there's no shock in his gaze. No surprise or relief.

He knew. He knows.

My forehead falls forward, and he meets it with his own, our eyes closing.

"Fuck the world . . ."

I can sense his smirk without seeing it as he whispers in return, "and everyone in it."

*

I should probably be concerned at how easy it is to walk out of Bastian's basement and leave Oliver's cold, dead body behind, but there's no time to focus on that. Not when it's eight-fifty-eight on the dot and we're walking through the gardens that lead to the new giant gate connecting Bastian's estate to the Greyson one.

As we reach the brand-new monstrosity, Bastian gives me a small nod, so I step forward, pressing my palm to the square reader, a replica of the one we use at The Enterprise, and what do you know, access is granted.

The first thing I notice when we step through the clearing is how there's no sign of all the busted rubble we left behind, someone has been working double time to erase the events of that night, but as we grow closer to the seating area of our gardens, my eyes are instantly called to the right.

Sai's soft, fading smile flashes in my mind and my eyes prick with the threat of tears, what I did and why I had far too painful to process right now, and Bastian knows it, his firm grip tightening in support.

I give myself one more second, then lift my head high, clearing my expression of all thoughts.

Movement catches my eye, and my head darts up.

Relief spills into me as I stare up at the balcony, finding my girls standing there, the boys at their backs. They give the subtlest of nods and then they disappear, and I know they have my back—*our* back—should we need it. We're definitely going to need it.

My dad. He is holding it in, but he is, without a doubt, boiling with rage, just waiting to be released. My feet hesitate, my body twisting to face his. "Bastian—"

No sooner than his name leaves my lips, I'm bent, tucked and rolled behind him, his left arm cased around me, locking me flush against his back, his right hanging at his side as his chin dips low.

Man after man reveals themselves all around us, creeping from behind every brush and corner, rifles raised, lasers pointed this way, and I don't have to be standing in front of them to know every single one is trained dead center on his head. The Revenaw team doesn't shoot to injure. They shoot to eliminate.

The double doors swing open ahead, and my father steps out, adjusting his suit jacket as he does, his face poised as he walks this way.

Bastian's grip on me tightens, but his hands don't shake. There isn't a single tremble or hint of tension running through his body.

My dad stops five feet away, folding his hands together loosely in front of himself as he tips his head slightly, his dark hair slicked back as always, sharp jaw perfectly smooth-shaven.

Slowly, a smile pulls at my dad's lips, a low laugh following, and my pulse jumps at the mockery he's making. "So, is this how you expected things to go?"

"Better question. This how you want to play things? 'Cause what you do here can't be undone, old man."

"I'm not the one with countless targets pointed at my skull, so yes, I'd say it is."

"If one of them spook shoots and she gets hit, every fucker on this field dies. Including you." Bastian pauses a moment. "Last chance, you won't get another."

I press my palms at his back in silent support, and his chest rises with a full steady breath, but then Bastian's arm around my body jerks, and I look over my shoulder to spot the tranq dart deep in his forearm, the liquid within disappearing into his bloodstream.

He whips around, gently tossing me out of the way as he rushes the man at our backs.

He's shot a second time in the chest, and his body begins to sway, but not before he's gripped the gun in the man's hands, torn it from his grasp and smashed it over his head.

He falls to his knees, fighting against the toxins bound to take control, and I dart for him, horror gripping me when I'm wrapped up from behind and lifted off the ground as a handful of men descend on Bastian.

They kick and hit him, punching every inch of his body they can reach. His skin splits, blood streaming from his wounds, his head and body flopping as he's treated like a rag doll, left completely defenseless.

I struggle and scream, and then I sink my teeth into the arm wrapped around me, shredding through the man's skin and sending him howling until I've been dropped at his feet. My knees smack against the ground, but I jump up quickly, stealing a rifle off the grass, but I don't point it at the pile of men beating mine.

I turn it on my father, watching as his eyes narrow and then widen when I place my finger on the trigger. "Don't make me do this."

His brows dip low, eyes searching, assessing, and I know the moment he sees it.

The moment he realizes I will pull the trigger if I must.

My father's lips press together firmly, sorrow drawing creases into the corner of his eyes just before they grow resolute, and he gives a small nod, but I realize too late it isn't in concession to my threat.

It is in acceptance of whatever he has planned and a silent order to the man who is sneaking up behind me, the one who puts me to sleep with my next blink.

Chapter 39
Rocklin

My head hits the warm leather of the back seat, and I fly upward, darting for the door, but it's slammed in my face. I scream, pounding on the glass but then whip around when the door opposite this one is yanked open and four guards file into the back seat, masks over their heads, glasses hiding their eyes.

Throwing myself against the seat, I'm careful not to touch the spot where my weapon hides, so as not to draw attention to it. My father would never disarm me, no matter if he is the very reason I'm sitting in the back of my very own town car right now, so I know it's still in place, *just in case*.

Instinctively, my eyes fly to the front of the town car, where Sai should sit, where in this exact moment, his eyes would snap up to meet mine, knowing I was looking, awaiting or watching for his brief second of reassurance. But it's Warren who sits behind the wheel, and my heart clenches at the sight as a bitter sense of betrayal forms in my throat. I swallow beyond the rising acid, eyes flicking from one dead man to the next.

"Where the hell are we going? What's he going to do with Bastian?" Not expecting anyone to answer, and they don't, but rage is building inside me at the thought of him back at the manor alone at the mercy of my father, who knows no such word.

Bastian took my father against his will, attacked him and his men and made him look weak, chained him in his basement and my father didn't even escape the situation. That's another slap at his ego, and he'll want vengeance.

481

He'll want his life.

Desperate, I throw my shoulder into the man on my left, headbutting the one on my right and kick my leg out, driving my heel against the throat of the man sitting across from me. The person next to him makes a grab for me, his hand wrapping around my throat, but then the person bleeding from the spike of my pump rears back and slams the butt of his gun into the man's chin.

The two at my sides go stiff, raising their weapons, but before they have a chance to put their fingers near the trigger, the bleeding man sends a bullet through both of their chests.

I sit back wide-eyed as a door is flung open, the driver realizing it a second later and beginning to swerve as the masked bleeding man tosses the guard from my right out, looking up at me as if to say *are you going to give me a hand*, or at least it's what I imagine he's saying even though I can't see his eyes or face. I quickly jump forward to the seat where the unconscious guard is slumped over, allowing him the space he needs to toss the guard from the left out just as the car comes to a screeching halt.

The bloody guard hops out and then there's another pop of a gunshot, followed by a thud as he removes the driver's dead body from the front seat. The squeal of tires from an approaching vehicle screech, clouds of dirt surrounding us as they skid to a stop behind us.

I grab the gun off the floorboard, pointing it out the door. My finger brushes the trigger right as Damiano comes into view. His eyes fly wide, and he jerks back, but I tip the barrel in the last second and the bullet only breaks through the edge of his jacket.

"Oh my god!" I scream, scooting to the edge, but I shuffle back when he begins to crawl in, Bronx and Delta right behind them, taking the seats in front of me, all three dressed from head to foot in black tactical gear.

All heads whip toward the opposite door when it's yanked open, but then the masked man simply pulls the unconscious one from beside me and tosses him to the side of the road before closing the door and jumping into the driver's seat.

Kenex and Kylo pull up in their own car, giving a small nod and then my eyes lift to meet the man in the driver's seat, watching as he yanks his mask off his head and glasses from his eyes.

Hayze winks at me and then hits the gas, sending us speeding down the road, but we're continuing in the direction the car was originally headed.

I dart forward, gripping the privacy screen, eyes narrowing. "What are you doing? We have to go back."

"Boss's orders, babe."

"I am the fucking boss right now. Turn the car around, Hayze!"

"Can't do it."

The click of a gun being cocked sounds, and then a steel barrel is pressed to the underside of his neck. Bronx leans forward, whispering in his ear. "Turn around, terror, before I paint the windshield the prettiest shade of red."

"Talk dirty to me, mama." The manic man laughs, but he only drives faster, tipping his head to the side to allow her even better access. "Dying to see those hands at work."

Bronx frowns, and then she shrugs and sits back on the seat, checking her bloodred lipstick in the reflective glass. "I'd shoot him if your man didn't like him so much."

"Maybe someone else likes me too," he quips.

"Maybe not." Bronx glares at nothing, looking at me. "Are you okay?"

"They beat the shit out of him." The muscles around my heart constrict, my lungs working overtime, still requiring a little extra time to heal. "He was unconscious, B, and they kept beating him." Like his father used to do.

Anger and hate and pure fucking sorrow threaten to swallow me whole, but I won't hide from the feeling. It's not fair to him.

He couldn't hide from any of it.

Delta's hands find mine, and she squeezes, our eyes meeting. "He knew something like this might happen. There's nothing you could do."

My mouth opens, but before I can speak, the car slows to a stop.

"Here we go," Hayze mutters.

Damiano flies forward, peeking out the window and his face pales instantly. "Fuck. He's really fucking here."

"Who?"

Damiano shakes his head, cursing under his breath.

"Damiano, *who*?!"

"Enzo." His brows crash, his tense eyes finding mine. "Enzo is here."

Holy. Fucking. Shit.

Bass

The fuzz in my head begins to clear, my limbs weighing ten times what they should as I try to shake the last bit of the horse tranquilizer they shot my ass with. That shit seems to be the weapon of choice around here, thanks to my girl and her inventive ways of sneaking out under her little lockdown sentence.

I know without the help of the *click, clack, clank* what I'll find once my eyes open, and I'm not disappointed. Thick, braided chains attached to three-inch-thick silver cuffs cover my wrists and ankles, but he was a little more creative than I was and strapped one to my neck as well. We're still at Greyson Manor, this time down in the training room, so he made these adjustments in anticipation of this moment, the moment he got to sit across from the peasant who captured the king, only to let him go in the end.

Rayo Revenaw stares me down from the chair he sits in, amber liquid of some sort splashing in his glass as he tips his head from side to side in that typical rich prick–type shit.

"If you ain't gonna drink it, shoot it my way." My voice comes out rasped, the split skin sticking from one lip to the other. I'm sure it's supposed to sting, but I've had more busted lips in my life than I've had steak dinners, so other than the drop of warm liquid that rolls over my chin, I show no sign of a beating well done.

It is a beating well done. My ribs are screaming, pretty sure my left shoulder is out of place, and I'll be looking like a fucked-up dalmatian by this time tomorrow, but it's nothing I can't handle. Nothing I haven't dealt with before.

Rayo's eyes narrow and he shakes his head, disgusted by the poor punk trapped near his feet. Because he knows as well as I do . . .

I'm the same punk he met months ago, just add a fistful of zeros to the end, and not much is changed. He still hates me and I'm still fucking his daughter.

What he *doesn't* know is that chaining me to the ground does nothing to change that, but I bet it feels good in his own mind to have the boy who got one over on the untouchable man bloody before him.

He watches me closely, doing all he can to pick me apart, to reach inside my brain with nothing but his eyes in hopes of pulling out some magical secret that justifies him getting got by a guy like me. By the scum he can't be bothered with, who isn't good enough to take the hand of his daughter on the dance floor, like his son wasn't good enough to take the seat beside his sister.

Imma get my dance.

Finally, after sitting there staring for who the fuck knows how long, the man shakes his head again. "Tell me something," He begins.

"What do I get in return?"

He lifts a single brow as if the answer should be obvious, but when I wait for him to vocalize it, he huffs, picking up a small black remote I didn't see tucked in his lap and holding it between his fingers, his elbow perched on the edge of the chair like a casual-ass motherfucker.

He stares me in the eye, pressing a button and my neck lights up, the muscles there spasming and stretching, straining against the cold metal as my teeth vibrate against one another.

I clip my tongue, the taste of copper filling my mouth. I make not a fucking sound, trained to take pain like a fucking masochist.

He presses another button, and that shit doubles, the electricity zapping through me and shaking my every limb, the veins in my arms pulsing and popping out over my flesh. My chest rumbles, low and long, and then he relents.

My body falls forward, chest heaving as sweat drips from my temples, seeping into what must be an open wound there, the second salty sting letting me know there's yet another cut along my brow. The droplets continue to roll downward, mixing with dried blood until it's falling into my eye, and I'm forced to blink rapidly to clear the fog.

Pulling in a long, slow breath, I sit back on my heels, shoulders slumped and arms hanging, but by some miracle, the left corner of my mouth rises when I want it to.

He tries to fight it, but a curious sort of frown flashes along his forehead. He leans forward with his elbows on his knees to cover it up. "Why would a man I've known all my life, who, at his own free will, was sworn to protect and serve my daughter until his dying breath, turn his back on us for some rankless fool with a death wish?"

"I don't know, old man," I trail off, cocking my head at him. "Why the fuck would he?"

This time his eyes do narrow. I know he hears the accusation in my tone, I put the shit there on purpose.

"You're not helping yourself here, boy. A cocky attitude won't do you any good." He sits back, lifting his drink to his lips once more for a ghost of a swallow. "You've already lost, so you might as well tell me what I want to know."

The smile he gives me has my pulse jumping, and I pick the card he wants me too.

"Where is she?"

He shows his fucking teeth now, satisfied. "Gone. Somewhere you can't reach, no matter how slick you think you are. You're still just a boy with a lot to learn. Not that you'll get the chance, so talk."

Gone. Somewhere I can't reach.

I fucking warned him, gave him a chance to hold on, even if it would have been with a weaker grip than he was used to. He failed my final fucking test and he failed it hard.

487

Nodding, I run my tongue along my teeth, tasting the blood there. I spit to the side, slowly bringing my eyes back to his. "Someone hurt your daughter."

His jaw tics at the truth. "And he has been dealt with."

"By me," I snap and his lips curl. "Don't fucking forget that."

"You want a fucking trophy?"

"Got me one."

He flies to his feet, jerking toward me, his control snapping. "You have *nothing*!" he booms. "And you will never have her. You are lucky you're still breathing. You think you can come into my fucking territory, pull the shit you did without consequence?!" he backhands me like a bitch, face sneering when my head holds straight.

My jaw is made of fucking stone, and I hold his eyes straight through. Anger boils within him and he grips my neck in the small space above the shackle, doing all he can to crush my windpipe, having no fucking idea he's touching the answer he seeks.

It's killing him not to kill me, but there's a tiny little whisper of his baby girl in his head telling him not to and it's taking all he's got not to listen.

"You've chosen the wrong circle to weasel your way into. Tell me what made Sai flip on the only family he ever knew!" he demands, releasing me with a shove.

A scratchy laugh leaves me and I shake my head, rising to my feet, ignoring the pain in my limbs and the yank of the metal locked around me, numb to the way the two shorter chains slowly cut into my skin. I strain harder, welcoming the metal into my skin, allowing it to shred and tear me apart, sending fresh trails of blood to the floor around me.

Small creases form at the edge of his eyes, but he says nothing, waiting.

"I watched your daughter from the moment I met her," I tell him. "Followed and tracked her damn near every fucking move. Even when she thought I was gone, I was there. I was the shadow in the dark you couldn't touch or find. Couldn't buy or blackmail, 'cause you're right, pops, I'm a rankless fucking fool. But you know what that means?" I yank on the chains.

"It means my eyes were fresh, my mind clear. I saw what you didn't and when that piece of shit got bolder, put his hands on her, I went into that dorm, seconds after he strolled in, and dug a knife into his shoulder, dragged the motherfucker out by the handle of the blade without being seen or caught. I crept through your house while you slept and took photos of her sleeping so you'd know, no matter where you put her, and you put her right where I wanted you to when I needed you to, by the way, you couldn't keep her from me.

"I followed the threat against her that led me to Daddy Henshaw, and I did what you couldn't. He was planning an attack. He was going to go to her room first with gas bombs and then real ones, and only after you heard them go off, heard her screams if she even had the chance to, he was going to come for you. I stopped him. I solved the puzzle you couldn't and then I took you. Don't forget you're only standing where you are because I fucking let you. Me. The rankless punk boy who—"

He clips me clean across the jaw and when he rights himself, I spit the blood he left behind in his face, baring my teeth this time.

"I told you what I wanted in return for the gifts I gave you."

"Her fate has been sealed!" he screams. "It's done."

"You're right. It is." I lift my chin, the lock slipping lower as I drop the bomb he never saw coming. "Her guardian made sure of it."

I've replayed this shit in my head a million times, but I only needed to once, 'cause in the end, the most obvious reason was the same, and when I came face to face with the man, suddenly, it clicked. Like her daddy said, that man promised to protect her with his life against all enemies and threats, and that's exactly what he did.

Rayo's eyes narrow and I bend my neck to the left, giving him a clearer view.

His attention drops to the area revealed, just visible beyond the lock. The fresh wound there, the mark familiar and of his own design, and he jerks back, stumbling over his own fucking feet.

Because he sees it.

He knows.

Sai Demonte didn't betray the girl he swore to defend.

He saved her from the biggest threat she'd ever faced.

He saved her from her father.

Chapter 40
Bass

Four Years Ago

When the dude said "somewhere near here," I thought he meant a couple hours away, but not thirty minutes later, we're pulling to the curb in front of an old busted-ass house that looks like it holds what nightmares are made of.

But what do I know?

My house had a fresh paint job and a wooden welcome sign on the front porch, but the devil lived inside it. Maybe the good is hidden in the ugly so it can't be corrupted, broken, or ruined.

My eyes narrow on nothing. "When can I see my sister?" I ask again.

The man climbs out of the driver's seat and slips into the back, once again sitting across from me. "The woman who runs the home across the way will come get you as soon as the doctors call to say she's out of surgery."

Surgery. Doctors. She'll be scared when she wakes alone, but what can I do?

"Cops won't be waiting there for me?"

"The second I leave you here, everything that happened before today disappears."

Finally, I drag my gaze back to his, doubting his every word. "How?"

"I work with powerful people."

Such a cop-out answer. But then again, maybe he does. The

491

ring on his right hand is a shiny kind of gold I've never seen. "And my mom?" My jaw tics at the thought of her.

He frowns, and when he speaks again, his eyes stay locked on mine, each word delivered slower than the last. "There is a man I know. He makes people disappear."

"Is that what's about to happen to me? I'm gonna walk in there and 'disappear?'"

"No." He dips his chin, almost as if he's lowering himself so we're equals, when that couldn't be further from the truth. "What's going to happen is you're going to lie low here. You're going to do what's asked of you and you're going to prove yourself. You're going to earn trust and you're going to learn the value of it. You're going to thrive and come out stronger. More."

Scoffing, I shake my head, watching as some kids my age come barreling out of the trees in the back, basketball tucked under their arms. There're three of them, and they run past, pausing for a short second to glare at the car I'm sitting in before taking off again.

"You don't know me, man," I tell the suit. "Maybe I'm gonna go in there and kill everyone in their sleep."

"Maybe."

My head snaps his way and I glare. "I will if I have to, and I won't even blink. I'll feel nothing." If they come at me, threaten me, I fucking will.

I won't live through what I did again. Not now. Not ever.

The man shocks me when he smirks. It's strange, but I get the feeling that was what he wanted me to say. "I believe you, kid, but if that doesn't happen, then I look forward to seeing you again."

A frown pulls at my brows. "I thought you said I wouldn't see you after today?"

The man steps out, and I follow, nothing but a pair of blood-spattered jeans to my name.

"I said you might not, but I'm good at my job." He looks toward some dude who steps out onto the porch and nods his chin our way before rounding the car and meeting my eyes over the hood. "So when the time comes, and I'm proven right, you will."

I swallow, not hating that idea.

"And if you're wrong?" If I don't thrive and I'm not 'more'?

The man smiles like he can read my mind but knows something I don't. "Then this is the last time you'll see me, and I'll be forced to find someone else for her." The man lifts his hand, touching a large burn mark on the right side of his neck. "But I'm betting on you, Bass Bishop. You're everything people in my world aren't, and that makes you perfect for it."

My eyes narrow, but when he finally looks back, he says nothing else, explains not a damn thing. The man just leans into the car, tossing me a white T-shirt and black leather jacket.

I catch the items against my chest, and he stares at me expectantly, so I tug the shirt on, followed by the jacket. No one has ever given me shit before, so I'm not sure what to say or think, especially since I like it. It's something I think I'd pick out on my own if I had the chance, not that I could ever afford an inch of real leather like this.

When I look back up, the man dips his chin, slides into the seat, and pulls away.

I stand there, staring after the car until the headlights disappear, and then, with nothing left to do, I'm forced to put trust I can't afford and don't believe in into a man I've never met. A man I know I'll never see again.

I walk into the fucking house.

Chapter 41
Rocklin

"Fuck!"

I grit my teeth, dropping to the floor as the others begin pulling out the minimal weapons they have, though they're not as panicky, remembering to keep calm and cool as they're trained to do. Well, fuck that. I'm so sick of this shit!

I toss the rug from the floor quickly, pressing my palm to the sensor, and the lock clicks. I throw it open, digging inside for the emergency gun, and unlike my father's car, mine isn't empty. I lift the gun, and a manila folder comes with it, literally tied to its handle, and suddenly my mind flashes back to a few days ago.

Sai's sorrowful yet reassuring gaze appears, and I drop back on my heel as his raspy voice rings in my mind.

"It's okay," he repeats yet again, his tone somehow managing to grow even gentler. *"It's time. My job is done now. My oath is complete. The safe. Everything he searches for is in the safe."* And then a ghost of a smile curves his lips as he says, *"Tell him I won the bet and that I had no doubt."*

Tearing the envelope free, I let the gun fall. I open the folder and pour the contents out, letting them spill around my thighs. Instantly, my eyes lock onto a pair of crystal blues, only they're younger, more haunted. *Void.*

His cheeks are littered with bruises, his body not yet covered in art but scars and angry red welts.

Bastian . . .

Why did Sai have this? Was he investigating him?

With shaky fingers, I pick it up, running my fingers over the fading image, noting the time stamp is dated from four years ago, and then I lift the next one and the next. It's like one of those grade school collages, each image offering a slightly older version of the man I love, his jaw growing sharper from one to the next, a new tattoo or ten added in each one, fuller, more pronounced muscles. Brighter, less tortured eyes.

Hayze is in the background of many of these, but Bastian is the focus.

This isn't a file someone dug up. This is a file someone has been building for years, and every image has Sai's handwriting printed at the top. The date, time, and place are written on each.

Sai . . . he's been following Bastian . . . for years.

Why?

I dig through the pile, my breath lodging in my throat when I find a photo I didn't know existed. It's . . . us.

Bastian and I, standing close, staring into one another's eyes in the center of the gala.

Bastian looking all kinds of wrong, yet utterly irresistible in his borrowed black suit, and myself in my evening gown. My fingers are folded over his, my head tipped the slightest bit. I'm looking at him like he's all that exists, and he stares back the same.

On the corner of this photo, Sai's scribbled note reads: Fate stepped in. He found her on his own.

I . . . *what?*

My heart beats wildly in my chest as I reread those words, my breath going out in short pants. I think back to that night, to how Sia disappeared as Bastian arrived. How, when Bastian approached me, Sai wasn't there to hover in the background the way he had all my life when someone he didn't know or trust came too close for comfort.

No, Sai had slipped away.

Hid away?

So he could sneak this shot?

Confusion clouds my mind, erasing everything else and leaving only my need to know, to understand and find the peace I've been missing.

I have to get back. I have to go home.

My dad, who knows what he's done. He might have killed him by now.

Oh my god, what if he did?! I—

I start to shake.

A paper slides a little to the right, and the photograph attached to it catches my attention. My eyes narrow, brows snapping together as I look closer.

This one isn't Bastian. It's a woman.

A pale woman with dark hair and light eyes, and I know instantly. This is her. The vile creature he's been searching for. This is his mother.

This photo is time-stamped as well, taken only three weeks ago, but the fact that she's still alive and this is current is not what shocks me most.

It's the woman herself. She's . . . familiar to me. I've seen her, but where?

And then it clicks . . . or maybe the click comes from the hard, cold steel now pressed against my temple.

"Out of the car, little Revenaw."

The photo falls from my fingertips as I look up directly into the dark, deadly eyes of none other than Enzo Fikile.

Fuck.

I'm bound and fucking gagged, glaring across the seat at a stone-faced Enzo Fikile. The man my father sold my sister to in exchange for an alliance, then went back on his word and offered him me instead.

It seems he's come to collect his prize, but rather than whisking me away to his private hangar here, the car is whipped around, heading back toward Greyson Manor. Panic like I've never known before engulfs me, and it takes every ounce of energy just to keep my lungs from seizing. I don't want to watch my father die, even though I might kill him myself if he took Bastian from me for good.

The thought sends a literal ache through my body, and my muscles stiffen from the pain.

I look to my girls. Bronx and Delta's hands are tied behind their backs, the boys just the same, and Damiano has blood dripping into his ear from where one of Enzo's men had clocked him with the gun.

We didn't stand a chance against them. They came far more prepared than we, barricading us in with no less than seven vehicles. I had no idea what was happening, how hard they fought against them. I was frozen, unaware, and shut down as I flipped through Sai's secret.

A secret I'm not so sure I understand, but there's no time to dive deeper because the next thing I know, we're pulling up out front of Greyson Manor, and I'm lifted, tossed over the shoulder of the man who came to take me home.

The property is oddly silent, with no sign of life as Enzo's men run ahead of us, guns locked and loaded and pointed around every corner as he carries me as if I weigh nothing into the foyer, across the hall, and down into the basement . . . as if he knows the exact layout of the manor and where my father would be within it.

I hear him before I see him.

His deep, angry growl rumbles, the clank of chains following and as I'm tossed to the floor, his chest rumbles louder. I snap my head up, my eyes locked with his wild, rage-filled ones.

"What the fuck?" Both Bastian and my father boom at the same moment.

My dad has his gun drawn and pointed at Enzo's head in an instant. All at once, my dad's men pop up from the surrounding space, circling us, but for every one they point at the men who have captured us, two point back at them. People shout and scream their demands, and when a few loose bullets ricochet around the space, I drop to the floor, eyes seeking out Bastian's.

497

A harsh hiss whooshes from him as I meet his eyes. He's busted and bloody, but he's alive.

He dips his chin as if to tell me it's okay, but the sharp, assessing gleam in his gaze gives him away . . . he's not a hundred-percent sure.

Then again, how can he be?

He's chained to the fucking floor and it's my father who put him there. Now an entirely new threat stands before us.

"Do not fucking shoot!" Damiano shouts, somehow free of his gag. "The future leader of our people is in this fucking room!" Surprisingly, all the men ease up a little, fingers still pressed to their triggers, though everyone in the room seems to take two steps backward.

"I give you the biggest fucking prize this world has to offer, and this is how you treat her?!" my father challenges, cocking back his gun and stepping closer.

Enzo's men jerk but make no move without his command.

"Untie my daughter. Now," his chest rumbles with rage.

"She is mine now, is she not?" Enzo speaks evenly. "If I want her tied, tied, she will be."

Bastian chuckles, but it's dark and deadly as he tugs on his chains, climbing to his feet, blood seeping from where the metal digs into his flesh on all limbs.

I take a good look at him then, my heart falling to my feet.

He's in rough shape. Cut and busted all over, but he doesn't seem to notice. Or if he does, he doesn't care.

I chance a glance at my father, who glares at Bastian before his eyes find mine. They tighten with what can only be regret, his lips flattening as he resigns himself.

"No," he says, his gaze leaving mine, his voice shaking, the odd sound drawing tears to my eyes. "No, Enzo. She doesn't belong to you."

I hold my breath, so fucking confused.

My father jerks his chin, keeping his gun raised at Enzo, and then my father's guard, Hue, kneels to the ground, and I stare, gaze snapping all around the room and back as he releases Bastian from his restraints with one cautious click at a time.

Bastian shoots to his feet instantly, blood smeared all over him as he brings an elbow back, taking Hue out with one hit, bending and scooping the gun he dropped in a single swift move.

He looks like the walking dead, slow and methodical, red all over as if the shade is simply a part of his skin, like the art decorating it. Skin dangles from his brow, his shoulder is twisted back, and his dark hair hangs in matted strands over his manic eyes.

He walks closer, and my heart beats double time as no less than five guns point his way, but he doesn't so much as flinch. Despite the gash on his wrist and the mess it's making, he holds his weapon strong, pointing at Enzo as he offers me his other hand. I eagerly take it with my tied ones, and he hauls me to my feet, untying me without looking or the use of two hands.

Once my wrists are free, he presses against me as I quickly untie the rope at my feet. The second my spine straightens, he cocks his gun, taking slow steps forward until it's pressed dead center into Enzo's forehead.

Not a single man makes a move, the room deafeningly silent, and then without taking his gaze off Enzo, his arm jerks to the side, pointing the weapon in the opposite direction.

He pulls the trigger, and my father falls to his knees with a harsh grunt.

Everything happens in slow motion, my eyes flicking wide, a sharp gasp leaving me as I jerk in his direction. Every Revenaw guard in the room now has their weapon trained on Bastian, who stands directly in front of me, his arm wrapped around my waist, keeping me from moving.

"Bastian!" I scream, fighting to see beyond his shoulders, but he keeps me tucked in tight and I punch at his chest.

Pushing up on my toes, peeking over his shoulder, I look beyond him, watching as my father's hand disappears beneath his suit jacket, coming back stained red.

I tear at his clothing, but his hold doesn't relent, and finally, our eyes meet. "That's my dad!" I scream.

Bastian's eyes turn to icy glaciers as they descend on mine. "And he disrespected *my* girl." He gets in my face with a menacing look as my lower lip trembles, his fingers rising to brush along it. "No one disrespects my girl," he murmurs, his tone deadly divine. "Anyone else, baby. Not you. This had to happen."

I swallow my denial, my head ready to explode from all the shit happening around me.

"It's okay, sweetheart," my father rasps. "I'm not dying today."

"See," Bastian whispers, his forehead meeting mine. "He ain't dyin' today."

I should not laugh, but a sob-filled one bubbles out of me anyway because what the actual fuck? He shot my dad . . . but wasn't I planning to shoot him myself?

Maybe he does deserve it . . . as long as he doesn't die.

"He might die today."

This comes from a deeper, older voice, and I snap my head toward Enzo, frowning when I realize his men are freeing my friends, my mind catching up to time, noting no one attempted to take Bastian out when he pointed a gun at their boss's head.

Bastian keeps his arm wrapped tight around my waist as he turns his body, giving me only enough room to twist in his arms so my back is to his chest as we follow Enzo's movement with our eyes.

He moves closer to my dad, who grinds his teeth as he pulls himself to his feet, unwilling to be looked down at. "You broke your word, Revenaw. I should break your neck."

I tense, but Bastian's lips find my ear, kissing me there as if to assure me it's okay. That I'm not about to watch my father get murdered as I feared I might.

My father holds his head high, small beads of sweat now breaking across his forehead, though he ignores it. "I was doing what needed to be done to protect my family."

"By fucking with mine?" Enzo snaps, pressing closer. "You called me here to take the daughter you favor, but I chose the one I want, and when I leave here, I will leave with her in tow. If you interfere again, you'll be dead before you can blink. Is that understood?"

Holy. Shit.

Never in my life have I ever heard of a man speaking to my father this way. Enzo should be on the ground, body already getting cold for simply setting foot on the property without permission, yet here we are, and my father isn't even reaching for his gun.

My dad's eyes tighten, and he looks to me, an apology in his gaze as he faces Enzo once more. "I don't know where Boston is. She found out you were on your way, and she ran."

Enzo growls, darting forward and gripping my father by the throat before slamming him against the wall so hard it shakes.

I wince, digging my nails into Bastian's arm.

We can't fight Enzo. Not when his criminal organization rivals my father's and not when his ways are darker than the new ways the girls and I are attempting to approach things.

"You lie," he speaks through clenched teeth.

"I swear on both my girls' lives. She's gone."

Enzo's chest heaves and Bastian's muscles flex against me.

As he must have suspected, Enzo spins, jolting toward us, but Delta has an arrow pointed at his heart, Bronx a dagger at her fingertips and then there's Hayze, garnering everyone's attention when he laughs. Our eyes snap toward the ceiling, and there he sits, high in the rafters with his feet dangling, a fucking axe spinning in his hand.

He smirks, catching the sharpest edge in his palm and pointing it backward at Enzo. "Go closer to my boy, I'll split your fucking head open while the rest of them take out your team. There're more of us in the hall, just waiting for you to make the wrong move. Be a good boy, and I'll lead you to your lady."

"You know where she is?" Enzo spits.

"I do. Saw the sweet little runaway. Caught her, trapped her."

Enzo rumbles, "I will feed you to my tiger limb by limb if you've touched any part of her."

"Only touched the good parts."

Enzo tears a gun from his pocket and shoots. Bastian spins, shoving me behind him and the two move at the same moment, guns pointing at one another's foreheads.

"We made a deal, Bishop." Enzo is panting with rage. "You got your woman. I want mine."

Aw, does he like my sister?

I snap out of it when Bastian taps at the trigger, his jaw clenching. "If he's bleeding, you die."

"You kill me, thousands of men will come knocking."

"Many will come knocking the second they learn Rayo Revenaw is no longer the leader of this place, regardless."

My head snaps toward Bastian, shock and horror threatening to spew from my throat like vomit, but then he says, "Hayze will tell you where your girl is, and when you leave here, you will spread the word. Let the world know the king has stepped down, and Rocklin is their queen now. To get to her, they go through me. To get to me, they go through Hayze."

"If Boston doesn't wish to go, no one will force her," my father adds.

Enzo's arm falls to his side and he looks to my father, staring him in the eyes as he adjusts his suit jacket. "If you made her feel she was worth half of what your other daughter feels, she wouldn't have been so desperate to leave in the first place."

My father's face falls and without another word, Enzo walks out, pointedly looking up at Hayze to make sure he's following.

I look to my friends, to my dad, and then finally to Bastian.

"Someone better explain what the hell is going on, and fast."

Bastian nods, grabbing my knuckles and pulling them to his mouth, but before he has a chance to speak, my father shocks the room when he says in a rush,

"Otto Henshaw is dead."

All eyes snap to his, but his are on mine.

"He murdered your mother."

502

My muscles clench.

"The youngest Greco is no Greco. He is your blood. My . . . blood."

My frown doubles, the air in my lungs stuck. His blood? What . . .

"And, honey . . ." Bastian's arms tighten around me, his lips finding my temple. "Sai didn't betray you."

My throat closes now, a wave of nausea falling over me, but Bastian knew that would happen, so his hold steadies me. That's . . . a lot. So much. *Too* much.

I can't even process what he's said all at once, but as my dad delivers his next words, I let go of all the others, listening with rapt attention to what he must have just learned tonight.

"Almost six years ago, Sai went searching and found someone, someone he believed in. Someone he saw something in, something strong and resilient. Someone not connected to our world who would grow without corruption or greed. Who came from darkness but still had a heart and would have a clear mind with fresh eyes."

My father's eyes lift, and mine follow, finding Bastian's gaze laser-focused on me.

In the background, my father continues, but I'm a prisoner to this man's eyes and don't dare look away.

"I lost my way somewhere, and you and your sister would one day suffer for it. Sai saw that, so he did what he swore to do—absolutely anything to keep you safe. He searched beyond his reach, where no one would know until he found what he was looking for in a boy he believed in. Bass wears the mark of the guardian now," he says, and Bastian lifts his chin, exposing his neck and my eyes fly to the spot, my insides burning at the sight of my mark burned into his skin. "You are his to protect now, to love, should you choose, and I will never stand in your way."

"I wouldn't let you if you tried," I find myself whispering without thought. "He would be mine regardless. He *is* mine. Mark or not. He's mine."

Bastian's eyes flash before me, my claim of him all he's ever wanted and not because others are watching, but because this means we're no longer on stolen time. There will be no bridge between us, no secrets left untold, no life without the other.

He steps into me, tenderly pushing my hair over my shoulder. "And you, Rocklin Revenaw, my rich girl, my little thief, are all fucking mine."

Behind us, a throat clears and we look over to find Calvin at the top of the stairs, his hands sliding into his pockets as he eases his way down, his face sharp and unreadable as he looks from the two of us to my father and back.

"I realize this might not be the time, but Mr. Bishop is right in what he said before. Rayo can no longer represent the Revenaw name as the head seat in the Greyson Union. The Bandonis, DeLeons, and Henleys," he says, adding the fourth, hidden family's name for the first time, and I lock eyes with the girls, "will not allow it. We do not go back on our word, and we do not put our own in danger. He has done both. Aside from that, I have to meet with the outside council later to reveal the treachery of the Henshaw family and see how they wish to continue. They will want the assurance our world is under control. I need to be able to give that to them."

Calvin holds my gaze, and I know what he's saying, know exactly what he means.

Sai's voice pops into my head, and I close my eyes a moment, remembering.

"Can I ask you something?"

"Since when do you request permission to ask me things?" I gauge him.

"This is personal."

Curious, I sit back, nodding slightly.

"If you had a choice, and it came down to leading your family name or taking the head chancellor seat at Greyson Manor, what would you choose?"

My mouth waters instantly, a tingling sensation sweeping across my arms, goose bumps rising. I look away from his prying eyes, unable to speak the words, but my hesitation, my delay in response, is answer enough. So, when I give one, we both know that while the words leave me, it's my father's voice that's heard.

"I would do as I must, no matter what." My eyes slice up and hold his. "Like a good daughter would . . . Sai, tell me what you're thinking."

"I can't do that, but I can tell you this." He spins to face me. "You are doing exactly what I hoped you would, and without the guidance I had planned to offer."

I blink, looking to the girls.

I know what they want. We've spoken of it many times, so I can say whatever I wish right now without conversing with them first.

Calvin is not intended to be the head of Greyson Manor. One of us is, and whenever he is absent, I stand in, the girls at my side. If I had to choose between being head of my family or head of the society we've created, of the family we created at the manor and school and all things Greyson, what would I pick? Me?

I look to my father. His entire life is dedicated to building the empire he has. He's sacrificed so much, lost even more, including his wife. If I don't take over the Revenaw name, it is all for nothing. The inevitable end of an era as Greyson becomes my purpose in life.

But as I look into my father's grave eyes, he ever so slowly lowers his chin and then does something I don't expect. He shifts them, looking to the man before me, the one still holding on and standing tall . . . the one who still has his gaze trained on me.

I look into his beautiful baby blues for a long moment, and then I step away from him, his hand only falling from my skin when it's forced to as I face Calvin.

"A Greyson is required to finish school at Greyson Elite Academy. I'm not done and I won't take the easy way out. When the time comes, I will take your seat."

I turn my head, looking up into Bastian's eyes once more.

He sees it, shaking his head slowly. "I did none of this for me, Rich Girl. I got what I want. I need nothing else."

I nod because I believe him.

His words are true.

He was never after taking my world, he just wanted me, but along the way, he earned so much more . . . including the respect of my father, as twisted as it may have come.

He stole for me, killed for me, risked everything and held back nothing . . . for me. Forced my father's hand, demanded he become the man I spoke of and take responsibility for his actions, gave him a chance to step back on the correct path. My father passed the test Bastian gave him, even just barely, but the only reason he was tested at all . . . was for me.

Not blood before all.

Love over all.

So I take his bloody hand as I look back to Calvin. "Call the union, let them know there is a new head of the Revenaw empire, and if they wish to meet him, they can come to him."

Calvin gives a single nod as he steps forward, offering Bastian a hand.

"Welcome. I hope your stomach is made of stone."

"Trust me." He smirks. "It is."

"You'll need to choose your team. Two guards at least to start, and I imagine one will be the psycho who left with Enzo?"

Bastian nods.

"And a second?"

He looks to Dom, who gives a curt nod as if the two understand one another, and a small bout of dread fills me at the thought of losing Dom in our day-to-day operations. "Does anyone really have to ask?" he says.

But when Dom doesn't so much as blink, rather standing tall and proud, I frown, glancing at Bastian, who looks to the right and drops his chin.

I follow his line of sight to Kylo, finding his tense gaze on his brother, but Kenex only grins, urging him forward, and my father's omission comes back.

His blood. His *son*.

My brother . . .

My emotions grow thick as I watch him come to stand beside us and—

Wait.

My eyes snap to Bastian's. "Where's Boston?"

Bastian's smile doubles, and I narrow my eyes.

Fuck. Here we go again . . .

Epilogue
Rocklin

One Month Later

He's glaring at the cuffs of his jacket when I walk in, so I lean against the frame to admire him a moment.

His staple leather jacket hangs over the edge of his bed, retired for the day . . . and he didn't have too much of a fit about it. Probably because this time, the suit he wears is one of the many he now owns. And goddamn, my man looks good wrapped in a sleek sheet of darkness, his hand and neck art . . . and the watch he was resolute about keeping—a good reminder to all, he said—only adding to the whole look at me wrong and die thing he's got going on.

He's downright mouthwatering.

"Keep looking at me like that, and we won't be making it to the car."

Smiling, I cross my arms. "Is that supposed to make me want to make it to the car . . . because now I'm not so sure I care if we go or not?"

"Liar." He spins, his marble-like eyes finding mine. He waits, silently demanding I come to him.

Eager to oblige, I push off the frame, my heels clicking along the floor and not stopping until I'm right before him. My eyes instantly seek out my mark on his skin, and he knows it, his head tipping so I can see it even more.

The double-walled *G* is slightly raised against his skin, and while it already was a bold marking on his flesh, it wasn't

508

enough for him. He went and added his own little touch, intensifying it with ink and lacing script into it.

Hers, even in death.

Those words alone stir something deep inside me and when the rough pads of his fingertips brush along my jaw, his other hand skimming across the bare skin of my thighs, I realize my eyes have closed.

Opening them, I lock on to his gaze as he drags my skirt up to my hips, palming my ass before bending slightly for a better look. I glance back as well, heat flooding me as my gaze lands on the spot he traces smack-dab in the middle of my left ass cheek.

He shifts then, dropping to one knee at my side.

His lips brush over the still-sensitive flesh and I drag my fingernails through his thick, black hair. "It's almost healed," he murmurs against my skin, eyes popping up to meet mine. "Does it hurt still, baby?"

Warmth spreads through me as I stare down at him, the man I never saw coming, who was working his way to me all along without our knowledge.

Slowly, I shake my head and we look back to the spot.

To his branding, fresh and proud on my skin.

The double-walled *B*, identical to the marking on his neck in design, the words woven in his very own handwritten script within it.

His, even in death.

Bastian pushes to his feet, his hand wrapping around my throat ever so lightly to guide my lips to his own. He waits, and I give him what he wants, a little nip to his lip ring.

His mouth falls on mine then, fingers absentmindedly tracing over the collar along my neck because, let's be honest, it's not a choker, at least not in his eyes.

"I'm gonna fuck you in this skirt when we get back," he promises. "Bend you right over the balcony that faces the manor, so everyone can see how good you take me."

My core clenches at his words and I melt into him, unaware my hand is reaching for his belt until his fist closes around my wrist.

"Touch me and it's over. I will shed your clothes from your body and the fifteen fucking minutes it took me to get this suit on will have been a waste 'cause it'll be coming off and won't go back on." His knee presses where I want him, and I suck in a sharp breath when his teeth scrape along the underside of my jaw. "I'm more than good with that option, so make your move, little thief. Pull my cock out or step back."

Goose bumps spread along my skin, and I blow out a long breath, hating being forced to go against what I want when, since Bastian stepped into my father's shoes, he's encouraged, dare I say, demanded I do the opposite.

It's liberating being his, and I am his in every sense of the word.

The transition from my father to Bastian was as smooth as one could expect, and while I was sure it would take time to get the men who work for and with my father a while to accept the shift in power from the top dog to a much, much younger one, it's been far . . . *cleaner* than I expected it to be.

It doesn't hurt that Bastian managed to do in three months' time what my father couldn't in six years—befriend Enzo Fikile, my sister's . . . well, that's a fucking mess I've yet to sort out.

"So, are you two fuckin', or are we leavin'?" Hayze calls from the doorway. "'Cause I vote for the 'bend her over the railing part,' but give me five minutes to get over there and bang down that wicked woman's door 'til she lets me in to watch."

"She's not going to let you in if you keep sending drones through her balcony doors at night," I tell him, smoothing down my uniform and spinning to face him.

Hayze grins, holding his hands out as if to say *tell me I'm pretty,* and he kind of is, in a rugged, troublemaker sort of way. Like if Barbie made a boy band doll and roughed it up a bit, that would be Hayze. He's not so bad, even if his new favorite pastime seems to be driving Bronx mad. It will be entertaining to watch him learn the hard way she hates to be chased. She's a hunter, my gorgeous friend. Easy prey is of no value to her.

Plus, she won't go near anyone who might actually like her for her, she's emotionally fucked up like that.

"If she'd go back to painting naked out there, I wouldn't have to, but that's a problem for another day. Now is anyone gonna tell me I look like a fly motherfucker in this?" He grins, sweeping his hands down his solid, royal-blue suit, a black button-up beneath it.

Bastian chuckles. "You look good, my man."

"Thank you, you look almost as good as me. Now let's go." With that, Hayze spins and walks out.

Bastian comes up beside me, grabs my hand, and leads me out of the room. We curve down the stairs, out the back door and around the fountain until we're walking through the connecting gate to the Greyson Estate.

When we reach the others in the foyer, I'm surprised to find Kylo in a suit rather than his Greyson uniform.

My expression must give me away as he nods his chin.

"He's moving in with me," Bastian shares.

I look to Kenex, expecting anger or, I don't know, sadness, but all I find is pride written across his face as if all he wanted for his little brother was for him to feel as if he belonged to the world that shunned him.

Even I shunned him, allowing my father's words to alter my opinion rather than forming one of my own. What I've come to realize is I quite like him, Kenex too. They kept things entertaining for us when the world around us felt mundane, in between scheming and whatnot.

"You look nice in a suit," I admit, and it's like staring into my father's eyes, the resemblance uncanny. "Almost as nice as our father."

Kylo's eyes widen the slightest bit, but I tug Bastian out the door before anything else can be said.

To say I'm as anxious as eager to get back to campus today is an understatement. The new students arrived this morning, Enzo's little sister among them, but it's more than that.

511

The day Bastian took his oath in front of the other Greyson families, swearing to protect me with his life, even though a guardian has never been the boss before, we swore to keep no secrets between us. He and I both know our lives could depend on it, but I held one back for myself. For today only, because it's more of a present than a lie. It's a prize he wants.

The gift of all gifts.

And I cannot wait for the moment his eyes connect the final dots.

Bastian

I never thought I'd like a monkey suit, but this baby is a solid A-fucking-plus. Dom proves himself more useful every day. His only flaw is one he can't control, and that's how every time I look at him, I think about how he knows what my girl's insides feel like. And that he wanted to see her in a banging white dress, promising herself to him for all to see. Pretty sure I'm gonna hold on to that grudge until he finds himself a new obsession, and if my intuition is as right as it always is, I've got a sneaky fucking feeling he might have found her. Not that he'll do anything about it.

No, she's . . . beneath his standards, or so a rich boy might say.

Might have to help the girl out, stirring him up a bit and see what comes of it.

"Nervous?"

I look over at Bronx, lifting a brow. "Do I look nervous?"

She leans forward in the giant stretch Hummer they've switched to rather than taking separate town cars. "You look delicious."

A smirk pulls at my lips, and I lean back, wiping at the Greyson ring on my finger. "I'm good, girl. Ready to get this shit over with so I can get back to work."

"How's the interrogation going, by the way?" Delta wonders.

I look to Ander, and he grins at his woman, jiggling his busted-up knuckles in front of her face.

"Going pretty damn good." I laugh. "Your boy is . . . convincing."

Alto scoffs and Anders's grin grows wicked, but I'm not touching that shit. That's between them, but I'll admit, I'd like to hear the story of how their little relationship came to be.

I look to my woman, knowing damn well I couldn't handle sharing her with someone else.

I don't even like it when she touches herself 'cause I want to be the one to do it.

Sensing my eyes on hers, she looks my way, and my eyes fall to her throat when it bobs with a soft swallow she tries to hide.

She's up to something, and it's got nothing to do with the little box she swiped from my pocket when she came to me in my room . . . which is exactly why I put it in my left pocket, to begin with.

It's probably burning a hole in her pocket, wondering what's inside. I know she knows it's not a ring. My brand is on her fucking ass and neck, hers on my neck and right hand. The world will never question if she's taken or mine. They will know.

Eventually, I'll tie her to me in the ways other people think are the most important and change her last name to Bishop, but I don't need a piece of paper or a party to show she belongs to me.

She just fucking does and that's never going to change.

But I think she'll enjoy the jewelry inside that black velvet cube almost as much as I'll enjoy feeling her put it on me.

Who knew they made pick piercings with initials on the tips?

Tonight, my cock will gleam with her name and then her lips with my cum.

As we pull up to the campus, it's like a fucking ghost town outside.

All the students are already inside, seated in the gym, just waiting for their queens and future chancellor to make their entrance, and I've changed the security measures for the estate.

There are no less than two dozen men scattered all around at all times, but you should never see them unless they're the ones at the entrance gate. Other than that, they're to be shadows—always there but never found. If they can't manage, they are cut loose.

Rocklin isn't aware, but I've also replaced several staff members with men Enzo vouched for. The man has proven to be more useful than I expected.

We climb out as a group, and I don't look behind me. I'll never get used to the gang of suits that follow my footsteps, but it comes with being the boss.

And I am the fucking boss.

The top dog.

The "go-to guy" took on another meaning and I ain't mad about it.

Rocklin squeezes my arm and I watch as she and the girls file inside, going ahead of us to make their entrance.

Buttoning the final button on my suit jacket, I slick my hands through my hair and look left. Hayze nods his chin.

I look right, and Kylo nods his.

I look up to where Dom and the other guys stand at the edge of the first step, doing the same. They part for me, and I lift my chin, making my way through the halls of Greyson Elite Academy, this time in a very different role. The last time I was an outsider who weaseled his way inside.

This time, I'm the guest of fucking honor. The man they're dying to meet 'cause they've all heard Rayo Revenaw has "stepped down," and his successor isn't who they expected it to be.

I step inside, following the path my girl just took to the double doors that lead to the gym. The doors are open, the floor deep down below a solid fifty steps or more, the bleachers lined along the wall where I'm standing, but they can't see me. They won't until I step inside.

Kylo and Hayze step up beside me, and the other guys slide by, heading down the steps, garnering the attention of several students.

They reach the podium in the center of the room, placing themselves a few feet back from the girls as they take turns on the mic, giving the new arrivals a quick rundown of expectations and more.

And then Rocklin removes the mic, stepping around the wooden box until she stands before the school.

"As you and your families were all informed, there is a new face that represents the Revenaw name, but I want you all to know he has one of his own as well." She pauses, her eyes connecting with a few in the front row. "Bastian Bishop. That's his name. He's rough, rugged, and utterly unpredictable. He's not cautious or contemplative. He's a volcano. Silent and steady one second, and a fucking nightmare in the next . . ."

The entire room falls silent, and it takes effort not to laugh. She looks to Bronx, from what I can tell, then quickly looks behind her before standing tall once more.

It's adorable, her little warning speech, and honestly, really fucking effective when her eyes find mine and she lifts her chin high . . . no one dares to turn.

I start down the steps, my boys at my back.

Heads stay pointed forward, but eye after eye finds its way to me and it's not until I'm four steps from the floor that she spins.

I'm not talking a subtle little spin.

Nah, my girl fucking whirls like she did that first day, skirt twirling around her and flashes every fucking person in this room who's watching her bare ass.

She flashes *my branding* on her ass, and I don't even fucking care.

Her boys might chuckle under their breath in good fun, her brother might grumble a little about not being warned to look away, but they saw it, and that was the fucking point, her little peep show stunt, her way of showing me she's ready for the world to know who she—who we—belong to even though most are already aware.

There's no doubt now.

As I step onto the floor, I turn to face the crowd, but I say nothing.

They needed to put a face to the name and now they have one.

Fear comes from the unknown, so if they ever hear the sound of my voice, it won't be in a crowded room in front of many. It'll be a warning whispered in their ear if they deserve a second chance at all.

Rocklin says something else, but I'm busy meeting the eye of some and scanning the face of every person in this place from top to fucking bottom.

It's not until I get to the last row that I hear her say, "And I'd like you to meet someone else. He should be treated as any person of power would, if not better."

She steps up. "Most of you know Kylo Greco."

Kylo tenses at my side.

"What you don't know is he is my brother, son of Rayo Revenaw."

Eyes widen, but when my head jerks toward the one person who makes a sound, the entire room swallows their words.

I don't have to look at Rocklin to know she's smirking.

The perfect princess is no more.

Fuck me if pride doesn't kick at my ribs at not only her words but at the way in which they're delivered.

"You can go now," Bronx speaks into the microphone dangling over Rocklin's shoulder, and slowly, row by row, the students head for their first classes.

It takes a solid fifteen minutes for the place to clear, our small group talking among ourselves as we wait because, apparently, we need to be the last ones in here. That's a dumb as hell security move, one I'm mentally adding to my list of shit to fix, but once the last person leaves and the doors are slammed shut, suddenly I'm not so sure . . .

Alto and Hayze roll a piano out of nowhere and Bronx hops up on the bleachers. Dom pulls a remote from his pocket and the lights above dim as he walks out, Kylo and Hayze right behind him.

Delta lowers to the piano seat, Ander right beside her, and the two begin pressing on the keys at the same time.

I don't know a lot about this type of music, but I know enough to know they're damn fucking good, and it sounds even better when Bronx starts singing from where she sits.

I'm frowning from one to the next, confused as shit when my girls' fingers fold over mine. I turn, finding her smiling up at me, dragging me to the center of the room.

I lift a brow, but she only laughs, shaking her head.

Rocklin places her hand on my bicep, moving mine to her waist, and then she lifts our connected hands on one side.

My lips twitch as I catch on, roughly tugging her into me.

She giggles slightly, pressing her forehead to mine when I lean in.

"Baby, you giving me my dance?" I whisper, my fingers spreading out across her lower back.

"I should have given it to you the night you asked."

I nod. "Yeah, you should have."

We sway to the music, spinning slightly, and I swing her around, dipping her back and she smiles up at me.

I glide my lips over hers, whispering, "I love you, little thief."

"I know," she breathes with a hidden smile. "And speaking of thieving . . ." She leads as we straighten and pulls the small box she tucked from where she hid it under her skirt. She smirks up at me. "Care to share what's in here?"

"Nope." I take her lips with my own, and she responds instantly, her arms wrapping around my neck.

Bronx's voice tapers off, and a moment later, the last note of the piano fades, quiet footsteps carrying the other away and then it's just me and my girl left in here.

Rocklin closes her eyes and she sighs against me.

When her eyes open, she steps back, a strange, soft, yet anxious gleam in her gaze.

"Baby?"

"Meet me in the women's lavatory on the Greyson floor."

"What are you up to, Rich Girl?"

"I'm giving you everything you ever wanted by finishing what he started." She squeezes my arm and then she turns and walks in the opposite direction.

Too curious to fight her over a few extra minutes, I do what she asks and make my way up to the Greyson floor, abandoning Hayze and Kylo, who are waiting outside the gym for me in the hall.

Slowly, I push open the door to the girls' bathroom, the low trickle of water from the sink the only noise to be heard and I smirk to myself.

How she beat me up here, I don't know.

I round the corner, hands in my pockets, but slow when I'm not met with a pink-plaid schoolgirl's uniform. Instead, a cream-colored jumpsuit is before me and a tangled mess of black hair.

Jet-black hair.

The woman swipes her towel along the mirror in small, useless circles, tipping her head as she does, and shock shoots through my veins.

Suddenly, Rocklin's words click.

She's giving me everything I ever wanted by finishing what he—what *Sai*—started.

The man who committed his life to protecting hers.

The man who found me the day I killed my pops and gave me a pass.

Who knew a man who made people disappear.

A man he wanted me to find and stop.

A man . . . who helped him make this poor excuse of a woman "disappear" within a place he knew I would find her. A place he planned to lead me to, but I came upon it before he could.

I stare at the vile creature before me, at the devil's apprentice, the woman who helped and held the hand of the man who used his to beat on those weaker.

Just like that, the final box on my list is officially fucking checked.

My chuckle is dark as I swipe my hand along my jaw, circling the small space until she's forced to look up, to look at me. I watch, reveling in the way she pales before me.

Her eyes fly wide, and she shakes, her voice nothing but a rattled whisper. "Bastian . . ."

"Hello . . . *Mother*."

Watch for Boston and Enzo's story BAD LITTLE BRIDE coming soon!

Sign up to be notified when it releases here: meaganbrandy. com/newsletter

Want more of Bastian?

Read BOYS OF BRAYSHAW HIGH and learn all about the

place Bastian comes from today:

https://www.meaganbrandy.com/bobh

MORE BY MEAGAN BRANDY

SERIES:

Boys of Brayshaw High
Trouble at Brayshaw High
Reign of Brayshaw
Be My Brayshaw
Break Me

STANDALONE BOOKS:

Tempting Little Thief
The Deal Dilemma
Say You Swear
Dirty Curve
Fake It Til You Break It
Fumbled Hearts
Defenseless Hearts
Badly Behaved

Find these titles and more here: https://geni.us/BMMBA